To 'Rod'
with fond best
wishes
Rod M...

Babbicam

Babbicam

Rod Madocks

www.hhousebooks.com

Copyright © 2015 by Rod Madocks

Author asserts his moral right to be identified as the author of this book. All rights reserved. This book or any portion thereof may not be reproduced or used in any manner whatsoever without the express written permission of the publisher except for the use of brief quotations in a book review.

All characters appearing in this work are fictitious. Any resemblance to real persons, living or dead, is purely coincidental. Any characters denoted by government office are entirely fictional and not based on any official, appointed or elected.

Hardback 978-1-909374-81-2
Paperback 978-1-909374-82-9
Epub 978-1-909374-83-6
Kindle 978-1-909374-76-8

Cover design by Ken Dawson
Typeset by handebooks.co.uk

Published in the USA and UK

Holland House Books
Holland House
47 Greenham Road
Newbury, Berkshire RG14 7HY
United Kingdom

www.hhousebooks.com

*"When you go to bed, don't leave bread or milk
on the table: it attracts the dead."*

R.M. Rilke, Sonnets to Orpheus: Sonnet 6

ONE
SPOOLS

PROLOGUE

You can start with those crazy-ass eyes. They've got an 'I'm gonna get you sucka' look to them. Blue as death and flickering with strabismal menace. You can tell I've been looking at his photo for too long. It's a portrait from about 1911. I've had it pinned to my wall for the whole of this last year. Yep, those eyes existed once now they live on through me. They say that the murder vic has the face of their attacker imprinted forever on their dead retinas but what about the perp? John Lee must have contemplated his handiwork in all its blood- bubbling grue. He has the gaze of a soul stealer. One of the court reporters said of him, 'there is something wrong with the eyes, they are such as you get in asylums.' Too right, buddy. Even though it's a monochrome pic you can still see them shining clear and cold as flint. They are beaming out at me, or through me or maybe around me—I'm not too sure. They seem like a portal, a vent down which has passed a goddamn virus download. That mutha John Lee has got inside me, a worm uroboros mining me out. How do you let a ghost crawl into you? By having too many empty spaces inside already, that's how. It's not over yet, I don't think it will ever be over.

I'd been hanging at a software place in Cudahy. I cut through the back streets looking for the Lake Freeway spur when I noticed that hand-written sign for a yard sale. It was at one of those big old places we call a Polish house. I stopped off, because I've always had a thing about junk and found objects. I can't resist scratching around in cruddy antique shops and boot sales, rooting through old photos and heaps of discarded things. I'm always on the trail, looking for something, I'm not sure what. Actually, correction: that's what I used to do. I've learned now you can pick up more than you bargained for and you might end up with a Pandora's box type deal.

There didn't seem to be much to interest me at first sight. Only some unwanted crockery, worn out electric tools and kids' crap laid out on tables. I was about to turn away when I scoped a pile of stuff under a table stored in an old cardboard container. Inside was a jumbled heap of dusty documents and old photos, just the kind of trash I liked. I got the whole lot for five dollars after beating them down from a ten.

I couldn't wait to dig into it once I got home. I used to get off on that vinegary smell of old papers, evaporated ink, mummified flies and all. There were no warning feelings, none of that premonition stuff. All it seemed to be was a heavy heap of old pictures, an album with newspaper clippings, sheaves of typed record cards of some sort, and lots of small red and yellow boxes that contained mysterious coils of silvery wire.

Poking around further, I could see at the bottom of the box the aluminum grilles of some sort of obsolete machine. I dragged the thing out. What the hell was it? It looked like some kind of primordial Geiger counter or maybe an ancient adding machine, and had the trade name 'Webster Chicago' written on the front in antique lettering. It took some on- line searching before I figured out what it was. I bet you've never heard of a wire recorder? No? It's a gizmo for recording sound. That's what that moldy lump turned out to be. A wire recorder from 1945, a Webster Chicago Model 80-1 to be exact. It printed sounds magnetically on spools of stainless steel piano wire. I read on the Net how the technology is now totally dead but apparently it flourished in the States in the years following World War Two before tape machines came along.

My first clue to what was on that machine came in the form of a crumbly booklet mixed up with the stuff in the box. It looked like one of those old dime novels and had a faded, fly-specked title: 'The Man They Could Not Hang: The Life Story of John Lee, Told by Himself.' There was a drawing on the front of man with a rope around his neck and a white bag over his head.

After a while I realized that the voice on the machine was the voice of the guy in the book. Once I'd heard his voice it was too late. Now I know I'm smoked and can never be rid of him. Back then I didn't know diddly about him and couldn't think why in hell a half-forgotten English criminal would end up in a backyard vintage recording in Milwaukee. Now I know better. How can you get to unknow stuff? Only by being dead, I guess. Maybe to be possessed in the first place there needs to be a vacuum.

There sure as hell wasn't much else happening anyway in my life at the time. I hardly ever left town apart from my yard sale raids. Mostly I stayed in a lot and watched 'Cops' on Fox each night. I was living off the last of Grandpa's money and kept on getting a bunch of rejections from poetry magazines. I suppose all that rooting in yard sales, buying up old photos on eBay and looking for found objects and trash art was a way of me trying to kickstart something in my life. It also seemed a way of distracting myself from the guilt trip that had been dogging me for so long.

It took a while to get the machine working. The tubes and speaker on the original machine were shot and it needed a 105 volt supply to work properly. I had to dig out some old radio engineers on internet forums to tell me how to fix it up. Some papers in the box showed that the wire recorder had belonged to a Dr Kaiser. There were documents there tying him to the Soldiers Home and the Veterans' Hospital at Old Main. I spent a deal of time going through Kaiser's surviving records but mainly I got grabbed by the amazing stuff on those spools. Kaiser must have got the wire recorder originally to modernize his practice, to dictate medical notes and such. Or maybe he just liked gadgets. For some reason he also recorded his patient, John Lee, during the last days of his life. There was an hour of that surprisingly clear voice on each spool.

I'd never heard anyone speak like Lee. It sure was a weird

accent. Real hard to understand his creepy way of speaking. There was another voice on the recordings. A flat Midwestern voice that cut in now and then. It had a sort of indistinguishable accent, a bit like old Walter Cronkite's. I guessed that voice must have been Doctor Kaiser's.

Who was that dude, John Lee anyway? I'd never heard of him. I looked him up on Wiki. He was all tied up in a killing back in 1884. The place the murder happened was called Babbacombe. I had no idea how to pronounce it at first. It's spelt every which way in all the historical documents but John Lee calls it 'Babbicam' and that's the way I say it. The place still exists. It's a quiet harbor on the English South Devonshire coast.

Lee's story when you got to know it was pretty amazing. He was convicted of murder but kept up a crazy, dogged claim of innocence despite all the evidence dragged up by his enemies and his disloyal kin. Everything was made doubly freaky when Lee predicted he would not hang—then escaped death on the scaffold after the execution setup would not work for some strange reason. There were all kinds of explanations offered for this.

It certainly was strange because there's a simplicity about the hanging block: it all works by gravity. Clunk! Trap door down and you're dead. In the States we like to kill our bad guys in complicated ways. It's routine in Texas to take several hours to stick poisons into the arms of killers as they buck and writhe on the gurney or to give extra cycles of juice to some sizzlin' scumbag in the electric chair. We even have our own low-life who survived the execution chamber like Lee. He's a sicko child killer from Ohio called Rommel Broom. They couldn't get the old needle into his coldblooded veins and so he survived. But he isn't at all as famous as John Lee got to be in his own day. Lee was called 'The Man They Could Not Hang' and he was known all over the world. He was the Houdini of the hanging block and he rode his fame for all it was worth. Then, to put a cherry on the cake, after a period of celebrity, he mysteriously disappeared, never to be heard of again. That's where I come in: these resurrected wire recordings hold the untold story of John Lee. If I had the choice again I'd rather not know it.

Okay, here it is, you asked for it. It's a transcription and I have thrown in my raw notes to show you the struggle to find the truth about Lee. I straightened out some of his words but left many in to give you a flavor of his speech. I'm concentrating on telling you what actually happened, no fancy mixing of fact and fiction. I've had to read a whole lot to understand it all myself. It's turned out to be one mother of a cold case review. I've tried figuring it all out. It's my own frickin' Wisconsin Death Trip. Watch out, homies, it might start something in you also. As for me, it ain't over yet, maybe never will be.

Spool One

The source:
Abbotskerswell, Devon, 1878

—What here? Is it on?

Doctor Kaiser: Yes, it's on, just speak into the microphone please.

—This end? ...Just talk? ...[long pause on the recording and the sound of tapping]... Starts with Ma I s'pose... Ma was a scryer, see. Those eyes could look into the heart of things. Every whips in a while she took me to a secret place called Ladywell. Whips in a while, that means every now and then, doc.

Doctor Kaiser: I see, go on, Mister Lee.

—The Ladywell was hidden away at the back end of the village. You could see your future there. The water was clear and bright but seeming with no bottom to it. Ma would throw in a bent pin and the pin would sink with no ripple. Ma said that what you dream of that night will be what you will become. Maids saw their husbands. I would see the man I was to be. I couldn't be fussed to wait for dreams and I'd go on at her 'til she told me what she'd seen. She told me that she'd seen me as a grand fellow, more important than any in the village. She said my name would be on the lips of all in the country. Well, she was to prove right about that, [laughter]. How's that sound, doc? Is that what you want?

Doctor Kaiser: That's fine, please proceed.

—In those days we believed in those witchy ways. That was how we was brought up, with spells and curses and the White Witch of the Moor and that. I never really thought much of it, even when the papers said I could never be hung because I was protected by a wise woman's spell.

Doctor Kaiser: You appeared in the newspapers?

—That's right, doctor. I was 'The Man They Could Not Hang". That was so many years ago. I'm going to try and tell you how I got to end up being that man. It's a twisty road that led to it but those horrible nights in Town Cottage were the start of it. It's all branded clear in my mind though I've tried to forget it. Time and again Millie and I'd be lying side-by-side. Ma would rake the fire and set the fireguard. She'd say goodnight to Granfer on his truckle bed in the front room then her feet would clump up the stair. The village would settle for the night. Maybe you'd hear the Bonds next door rattle a bucket and further off beasts calling in Maddicott's yard. Everything seemed to hold its breath. Then we'd hear it. First, a man's voice and someone laughing. They'd be coming up Slade Lane from the Tradesman's Arms. Then the voices getting louder, the scrape of boot nails and the sound of a song. The Bond's dog would begin yipping until someone quieted it. Downstairs, we'd hear Granfer clear his throat. The front door latch would sound, boots coming in with a crunch on the parlor tiles. Pa's voice, "We have spent all our tin on women and gin, all on beer and tobakker." That's a drinking song, doctor.

Poor Millie used to whisper to me to hide away, for here he was agin, coming home drunk as a drain. Boots on the stair, a lamp sizzling as it swung in his hand. His big shadow on the wall. His crook-backed shadow as he leant over Millie's bed. He'd whisper her name and call for his little cubby-down girl. She would just stay quiet. He'd often sit on her bed, I could hear it creak. Sometimes I peeked out the blankets though it could get me a larruping. I'd see his hair, wiry in the light, a red neckerchief still on but with braces down on each side. Sometimes he'd ask her why did Ma hate him so. The lamp would go out. There'd be something happening in the dark that seemed to go on forever then all of a sudden Ma's voice scraping out from the other room. Calling him to stop paiks'n about and come to bed. It would sound like a command but there'd always be fear in it. There'd be quiet for a bit then the scratching about would begin agin. Once more Ma calling out his name. He'd answer that he was coming dreckly but he'd go on crooning after Millie under his breath. She'd be dead quiet. Then there'd be a banging and knocking and he'd be back on his feet moaning that Ma was a sour zab crow and worse. Boots would thump off. Loud spitter-spattering, probably the chamber pot then the bedroom door would bang shut. It would seem so dark in that room afterwards. I'd ask Millie if she was alright 'n she'd tell me to go to sleep. Said it was nothing. Soon mended, soon mended. So many nights we'd lie together like that.

Shall I go on? You don't mind me talking like that? [no answer on the recording, maybe Kaiser only nodded] I liked to watch Millie of a morning. That glimpse of her bare back, those two little dimples just above the waist line of her drawers as she pulled a shift over her head. Then she'd comb her long hair before pinning it up to show her lovely long neck, like a swanner duck. I seem to see her again sometimes now, just when I'm waking, a shape against the window there.

Doctor Kaiser: So you were raised in the country?

—In a village, sir, in deepest Deb'm, back in England. There's nothing like it here. It was a close-knit place. Heifers would be roaring at Maddicott's and carters rattling on the lane and the dung-heap roosters calling all the way down through the village. That would be the next dawn or any dawn when I were a boy. Pa would usually be up and gone to the quarries, thank the Lord. He'd pull on his clay-smeared gaiters and spare us having to see him over breakfast.

I'd get out of that cramp cottage and go up past the dirty old yards of Town Farm and Maddicott's and over the brook past the Ladywell. The wind from the moors would clear my head as I went to my penny jobs. Maybe working with the shepherds, carving at the winter-rotted sheep's hooves or docking the tails of the new lambs. We would throw the scraps to the dogs. I learned to cut strong and clean. The shepherds told me that it was best to cut on a waning moon, that way you avoid bleeding. I knew not the truth of it. Or there'd be work feeding the beasts at Town Farm. I sometimes worked the chaff cutter and the root slicer there, cutting the mangels to feed the shorthorns. Once, Farmer Maddicott let me look after an orphan white calf. I taught it to suck milk from my fingers and took my duties so serious-like that I'd get up special early to feed it. I loved that calf. It came to my call and I gave it a name. What was it? Ess, here it comes—Tafferty. Not bad, eh, doc?

Doctor Kaiser: Please continue.

—One day I heard the calf calling and found its byre empty. I ran about the yards and found Maddicott's men dragging it by a rope to a barn. They cracked poor Tafferty between the eyes with a maul and cut his throat. One farm hand told me that all knows that 'ee gives no name to something that will not live long. He said they were veal calves, didn't I know? No, I had not known but I soon learnt that all comes to nort in the harsh hand of nature.

Doctor Kaiser: You have no happy memories of childhood?

—Not while Pa was around. He'd come home nights wanting to make amends. He'd sit at table talking to himself or us, it was hard to tell, muttering how he'd taken on a load that previous night, oh ess, oh Lord ess. He'd be rubbing at his face, his eyes looking all uneasy, oh ess, a roit load.

As evening came on Pa would become more cheery. He'd call for zyder hot and he would try and push Granfer on to join him in a drink, but he would usually refuse. At other times he'd make play to chase Millie round the kitchen table. She'd try and get away as his big red hands pulled at her pig tails. He would become more fretful as the evening rolled on until he'd suddenly rise, saying he was seeing a man about a hoss, and he'd be gone down the lane. Then we could all rest easy for a while.

Stains

The ceiling above my bed is all freckled with brown stains. Creeping khaki blobs. The landlord said it's mold and I don't open the windows enough. I've tried cleaning it with bleach and Clorox Clean Up but it keeps coming back. In fact, I seem to be seeing stains in everything: saffron halos on the sheets, diesel plumes on the river's back, muddy tattoos on dark skin. Don't worry, I'm not going to get all metaphorical on you. I guess contamination is part of the process. That voice of John Lee just seems to make me question everything.

Go ahead, I know you think I'm nutso. You think I'm making it up. That voice from a fusty-ass English past cannot be for real. I tell you he is. He is invading and pushing on through. There is one law I've learned in my whole short life—big fish always swallows little fish. Trouble is, I can't decide which fish I am in this story.

Okay, settle down, hang tight, get yourselves comfortable. It's going to be a long haul before I can draw a good bead on him. Here he comes again…

Spool One

Signs & Portents
Abbottskerswell, Devon 1878

Doctor Kaiser: Tell me about your Grandpa.

—Granfer went some way to heal the hurt. He had been both cobbler and shoemaker. I can see him now, doc. He patched the boots of the field hands and quarrymen and made new shoes for the children of the gentry and their servants. He made sure we had beautiful boots for school but he did little work himself in the last years as he was old and weak. His own feet were all swole up and he wore bootees made out of carpeting. He still liked to get his tools out in the front room, turning all those the nippers, punches, pattens and lasts in his hands and letting us hold them as he showed us how to work them. He liked to say that you can tell everything about a man by his shoes.

Granfer was the only one we could really ask about the doings of the world. We bothered him with all manner of things that were in our heads. We'd ask him if the Ladywell could really tell the future? Or would the White Witch come down from the moors and take us away if we were bad as Ma said? He found a way of answering us without harming the mystery of things. He would teach us in a way Pa never would, explaining the doings of the village, why the fields had their own names, things like that. Mainly he liked to talk about his craft. He would sit in his old chair holding his favorite tool, his number one hammer, an 'andsum thing with its oak handle, telling about how the face of the hammer is crowned and has a narrow throat which gives it power, just ezzackally zo, tapping at a make-believe boot on his lap. Sometimes he'd drift off to sleep holding that hammer.

He once tried to explain to us why Pa was the way he was. He told us how Pa went off to be a tinner on the moors. They were a wild crew and he learned his drinking up there. He explained how when the tin and lead ran out Pa took to farming but he'd suffered over the wet harvests they kept having then. Granfer didn't know why but the weather had been wrong, only oats were good and wheat failed two years in three. He told how Pa went cap in hand to Farmer Maddicott and made an agreement to work for no wages but to take a share in profits. Turrible traited he were. He lost money and was cheated out of his expected rewards by that cunning, maister farmer. He got nort for six years of labor on the land and that was why he drank. Granfer said we must understand, whatever else happened, that he brought food to the table and there was nothing worse than want. He was to be respected for that. We listened but in our hearts we had condemned our Pa. Can you understand that, doc?

Doctor Kaiser: I can see how difficult it was for you. Now, how was your schooling?

—The new Board School stood along past Sunnybank. The youngsters went as a mob in winter but many were fetched out at harvest time. Eddikayshun took second place to the fields. I was a solitary young dog since I was a babby and found it hard to rub along together with the others. I particularly had it in for Sam Bartlet from Prospect Place. He came on the bully and thought 'ee was a cut above the others because his father had moved up in the world and gone to work in Henley's Cider Works. We were all bunched together from the age of six to fourteen. We sang out the names of the seasons and the rivers and the tables of figures while Miss Cornish waved a cane above us. Sometimes she'd allow an older one to be in charge of the really small nappers while she saw to the others in a curtained-off part of the school room. Those monitors would lord it over us little 'uns and twist our arms later in the yard or worse, they could hang you by the feet in the woodshed. They had a little song when they did that. I can still remember it. It went, 'and round and round the oaken beam a hempen cord they flung, and like a mighty pendulum all solemnly he swung'. Spooky, eh, doc? That little poem came to mind later in my life, I can tell you. The ones what did it, girls like Mary Venning and Katey Mogridge were quiet and shy when you saw them on the lanes outside but they became roit demons in the school play ground. They liked to surround us boys and weave around us with their evil little sayings—'Nimmy nimmy not, yer name's tom tit tot' or 'Mary Ann Cotton, she's dead and she's rotten'. I tried to keep away from them and clumped with those boys who were at least not enemies. Lads like John Chudleigh and Charlie Emmet. [long pause in the recording] Mary Ann Cotton, doc. Heard the name?

Doctor Kaiser: No, I don't believe I have.

—Well, she was hanged she was. A poisoner, they said.

Doctor Kaiser: You certainly seem to have been raised in a grim atmosphere.

—Grim? [chuckling sound] Ha, maybe. Miss Emma Cornish wasn't a bad 'umman though. She made a big impression. I'd never seen anyone like her. She wasn't a local. She did not speak in Deb'm-talk. I suppose she must have been in middle-age. Quite young really compared to what I am now. She was always in a long black dress with white cuffs. She had kind eyes which often looked a little teary after tussling with those angry fathers wanting their boys for farm work. I sometimes looked out for her lamp still glowing late into the nights in her cottage rooms up on Buckpitts Lane. A lonely spinster woman but she was a godsend to us ignorant little varments.

I used to fight with the older boys all the time. I'd jump on them right quick even though there was only one of me. I knew that getting angry could carry you farther than strength alone. I was made hard as a stone from a babby. Just born 'crabbit' Pa had said. Anyhow, Miss Cornish caught us fighting once. The others ran for it but she took me back to the empty class room and sat me down and stared at me with her soft eyes. She spoke some words in a furrin tongue and asked me if I know what it meant. Well, of course I didn't. She told me it was Latin. It meant, 'Man is a wolf to man.' Bet you know it also?

Doctor Kaiser: It does seem familiar, Mister Lee.

—Miss Cornish, she said that she was sick of us chillern clawing at each other. Her queenly face looked sad. I liked that 'man is a wolf to man' bit though. I ain't never seen a wolf except in Milwaukee Zoo here and that was years later but still I knew somehow what she meant.

Miss Cornish woke me up to another world and I'm grateful to her for that. She was forever talking about how grand life was in Exeter and London and I could not hear enough of it. Life in that dirty old village seemed as empty as a drum. I must've been all worked up at the time because I began walking in my sleep. Millie would have to get me back to bed. One time Pa caught me wandering and set a bowl of water at the foot of the stairs. I woke up all covered in wet with Ma screaming for Pa to stop in case I was frit out of my senses. He sent me back to bed with a kick, yelling at me to stop wakin' the vamlee up with traipsin' around in the night. Every time he belted me he'd roar out that I was a bad lot, a dirty little tacker, half scat, not roit in the head. Do you still think I'm roit in the head?

Doctor Kaiser: You sound as if you are in your right mind, Mr Lee

—Well, I need to be with what's facing me. That last summer in the village seemed special hot. The stream that ran through the village dried out for the first time ever the old folk said. Granfer was ailing. His feet were swelling and he gasped for breath. I seemed to be full of trouble. I never could be still, I was like a bag of fleas. I did not understand it then but I see it now. Growing hair in new places, having all sorts of strange and shaming thoughts. Millie had to lie with me sometimes. She let me rest my head on her belly while she stroked my hair. She'd ask me why I was so troubled and always atwitching and asighing. I didn't know what was wrong with me I just knew my heart was like a shaken fist.

The travelling folk, the ditties, came drifting in at harvest time like always. They'd suddenly appear one day on the fields below the convent on the north side of the village. They were wild ditty-guys, you know—gypsies. Come to think of that I've never seen gypsies here in America so maybe you don't know. Anyway, we young 'uns couldn't wait to spy on them. Charlie Emmett and John Chudleigh told me about them once while were sitting out by the rail line waiting for the Plymouth Express to come roaring past. It was racing to better worlds than ours, we thought. Charlie said we should peek on them ditties while they were washing in Aller Brook. He told us that one of the girls would lie with you for a penny, though she was fearful ugly.

Everything got swept up that summer by the news that Millie was soon to be taken from me. Ma told us she would begin service with a lady in Babbicam at Lammas before the harvest was finished. Lammas, that's the beginning of August when servants got taken on in the old days, you see. Ma had been down to see the lady by the sea. I knew her later as Miss Keyse. It had all been fixed up. Perhaps she wanted to get Millie away from Pa. Things were made worse when Pa caught me lying with Millie in her bed. He gave me a pounding, shouting out that I was a bad lot with each meaty whack. I'd hide out in the back garden under the big old rhubarb leaves to heal my bruises. I'd pass the time by catching beetles and throwing them in to the bee skeps to watch the guard bees kill them. Granfer faded fast that summer. Even Pa stood over him looking uneasy. Ma tended to him all the day long, spooning gruel into him and fanning him when it was hot. It was horrible to see his purple feet all swollen up and squeezed into the bootees. Bit like mine are now. His breathing used to rasp through that little cottage like a corncrake's cry. On and on all night. The villagers knew of many signs that foretold a death. It could be fire remaining alight through the night or if a dog howls at midnight. It could also be two spoons left in a cup or a clutch of pigeons gathered on a window sill. Ma looked for the signs each day. The hours crabbed along slow as winter treacle and Granfer's sawing breath filled the house.

August the 15th was my birthday. I certainly remember that day. I was fourteen years old. Ma baked me a plum cake and Pa left thruppence on the table before he went to work. He didn't usually do that. Maybe he felt bad about something or other he had done to me. Granfer seemed like a drowning soul that morning and Ma sent for Old Thirza, a healing woman, to look at him but she just shook her head when she saw him and left some poppy juice in a bottle to ease him. No one thought to fetch Dr Adams, the hard-handed local doctor. He wasn't like your good self, oh no. Ma didn't see no point in fetching a doctor, good or bad, for Granfer. A mouthful of earth would be Granfer's only remedy soon enough, she said.

The harvest was at full whack and all were in the fields. I left Ma tending to Granfer and went up through the woods and headed for the ditty camp. I sat in the trees for a while before coming up to the tents and caravans. A young girl came out. She was wearing a long skirt, full of holes, and her feet were bare. I held out my thruppence. She was young, perhaps my own age. She drew her bright scarf across her face. A secret people I thought 'til she let the scarf fall. It was a shock to see her face all riven up by a split from nose to lip. Her teeth glaring out from the hole. Ma had told me that some people had gash mouths because they had been frit by a hare. I guess you think that's stupid as a doctor? But we were just country folk. [no discernible reply from Kaiser]. I suppose that girl was waiting for me to turn her away but I still offered those coins to her and she led me to her bower made of canvas and hazel twigs. There was a smell of fresh hay inside there, I remember that so well and that thin little hare-lip ditty girl.

When I came home I thought I saw a white dove fluttering at the eaves of the cottage roof. Granfer's eyes had gone all milky and he seemed to be smiling. Out in the fields the last stands were being cut down. I kept thinking that I was a man at last and I had taken a woman though she was a monster. I tried talking to Granfer, telling him how much I hated my dirty village life. He smiled and pointed to his old working apron. I dug about in there and fetched out his number one hammer. He held it in his purply fingers and that seemed to settle him. Sometime later Ma came into the room, and told me he was gone and we'd have to put him to bed with a shovel now. The custom in the village was for the sexton to ring three bells for the death of a man and two bells for the death of a woman. Ma turned the hives round and wrapped them in black crepe so the bees could mourn also. [pause, sound of rustling] You have a mourning band on your sleeve, doc?

Doctor Kaiser: Yes, a family member. Just proceed.

—Well, I'm sure sorry to hear that.

Doctor Kaiser: Thank you. Do go on.

—That three-fold tolling brought forth a fine gathering for the whole village wanted to see my Granfer off. With the body set in the grave and the priest leaving, Ma waved to a strange little man I did not know. He came forward and said a sort of prayer over the open grave. Everyone said 'Amen' and Ma gave him some ale and a piece of fresh-baked bread. The stranger ate and drank by the grave then I saw her give him a coin before he went away. I asked Ma who he was. She told me it was Emmanuel Burridge, a wheelwright from Wolborough. He was a sin eater, Ma explained. He had come because she'd asked him to. He took on the sins of those who have gone off quick like. Strange to talk of Granfer's sins because I thought he had been a good man. Ma told me I didn't know all that had happened in a life. She said that the old were peaceable because all the living has gone out of them but our past deeds live on with us. I guess that's also true of me now. I asked Ma if Mister Burridge had be a bad man hisself to take on sins like that. She told me that no, it was a calling. You are chosen to be a sin eater. Something in your life draws you to it. Strange thought isn't it?

Doctor Kaiser: Was this a common practice, this 'sin eating'?

—Not ezzackerly common. But it went on around us secret-like in the villages. Maybe it still goes on in different ways. Maybe we could all do with someone to take our sins off us?

Doctor Kaiser: It's an interesting notion. Okay, please continue. It was the day of the funeral?

—Ess, Millie had come back from Babbicam for the funeral and we all went 'ome. Pa went off to the Tradesman's Arms. Men were buying him drinks to ease his loss. He came back to the cottage later that night and began to thud up the stairs moaning about his old feller being gone and where was his dear Millie. Well, I caught him on the stair and kept on hitting him until he backed down again yelling that I'd murdered him. He remained quiet for the rest of the night and Ma found him asleep in Granfer's chair in the morning with a kitchen cloth wrapped around the bloody welts. No more was said of it and Pa stopped seeking out Millie in the night after that but I kept Granfer's hammer under my pillow from then on. What do you think of that, sir?

Doctor Kaiser: You did what you thought was right at the time.

—Ha! I've got into a deal of trouble in my life doing things I thought were right at the time.

Doctor Kaiser: And the gypsy girl?

—I went back to the ditty camp quite a lot. I used to lie with the girl after throwing a bit of sacking over her head. After a while though I became used to her face. She told me her name was Amy. She stopped asking me for money and I began to call every night. I found it quite peaceable with her there, the blue smoke coming off the camp fires and the dogs all ranged about. Summer was ending though, the swifts were screaming about St Mary's tower and then all of a sudden they were gone. Ma said that they had dived down into the mud at the bottom of Aller Ponds and would only hatch out when spring came again. Farmer Maddicott had marked the rams with red paint on their bellies so as to show which ewe had been tupped. He got me to count the sheep that bore the rodding stain. As the evenings cooled and harvest was over the gypsies were gone one night, only leaving cart tracks and the circles from their fires. I never said goodbye to Amy. I sometimes walked over their camping grounds afterwards and turned over the old fire logs with my boot. Millie had written that there was a place for me in her mistress's house at Babbicam. I was to tend the grounds and to look after Miss Keyse's old pony. The coming change eased the pain that I could not name. I was all hollow, like a well when you drop a stone down it and wait to hear the splash. Only with me you could never reach that bottom. [sound of clinking and water pouring] Ma used to collect the honey only by killing the bees. She explained to me that she let two skeps live to continue the bee tribe for the following year and the rest would die to give the harvest. She would light up sulphur rags and stick these into the skeps. The bees would come tumbling out. She then picked the skeps up and squeezed them until a brown mess of honey comb mixed up with dying bees began to slide out. Seeing her struggle with the weight of them, I'd help her, dragging and pummeling the skeps until they were flat. Ma said I was her strong, bigabout lad. Before I left she taught me how to kill the old hens who had gone past laying prime. Cutting off the heads, feeling their last life flutter out under my hands. Arms out straight to stop the blood getting on my sleeves. Hold on, I think that's Addie coming up…

Automaton

You get used to the flavor of it. I've heard his voice for so long now I forget how weird- sounding it is when you first run into it. That voice has been my chance to reboot and start over. At first, I was fooled into thinking I had stuff in common with John Lee. I was brought up by my Grandpa after my parents died, and I was also lonesome as a kid—although I'm not as tough as Lee was. I guess I'm still lonesome now, especially after my girlfriend left me. I used to spend my nights sitting up in my truck watching the mayflies swarm around the lights on the River Walk in this little town. Going through all this John Lee history has filled up those empty hours and I don't worry so much about being on my own. I've found it hard to make friends. It's not helped by this damn flickering and shaking I do. The doctors have done a deal of tests. They say it's an 'essential tremor'. It's benign and maybe inherited. My head just does this involuntary movement. Mainly it's a no- no shake but sometimes a nodding yes -yes. Whatever, it's a social downer and it always gets worse when I'm stressed. When Kimmie was around it nearly disappeared. I grow my hair long nowadays and it hangs down in front of my face to disguise it. But it always seems to show when I look into the eyes of someone else, especially girls. I guess that's why I've become an alpha nerd and an internet freak, always chasing after arcane knowledge. Maybe I'm looking for how to cure myself. And, yeah, I know what you're thinking. I am not, repeat not, a goddamn autistic. Not an aspie, not a neurotypal nor a high-functioning skid-brain or whatever other cliché you are groping for in your ready-made bag. Labels suck, so do labelers. Besides just about every literary guy gets the Asperger's badge these days. My problems are altogether more slippery. You can dump anything you like on me but not that.

When I was 10 or 11, my Mom and Dad took me to that attraction called the House on the Rock near Spring Green. That was when my folks were still around. The place was an amazing building on top of a rock going out into a lake. There was a big room there filled with every sort of orchestral musical instrument. All of a sudden they'd come to life and start playing by themselves with no musicians. I thought it was so cool although Dad said they were automata and the sound came from hidden organ pipes and they weren't really playing at all—but I preferred to believe in the illusion. John Lee's recordings are a bit like that. They seemed to just start all by themselves out of that old Webster machine and a forgotten faraway world jerks into life.

Lee has a strong growly voice on the recordings. He doesn't really sound sick and at first I wondered why Doctor Kaiser was recording him. It's clear that Lee is in bed as he speaks into the machine and he seems to be at home. There's so much unexplained stuff leaking out of these wire loops. All I can say is, 'caveat viator': that means, 'let the traveler beware'. I might as well warn you now. I'm nuts about Latin. I use it all the time. It started as a defense tactic in Waukesha South High School. They kept on hazing me because my head shook like a bobble-head doll all the time. And because I was weird already. I started learning Latin so I could put freaky-sounding hexes and spells on the mean dickweeds who kept on bullying me. It didn't stop Cody Breadwood from beating me to pulp in the swim team locker room though but it did make me feel better to have a secret language that no one else understood. Okay, back to Lee. Let's lay it out. There is little about the next three years of Lee's life on the spools. The thin wires could become twisted or broken. If they snapped they formed a bird's nest around the driver spool and they were a pain to rewind. Quite a few had to be spliced and so they might seem a bit herky-jerky at times. I've had to reconstruct some of it.

It turns out wire recorders hung on for a surprisingly long time though tape machines gradually replaced them. They gave off a pure sound as they spun out at two feet per second, no background hissing like those granular magnetic tapes. They were still being used in aircraft black box devices and cockpit recorders as late as the 1970s. I keep thinking of all those doomed voices, the dead crews' last messages held on the indestructible wires.

I've done a whole lot of checking to get clear about those bits of Lee's story that the recordings miss out. It seems he first went to Babbacombe when he was barely a teen. The Glen itself was a quiet spot, a white-walled place right next to Babbacombe Beach. It looks somehow different in each photograph I have seen of it. The thatched roof gave it the look of a cabana but it was a big place with ten bedrooms, a music room, dining room, conservatory and ante-room. Behind the Glen, steep slopes and deep beech woods led to The Vine, another even larger house belonging to Miss Keyse. She kept that place for guests. Her whole lot covered thirteen acres. Beyond the Vine you went up Beach Road to Babbacombe Downs on the crest of the bluffs. The big houses and great hotels stood there where the well-heeled elderly and invalids came to spend the warm winters and to soak up the healthy climate. Here also was the property of Miss Keyse' half sister, Mrs McClean. Her place was called Compton House. Beyond lay the suburbs of Torquay (let's get stuff straight, the Brits pronounce it to sound like 'tor-kéy, with the stress on the 'e'). They called this suburb St Marychurch. It was where Miss Keyse shopped, worshiped and socialized. The main part of Torquay was spread out to the south of St Marychurch around the next headland. It was a popular market town and resort, famous for its warm weather and good class of visitor.

Miss Keyse herself had never married. She was sixty two years old when Lee first came to the Glen. She was very religious and a tad left field. Her loyalty to the unreliable John Lee was one example of her kookiness. Her neighbors tolerated her weird ways because she was well-connected but she was gradually sliding from high society as her money drained away over the years. A whole lot was made of her royal connections. The British Royal Family had visited Babbacombe several times when the Royal Yacht had anchored in Babbacombe Bay. Miss Keyse had entertained the Queen's husband, Prince Albert, and his sons a few years before and there was another visit a few months before Lee arrived. A bedroom called 'The Honeysuckle Room' was kept always ready at the Glen for any future regal appearances. Lee didn't seem to like it at the Glen that much.

He stayed less than a year then set his mind on joining the navy. His Pa apparently tried to prevent it. He didn't want the boy ending up like his Uncle Fred who had left to be a sailor and had never come back. Lee seems to have resisted both his Pa and Miss Keyse who also tried to make him stay.

On enlisting at fifteen, Lee was sent to nearby Devonport and served as ship's boy on the Napoleonic hulks that were used as training ships. These were old boats from a previous century. You can see details of him and his crew mates in the online census records of those days. He was not to find a settled life in the Navy though. At first it seems he did reasonably okay. He was proud of his Admiralty Prize awarded by the Commodore of the training brig. The records show that he caught pneumonia and was invalided out the service after a year but in reality he was probably an awkward, creepy-ass kid who did not fit in with the smooth-functioning life on board. The census showed he was' second class boy' while most of his contemporaries were 'first class boys'.

Discharged from the service, he went to be a pot-washer at the Yacht Club Hotel in Kingswear, along the coast from Torquay. Rumor has it that he was thrown out for breaking the crockery. He came back to Torquay to work on the railway at Torre Station, toting luggage in the goods room. He did not get on too good there either, nothing much seemed to suit him and he resented the gruntwork. Miss Keyse freed him from that labor and arranged for him to start at Colonel Brownlow's as a house servant. The Brownlows were established high society from a Scottish noble family. The Colonel was a retired commander of militia. He kept a fancy household with a Cuban wife, French butler and Swiss maids in a big villa called Ridgehill in the Warberries, a twenty minute walk from Babbacombe. Within a few months Lee soon betrayed all the trust laid in him. He was caught stealing from the Brownlows' and sentenced to six months hard labor in Exeter Prison.

Five years after Lee had first come to Babbacombe, Miss

Keyse's door was opening once again but Lee didn't act too grateful about it. He was coming on to nineteen years old, just out of jail and all hung up about how life had treated him. There are no photos of him as a kid but we do see him as he was at about this time in a cabinet photo that survives. He stands square on to the camera, wearing a servant's linen jacket with a white necktie thing which I believe is called a 'stock'. One arm is nonchalantly leaning on a stage prop lintel. You can see how big his hands were. Too much testosterone gives a guy a rounded face, a round-faced man is an aggressive man. Lee's face was shaped like a beet. He had a tip nose and fleshy protuberant lips that seemed fixed in a scornful smirk. It was those pale eyes that made folks remember him though. How they bored out at you under the shadow of the derby hat he always wore. They were gun sight eyes and you'd better watch out if they ended up focusing on you.

Spool two is one of the longest of the recordings. On it, you can hear Lee's voice as he cranked out his story covering all those eleven months from January to the murder month of November 1884. He probably recorded it in one or two sittings. You can usually hear an audible feedback clack on those Webster machines when the record lever is switched and I could only count two of those on the whole reel. I've split them up into sections to ease the story as sometimes he tracked back and forward.

Lee's recordings of this time period start after Miss Keyse had written a letter to the Reverend Pitkin, chaplain of Exeter Prison where Lee was locked up. You could say that the letter created a chain of events that led in one way and another to a killing. On the face of it Miss Keyse had written to Pitkin asking how Lee had acted in the county jail but in reality she had obviously already made up her own mind to have him back in her home. She stated in the letter, "He will live in the house and sleep as before in the pantry." It seems that she was set on him joining her at the Glen once more despite all that had happened at Colonel Brownlow's in the previous year. It was a hell of a thing in that age for a woman of breeding and with a position to keep in society to so concern herself with someone like Lee. He had come from nothing and he was a jailbird. Perhaps she wanted to reform him or maybe there were other motives there. Whatever her reasons, it was mighty risky for her to want him back because he had already shown that he could not be trusted. Still, she set it in motion and the wheel turned. All behavior has its consequences, some more scary than others.

I've got a picture in my mind of the Glen and the bay community on that New Year's Day of Miss Keyse's letter. I've built it up from all the reading I've done and there's been some personal experience but I'll tell you about that later. The place was keeping its calm like a pond before a stone gets hefted into it. Work at Gasking's boatyard had likely been suspended for the day but the Cary Arms pub was open as usual. Fishermen sat outside of their cottages and tinkered with their nets down by the beach. A few townsfolk strolled on the Downs and on Walls Hill which overlooked the spot. In the Glen, Miss Keyse probably sat writing her diary at her lamp-lit desk. The place was always dark in winter and the rooms were shadowy even at noon. The household was very different from that of three years before. Millie had gone to be a servant in Newton Abbot, a nearby town. She was a sickly girl and maybe needed to be nearer home. Lizzie Harris was now the cook, she was Lee's half-sister by his mother's unwanted teenage pregnancy. She had come to the Glen that year. She looked just like Lee. She had the same stone-shaped face, pursed mouth, tilted nose and chiseling blue eyes.

Eliza and Jane Neck were still shuffling about the house. They had been servants to the Keyse family for forty years and more. It was hard to tell the sisters apart. They probably whispered to each other that the old woman must have gone crazy-mad. That boy would surely go to bad again and they were too old to be dealing with his yardbird ways. Well, that's what I imagined. I need to be careful though. I owe it to Lee as much as to myself at least to get things right. I wouldn't want to get him pissed with me either. The truth, it does matter doesn't it? After all it's the only thing that will set you free in the end. So, if I am forced to imagine stuff in between the gaps in Lee's recordings—I'm only drawing it out from the known facts. I'm going to call it. You have my word on that. I intend to be straight with you, guys. That's a promise.

SPOOL TWO
Promise and Temptation
Babbacombe Bay January 1884

—Strange coming back to that place at nineteen.

Doctor Kaiser: To Torquay?

—To the Missis' place, The Glen, down by the beach on Babbicam Bay. Just round from Torquay. Going back there knocked the spirit out of me, I can say. I'm sure it was wisht. Don't suppose you knows what 'wisht' means? Well, if you hung about there long enough you'd have found out. It means there's a curse on it. The dark made you keep your head down and the shadows swung around your lamp. There was always something cramped about the place. It was truly a maze and with ugly secrets round each corner. As I remember it, it was filled up with the smell of camphor and Alexandria oil on account of all the lamps and candles that burned day and night.

Something about the place had gone down since I was last there. It seemed that the Missis had stopped spending money: some things were obviously patched and not replaced, and the thatch had also begun to drip here and there. My little pantry room looked much the same though, with the same pull-down bed and rows of cupboard drawers above me and cans of lamp oil ranked at the foot of the bed. I was thankful there was nothing showing of the crooked Sam Bartlet who'd camped there the previous years. The first thing I did was slip Granfer's hammer under the pillow.

The sea was churning away a few paces from the pantry door. At night its cold fingers would come in under that door. I had a bad feeling at coming back. It seemed narrower even than my cell at Exeter.

Lizzie would make me tea and vittals but she was in no way like dear Millie who alles looked after me. Lizzie was quite a different character, though she seemed like family. She had the same look as all of us. Maybe she was made special hard on account of her birth. Millie had only told me the truth of it a year or so before.

Doctor Kaiser: What do you mean by "her birth"?

—Ma had been taken with child when she was young and in service to a rich farmer called Esterbrook over at Widdecombe. She left in disgrace and gave birth to Lizzie. Ma married Pa a few years later but he would not have the little girl. She was raised by our kin at Pepperden Farm at Kingsteington. It was a rough place to grow up in, near to the race ground where the horse dealers hung about. Pa would not speak of her but Ma sometimes took us to visit when I was small. I remember her as a quiet, staring girl.

Lizzie had grown to be an 'andsum maid with a free and easy air. She took to joking and a-jesting with me. She told me we were a family of servants begat from masters and warned me to mind how I spoke to folk. She didn't seem like a sister. A sparky maid, I thought, there to be tamed. I liked the way she moved, a nice shape and full under the grey cook's dress. I like a girl who had something to jig around with—poor Millie was so reed-thin. I started grabbing at her. I were a hot young dog you see. You can look at me like that, doc. But that was how we was in the villages. Brother belonged to sister often enough and 'tother way round.

Lizzie gave me a warning look after I had tried it on with

her but didn't move away. She told me I had bravish wandering hands and she had enough of those on at her already. She told me to mind how I behaved.

She also told me what I did not know, that Ma had come down to Babbicam to beg Miss Keyse to take me back. So Millie didn't want me to go ruining everything. She warned me the Necks didn't like me, especially that old crow Eliza. Eliza had tried to persuade the Missis against me but the Missis would not have it. Lizzie couldn't work out why Miss Keyse liked me so something marv'lous. I knew though, or so I thought in my unformed mind. I did not want to brood overlong on how folks took to me anyway. I didn't like to think on that empty hole inside. Better by far to roll on and take what life gave. I wanted to throw off all memory of that cold cell at Exeter, and the naval barracks there. I was going to forge on and take what was due to me.

Doctor Kaiser: Did you find it hard to fit back in to being a servant?

—Nay, I soon went back to my old ways. Hiding out in the servant's privy up some stone steps on the edge of the cliff woods. The paper on its hook used to rustle in the draught from the sea and there was always a dripping sound from the rocks behind. I liked to sit in there and imagine Lizzie pulling up her shift. Woodlice and all sorts of crawlers used to stir about my feet. 'Chuggy pegs', we called them at school, although Granfer called them 'rabberdasters'. It seemed there were several names for every living thing in Deb'm talk. I wanted to give up speaking like that though, it smacked of the fields. Funny how it comes back now. I used to peer through a knothole in the privy door to keep an eye on the doings at the Glen. I could pass all morning spying out from there, awaiting Lizzie to come out where I could surprise her and be away from the sharp little eyes of the Necks.

Doctor Kaiser: And your employer, this Miss Keyse?

—My first interview with the Missis was ticklish. One of the

Necks told me to report to her dreckly in the drawing room. It was the best room in the house. Full of those stuffed birds pinned to wax flowers. They were all along the cabinets. There was the odd bit of silver and that, oh, and a nice gold clock. I used to love that clock. The room was a chill place with no fire in the grate—the old lady had forbidden fires in the day, the crabby nip-cheese. The Missis had her back to me at her desk. The Necks stood along one wall and kept watch. The Missis turned and told me to come nearer. She had a thin scratchy voice that could jump up to a scream. She was still all wrapped in that black bombazine stuff, you could hear it rustling at night. She caught me in a crimping stare and kept calling for me to come closer but I really didn't like to. She was a plain old thing with a beaky nose. I had to listen to a long speech about her disappointment over the Brownlow business. She said she did not want to add to my punishment. But really she did punish with her crabby words.

The Missis went on about going forward into the light and helping me find the character that I had lost.

Doctor Kaiser: Character? What is that?

—That's like a good reference for your conduct. She also told me she could not pay me much and I would have to be steady and keep in of an evening. She made me promise that and much else. I promised away but in my heart all I promised was that I'd survive her. She told me that if I proved myself she'd help me get to the colonies or some other fresh start in life. I wanted to ask her just ezzackally how I'd get my character but I decided to keep my trap shut. It'll keep, I thought. Prison gave you that. A fellow can wait on for a while. Best not bark too loudly but dog would have his day.

Miss Keyse told me that the household had all liked me before and would do so again. She gave a sharp look to the Necks when she said that. Then that crooked stile of a mouth rapped out more orders, it could have been getting kindling, loading coal, trimming lamps—there were so many jobs keeping that old place going. She complained that Sam Bartlet used to do a lot and now he had unaccountably disappeared, gone back to Abbotskerswell and never returned. She asked me if I knew where he had got to. I said he was taken terrible sick. He'd got the coughing sickness and not likely to come back. She was most discomforted about that. The Necks went on at me later, saying I was a dezaitvul boy and asking what had really happened to Bartlet. I just laughed and said he must have fallen scat on his face. What I didn't tell them was I had just caught Bartlet and given him a hell of a pounding and I told him to never come back to Babbicam agin. The Necks still kept on about where he was until I yelled back at the hags and threatened to stop their squawking for good. Lizzie had to calm me down, told me servants had no call to get in a stewer about things. 'Twas danger for us.

Lizzie was soft with me in them days though she was hard with all else. I fancied she looked at me with a touch of sparky promise. We were strangers yet kin and I kept being drawn to her. She told me how hard her life was, up at crow fart every morning, sweeping out, bringing in the coal, buying and preparing provender, feeding the old mistress dawn 'til dimmet. The Missis went about her devotions and got us to trim all expense but she guzzled away at her dinners like an old sow.

I had to serve at table, putting on those white gloves that Bartlet used to wear. She'd moan about how the dumplings were not right or how the soup was too salty and Lizzie would say to me, "Let her choke on it" and we'd both laugh. The Necks always looked frit when they saw us whispering and laughing together. Maybe they were right to be. [sounds of clinking and bumping. Maybe someone clearing away something. A long pause…] How their faces come at me, called up, floating up, coming up, like reflections in the Ladywell. Bartlet, Gaskin, Templer and most of all—that Harrington.

Doctor Kaiser: You will have to explain to me who these people are.

—All in good time, doc. Gaskin now, he spotted me mortal quick once I got back to Babbicam. He had a habit of creepin' up. He'd get me when I was lamp trimming out in the yard or maybe in the woodshed. I liked to go in that woodshed where I could be out the way. Old Tib, the tom cat, lived in there. He'd been there when I was a boy and was quite a sort of friend to me. Anyway that Gaskin must have seen me and crept up behind. He always seemed to get the jump on me. He liked to call me "mackerel", a sort of joke but I didn't like it. He was an evil-looking old goat. His face looked like it was covered in old leather, all drawn back with no lips and teeth the color of roof tiles. He wanted to know what I was doing and what I had learned in clink. I itched to see him off. Although he was old those twisted hands, like big brown crabs, could still hurt a man. He told me to keep to my hammock of nights, to mind where I be going in Babbicam and all will be well. No wandering of a night. No looking at things that didn't concern me. He complained that the Missis was a nuisance with her night walks and praying to the moon. Lizzie had warned me how Gaskin had got stronger while I was away. His business had spread from Anstey's Cove to Watcombe, and they said he had gangs running barrels of brandy from French schooners in the dead of night right down the coast. He said nothing good about Lizzie. She was accommodating of a night he'd said. He told me that was another good reason not to go creeping abroad. He wagered she would be keeping me in anyway. He called her 'Lizzie lift-skirt'. It was all I could do not to smash him right there but Lizzie kept a hand on me. She told me not to make enemies. Gaskin could see in my eyes that I did not like him. "Now, now, young heller. Dog does not eat dog, mind," he used to say.

Doctor Kaiser: And those others you mentioned?

—Worst was a lop-sided shape I knew. I made him out soon enough at Babbicam. A figure often perched on the seawall smoking a cob pipe. I could see at once who it was. He was always hanging about just watching. I kept away from him 'til Lizzie asked me to meet a friend on the beach. He came over, a small, well-made man apart from the limping gammy leg. In a sou'wester hat and an oilskin weskit. The same rolling step although his face was at first hid by the hat brim. I knew him. Oh ess, I did know him. Looking a little more weatherworn than a year before but still with that sharp gaze, eyes like hot coins, something steely about him. He could look sharp and cruel from one side but were fair and 'andsum seen from another. Lizzie'd said, "This is Cornelius Harrington." But I knew that already. Lizzie told me he was a 'friend'. I did not like to think what that really meant. She said he was a Janner and was in Harris's fishing crew.

Doctor Kaiser: I'll have to stop you. Did you say a 'Janner'?

—From Plymouth. They pronounce their 'o's to sound like 'a's so my name became 'Jan'. You see? Also, a lot of them hawkers that came round selling things were from Plymouth. Over-familiar they were, calling you Jan-this and Jan-that. So Janner also means a fellow who needs to be watched, a bit crooked like. Cornelius, he smiled and called me "Brother Jan" and made to know me but I said we'd never met and he was a stranger. He still smiled and chaffed with me and made no mention of our previous acquaintance.

Doctor Kaiser: When had you first met him?

—I'd come across him the year before when I worked for the Brownlows. It was because of him that I'd got into such a fearful mess there and ended up in clink. Even though I felt so bitter about the business I still couldn't seem to say 'no' to him. Lizzie thought him marv'lous and was always full of his latest sayings. I wanted to judge if he would say anything about me to Harris, his boat master. He said he did Harris' bidding on board but held no bond on shore. Lizzie kept on asking if we had previous acquaintance. But I could not speak of it. The hurt of that Brownlow business was too much.

Doctor Kaiser: You will need to explain what happened

there.

—I will, I will, sir. But first I need to finish about the Glen. It's important to understand.

The Glen was at the heart of everything rotten. Nights were the worst thing about the place. Lizzie would seem sad and lost, looking out at the yellow lights of the Cary Arms and saying the boys were on the rantan agin. At about ten of the clock we'd have prayers with Miss Keyse reading out awful long Bible bits. The Glen was a ghosty place at night, full of creaking and clicketting. Lizzie used to come down in a night gown and wish me goodnight, "Let not dreams fright 'ee," she'd say and laugh but there was no merriment in her eyes. I hated the cold sheets of that thin pull-down bed. It had fitted me as a boy but now my feet hung over the end. The pantry door was left open— Missis' orders. Jane Neck would rattle the bolts on the lower ground shutters and clatter about in the kitchen, then I'd hear the scrape of a pan on the range. It was for milk left to heat for the ole dumman. She liked to stay up writing or reading at her desk. I used to fight off sleep, for it was important to remain sharp. The sea would boom away and my eyes would get heavier. Then there'd be shuffling steps and the rustle of bombazine. The door would creak. I'd hold my breath, eyes open in the dark. Someone would be standing there in the room. They'd be there for a long time it seemed then there'd be another creak and something would come bearing down on the edge of that rickety bed. I'd hear the click of a chain catching on a brooch. Something'd move near my face. There'd be a strong scent. I'll always remember it. Attar 'o Roses soap and old flesh. A hand stroking, creeping. I'd bite on my blanket. Then as suddenly the pressure would go off. I'd hear slippers scuffing, a cup being poured in the kitchen then after a moment the creaking of the stairs. In the mornings I'd find little white cards left by the bedside, in a familiar hand. They said things like: 'John, the workman must be worthy of his hire'. That sort of thing.

BLOOD AFTERGLOW

It's been slow work transcribing the recordings and looking up all those history references to get a handle on what was going on. I thought I was starting to feel acquainted with John Lee as much as you can feel comfortable with a violent guy with a thing about his sisters! There were gaps and breaks on the spools though, like the cloudy stains you get on old photos: the mind wanted to fill in the vague and formless holes. For example there is all his folk history stuff. Lee talks about being 'wisht' and there was that 'sin eating' business that Kaiser picked up on. I can't find out much about that kind of thing. I do know there was a massive event that happened then. Krakatoa had blown up in what is now Indonesia just about the time when Lee was first sent to jail. That humonster explosion threw up a cloud of dust that turned the skies fiery red all over the world in the winter of 1883 and 1884. The skies still glowed ominously on January and February mornings when Lee returned to the Glen.

The Victorian time was supposed to be one of science and reason and all but there were plenty given to prophetic signs who said the bloody skies were bad hoodoo. The English papers were full of speculations about the meaning of the atmospheric effects. They even cooked up freaky headlines about the red skies. They called them 'blood afterglows'. Maybe every period is always worrying about something bad coming up over the horizon. I guess there are some dudes who are actually looking forward to the ugly shit happening.

Spool Two
A Babbacombe Murder
Babbacombe Bay, January 1884

—I'd have the run of the place in the early mornings in those red dawns of late winter. The Missis did not usually break cover 'til much later on account of her night time wanderings. The witchy light and the sea mists set me to all sorts of thoughts and fancies. It didn't take me long to do my jobs and then I'd be free 'til the mistress came to snap out new orders. I'd climb up the cliff path and watch the bay from one hidey place or another. I did not need bloody skies to scare up any thoughts and fancies for there were bad memories enough clinging to the place. For a start there was the ghost of the hopeful little tacker I once was.

Doctor Kaiser: Tacker?

—A kid, the dumb boy I used to be. I'm sorry doc. I get carried away and forget that you don't know Deb'm words. Mouth spaich, we used to call it, Deb'm talk. So, let's go back then, it seemed so long before that I'd spent that happy first Christmas at the Glen with Millie looking after me when I first came to the place. She had been so much milder than fierce Lizzie; Millie with her thin girlish wrists and soft words. Still as a cat, she could be. But she made my blood leap with her touch and there was sadness in our parting. Then, there were the sailors who told me tales that set me onto the ill-starred road of going to the Navy and all that led after.

There was also that famous murder, a bloody tale about Babbicam that I had learned early on. It was Richard Harris who told me about it. Harris was an old salt, lived at Beach Cottage and ran a boat crew. A sort of father to me he was then. Harris put himself out to be a friend to Miss Keyse and it was said that she had a mind to take his advice. He was an explainer of the doings of the Bay and of the world in general. He also told about how years before a sailor called Robert Finson had cut the throat of his wife right on the beach there after she had maddened him with her man-cheating ways. They had lived on the very same spot where Miss Keyse's house now stood. Harris told me that when Finson was done slitting up his wife he slashed at her invalid father, and wiped his bloody hands on the hair of his little niece who was staying with them. Then he tried to kill himself out there on the beach, falling on the blade and a-cutting at his own throat until the fishermen seized him. Harris told me that Finson he was tried at Exeter. They turned him off at Northernhay.

Doctor Kaiser: "Turned him off"? I don't understand that term.

—That's old words meaning a hanging. A few from Babbicam travelled up to see him die. Harris' father saw it as a boy and Gasking also. They say Finson died brave. They broke up the murder house soon after and built a new place on the site. The Keyse family came soon after. And Robert Finson's crime was all forgot except by the fishermen for Harris said they knew what it is like for a man to lose all sense in a passion.

Doctor Kaiser: So, you are saying that Miss Keyse's house was built on the site of a murder?

—Ezzackerley, you've got it doc. That shivery tale about the Finson murder stayed with me as a young 'un and later it came back to me as I lay in Exeter gaol that first time. Those notions had been all stirred up by the tales of the Exeter 'death house' from the older prisoners. The 'death house' was a brick shed tucked against the block wall off the governor's garden. They kept the prison wagon in there until it was needed for a hanging. No-one was hung while I served my six month sentence but the old timers liked to frit the young felons and often filled my head about the hanging of Annie Tooke, the nursing maid, a few years before. I think she had chopped up an infant and left him in the sluices of the Powhay Mills. No-one knew why she did it.

It seems she just could not manage the child. Anyway, they said that on her execution morning her screams echoed all over the blocks when she was being taken down. She cried out, "Save me! Save me! Oh don't do it! Don't do it!" to all who would hear her as she took the last walk but there could be no saving of her.

DEATH PENALTY

You know that in 1851 the state of Wisconsin hanged an Irish immigrant farmer called John McCaffary for killing his wife by drowning her in a backyard cistern. They strung him up from a tree outside of the Kenosha court house and jail in front of a big crowd. They screwed up the hanging and McCaffary remained kicking and gasping at the end of the rope for nearly half an hour before he eventually died of strangulation. It was apparently such a gruesome spectacle that the state legislators passed a law that abolished the death penalty and replaced it with a penalty of life imprisonment. And so it has remained. We are the only state in the Union to have only ever executed one man. I find myself wondering if Lee ever got to know about that little history factoid.

SPOOL TWO
Lawyer Templer Comes to Dinner
Babbacombe, February 1884

—There was always a rattle and a rush in the Glen when 'Soapy Reggie' came a calling—

Doctor Kaiser: Who was that?

—That's what Lizzie called him. Reginald Templer was his real name. A thieving lawyer always scratching round the Glen that year. Lizzie seemed to know all about him. A shadow used to cross her face when she spoke of him. She told me the Templers had long been the acquaintances of the Keyses and Whiteheads. Whitehead was the name of the Missis' family. She said she knew Reg Templer in Teignmouth, often saw him walking the promenade trying to get girls. She learned not to stand near him at the dinner table when she was in service with the Chants. His parents lived at Newton close to where Millie worked.

As I said, there'd be a hurrying when he was coming for dinner. I'd be shuttled up to Marychurch for extra provender and the butcher's boy would come calling. Jane would set to polishing the silver, it was usually kept locked in a chest in the Honeysuckle Room.

Lizzie would get into a stewer whenever Templer came creeping round. I often found her crying into her apron by the range. Whenever I asked her what ailed her she'd say something like it was because she had not prepared the pudden in time. As far as I was concerned they could shove their pudden but sometimes I'd ask the Necks to help in the kitchen if Lizzie was too overcome. Eliza would say that Lizzie could go and swim in her own juice but Jane used to help. I asked Jane why Templer kept sniffing round the place. She told me that there was something boiling with the estate. It was not friendship for Templer was a strange fish. Jane said they always shut themselves in with papers after dinner. She also told me to ask Lizzie about Templer. She was the goose that sits on the eggs, said Jane. I knew not what she meant at the time.

Doctor Kaiser: What did she mean?

—I think now she meant that Lizzie controlled what was going on in and around the house more than anyone realized. The house would get all jumpy as evening came on. Lizzie usually reined in her tears and came out to sort out the dinner but her eyes often looked puffed and the mistress also paced around and would likely ask me to fetch out something special from the wine cellar. Templer was a strange fellow. A slight gent with skin as shiny as soap and splintery little eyes. I didn't know what the fuss was about. He was most interested when Miss Keyse told him I was Lizzie's brother. He told me to look after her and make sure she took the right path. He seemed to find that amusing and laughed a lot. There was something that was odd about him on a closer look, something about his thin eyebrows, the way he moved his neck as if it was stiff and the slight shaking in his hands. Miss Keyse thought him well-made though. He seemed to put her in a confusion with his coarse jokes and chat. She came over all girlish and tendersome in a way I had not seen before. I tried to find out what they were doing over their papers after dinner but Eliza kept the doors shut. As he left the Glen, often quite late, Templer would seem to sway a little. It seemed as if he was toss-pot drunk. He'd tottle about like a seaman with the staggers and his face would be afire with a red flush. He'd call out, "Let me thank the cook!" [Lee shouts this] Lizzie would stand there with her back to the range. Templer used to try and make a grab for her, he'd say things about how such fair hands were born to do more than hold a baking tray. Lizzie always moved away out of his reach. Behind her back I could see she would be pressing her nails hard into her palms.

Doctor Kaiser: So, what was she so upset by?

—Lord, it was hard to find out what was really going on in that house. One afternoon I was in one of my hidey places in the grounds when I saw two figures flittering through the trees at the back of the Glen. They went through the covered path that led to The Vine, which stood deeper in the woods. I moved to get a better view but it was hard to make them out. I thought it was Lizzie's grey cook's dress, she seemed to be with a taller shape, a man. Then they were gone, hidden by the laurels. Later, I tried to question her, asking her about who be that stag out there a-squiring with her in the woods? She said I had no rights to question her. She'd put me in a right stewer. Oh, the passions of long ago. Now I have hardly any feelings left, only sadness at hurting Addie by not telling the truth. But in them days I was pulled about by 'em all over. I was powerful drawn to my half-sister. That's true. I had not met anyone like her before. She was a bold piece yet kept something back from all who tried to hold her. All I wanted was to tame her, to crush her down like a farmyard cockerel pressing on a hen. She was my blood yet not of my blood and I could not help thinking of her at night in my tight little bed. Her refusal to confide put me all in a rage and I often went banging the doors of the Glen. I often heard Eliza saying after my fights with Lizzie that them Lees are a passel of trouble. Little did they know how much trouble we'd really be.

Doctor Kaiser: It sounds like there was lot of tension in the household?

—You could say that, doc. Those nights in the Glen cramped me in like a fox in a snare. I had no money and I was forced to keep to my rooms especially during Lizzie's disappearances. She often couldn't be found anywhere between supper-time and prayer-time. If I did go out often as not I'd bump into an unwelcome figure. I might be in the woodshed with Tib the cat or on the terrace watching the doings over at the Cary Arms. Wherever it was, he'd come slinking up—Cornelius Harrison. I'd blast him for his creeping. He'd try and call me "Friend Jan" but I said I was no friend of his. Not no more. He tried to warn me about Gaskin. He wanted to lay aside what had happened between us at the Brownlow place. I'd be all bunched up and ready to fight him but something about him made me as weak as a woman. It seemed like I was always putting my neck on a block for him. Lord knows why. I still can't understand it now. I noticed once when he made play to help me chop firewood in the wood-shed with the old hatchet that he was click-handed, he favored the left like me. They said in the village one should never trust a dolly paw, a clicky hand, for they are ill-omened. I asked him if he was courting my sister but he just said she was as free as the wind. I was a gert vul anyway to think I'd get a straight answer from him.

Doctor Kaiser: Couldn't you have just left and got a job elsewhere?

—Oh Lord, doc you really have no idea have you? I'm sorry, I meant no rudeness. The truth was that every door was shut to me. No one would take on a felon with no references. I knew that Miss Keyse would ruin any chance I had of getting away, she liked me at her beck and call. She used to hammer on at me of an evening once she had slopped her way through her food. She would even call me in from the kitchen while my own dinner curdled on the plate. I never could tell what she would come out with next. Farming life in Scotland or showing me advertisements in the paper about ships for Canada. The old witch didn't know that on two and half shillings a week I could barely get to Plymouth. She also went on about lie-telling. She always said that she could not bear a lie from any of her household. Some nights she'd rant on about all sorts, said she'd seen a strange thickening of the cloud wrack against the moon, said she could not sleep. Thinking of the moon as blood came to her at night. Said she strove so hard to be right she didn't want no crooked timbers about her. She felt God's message more clearly in the dark, she said.

She'd keep up these rantings all the while I followed her on the winding track to Babbicam Downs on our weekly shopping trips. She liked to walk. Her humpy back would bob in front of me as she went along surprising lively on her thin legs once she'd set to. I would entertain ideas. What if I thumped her and heaved the dry sack over the cliff? So nasty when her hands twitched over me, straightening my tie, scrubbing at my face with a spittle-wet kerchief. She said I had to be presentable before getting on Fore Street with the milliners, drapers and grocers piling their parcels onto me to carry. The shopkeepers at their doors used to go shaking their heads to see me walking out with her. I guess they thought me a bully boy. Constable Meech used to stop us sometimes and ask if I was going along steady. He'd give me a look to signify he was keeping his eye on me.

Miss Keyse didn't used to like that and she'd go on about how it was so vulgar to have a policeman talking to one on the street. [sound of coughing then a long pause. Footsteps.]

Doctor Kaiser: I think that is enough now we don't want you getting tired.

—I'll rest soon enough. Don't you worry yourself, Doctor. I can hear that spring wind a-knocking at the window there. It's signaling a coming change. Time for me seems to be a racing to its end. The winter in this bedroom has gone by in a flash and the gulls outside are telling me something. I do not think I will see the summer this year. They say the war is coming to an end, I've seen the planes going out to finish pounding the Japs and those munitions trains keep me awake, racketing through each night to the Cudahy yards. They are all racing to an ending just like me. Strange that what went off at Babbicam is more real to me now than these last thirty years in this country. [more coughing]

We used to get spring gales off the sea at Babbicam. and sometimes I'd look out into the wind-tossed woods and fancied to see a figure going through the grounds. I was sure it was Harrington. I'd complain about it to Lizzie. She'd tell me to shush but she would look out the window with a faraway look and a little smile. I could hardly make Lizzie out. She was either flighty or she was burning like a fire. I never knew how I'd find her. I found myself wanting what she had under that servant's dress though.—indeed, every part of her called to me. I'd make excuses to get up close, trying to help her peel the vegetables, seeing her strong hands pulling the greens apart. She could quickly fly me and yell but in truth I liked all her moods.

I felt as if my heart was threading through a tunnel when I see her flinging back her wet hair after picking crops in the Vine's garden in the rain, or bending over a tub in the wash house, her bare arms in the light. They say we love those most like us and indeed both of us looked cast from the same mould. The sounds of the sea would follow me, sighing and slapping about the rocks, for the sea had its moods like a woman. At night I'd lie abed thinking of Lizzie only to wake later to the swish swish of a bombazine dress and the creaking of my opening door. I'd had long practice at living with ugliness. In truth, I knew not what I wanted most though. I wanted escape from the dry hands of Miss Keyse. I wanted to know what Cornelius was after. Most of all I wanted to fly like a crazed night moth straight to Lizzie's flame.

It's strange now that all feeling is slipping away from me to still think so much of that fearful passion for Lizzie. On Friday nights before prayers she would take a bowl, spread a towel over it, fill it with water and step into it naked and sponge herself down. The spread towel stopped her from slipping and muffled the splashing. She enjoyed that warmth in front of the range. I used to leave the pantry door open and look at her with a mirror. Later I just stood and stared. There was a beaten look somewhere deep down behind her eyes. I thought maybe she would let any man do as he willed with her. Sometimes I'd question her. I tried to dig out of her what was the truth of her and Harrington and that Templer but it was like catching water dealing with her. I'd demand to know the truth from her but she'd always say that a truth spoken before its time was dangerous.

DESIRE

Lee starts to mention Addie early on in the recordings. She appears to be a woman who is living with him. Maybe his wife. He is often worried that she will be upset by stuff he is saying and she certainly isn't present during the recordings. Women seem to play such a big part in his life. When I first started to listen to these recordings I began to have the notion that Lee was somehow letting me get the idea of what it was like to really feel something. It was like a sort of gift. He was allowing me into his world. It amazed me how passionate he was about everything.

I am such a fuck-up where feelings are concerned. I seem to be so bothered with managing myself that feelings somehow escape me. I do miss Kimmie but she's vanished, leaving a hole in my life. There's only emptiness and absence. That's all I can get a sense of. I've got a vid of Kimmie singing one of Katie Scullin's songs. I still look at it now and then. Kimmie wanted to be a singer herself. She even looked a bit like Katie. Katie Scullin is a big deal round here. She's from Fort Atkinson herself and performs around all the bars and diner clubs. She does cover songs and some of her own stuff. Kimmie and I used to follow her gigs. She's got a strong sweet voice sort of like Amy Winehouse, Ann Wilson and Gotye's Kimbra all rolled into one. That song that Kimmie was singing and strumming along to in the vid was called 'Sunny Dayz'. I asked her once what it meant to her and she said the song gave her the feeling that she could do whatever she wanted with her life. As soon as she said that I kinda knew that she would leave me sooner or later. She was so much freer than I was.

Spool Two

Return of an Enemy
Babbacombe, February 1884

—I caught a smash to the gob. I was on my hands and knees in the dirt. Like a veal calf waiting for the maul. Like a damn beetle with its legs tore off. Then that Bartlet had me again. This time by the neck. Choking me in a cranking grip. I wouldn't give in though. I kicked out at him 'til the grip went off a bit.

Doctor Kaiser: So you ran into Bartlet again?

—Ess, that's right. He jumped on me at the Cary Arms, just along from the Glen. I don't suppose you've been in a real fight, doc? Not when the other feller has really meant it? If you had, you'd remember it, all of it, as if it was yesterday. The button-hearted devil Bartlet had been waiting for me in the bar. Heavy-set he was and hard to beat. He'd learned from my previous hammering of him and guarded himself better. He'd started it by shouting that I should clear out and give other fellows a chance of warming the bed of that sister of mine instead of me. That gave the fishermen a big laugh. Then we went at it. They all called out to him to give me a drashing. None were on my side. First in, first blooded. I cracked my fist into his face. He could take a blow though and kept on hooking at me. One caught me. A glancing strike but it hurt. My head rattled like a pot of dry beans. The pub raised a cannibal cheer. The big lump faced me and swung again but I dodged away this time then came back in and caught him with a clappering punch—hard and straight just below his heart. He stripped off his shirt. That signified he meant business.

"Go on, boy," they all yelled. I saw there was a red mark under his chest. He came at me, hands forward like the nippers on a great big crab. I took a clunk in the innards. Then that smash to the gob. Bartlet's arms got around my neck and choked me. I took back hold and kicked out. The boot plate went down his shin and splatted his toes. Then I got to work.

I kept on punching him in the same place in his side. I kept away from those big hands. A bruise started up and grew under his chest. He stopped to touch himself then came at me again— Whap! I got another into his side. He gave a groan then. The fishing crews went silent. I think his turnip wits signaled at last that he was in considerable trouble. Whap! Once more, same place. This time the big lump gave out a shrill womany scream then it was over, or it should have been over if all been fair but life is not given to fairness. I was all ready to stamp him flat. I came to finish him off but one of the Stigings crew put out his sea boot and tripped me up. Gasking roared, "Get rid of the mump aid." They all fell on me, kicking me, slamming me with bar stools then dragging me by my shirt across the floor. Bartlet got back up, hobbled over and joined in. Then they threw me out the door and onto the fish-smeared slip way. I got up to try another go but there was a mob of them now standing at the Cary Arms doors. Bartlet yelled that I was finished and I should crawl away somewhere. My hat came skimming after me. I knew that was it.

I went hirpling into the woods, wet my puffed face in a rock pool and wondered what to do. I was sure I was finished. Bartlet and Harris would go to the Missis and that would be the end. I'd tried to do what they always did in my book, Bear Hunters of the Rocky Mountains. In the book, they struck at their enemies at once and all came right. Everything kept turning out unlucky for me though.

Doctor Kaiser: So, what did you do?

—I crept back to the Glen in the end. I was expecting to see my things slung out on the kitchen step. I'm sure the Missis would not tolerate me fighting quite apart from the bad things Bartlet could say about me. Just as I turned up I saw there was a right bobbery going on. The Necks were running in and out with bowls of water and towels and Lizzie also. Lizzie asked where I'd been and told me the Missis had been taken sudden sick and I needed to run up and fetch Dr Chilcote.

At the doctor's they at first thought it was me that needed the attention, what with my cuts and bruises. I had to push through the crowd at the poor clinic with their coughs, goitres and yellow faces. Dr Chilcote was fetched when it was made clear that it was Miss Keyse that needed seeing. We rattled back in his trap to Babbicam. Chilcote asked what ailed me, he said I looked winded. I told him it was a fall but he said something about how I always seemed to be looking for trouble. Miss Keyse must have spoken to him about me I expect. I told him that trouble afound me where'ere I went. He told me to never mind. He said that if it is not for bitterness we would not recognize the sweetness in life.

Doctor Kaiser: Then?

—I stood and looked after the trap at the top of the beach track while Chilcote hurried down the cliff path. I stayed all coiled up. I expected the crowd coming up from the Cary Arms at any time. Chilcote eventually came back into view in the dimmet, he told me to cheer up and that my mistress would be fine. Back at the Glen they were giving Miss Keyse a potion for her pained guts. I felt on the edge of a great cliff. I kept thinking of them all kicking and pounding at me. Lizzie came and washed my face and dressed my cuts. She asked what I was going to do, and I told her I must meet my troubles or run and I was not going to run. All of a sudden she got holt of me and we kissed. It was as if we wanted to suck all of the bad past out of each other.

Harris turned up later a knocking on the Glen door and Eliza Neck put on a spider bite smile to see me about to come to ruin. But the Missis sent him away without seeing him.

I was left to stew, fretting about what I was going to do. I had thoughts of burning the whole lot of them. I started to count the paraffin cans at the foot of my bed. It was Lizzie that stopped me. She came back later, her cloak all wet with sea spray, said that Harrington wanted to see me. I was so addled and confused I did not even know how to be angry. She led me to Harrington. He told me he had fixed Bartlet so he wouldn't be worrying me agin. I wanted to know more. "Got rid," said Lizzie, laughing. "Got rid," that's all they'd say about it.

I felt strangely overthrown. It was a confoundment. I needed to be my own man and now I was depending on Harrington. He already had too much of a hand in my affairs. Also, there was disappointment for a part of me had been looking forward to wiping out the Cary Arms. Lizzie told me to just be thankful and not enquire how Cornelius had dealt with Bartlet. We need to keep our place, she kept saying. Harrington told me to be easy I had kept my silence about his past misdoings at the Brownlows and he would stand by me. Lord, All I could think was I had put my head in the noose again and I knew not what would make me free.

Disappearance

Maybe it's in the nature of old men to make confessions. A little girl called Georgia Jean Weckler went missing from a farm near here on Highway 12 close to Red Cedar Lake. It was back in 1947. She must have been snatched by someone while getting mail from the mailbox in her farm drive entrance. Volunteer posses combed the woods and slushy bottom lands and they dragged the nearby Wisconsin river but no trace of her was found. Then Buford Sennet, a potato-faced sex offender and murderer, confessed to kidnapping her. A while later he recanted. Searches went on all over again with no result. There was a theory that Ed Gein, the Plainsfield Ghoul, had got her but that was discounted. In the 1970s, another elderly murderer already in jail said he'd taken her and burned her in a field. Again they poked around for her but nothing came of it. A few years ago an old guy said he'd seen her being buried under a Delavan greenhouse and had become perturbed that he had done nothing about it at the time. That was also looked into and eventually discounted. The spotlight came back on Buford Sennet, still rotting in a Wisconsin corrections facility, but he went and died in 2008, buried in Cattaraugus, and that thread died with him. The whole thing flared again recently when an 80 year old tipster told Jefferson County police that he'd seen the little girl in a grave all those years ago. I watched on Channel 3000 news while they showed a backhoe digging up a plot in Janesville. They had squads of police forensic searchers and cadaver dogs and all: but poor little Georgia was not found.

Grandpa once showed me the Weckler place. We stopped in his truck. Everything was as blank as a bubble, just the grasses blowing by the roadside and the water churning like an engine under the Blue River bridge. We watched as gulls bobbed about on the water like pieces of Styrofoam. Grandpa said that a family must never get used to losing a kid like that. I got this idea of little Georgia floating like a wraith, merging with those gulls, trying in vain to signal to us where she was hidden.

Not that Lee sounds confessional at the beginning of these recordings. I kept hoping he'd blurt it all out but he'd got his own plans. He sounded not at all contrite—mean and snarly more like. The really bad stuff has yet to happen, all the ingredients were beginning to boil about though. Take his comments about Bartlet. Bartlet was a weird character in the whole Lee story, and I've not been able to fully figure it out. He was raised alongside Lee in Abbotskerswell. He is pictured by Lee as a bully and a rival. I sometimes see him as some kind of an unacknowledged feral brother to Lee. He replaced Lee at the Glen during Lee's years in the Navy and the first prison sentence. Bartlet was there with Millie in 1880 when the Brit heir to the throne, the Prince of Wales visited the Glen and gave a gold coin to each of the servants. Lee mentioned two clashes with Bartlet then there was silence. I've not been able to find him in any documents after 1883. You can read a whole lot into that void. Lee seems not to have given a damn whether he was alive or dead. Let's leave Bartlet to hang around a while longer.

I might not have been able to find Bartlet but this English old world scene teems with suspects, it's close-packed like an old-time Sherlock Holmes murder mystery. Crime around my own parts is a different deal. There have been no murders near here in more than 10 years but when they do happen it seems like people disappear into a vacuum. Girls disappear like Georgia, killed by drifters, the truth is never found, and the families' loss is left to be eroded by the hungry years. The crimes we do have these days are mainly thefts. Also the Net tells me that there are 51 registered sex offenders in our little town. Jeez, that sounds a lot, that's one for every 200 or so inhabitants. I'm not sure why they are all here. Maybe they know something I don't.

It's no accident that I'm drawn to guilt and to secrets. Maybe that why I've also chosen this little town to hide out in—I've got stuff of my own to cover up. You could say I was dogged by bad spirits. I'll tell you about it before long. Maybe that's why I've been drawn to John Lee's recordings. His tales of grue with ghosts is an antidote to how bland life can be here. We are a hopeful people. We want to dare to live the dream. In America, we always seem to be looking for salvation and redemption stories to keep us alive. "Learning today, leading tomorrow'. That was my High School motto. But I didn't join all those activities that could have shaped me: best buddy groups, American Field Service and National Honor Society. Nope, I just stayed in, playing Kings Quest at night and learning all those Latin words in secret. That's why now I'm drawn to that hollow- face Lee character, instead of joining my peers who are chasing the Dream, raising families, chillaxin with a brew or sharing honey wings at Fat Boyz downtown.

Spool Two
O the hog-eye man is the man for me
Babbacombe, March 1884

—Spring was a hard time for the fishermen at Babbicam. There weren't much to eat, you see. Maybe March is hard all over the world. I've seen the snow at the window. Sometimes I don't think I'll see the sun again. Good of you to come out on a day like this.

Doctor Kaiser: You were saying last time that things had gotten tough where you were working?

—Ess, you could say so. I've been thinking a lot more about it all since starting with all this recording business. I've been remembering how at some stage I got news from Millie. She was in service in Newton Abbot and wrote that she had arranged for me to meet someone special. Her name was Katie Fisher and she lived with her mother on Grafton Terraces at Ellacombe in

Torquay town. She knew Millie because her house was a few doors down from my Auntie Amelia. Millie often visited my Auntie. Millie came to town by train and we all met at the Pleasure Gardens. Katie was an 'andsum girl, always turned out nicely too, hats with feathers and the like. A nice face with kind cob-brown eyes, a top-heavy maid like a pouter pigeon and with little weak ankles. She was good to me though. Katie had good schooling, a bit shy but her head was full of dreams. I found no end of those 'sensation' books hid away in her bedroom. She liked me too and we soon struck up an understanding. Millie warned me to look after her and to mind how I went, not to run at gates and make a mess o' things. Sweet Millie, I thought she looked awful thin when I saw her and she had this cough that would not go away. She said she caught it at the Glen with all that cold and damp. She also warned me about Lizzie, said she was a wild, self-seeking girl with gentry blood in her.

Doctor Kaiser: Weren't you worried that Lizzie would find out and be jealous?

—I never said anything about Katie to Lizzie. She'd sniff me out anyway. We'd stay up late after prayers with an ear for the mistress' tread down the corridor. Lizzie pinched the Missis' Madeira but I refused it. I've never drunk likker on account of not wanting to be like my Pa. Well, I should say I've not drunk 'til a few years back when I did let go with a bottle of brandy. That made me prapper sick and tissicky and I spilled out all sorts of nonsense to the neighbors. Said more than I should have.

Lizzie wasn't so fussy about drinking and could knock it back. She'd roll about on my bed, her hair springing up from under her cook's cap, taunting at me about who I was a-courting. She used to say that all the Lees were cold, always turning their backs on her. Then she'd ask me for a goodnight kiss and pull my hands over her. She frit me with her passions. I liked to be the cock bird, the one in charge. When I in turn tried to hold her she'd knock me back, telling me not to buck her hair. Much later in the nights, I'd go creeping up to her room but more often than not the sheets would be thrown back with just a shape let in the bed where she had been lying. The backstairs nursery door would usually be left open with only the sound of the sea outside.

Doctor Kaiser: So, you began to date Katie?

—I suppose so. We'd call it 'walking out'. I'd see Katie on Saturdays. We'd stroll around and watch the gentry at the big hotels or stand outside Shapleys on the Strand and smell the coffee, cheeses and hams. I'd promise her that I'd get her good things like that one day. Or we'd go up past Anstey's Cove where the Sunday trippers went and up above Babbicam Bay on Walls Hill by the quarries. We liked to look out over the sea. I'd explain that the mewie birds were the spirits of dead sailors and such. She liked my stories. She had troubles of her own, poor girl. Her mother had been ailing with a cancer eating into her breast, and the family were in want of money. Katie took in pieces of work of an evening to pay the doctor's bills. She had one brother who had left home and one younger brother, Ernest. She worried what would become of the boy. I told her that all would be well. Fat lot I knew.

Babbicam was full of beady eyes and all the old witches liked to pick the bones of gossip. One night after prayers Miss Keyse summoned me to the parlor and told me that a lady should not have to put up with irregularity in her household; there should be no 'communing with undesirables'. She told me to keep to the house more. I told her I was not keeping bad company but she said that any company was bad company for me.

Miss Keyse probably told Lizzie to make sure I stayed in more though I managed to send Katie little notes and messages. We'd also meet in Marychurch while I was supposed to be on my errands. Miss Keyse rarely stirred between nine of an evening and prayers at ten thirty and it was also safe then for me to go out then, running along Marychurch Street down to Ellacombe for an hour or so. Here, I would cram up to Katie in her bedroom where she would allow me liberties while her mother groaned and gasped in the next room. She wouldn't let me to lift her skirts though, always saying, "Not yet, Jack, not yet" Then I'd pull away and go running back to Babbicam along all the back ways. I nearly ran into trouble on some of those nights. Cutting back down the cliffs in the dark by the Oddicombe path I'd see men, sometimes a dozen or so, outlined against the grey moonlit sea. Humped with bales and chests coming up the cliff path. I'd hide in the bracken until they passed. Sometimes I'd look up and see the blue spurt of a match against the headland high above. Other watchers were always up there.

Doctor Kaiser: So, who were those fellows?

—Smugglers, doc. Bringing in stuff off the French boats. I'd come across them before when I worked for the Brownlows. They weren't around so much in the summer months, too many folk milling about then with all the trippers. You knew summer had arrived when they'd dragged out those big white bathing machines from Gasking's yard and bumped them down over the shingle. The Cary Arms garden would get all filled up and little nappers swarmed the rock pools with hand nets. The fish catch would usually pick up then also and lines of ponies went up the cliff path carrying fish baskets to Newton Abbot market. About then Miss Keyse used to send me out to note down which fishermen were too close to her house. She threatened Mr Templer on them. She refused to see Harris or Gasking to sort out the matter and an angriness grew further between her and the fishermen.

I started to reel other maids into my nets. Meeting Katie had made me brave though really I see now it was all foolish pride. Maybe also it was a way at getting back at Lizzie. Anyway, I thought I could range free among the Marychurch housemaids, barmaids, nursery-girls and fishermen's daughters. One was Eliza Maile, a pretty housemaid from Shaldon. I had taken to chatting to her and making all sorts of promises on those garden seats in the Glen grounds when I should have been working.

I found that I could easily keep up a foxy double-dealing way which meant that no-one really knew what I was about. For me then, the truth could be whatever I thought it should be at the time.

I spent most time with Katie on Saturday half days. Sometimes she wept for her mother's sickness but usually she tried to hide her grief from me. She fed me, she allowed me to fumble at her and she listened to my ranting on about Miss Keyse. She gave me a steadiness, a chance to be admired. Heaven knows what she saw in me. I suppose I gave her hope of a settled life. In time we went out and about less. I told her that the Missis was always spying on me. It suited me to keep her out of the way, my life was getting all snarled up. Lizzie kept calling me a 'ram-cat' every time I came back from Ellacombe. That's Deb'm for a tom, you know. Miss Keyse started to pile jobs on me. Once I told her I could not manage on two and six a week and needed to know if she could give me a character. She flew into a fizzing rage and said I was going on most unsuitable and needed to buck up. I could have swung for her right then but one of the Necks came by. The old crow reminded me that I'd have done even more time at Exeter clink if she had not spoken up for me at the magistrates. "Think on" she kept on saying, "think on." I was thinking alright.

I fell into staying out late and sometimes I'd come back to the Glen and slam the doors to frit the Necks. They got on my goat. Days would pass when I didn't see Katie and she'd send notes asking if I was well. However much I sniffed around the other girls, I still kept coming back to Lizzie. I spied on her and chased her but she'd pulled away since Katie had come on the scene. If she found me creeping up to her rooms more often than not she would yell that I was a daw-bake and slam the door. I kept filling up with angry feelings. About this time on one of my shopping trips for the Missis I spent my money on a knob-ended cane from Mr Salter's although I could scarce afford it. I used to knock the heads off Miss Keyse's flowers and waved it at the rough lads in St Marychurch and ask if they wanted a lick of it.

Doctor Kaiser: Weren't you scared of getting into trouble with the police again?

—Everyone seemed to be down on me and I was beginning not to care. The Glen was always surprising me by unlooked-for visitors. One such was Tom Bennet the coast guard officer. He kept bothering me and asking if I had seen anything of a night. When I denied it, he threatened me, said I was a bad 'un, one word from him would get me in trouble with Torquay police. All had their hand against me; so it seemed. Miss Keyse must have seen Bennet scratching around, for she came to my room at night and whispered with her dunghill breath, "I will protect thee, John but you must be a good boy." It would seem better in the daylight. I'd go up the cliffs and watch for the blue shadows of warships out at sea. I could have been with that channel fleet if only I had been luckier. You could see so far at Babbicam— not like this muddy Milwaukee light, the air full of taint from the factories and such.

Doctor Kaiser: Tell me more about what was really happening between you and this Miss Keyse.

—I don't like to say it. She was like a bad-smelling cloud all over the place. In the hot afternoons there was the distant thuds from the quarrymen blasting, that seemed to shake the air. Miss Keyse kept on complaining of the creaking and clicketting of the capstans and the rough songs the men sang. She was always asking what "hog eye" meant. She must have heard the sailors singing it. The Necks said they knew not what it meant. Lizzie said she was a silly old woman, all the girls and boys knew what a hog-eye was. [sounds on the recording, coughing/ laughter?] It wasn't just Miss Keyse, doc. I was in trouble every which way. I kept away from the night beaches for fear of the coastguard and of what else moved there in the dark. Still, trouble seemed to find me. I courted maids whenever I could, something drove me to it. I was now surrounded by women. I could often hear Lizzie singing in the kitchen, "O, the hog eye man is the man for me; he comes a sailing straight from the sea." She did it to get a rise out the Necks I suppose. She would not explain the bruises she had on her arms and neck. When I tried coming up to her she would slip from my arms with a biting word. She now kicked the kitchen door shut when she took her bath.

I sometimes peeped on the female bathers by the shore. Harrington was often sniffing about there also. He was usually perched somewhere whittling with a big sailor knife, his pipe puffing, his eyes busy watching. Those blue-green eyes looked at you like they were getting to the marrow. He always seemed to be drawing me back into a game I could not understand, holding out a hand to me—but to what purpose I did not know. I felt myself pulled to him like a boat that drags its anchor in a rip tide. Maybe I wanted to be like him because he did not hide his true nature; you see, I did not know my own nature at all.

Harrington got me into trouble with those Fey girls. He seemed to know about my tom cat ways. "You do pick 'em," he used to say, "they come at you like flies." He offered to arrange for a meeting with two sisters in service to the Mount-Temples. We cornered them on the Ilsham footpath. One was called Sarah, quiet and deep she was, and the other was Mary Ann, a fair haired maid who kept gabbling on ten to the dozen. That Harrington was a silver- tongued bravo, he got them to drink cider with us in the bracken. They soon were drunk and Mary Ann was mizzy-mazy. She kept on about how the gulls spoke in God's language. Harrington kept on filling them up with cider until they were rolling about as drunk as drumbledranes. He got me to choose which one I wanted. I chose Mary Ann, God knows why. Harrington laughed about it at the time saying everyone to his own taste as the old woman said as she kissed the hoss's arse.

That broken bracken gave off a sharp stink. Can smell it still. I felt sick when I pulled away from Mary Ann. Her goosegog eyes had never left the circling gulls as I rolled her onto her back. Harrington seemed to find it funny, asking if all had had their fill. He clapped me on the back telling me not to look so concerned. Said he wouldn't tell Lizzie. I was in a confusion for a while after that, I felt strangely frit and kept washing my itchy privates. I hurried up to Ellacombe as soon as I could and blurted out to Katie that we should get engaged. Well, it made her happy. And we went out and about a little more. I never got her a ring. It seemed to settle me for a while also. We used to walk on the beach near Watcombe, and I'd moan that the crows hopped on the sand after us just like my bad reputation followed me everywhere. Katie used to say that the difference was that now I had her on my side.

SHANTY

I've looked up this 'Hog Eye' business. Apparently it's a sea shanty, sung by oldtime sailors when they pulled on the rigging and wound their ropes. A shanty is like a work chant. They say the name come from the French 'chanter' to sing. There is a whole load of versions of that particular Hog Eye song. Some of the words are not so complimentary to the bros. Let's say you wouldn't want to be singing it down the hood. There are some who think that a 'hog eye' is some type of barge but I pretty much think that the idea of it meaning female private parts is the right one. The song is all about the bad things guys do to a girl called Sally. No wonder it made Lizzie laugh to hear it. It's got some cool verses and I found myself singing them while out driving or murmuring them as I went down the aisles at the local deli. My favorite stanza goes "Sally's in the kitchen punchin' duff, the cheeks of her arse go chuff, chuff, chuff. Chicken in the bread pan pickin' out dough, Sally will your dog bite? No child, No. Daddy cut his biter off a long time ago." There's something a bit scary about the words, ain't there? They are songs for hard men. There is something about the shanty's crudeness that has lifted me up a little. I've gotten to be too sensitive, I reckon my sensibility has been dragging me down.

There are many other shanties. The one I like best is 'Lowlands". It has all the economy and passion of a fine poem. It's all about dreaming of a departed lover then realizing they were dead. There are a lot of revenants and returning dead in shanties. I've found it pays to look at the seafaring songs closely if you are picking about at the life and doings of Mister John Lee. There is one strange one called "Hanging Johnny" which riffs on different ways to hang people. It has sinister jokey lines like "They calls me Hanging Johnny, Well I'd hang the Holy Family, 'cause hanging is so funny." I wondered whether John's shipmates on The Implacable used to kid him about it. I somehow got the idea of having the Hanging Johnny tune sent to my cell as a ring tone. You can see I'm real dedicated to research. Not that anyone ever much rings me, it's mainly cold callers and finance companies.

Lee's world is keeping me busy but the sad stuff still leaks back in time. Nights are the worse. Lying there with the TV off, hearing the rumble of the big rigs out on Highway 12. My rooms seem to shuffle around with muffled noises. I keep turning the light back on but there's nothing there. I spend the days filling myself up with nootropics I've bought off the Net to try and help me function better but they make my head race at night. All that Gaba, Citicoline and enhanced Vitamin B12 swirling about. I guess for a lot of folks you can measure how well your brain is doing by comparing yourself to brothers and sisters and to parents. Now that Grandpa's gone I've got no- one against whom to measure how screwed up I really am.

SPOOL TWO
Gasking's Race
Babbacombe August 1884

Doctor Kaiser: Good to go, Mister Lee.

—Don't know what to say today. Keep thinking of the ole dumman. I tried to keep in with Miss Keyse that last summer even though I didn't realize that my life was like a ball of string about to come all undone. I went to St Mary's with her for Sunday services and fussed over her special in the house. She was never satisfied whatever I did. The harder I worked the more she wanted me to do. I remember particular I had to dance attendance on her right through the summer sea races. They were the high point of the year at Babbicam. The Regatta they called it. Gasking used to arrange it. There was no end of the pies he had his fingers in. A lot of craft came and filled the bay. The bandstand on the Downs got a lick of paint, a greasy pole was put up for games and flags were flying along the tops.

I had just harnessed the dog cart to take Miss Keyse up to join the gentry in the viewing stands when the screaming started. A woman calling out for 'Johnny'. I could see at once it was Mary Ann Fey.

Doctor Kaiser: One of the two sisters you mentioned?

—Ess, crazy she were. The Missis asked who the woman was, 'n I told her it was a mad woman and whipped up the dog cart to get through the crowds. Miss Keyse was frit about us toppling over on the steep road and it looked like Mary Ann was gaining on us for a while. I caught a sight of a man in a naval jacket and cap who jumped into the crowd and got hold of Mary Ann. She gave out a hell of a shriek then was pulled away behind the Cary Arms. I cracked the whip again and the dog cart dashed away with Miss Keyse hanging on. Things calmed down after that and I put the ole dumman down by a viewing stand along by the bandstand. I could see the Mount-Temples were there and Colonel McLean and the Missis' sister. And Doctor Chilcote, bless him. Thank the Lord the Brownlows weren't there. I had a job with the hoss because of all the racket—brass band playing, fire brigade bell ringing and that shouting crowd. I was also worriting that Mary Ann might pop up again. Presently, Harrington and Lizzie came. Harrington told me that if I lay with a mad woman then I would beget a harpy. He seemed to find it funny. I realized that it was him that had grabbed the Fey girl, so I asked him what he had done with her and he said that the mazy finch wouldn't sing for a while. You could never get anything from him straight. When I pressed him he said that he'd saved me again but next time I was going to save him.

The racket moiled on, drunken fellows attempted to go up a greasy pole. The Marychurch fool was made to sing and dance for gangs of chillern. A big fat girl they called 'The Maid of Babbacombe' stood on the rock above Lovers Leap and started the race by waving a yellow scarf. The whole bay was spread out with boats—navy steam cutters, fishing ketches, the Avon—a training ship for boys, schooners, yawls and dinghies. The big money was on the six-oared seiners, owned by Gasking, the Stigings and Thomas of Anstey's Cove, all smugglers in one way or another. I let Lizzie stand in the dog cart to get a better view. I don't remember who won. Most of them were related to Gaskin so the prize money likely went back to him.

I had to walk the pony back to the Glen through the thick crowds. Miss Keyse liked to wave back at the tradesmen and other locals that were greeting her. We were blocked at the top of Beach Road by a figure coming through the crowds. It was Gasking being carried like a king on a chair on the shoulders of fishermen. He passed Miss Keyse and turned his brown face to glare at her as he passed. Some of his gang began to boo and hiss at her and shout things like, "Old crow! Old crow!" and, "Not dead yet? You old biddle."

I could see that Miss Keyse was crying. She said something to Lizzie about how sad to have lived there so long and not to be loved. Later I went down to Grafton Terrace to see Katie. There were rockets going off above St Marychurch. All of a sudden Katie decided I could take her in her bed. I remember all the time I was with her that night her mother kept knocking on the wall with her stick. I thought in my foolishness that at last I was treading a smooth road.

REAL LIFE

I've been looking at most of the stuff on an online British newspaper archive but the real buzz was getting the A1 size paper copies in a big brown envelope carrying English stamps. The stamps had colorful images of butterflies. The types were written on the stamps 'White Admiral' and 'Chalkhill Blue'. There was something so non-American about those names and those stamps. They seemed like emblems from another world that confirmed me as a true seeker. I'd ordered copies of journals like 'The Torquay Times and South Devon Advertiser' for 1884. My eye greedily caught on to all sorts of stuff about the times my characters lived through. I have to pick my way carefully. I don't even have a drop of English blood to help me. No ancestor vibes. I'm German with a dab of Norwegian just like the blood line of Ed Gein—or Jeffrey Dahmer's probably for that matter!

Once I got to look through the Torquay newspaper stuff I particularly dug the adverts like: 'Chlorodyne, it assuages pain of every kind' and 'Try Mrs. Winslow's Soothing Syrup, The Mother's Friend'. I'd got the idea somehow from the movies or the History Channel that once you put Jack the Ripper to one side then the English Victorian times were a settled sunlit time of peace and prosperity but the papers seem actually full of a jittery sense of threat. There are weekly references to how many people were dying in Torquay. In August 1884 it was 9.6

per thousand, the death rate ebbing a little due to the cholera being under control. Fear seemed to move in Torquay in many ways. You can feel it through the flow of events as you flick the pages. Prisoner John Bray escaped from Dartmoor Gaol running south, last seen at Lustleigh. The public were warned to be on their guard. Yet other unseen dangers were lurking. Lee mentions somewhere that Miss Keyse read the papers a lot and got her servants to read out bits to her. I tried to imagine what she must have made of all the stuff that was in the courts each day. Harriet Brimmicombe, fisherwoman, found lying dead drunk in St Marychurch, William Rouncevel, labourer, charged with wounding his wife 'by incising her neck with a penknife', Rebecca Loveridge, Infanticide, drowned her baby in the Teign, 'her dead baby found by gypsies', PC Meech found a donkey and cart abandoned on Babbacombe Road, no explanation as to its vanished owner. There certainly seemed to be a notion that something bad was just around the corner. Sheep scab was on the rise, deaths recorded for all sorts of reasons from a stroke in the street or a carriage accident to a tree falling on a passer-by. The inhabitants seemed awful keen to cut throats, their own or others. The paper reported a veteran of Waterloo, 85 years old, killed himself with a knife because he feared he was going blind. There were also long articles about milk being a source of disease and instructions to buy 'Rough on Rats' poison to prevent being overrun with pests. They recorded that Dr Chilcote was given extra parish monies to build an isolation ward for infectious cases among the poor.

As I went through all this stuff the same names that Lee mentions on the wire recorder kept bobbing up and that gave me confidence that his strange ramblings were not plain fantasy.

Spool Two
Two Deaths and a New Life
Babbacombe, October/November 1884

—Kisler, Keeseler, Kissler, that Frenchie bastard, however you said his name. He used to call me "charlatan". I didn't know what it meant but nothing good I'd bet. Lizzie had to hold me back when we bumped into him on Fore Street. I'd have belted him with my knob stick if Lizzie hadn't dragged me off. It got hard to be anywhere in that place without trouble.

Doctor Kaiser: You have not mentioned this man before

—I'm sure I must have, doc. He and Harrington got me six months prison time. It's hard to explain it all but I'll get to it. At the time I had no end of other troubles. Down on the beach the fishermen snapped at me as the creeping servant of that old toad, Miss Keyse. And at Grafton Katie had cooled a bit. That, or she was too worn out caring for her Ma. I also thought that she'd grown fed up with me ranting on about the Missis or about Kisler. She made excuses and kept her arms hanging by her side when I tried to hold her. The Missis bore down on me, alles groaning on about grease spots on my jacket and checking on me and chivvying. She sent me to the post three times a day and found no end of pointless jobs for me to do. She said how even that rough stupid Sam Bartlet who had so strangely disappeared was a better servant than me. She was not content with any of us, kept sending her meals back to be done again, complaining about her linen, hinting that she could do without me and all of them and would soon go to live with her sister at Compton House. Later I would hear her crying and she'd try to creep into my room as if to make amends. She told me that she was sad to think of the grand parties and the life she once had there. Said that her brother St John was quite a blade. He had blue eyes just like mine according to the ole dumman.

I asked Jane Neck about this brother of the Missis. Jane told me she was often sad in the autumn as it was the anniversary of her mother's passing. She'd had many deaths, Miss Keyse. She never knew her father, he died afore her birth. Her other father Mr Whitehead was long dead. He was cruel to her. And her Ma was also dead many a year. All her other sisters gone except for Amelia married to a reverend in Hereford, and her half-blood, Mary, at Compton. The one she grieved most for was her brother, St John. Jane pronounced it 'sin jen'. They used to call him 'Jack', just like me. There is a mystery there. He went to Canady as a young man, got married then came back to Babbicam all on his own, then cleared off with Annie Bennet, a local girl. A bit of a bad 'un was Jack Keyse. The mistress still cried for him. Some say he was killed in the South Seas ten year before. A seaman had brought news that he had been murdered by a native though the Missis would never speak of it. She still talked to his portrait as if he was alive. I had no time for her woes but I wanted to understand why she kept me on.

Doctor Kaiser: Let me get this straight. You say that Miss Keyse's brother Jack was murdered?

—That's the size of it, doc. There was all sorts going on in that house once you started looking under stones. Take Lizzie for example. The leaves were on the turn in the cliff woods when I first began to notice that there was something wrong with Lizzie. She seemed unsteady and fearful, ringing her hands and not saying what troubled her. I kept finding her looking out the kitchen window up at the tangled cliffs. When I asked her what was the matter her eyes filled up. I heard the Necks whispering about it, about when women have troubles 'twas a man that had sent them. On top of worrying about Lizzie I had the Missis even more on my back. She wanted the Glen to look more presentable and she had me at half a dozen jobs a day: leaf sweeping, watering the music room ferns, painting the doors to the coach house. Little George Russell the chimney sweep came down with his bags and brushes to clear out the Glen's chimneys. He was stretching out his canvas covers over the dining room carpets when Miss Keyse came nipping at him with orders to keep the place clean. After she had gone, he said that the old bird was sparky. I told him I'd stuff her sparkiness down her throat or some such. I was fed up with her on my back all day, the crow.

Doctor Kaiser: Had Katie dropped out the picture then?

—Katie was all tied up with her Ma being so sick. She was took really bad. Miss Keyse was angry at me for taking time away to go down and see her. Katie's Ma asked to see me on her sick bed. The room stank like death. She asked me particular to make sure I looked after Katie when she was gone. I promised her I would. I had to be careful coming back from Grafton as Mary Ann Fey was often on the prowl. She'd be waiting for me and she'd jump out, saying I had destroyed her peace and I was a liar and a cheat. She said she'd tell Miss Keyse that I'd seduced her with strong drink. I'd scream at her to be off but in my mind I wondered what was ever going to stop her. We buried Mrs Farmer at the new cemetery at Hele Road in early October. There was a small gathering. I walked with Katie arm in arm down the chapel steps and told her we are free now. She cried her eyes out.

Doctor Kaiser: Did you intend to settle down with her?

—The poor girl was probably crying not only for her Ma but also for how unsteady I was. To tell the truth the troubles at the Glen got to be bigger than any worries about Katie.

Us servants were in a right bobbery. There were so many coming and goings. There was Templer and Carter the legal men, there were commercial men who looked about the place. The Necks spotted Tregaskis, a hard-bit local dealer and bully-boy walking up and down the quay, sizing up the place. One day Jane Neck held up Miss Keyse's copy of The Torquay Times. It had a big hole cut out of the Notices page. "Why would the Missis do that? 'Tis strange," she said. I ran and got a late edition from one of the Ellacombe shops and there it was, an advertisement for Bonds the auctioneers. The Glen was for sale and all that went with it. Jane wondered what will become of us. My Lizzie said that we'd be going down the road with our notices.

Lizzie had written to Millie and she came down to see Lizzie at our Aunt's house. I went out to visit Katie at the same time. We quarreled. I accused her of making up to gentlemen customers in the millinery shop and shouted that I would leave her and leave Torquay. This frit her and she tried to soothe me but I felt all riled. Later on I walked Millie back to Torre Station. She told me Lizzie was with child and Lizzie would not say who the father was. She was sure Lizzie would lose her situation when Miss Keyse found out about the babby. Millie thought it best I came home. I said I would last out a while. Millie went on about being frit of something happening. I could not fathom this news about Lizzie's baby. I got another knock about then when Miss Keyse told me she was not satisfied with me and I would now get only two shillings a week. I told her I could not manage on that. She said that we all must cut our coats according to our cloth. That really put me in a rage.

That's when I ran into Bill Richards. He used to call out to me as he cycled down the Beach Road to deliver the post. I'd known him since I were a napper. He liked to talk, old Bill. Little did I know how our words would be used against me. It was in early November, I was slomicking about, flicking at the leaves with my knob cane while we had a chat. I was moaning about the Missis. Said I was tired of it, felt like putting an end to it or some such. Bill liked my stick and tried to buy it off me. I said I needed it to crack heads. He laughed and told me to mind I stayed out of trouble saying things like that.

Everything began to pile up after then. They brought in a fisherman onto the beach at about this time. He had fallen into the nets at sea, got caught up and drowned. PC Meech and Sergeant Nott were down there bent over the body with their notebooks out. Harrington told me that the Stigings had pushed him in and drowned him because he'd gone a-blabbing to the coastguard. He told me to guard myself and that he might need my help soon. I was still seeing Eliza Maile up in the cliff woods. I'd ask if she was frit of me. "Should I be?" she kept asking. She laughed all nervous-like. She used to let me feel her bubs but nothing else. Said that I had to prove myself if I wanted more. I don't know if I wanted to have a clearer run at Eliza or if I just wanted to keep poor Katie out of the mess of my life. Whatever it was, I ended up writing that stupid letter about then. Telling Katie that I wanted to end our engagement. I worked a long time on it and posted it quick before I had second thoughts. Mary Ann continued to harry at me. She'd fix me with her mad spider eyes and try to get me to lie with her in the tallett loft above the wood shed. Even though I'd freed myself from Katie I would not dream of touching Mary Ann again. How she used to curse me when I shook her off.

The Glen was no refuge either. The house almost cracked with the strain although the usual jobs ran on. Miss Keyse still did not mention the coming sale. Lizzie was stopper-mouth quiet but I could see she was considering something. I couldn't help but keep staring at her belly. Jane Neck kept dropping things and bursting into tears.

Doctor Kaiser: You wrote to Katie ending your engagement?
—Ess, that's correct.
Doctor Kaiser: How did she take it?
—I got her reply by return pretty much. I could not bear to look it at once and saved it to read in a private place down along the sea shore past the Stigings' cottages. It shamed me to read her words and I no longer really wanted to be free of her. Hell, I didn't really know what I wanted by then.

LETTERS

These are the original letters in full, preserved in the archives and much published at the time. It's so weird how literate and formal they are when everything was on the brink of such savagery. I've hardly ever written a letter myself except some email pitches to poetry publishers. Lee's written voice as a young man seems different from the mature world-weary voice on the spool but occasionally there is prefiguring. Some of his wording is unexpected. Did he get someone else to pen it?

Here's Lee—

> *My dearest Katie,*
>
> *I am very unsettled in what I am going to do in my future life. I am tired of service and am going to look out for something else and to do something which may not be to your liking. And my dear don't let me keep you from going anywhere where it will be for your good. You may get a better chance by going away and we might not always be the same as we are now. My dear, I implore you, if you think we shall not come together let us break off our engagement before it is too late. I am beginning to love you so much it will break my heart if we should leave in time to come. Do let us break off at once. My dearest let what we have gone by die out of our thoughts but our love never can. My dearest you have been the kindest I have ever met with in love and all things. I shall ever love you the same and I shall leave the town as soon as possible. I shall feel it very much my love. If I had kept your company when first I had seen you I would have married you and made you happy. I am unsettled now and don't know what my fate will be. My own love.*
>
> *Goodbye my sweetest love from one who will ever love you the same.*
>
> *John Lee*

And Katie's tender, passionate and strong-minded reply to the flaky, insincere-sounding words of Lee—

> *My dearest love,*
> *Your letter to hand which has caused me the greatest pain and grief. What can you mean by telling me one time you will leave me and then writing to me to know if I wish to break off our engagement? I cannot make it out. As you are so undecided about what you intend to do for the future, are you also undecided about me? I tell you now the same as I told you before, our engagement shall not be broken off with my consent. As regards what you intend in the future, if it was to be your lot to break stones in the street I will not say no. Have pity on me and think how dearly I love you. Perhaps if I loved you less you might have valued me a little more. As to my getting another chance anyway, do you think I want anyone better than the one I love? If you knew how you were deceived, you would never mention it. Why not have told me last night when you mentioned about going away? There is one thing I wish particularly to know, that is do you think I wish you to marry me before you see your way clear? I am prepared to battle my way until you see fit to make me your wife. I will never be the one to mind waiting for you, Jack. I think if we part you will be the cause of grieving me to death. After what you said to me on Sunday I never dreamt of your writing me in the same strain as your last letter was written. But I freely forgive you but at the same time will not give you up. My mother will naturally come to your mind. Would to God it had been my funeral you went to instead of hers. Then I should never had got your letter. And you would never had written it. She was my only friend but I have always depended upon you to be something*

more than a friend to me. You have been my friend in all my troubles and helped me to bear them better than I could else. I should much like to see you as I have something to say which cannot be written. Grant my last request by coming down tomorrow evening
    My fondest and truest love and believe me ever your true love
Katie Farmer

SPOOL TWO
Consequences
Babbacombe, November 1884

—I went back to Grafton Terrace after delivering the post the following evening. Katie sent Ernest out for some penny sweets. She told me how she found my letter in her hallway. Her cat had brought in a pigeon and killed it. Its blood had got on the letter. She sat on my knee as she recounted this scene. I was stirred by it and we made up. Katie had crumbled my wish to get free of her. I had become as weak as a worm.

Doctor Kaiser: When is this, Mister Lee? I'm not sure where we have got to.

—It was a few days in November before the whole thing went bust. I ran into the busybody chimney sweep, George Russell, about then. He was walking up to Wellswood with a lantern. He asked me how's the old woman was keepin', I said something mazy like I wished I could push her off a cliff. It was a foolish thing to say but it got rid of him. That last week is all smudged in my mind. I know we got a big delivery of Alexandra oil, it made my little room and my clothes stink of the stuff. Harrington told me that the younger Fey sister, Sarah, was dying of poisoning in her innards. Doctor Chilcote was not likely to save her and her sister Mary Ann was fair out of her head with grief. I took it as a warning.

Doctor Kaiser: A warning of what?

—Of the terrible business that was about to jump out. That last Friday the 14th November dawned with a flat sea and a red sky. It put me in mind of what they said in the navy, evening grey and morning red makes the sailor shake his head. The mewies came ashore all morning flying fast and low inland, I remember that. Sails moved west to Brixham as the fishing fleet took shelter. We kept hearing the rattling of the capstan as the seiners were dragged up high over the shingle. I overheard the Necks saying that the Fey girl was dead. They always got to hear bad news first. Miss Keyse wanted to go to Marychurch after luncheon. I helped her go up to Weymouth's for cakes and to Bardle's the stationers for writing paper. The ole dumman took her time choosing the right type of paper and paid out her money coin by coin in a careful way. She passed the time with a few gentlefolk who greeted her in Fore Street then as slowly we made our way home.

THE LAST TIME

That's Lee's description of his last hours with the old lady. I've got this image of them returning from St Marychurch and standing there for the last time on the crest of the Babbacombe bluffs, looking out to sea, with the old mistress leaning on her stick, her hair flying in the wind by the empty bandstand, her servant just a dark shape behind her. Maybe it didn't happen like that but that picture of them fixes in my mind.

I keep telling myself to stay ahead of goodbyes, I want to anticipate them and roll through them like some winter season you've already survived. I keep thinking of that last night with Kimmie. She never told me she was going to go. I guess she was worried that I'd freak out. She spent the last evening strumming songs on her guitar. I realize now she was playing them especially for me. Later, I came back to the apartment after attending a poetry reading and found she had gone. Maybe we just remember stuff backwards, inventing, always inventing some explanation for why bad stuff happens.

Spool Two

The Storm
Babbacombe, 13ᵗʰ November 1884

—Evening came on. Miss Keyse kept tapping the glass in the hall, and it was falling like a shot bird. We all knew a storm was coming. I lay on my bunk a lot. At five of the clock Lizzie went to bed saying she was poorly. Rain began scammeling in the down pipe of the great water cask beyond the nursery door, and the thatch began to drip. Miss Keyse, in a mob cap and wrapped in a shawl, allowed a small fire in the parlor. She sat at her desk all evening writing her diary in the lamplight. I went out to get more coal for the range. A strong westerly was bringing dead branches down in the woods and the sea was boiling out in the bay. Three of us servants ate supper in the kitchen, Jane had fried up some leavings in a skillet.

Doctor Kaiser: Anything unusual happen?

[indistinct answer from Lee]

Doctor Kaiser: Did you see her again?

—One time Miss Keyse came out from the parlor and asked where Lizzie was. Jayne said that she had gone to bayd with a woman's malady. The storm pressed on, blowing smoke back down the chimneys. I ran down to Grafton Terrace to see Kate and was back an hour later. The last of the Glen's life played itself out for a few hours more. Prayers were called at ten thirty, we came together in the cold dining room and faced the mistress, her face all pinched up and her spectacles shining. She read out the prayers, raising her voice against the sound of the sea and wind. The prayers, they seemed fitting as if she had chosen them special. Particularly that one about lighten our darkness and defending against all perils and dangers of the night. We said amen and parted with no further words. After an hour Jane pulled the downstairs shutters to and bolted the front door, conservatory door and the kitchen door. I listened to the clinking as she took the house keys off the sideboard in the hall and carried them upstairs to her mistress' bedroom. Eliza filled a hot water bottle for the Missis. Someone rattled the bolt to the nursery door—probably Eliza. At midnight cocoa was on the nib ready for the ole dumman to take to bed later. Still Jane scuffled about tidying things, for an age it seemed. Once she came into the pantry to take out a candle and some matches, an' I kept my eyes shut as if asleep. She shuffled out again. Miss Keyse made no sound, she stayed at her desk in the cold parlor with the dead fire. At the last I heard Jane calling to the mistress, "'Tis twenty to one, Miss Keyse, Good night." I listened to those last rustlings of the household and to the rising thunder of the sea. I lay full dressed under the blankets, nerving myself for what was to come.

FROM WHOSE BOURN

How Kaiser did get it all out of him? It's like a tap being turned each time the recording loop winds round. There is a gasping urgency in the recordings here and the memories seem to really stress him. There are gaps and the frequent clacking of the on/off button. There are hoarse, scratchy sounds. Could they signify heavy breathing or tears? Lee seems to jump forward and back, his mind sticks on some events. I've had to work hard to get it all down right. I feel I have to finish up this job before getting on with my life. Sometimes I wish he'd just spit out what really happened and give us the money shot. I'm not big on this 'closure' business in general. I don't think people really want their lives fixed. Nobody wants their problems solved or their dramas, distractions and stories resolved; their messes cleaned up. Because what would they have left then? Just a big fat zero, blankness. What would Lee have been if not for being thrown into the fire like this? A forgotten, know-nothing hick—that's what. Lee is sneaky though. He protests a lot about the shit situation he's fallen into but he won't stick to the chronological. He jumps all over. Maybe he feels he has the right to deceive us, after all, how many bad cards can a guy get? Here's the kick in the crotch card, John, followed by the shot at dawn one. He is a premium class, grade one, bad luck story so far but that experience gives him special qualifications. He's a survivor, someone back from the brink of death. He has peered round the curtain, just about bought the farm, nearly got a pine condo and crossed the bar. Hell, he's checked out and goddamn come back. He has had a 'near death experience' in more ways than one.

Spool Three
The Hangman Mr Berry comes calling
Exeter Prison, February 23rd 1885

—I told Mister Bennet about my dream at dawn on the day set for my hanging. I told him that I dreamed the time had come and I was taken to the hanging place, the rope squirmed at my neck but nothing happened. He seemed discomforted by my account but kept on laying out my breakfast. Told me to think no more on't. They were trying to keep things clear and calm for me and everything moving forward all purposeful-like I suppose. Those warders, Bennet, Halse and Tom Snow, they'd become like family, waiting with me and tending me for nineteen days. I felt warm about them and grateful for their company.

Doctor Kaiser: You've jumped on now. When was this?

—It was the day they set to do me in. Strange thing isn't it? Bet you've never had a patient who was supposed to be dead already?

Doctor Kaiser: You mean you had received the death sentence?

[break in the recording]

—You've got it. If you had been reading the papers sixty year ago you'd know that I was due for the jerk that day. It was a Monday like any other for most folks. Spring was around the corner, I could hear the birds singing more loudly in Norny Park beyond the prison walls. First it had been weeks, then days, then only hours were left. Those last two hours are printed on my mind. They fussed with my breakfast. Their boots creaked as they moved. For some reason I fixed on the fat neck of Warder Halse. Curious to think of that neck living on and me not. And the spiders scuttling along the walls, they'd still live longer than me. I had settled in my mind that I would be gone at the stroke of eight yet I felt somehow untouched. In my head there rang a voice that said: I have done no wrong and all will be set right. Besides, my dream on that last night had surely told me that there was nothing to fear. All the arrangements going on around me were surely flummery, a shadow play to frighten children. I sat to breakfast. Prison enamelware with its blue government arrow. I tapped at it with a tea spoon and it gave forth a solid clunk. So solid and real. I found my breakfast hard to swallow. I kept on jumping up and pacing around. All the warders kept hopping up also every time I did that.

"All right, boy, it will be all right," Tom Bennet kept saying. He told me that the Reverend Pitkin would be along presently. I laughed and told him to spare him the trouble, I was alright, happy even in a way to see all events come to this pass. By the breakfast table lay a pile of letters that I had written the previous night. Those were my goodbye notes. To my Ma, I had written that I was prepared for my home above, the Lord would give me strength to meet my doom which I deserved for not opening my mouth. To Millie, I had said that I would meet her in heaven. I said the truth will come out after I was dead. They had not told six words truth. That is the servants and that lovely stepsister who carried her character with her. I also asked her to forgive Lizzie. I did forgive her myself. It was my fault. I ought to have opened my mouth before. Goodbye, goodbye forever in this world. To Katie, I put that I deserved hanging for being foolish enough to let things go.

The papers were all piled. In them were my words, some regrets, and hints of the truth. To my mind then the truth no longer mattered. It was all too late. What did it matter anymore, I thought? My innards kept cramping. They had a new-fangled water closet in the cell. I'd never seen one of those before. Kept on flushing it to see my waste hasting out and down the pipes to freedom. I kept on thinking of what Pitkin had said to me that last night. You remember him from my previous time in Exeter?

Doctor Kaiser: Sure, the prison chaplain.

—That's him. He said to me, "You are on the brink of eternity." Back he came to have another go at me. Barrett asked if I was ready for him. I joked that was he ready for me? The warders shook their heads and looked frit. To them, I must have seemed an unaccountable lad, behaving as if there was naught on my conscience. They had heard me laughing to myself in my cell. Maybe they wondered if I would try to fight them when the time came.

Pitkin had been disputing for my soul for a good while now. He often came to my cell when I was there in prison a year before. You remember it was he to whom Miss Keyse had first written asking after my progress. Back he came to pester me in my last moments. A fidgety man, his peepers skittering behind spectacles. He waved to the warders to leave and took out a prayer book. He wanted me to pray but I would not kneel or bend before him. He went on anyway reading from his black book, went on about God's wrath lying hard on me and for me to get a right understanding. He tried to weaken me, waving that prayer book and asking me to repent and confess the crime. I was tired of him afflicting me. I said that I had nothing to confess, I had finished with this world. I wanted to think about the things of the next. He said that was pride, a form of pride. I must confess, he kept on saying. I called to Barrett to say the Reverend was done and in the end he took himself away.

The warders tried not to stare at me too much. They must have been curious to see a man who was soon to melt in quicklime. Some of them were there four years before when Annie Tooke went shrieking down the blocks to be hung—now that had been a bad job by all accounts. I've told you about her before, haven't I? [No evident response from Doctor Kaiser] I had decided already to be no such trouble to them. The prison was very still that morning. There was no prisoner movement on the day of an execution. I sat back on my bed although I felt the need to pace about, and kept on pressing a finger to my neck to feel the blood knocking away steady as a clock. The three warders sat around me. They no longer played brag like they used to. Now they were quiet and solemn like men listening to a sermon at Sunday meeting. I had said to Mister Barrett that I did not know how this had all come to pass. He told me that the world's a forest where all lose their way but each by a different path they go astray. I liked that. The world a forest. Each by a different path. My path had been a special one indeed. The Ladywell had been right. I was the talk of the nation. I felt a power over these humble warders for I was a chosen man. They knew not how they would meet their fate. At least I knew it and lived with my sentence like a man. I knew and did not know. It is hard to put into words but I somehow felt I was going to go through a change that day but I could not call it 'death'. I felt a bigger man for it. I was special and my nature would see me through. It gave me a power over all that tried to push their will on me.

Doctor Kaiser: How did you spend your last hours?

—Time really gnawed at me at the end. I watched the warders clearing breakfast things and folding blankets. I saw a shaft of light slanting through the high cell window. I wondered why I had I never really appreciated the light. Down that ladder of light seemed to come all the ghosts: Granfer, his knuckled old hand gripping his hammer; Miss Keyse staring through cobwebs of hair; Mary Ann Fey, blue and dripping. I stood up, trying to shake the spirits off me. There would be time enough for them when I was cold. The warders remained sunk in their tasks. The light coming into the cell held everything in the one moment. It was as if I could slip through that light. I kept thinking how I'd tell Ma, I had a dream I could not be hanged. The door swung wide open and Chaplain Pitkin entered my cell in full robes. A bell began tolling somewhere. It was three minutes to eight. All my roads had led to that moment, all my paths through the forest. Many feet now sounded in the corridor. They came to a halt then they all poured in and the warders stood up and straightened their tunics. First there is a solidly-built man I had never seen before. He wore a sandy chinstrap beard; his dark eyes were like stones; there was neither pity nor blame in them. In a soft Yorkshire voice he said, "Poor fellow, I must do my duty." It was the executioner James Berry come for me. Governor Cowtan sprung forward and insisted on shaking my hand. For a foolish moment there was a sort of tussle between Cowtan and Berry. Then Berry took control, binding my elbows and wrists to a broad buckled belt. He murmured words to me I could only half hear. He said, "Time is a passing, you will give me no trouble, lad?" I smiled at him and shook my head.

Fever

I've thought I've been riding comfortably with John Lee. I'd just about had a line on him. Got him fixed in my mind. This transcription business is a chore but I'd found a tight rhythm and was getting it done. I used to work through the afternoons and into the night then go to an eatery, mainly Scottie's—I never cook you see. I can't manage all the mess. Then later, I'd drop into the convenience store off Main on my way back to pick up candy or snacks for the next day. I'd noticed a cool girl in Picks—that convenience store. Her name badge read 'Jenna'. I thought she was really friendly to me but I never said more than a few words to her at first though I hung around a good deal. One night I saw that the owner had pasted a staff list on the wall next the cash register. I saw a 'Jenna Neidecker' listed. I took a risk and asked her if she was any relation to the poet from Black Hawk Island. She was real pleased that I had recognized the name. She said Lorine Neidecker was her great aunt or something. I told Jenna I was a poet also and she said that was awesome. That's about all I managed before I began to get sick. It built up over a day or so. A grinding headache started. I thought at first it was too much computer time then a fever built. I found myself sweating and woozy and all I could do was lie down. I began having weird dreams that sharpened into hallucinations. I kept seeing a picture that was rerunning all the time. It was of grasses blowing in the wind and something glinting there by the roadside then there popped up a pair of blue eyes staring out of a waxy face. Those eyes were as hard as diamonds. Holy crap! I had the thought it was John Lee creeping up on me. I got up, determined to crawl away from my haunted apartment. Wobbled, all shaky, to Picks. There was Jenna giving me a sweet smile, I asked her if she sold any Advil or something. That's the last I could remember.

The responders later told me that I'd fainted and the checkout girl had rung for an E.M.S. I turned out I had the flu real bad maybe combined with not looking after myself too good. I thought it was something else though. During those sweaty hours of fever I got the idea that someone or something was leading me, dragging me down a road. Maybe it's a much more serious deal than I at first thought. Somehow Lee's troubles were becoming mine. He'd sought me out and now he was testing me. Seeing if I had the fiber to stick it out. Seeing if I had the right stuff and checking if I'll step up to the plate whatever the cost.

Spool Three
Somewhere to hide
St Marychurch, November 14th 1884

—I ran up to Compton as if devils were at my back. The gale was pushing me along and twisting at the lantern in my hand. I felt I was running from death and my own bad self.

Doctor Kaiser: You are talking of the night something bad happened?

—It was that next dawn. George Pearce, the custom man, had screamed out to me, "Oh Lord, look at Miss Keyse. Dead as a herring!" He'd caught sight of what was left of her after we dragged her into the boat house. Jane Neck, smoke-grimed in her bloody nightdress, had croaked that I'd better go up to Compton House to tell Mrs McLean her sister was dead. Tell her gentle-like, she'd said. I'd asked Sergeant Nott if that was all right. He'd just nodded and watched me go.

I belted on. The running seemed to ease the fearful hurt of my wounded arm. My hand on the lantern handle was all sticky with blood. At the Downs in the grey light I saw the fire brigade coming ringing their bell and flogging their horses on the upgrade of the Babbicam Road. They would never get down Beach Road in that fire wagon. I also met another of the police, hurrying along, "Where away is the fire?" he shouted.

"There away." I pointed back.

Down St Alban's Road I stopped, and pulled off my collar

and tie and put them into my greatcoat pocket. I looked over garden walls but could see nowhere that was any good. I had something to get rid of, see.

Doctor Kaiser: You wanted to hide something? Can you tell me about it?

—Caw, doc. You surely like to rummage through everything. It was my stick. My knob-ended stick. It didn't look like a good thing to be carrying around. As I was saying, I arrived at Compton House and threw gravel from the drive up at the servants' window. Anne Boulder, the fat old cook, stuck her head out and asked me what was the matter. I told her Miss Keyse's house was on fire and she was burnt to death. She and the maid, Mary Blatchford, let me in at the front door and I stood by the potted palms at the foot of the stairs. I moaned about my arm but they wanted to know what had happened. They kept asking where Miss Keyse was and I told them again that she was dead and that they had to tell Mrs McLean.

Next, I ran down Plainmoor Road, away from the Glen that is. The day was getting light. Somewhere past Rose Villa, Joshua Horn's's place, I chucked my knob stick into the bushes. I kept on going through the Cary lands up to Wellswood. I could see the snowy moors twenty miles away over my right shoulder. The first folk appeared, milk carts, servants going to work. I thought I should really go running down to Torre and get a train, or go north towards the moors. But something made me go on. All the faces of the parish seemed to come out that awful morning and news travelled quick. There was Charlie Sutton, the barber, he stopped me and asked about the fire, I told him that the lady was burnt to death and that I should have been burnt to death too if it had not been found out. Far too many folk came past but I kept hammering on up through Wellswood to the Warberries and to Katie's place. The pocket of my long coat bumped and banged with something heavy at the hip. I was carrying something else, see. Mazy Jack, mazy Jack. That blasted song kept sounding in my head, can hear it still. I ran into the chimney rat, George Russell—he was worried it was a chimney fire. I told him that we should all have been burnt to death if it was not for my sister. She smelt smoke, came downstairs and saw the sofa afire in the drawing room. Then I said that most gert foolish thing that near guaranteed a rope around my neck, something about how I was very sorry for it but as she was dead we shall never know how 'twas done. Mazy Jack, mazy Jack, What was that in thy head? Ah, ess, Mazy Jack, what have you done?

The girls singing it and pointing at me at school. Mazy Jack, what have you done? Gone a-ploughing with your slippers on. I also couldn't get out of my mind what Lizzie said to me the day before the whole horrible mess. She'd fixed me with a look and said, "That babby is yorn," and tapped at her belly.

On past the palm trees of the big villas where the cursed rich folk lived. Daylight came on fast as my boots went slamming along those high-walled ginnels that led past the big gardens. I stopped at the junction of Lower Warberry Road. There was a trough there set into a hole in the wall. The pack horses carrying fish from Ilsham used to stop there on their way up to Ellacombe. A stone trough fed by rain, set in the red wall. I pretended to do up my boots then took it out my pocket and jammed it behind the trough. There was a narrow crack and ledge. No-one would think to look there. It was a secret place. I had used a year before with Harrington. It was our hiding hole. Lightened, I came by the back steps to Grafton Terrace, hammering on Katie's door until her pale face came to the window. Katie, her hair down, let me enter. How everything in her little place seemed so peaceful, so unspoiled after the wild bad dream of the night.

"Katie, Katie!" I had cried out, "I was asleep, heavy asleep and woke to hell. You'll see us all marched off to a police station." I really needed her then just as everything was folding up.

Katie made me go back. She made me believe it would be

all right although my senses told me to keep on running. My feet seemed to drag as I dropped back down Beach Road to the smoke-logged bay an hour later. It was six and thirty and quite a crowd now swarmed over the Glen. Firemen had finally made their way down and were busy dragging burnt thatch off the roof with their hooked poles. The custom men were stacking furniture on the terrace. I was met by many a sidelong suspicious look. Gasking and the fishermen gathered in murmuring groups and stared at me. That lawyer Carter, one of Miss Keyse's legal men, was also poking about. I remained free for an hour or two longer, wandering around the ruined house, shivering. Doctor Chilcote bandaged my arms. He said nothing to me but gave me a worried look now and then. Then Nott and two constables came up to me.

"I am arresting you on suspicion of having committed the murder of the deceased Miss Keyse," said Nott.

"Oh, on suspicion?" I answered.

They said I had to go with them to Torquay. We began walking up the cliff road, me in front. Lizzie ran out and asked me where I was going. I told I was taken on suspicion.

"I know you didn't do it!" she shouted.

Gasking began yelling that I was a foul beast for what I had done. I knew then that a gert dark hole was opening up for me.

Nighthawks

I've got back on my feet. Taking extra vitamin complex with additional Selenium. I've also returned to my routine. Jenna seems to have disappeared from Picks though I keep looking out for her. The season is tightening up here. The lights of Scotties eatery are like an Edward Hopper scene. Everyone hunched over the cherrywood counters. There was a black dude in there yesterday, a rare sight in this town. A heavy-set guy who kept his head down and carefully read through a magazine making careful markings on page after page with a yellow hi-lighter pen. I kept trying to see what magazine he had. Even asking him to pass me the sugar and peeking over his shoulder but I couldn't make it out. He kept the magazine carefully scrolled as I watched him go out into the lights on Main then get swallowed up in the darkness beyond. I'm tackling my research carefully. I want to know stuff. All poets hate the approximate. I'm also checking for emissaries. You never know who Lee might be sending.

Spool Three
On Suspicion
Torquay, November 15th 1884

—In Torquay police cells at the Market Street station a day afterwards, I still had little understanding of all that was happening. I sat in my cell, the crazed doings of that Friday night running in my head. My arm hurt and dried bits of blood kept dropping from me. When I washed in a bowl the water was pink-stained. My braces and bootlaces had been taken from me in case I tried to make an end of it. PC Meech had brought me my Sunday suit, my other clothes had been taken for evidence. I kept on coughing. That smoke had got into my lungs. I had no appetite for the meals delivered from Gibbons Commercial Hotel. That was Tregaskis' place, and that bully had been sniffing around trying to buy Miss Keyse's silver. What a meshed town that was. I wondered what Katie was doing. Outside I could hear the sound of carts going to the covered market down the hill a way. I kept being disturbed by the clicking of the eye slit as officials came to stare at me. There was a constant racket in the cells from the drunks, tramps, flower sellers and beggars that had been hauled in over the weekend. Torquay was a rowdy place. I was in a lot more trouble than they were though.

Doctor Kaiser: So, had they charged you with anything?

—On suspicion, that's all I was told, I was held on suspicion.

FORECAST

I've got this weather finder app; I like to let it run. It's a kind of doppler radar. Weather shows as pulsing bursts of color speeding over the landscape: I zoom in east of Lake Michigan, the shimmery bursts go green for heavy rain, blue for drizzle—the deeper the color the heavier the downfall. Today the color bursts are spreading from the north, Canada, so it's not looking good. Outside of the window my birdfeeder swings like a metronome. I won't go out today, too much to do any way. I've decided I've got to get a grip of what went on around John Lee's trial. If you can examine the facts straight after an event that gives you much more of a chance. I'm going to work it out; I've got to understand. Then maybe John Lee will leave me alone.

I've had the freakiest dreams recently. I keep going back to a scene when I'm running in a storm, blood is glistening somewhere, all of a sudden a woman comes screaming out the smoke. At first I thought it was that Lion's Mane mushroom extract I've been taking. I've got to concentrate. I have ramped up the amount of nootropics I'm taking. They say that this idea that most folks only ever use 10% of their brains is a myth started by William James, one of the first American psychologists, but I'm sure there is truth in the story. You need a goal to measure up and push your brain furtherer than it's gone before. Even a bad brain like mine. If I really stretch it then maybe I can get to be some type of a standup hero. Maybe I can juice all those ghosts that are ganging up on me.

I've got a new bunch of papers. I paid good US dollars to a Brit archive cache. I've printed them out and the papers are spilled all over the apartment floor. The old Webster has been lugged to one side for now. There is almost too much information to take in at this point: There are the inquest and court records, the notes the Torquay cops made and of course, the detailed stuff that filled the newspapers of the time. The hound-dog reporters apparently came in packs to Babbacombe. The inquest was opened three days after the death of Miss Keyse. It was set up much like the inquests we get now in the States only they had jurors then. Twelve of them were selected and told by Coroner Hacker to go with Sergeant Nott to the Glen in order to "Super visum corporis", the first stage of all inquests of the time. I guess most of you do not know what the words meant. I do though. Hold up, dudes. We'll be getting onto Latin later. OK, I'll tell you—it means "On a view of a body". I've got the idea that PC Meech stayed at the front door to push back the crush of onlookers. I can see the crowd pressing up to the Glen's doors, murmuring like bees, some were probably drunk already. Miss Keyse had been laid out in Lizzie's bedroom. Let's explore it in the mind's eye. We know this room had been untouched by the fire. Lizzie herself had been sent to stay with her Aunt Millie in Tormohan. The sea outside was now calm, the storm spent, and the beach was strewn with wrack and trampled by onlookers come to view the site of the terrible crime as news spread right through the parish. The papers told me that the jurors were taken through each room. I can see them shuffling reluctantly into the bedroom. Some reporters followed them. Everything must have been permeated by a bitter smell, a tang of burning combined with the stench of dead flesh, kerosene and wet plaster. The jurymen all came from the parish and all likely knew Miss Keyse in life and most of them also had seen Lee about in St Marychurch. It's clear they thought he was a cold-eyed son of a bitch.

They followed Nott in to look at Miss Keyse's body. They had taken off her scorched night dress and wrapped her in a sheet. Her face was yellow against the white fabric. The only really recognizable feature was that strong nose made sharper in death. Nott showed them the injuries. I've seen examples of head trauma in grue sites on the Net and I'd looked at the sicko illustrations in Kerr's Forensic Medicine, a 1947 manual I found in another yard sale. Miss Keyse's head must have been a tangle of snowy roots and henna-stained locks glued together by stiffened clumps of black blood. The skin would have lifted from the wound as if some creature had ripped its way out from Miss Keyse's head. Nott then probably showed them the other massive head wound, a great dent to the right side of her temple. Her features would have been drawn in on this side by the impact. They said he even lifted the body a bit to show them the throat wound, a blackened trench which gouged right across. The stem of the neck was quite gone. I guess all they could do was stand and stare. I bet none of them would ever forget that room and the smell. Nott plodded on. He'd been told to show them everything and he was a thorough man. He raised the sheet to reveal her legs quite black and oddly smooth and shiny like carbon pencils, and at the bottom of the bed her scorched feet, the white pegs of the toe bones sticking out through the charred flesh.

They stumbled on through the murder house, following Nott, who went ahead with a lantern. He showed them the torched bedroom, the Honeysuckle Room with burnt laths poking out the walls and straw shreds from the roof thatch floating in puddles. He pointed where they had cut out bloodstained portions of the stairs and hall carpeting for evidence. At the foot of the stairs he told them this was where there were the most blood stains. They looked at the large patch of black there on the floorboards. Nott pointed to the splashes like tadpole blots on the walls. Nott explained they were marks from jetting blood as well as the thrown blood from an uplifted weapon. He showed them the trails all over the floorboards from dropping blood and the streaks along from the hall to the pantry and told them that was smeared blood.

The chiffonier in the hall was open, (a chiffonier is a kind of wooden closet, guys) and heaps of half-burnt newspapers lay about everywhere. The walls were soot-stained. In the dining room where the body was found, burnt paper and shreds of household furnishings blew about in a breeze that came through the shattered windows. There were dark smears and stains on the remaining window panes. You could see right through the scorched ceiling to the walls of the Honeysuckle Room on the next floor. The Glen had been gutted and trashed. All the dresser drawers were pulled out and furniture was toppled and piled in corners or lying out on the terrace. Everything stunk of kerosene. The place must have had a poisoned, violated vibe.

Lastly, Nott wrapped it up by showing them the narrow butler's pantry with its fold-up bed and the set of drawers with one drawer open and a blood smear on the edge of the handle. They all shook their heads when they saw the lair of that untrustworthy young servant.

They were glad to get out the front door and past the doctors who had gathered for an autopsy. Red-faced Dr Chilcote with his droopy whiskers standing next to his small neat rival, Dr Steele. Both held instrument bags. Inspector Barbor of Torquay Police stood next to them holding a bundle wrapped in oilcloth out of which stuck the shaft of a hatchet. The crowd groaned with anticipation as they emerged. Everyone in the place must have been having a hell of a day. Then as now, a murder really brought the neighborhood to life. They all came pouring up from the beach towards the Town Hall. There, Coroner Hacker was preparing his papers. This was truly going to be a big case, a historic occasion, and. he was set on making the most of it. Sampson Hanbury, being high class gentry, was inevitably elected as foreman of the jury. The court artists sharpened their pencils. The press was hungry for this major story that was to reach around the world as quick as telegraph could signal. This leap year had been a strange one with its volcanic red dawns and sunsets and the nation needed something to distract itself from the looming fate of General Gordon surrounded by hordes of Islamics in Khartoum. The other juicy case that week—the case of the shipwrecked men from the Mignonette who had eaten their cabin boy in a gore fest of cannibalism—was now bogged down in legal arguments. Attention locked onto the Babbacombe murder. The nation needed a freak to be caught and punished. A faithless murdering butler made gave them all the chills when every big house kept a servant. The case had also stirred the parish to a bat-shit frenzy and a big noisy crowd assembled in front of St Marychurch Town Hall and overflowed back down Fore Street and Hampton Road. That's the scene as much as I can picture it.

Just got up to stretch and look out the window. Rain still building outside. A red-bellied woodpecker on the feeder real close to me. Water drops on the brindle-barred camo feathers on his back. He had so much more energy than the sparrows and chickadees. He hung there, wildly stabbing with his beak, really whacking at the fat. He stopped for a moment and glared at me with his savage pin eye in a disc of grey, then—Boom!—he whirred away leaving the feeder swinging even more wildly.

Spool Three

The evidence heaps up against him
St Marychurch Town Hall, 1884

—They all showed up to say something bad about me. The witnesses were ranked up on benches at the front. There was poor Katie, all whopper-eyed under a black bonnet. That's what Devoners called being tearful. Lizzie was sitting next to her. She looked brazen-faced. The crowd was asking why she was not dressed in mourning for her mistress. There sat also the Necks, two bookends, wrapped in black crepe. I was pushed forward and the crowd rustled like dry leaves.

"Lee, Lee, it's John Lee!" they kept saying. All seemed to know who I was. They put me on the same bench as Katie and

Lizzie, and Katie leaned forward as if to touch me, but PC Bastin stopped that. I stared around the crowded room in a bold way but inside I was shakin'.

It had been all right at first, put into a cab early that Monday morning, my unbandaged hand cuffed to Bastin's fat red wrist, the cab pony's canvas tucker bobbing as we went up past Ellacombe then by Katie's place. She was probably still asleep in that bed I would never lie in again. Past the Warberries, going up the hill, I sneaked a look back towards that water trough cut into the wall on Lower Warberry.

Doctor Kaiser: I don't follow.

—The Warberries was a place where the rich folks lived. I hid something along there. Something involved in the murder I wished I'd never had. At the time it was all a confusion. All them faces staring at me as we went up Marychurch Road past Compton house, then the first crowds already waiting. They had got me in early to the Town Hall in case of trouble with the crowds. I struggled to keep pace with it all. My mind would not obey me, pictures of blood and fire kept coming to me.

I got the idea that there had already been proceedings by the time I was taken into the court room. In the cells, I asked Sergeant Nott who would be there be to speak for me

"No-one," he answered. He said that I was under the coroner now. I could ask questions but not make statements. He said to best ask the coroner afore you do say anything. I was confused if this was a trial or no, it certainly felt like a trial. Coroner Hacker with his big black beard acted like a judge. He seemed to be in the middle of addressing the jury when I was pushed in. They looked already fed up with his prideful manner. He turned to me and gave me a long talk about how this was an enquiry into Miss Keyse's death. I could ask questions, and if I did say something it could be used in evidence against me. He said it could turn out serious for me. He was right there.

I nodded. What a to-do. This was the wustest trouble I'd ever been in and none to speak for me. I knew most of the jury by sight; none looked friendly. I kept thinking—how came I here? What a buffle-aided fool I was to be sitting here where others should be sitting.

A fat little man with the beady gaze was sitting next the jury. He kept glaring at me and I asked Bastin who he was but he signed for me to shut up.

The first witness was a dusty little clerk. Surveyor to the Council or board of something, I never caught it. He'd drawn a map of the Glen, set up on a big easel. He pointed out all the main rooms and features. Ah, the Glen, that place of passages and dark corners. I remembered it differently. No map could catch its mazy ways. The clerk went on a long while. A strange weariness came over me and I kept looking out the windows at the clouds and at the mewies skidding across the sky outside.

The old fat fellow with parroty beak for a nose was called up next. He still kept eyeing me with a hard look.

Doctor Kaiser: Who was he?

—It turned out the old buzzard was George Whitehead, a gentleman, "brother to the deceased" is what he called himself. The old scrutt was kin, a half-brother really. He'd never bothered with Miss Keyse 'til this happened and I'd not seen him before. Still he was blood to her and he would want blood in return.

He said that he knew the house well, that he had examined it and no house breaking tool had been used on it. He was certain that no one could have got into the house unless they had been admitted. Again he turned and gave me an evil look. Well, I thought, no-one got in unless admitted. That left quite a few to be accounted for.

They whirled Lizzie up next. It seemed like Sergeant Nott was really in charge, pointing to the witnesses where they should go. Lizzie took the stand. She did not look at me once. She was handsome standing there though, her hair shiny under her bonnet. I marked her neat little earlobes that I so liked to bite and suck on. She walked with a careful wide-set gait and there was something in the way she stood that showed her as being with child. I was sure that all could see this also although she was early on. She took the oath, speaking in a low voice. Hacker asked her when she last saw the Missis. She said she saw her for the last time in the morning before the murder. That was at morning prayers, in the dining room. She said she had not felt well that day and slept 'til 11 o clock of the night when Eliza looked in on her. Then she slept again until three or four when she awoke smelling smoke. She woke the Necks and tried to throw water on the upstairs fire in Miss Keyse's bedroom and the Honeysuckle Room. She spoke of how all was thick smoke and she saw me helping fetch water.

The coroner pressed her as to whether she had seen blood on me. The crowd gave a rustle at the question. She denied seeing any blood on my person. It looked good then for a moment. She said that the back nursery door to the water casket was open and she did not know who opened it. Hanbury the Foreman then put his hand up and asked Lizzie a question directly about when she saw me that night. The other jury members nodded like mad at the question. She said it was about five minutes after calling the other servants. Hanbury drove on at her, asking how she knew her mistress was murdered. For the first time she looked frit and muddled. She said she did not know what had happened to Miss Keyse. They all started on at her then. Mr Bendle called out about this illness, had she been ill long? No, she said, she'd not mentioned it to Miss Keyse as she might think more on it than was necessary. Oh aye, I bet she would have. Miss Keyse would have gone mad if she found Lizzie had a rabbit in the burrow.

Hacker then harried her for a while longer about how sound she was asleep, then he hit with the big question. He asked her if I held any grudge against the mistress. The room went like crazy and a mass of heads turned and whispered each to each. Lizzie stood silent, looking down. Hacker shouted that she must answer. She began to speak, at first so low you could scarce hear it, then stronger. She'd said that in late October I'd come into the kitchen crying. She'd asked me what I was crying for and I'd said the Missis had cut my money. She said that I then grew very angry saying I would not stop another night and before I left I would have my revenge. I jumped up to say something but Bastin put his hand on his shoulder and forced me back down. I yelled out that I niver said such a thing. I had to stop it. There was a commotion in the court Hacker told me to put my hand up if I wanted to question the witness then he told her to go on but Lizzie whispered that was all she could say. There was still a furious gert noise in the room and Hacker kept yelling for order. He told Lizzie he may have to recall her. I kept on shouting that my sister had not told it right and Hacker said that it had been noted.

Don't Be Afraid

A while back I heard an old poet had died in another country. He was someone revered by the whole world as a bard and inspirator: Heaney, Seamus Heaney, of course The news here is mainly local stuff: car wrecks, new Assembly leaders, worries about listeria in cheese products, I usually screen that crud out. I like to keep a TV or radio burbling on in the background. That way I think I have company. In fact I was actually asleep in my chair when I heard about the poet's death but somehow a waking part of me heard it. I found myself sobbing out loud, partly in dream, partly waking. There is something so horrible about a great poet dying. Perhaps that's the only way my male brain could allow a display of feeling. My asperities usually cancel out any other attempt. A later report said that the last words that Heaney had come out with were: 'noli timere'. He texted it to his wife. I loved that. It was so cool that he loved Latin also. I think that should be my motto. It might help when I feel the spirits of my parents brush past me in the dark. Also when accusing versions of the self say it's all my fault they are not here.

Noli timere, don't be afraid. Maybe that's what Grandpa was grasping for after the funeral when he said, "If you're going through hell kid, keep going." I never went to my own parent's coroner's inquest. The cops had me write down what happened but I was never called. I might not have gone to my folks' inquest but I've sure had to wrestle with the one Lee got dragged to. Maybe there is a parallel here. Some lesson I've not cottoned on to yet. Mainly I've used all these transcripts to test out if he is lying on the recordings. They are the one chance to check the accuracy of Lee's memory as recorded on the spools. It's awesome the way they do match with Lee's account. Often they follow almost word for word, although sometimes he mixed the order in which the witnesses were actually called. Lee might have accurately remembered what people said but as to who was actually telling the truth on the stand, that was quite another deal.

Spool Three

Who is There to Speak for Me?
St Marychurch November 1884

—I was on about the inquest, doc. Jane Neck was taken up to the stand by Nott. He also brought out a candlestick, a box of matches and an oil can. I waved my hand about at Hacker and asked him when I would get a chance to speak. Hacker kept calling me "prisoner". He said that those proceedings were not concerned with my witness, I was to be quiet.

Doctor Kaiser: Who else was called to give evidence?

—Jane, all in black, her face like a brown leaf. I thought surely she would be gentler and not say ill of me? She said she had been in employment of the deceased for forty years and more. 'Twas strange how they all spoke of the "deceased". What word was that? Dead is what the Missis was. Deed as a maggot, deed as a stone as they said in Deb'm spaich. What divvurnce was it then, what was the point of all that talking once she'd gone? That's what I thought then in my young simple mind. The Missis had once said to me that she was not afeared of death, for she would meet her pilot when she had crossed the bar. Well, she had well and truly crossed it, that was for sure.

Jane went on about how on that last Friday we had prayers at about ten thirty. After that she saw me go to bed. She said she went into my room for lamp oil at about eleven and found me asleep. Good old Jane. She left cocoa to warm for the Missis and last saw her writing in her diary at twenty to one. She left the house keys by the Missis' bed and went to bed herself. She said she had bolted most of the downstairs shutters but left one open because the Missis liked to go out on the terrace sometimes. That was important but no one made much of it. Jane said she was woke by Lizzie crying out about smoke. She went to the Missis' bedroom and found it empty and ablaze. She heard her sister calling that she had found Miss Keyse downstairs. She said that she saw me in the passageway outside Miss Keyse's room on the first floor. I took her arm and guided her down. She said that the only words I came out with were, 'Good God, the fire!'

Jane kept twisting a handkerchief in her fingers as they batted at her with questions. She said that the fire broke out about four or five in the morning and the house was filled with thick smoke. Hacker was most keen at finding out about the dining room shutters. Were they open or not? he kept on asking. She said that they were not open when she first came into that room with me. The only light was a glow from the fire. It was a while before she realized it was her mistress burning there on the dining room floor. She wasn't sure who opened the shutters, then they were broken and she was able to open a window and shout 'Fire!' out the front. They kept on asking her how was the glass broken but she couldn't tell them clearly. I jumped up any number of times to try and tell them that it was me that broke them but I kept being shouted down. They made it clear they did not want to hear from me. I even waved my bandaged hand at Jane and she then gave me a quick look across that crowded room. She looked plenty frit also. Then she told them that I had been up and dressed when she first saw me and that yes, now that she remembered, I had broken the windows and hurt my arm doing so. She said that she had then sent me to fetch Gasking. They kept on at her trying to see if I had said anything to her about Miss Keyse but she denied it.

About then the jurors talked among themselves and then Foreman Hanbury got to his feet and called out asking Jane to tell why would Miss Keyse come down from her bedroom in the night. Jane said the only reason would be to leave a message with me, John Lee. Yes well, I knew what else she'd be minded to do. I tried to say that Miss Keyse had already given me a note that night to take a brace of pheasants up to Compton House and had no need to speak to me again but again Hacker told me that was enough from me. The jury stared at me as if hearing yet another thing that told against me.

Doctor Kaiser: Let me understand. Your mistress had already left you a note that night? So, she did not need to return downstairs to tell you anything else?

—You've got it, sir. But the court weren't bothered about hearing it. They finished with Jane by getting her to identify the Missis' candlestick and the can of lamp oil that was usually kept in my room. Jane said the can was near full on that Friday night but now 'twas empty. They kept the biggest question to last, asking on the relations between the servants and the Missis. She said that all the servants were on good terms with Miss Keyse. I could have hugged the old bat then though she began to say something else, something about the Missis getting me to emigrate and about her advancing me some money. That made me laugh out loud. The tight crow would never do such a thing. Why silly old Jane came out with that, Heaven knows. I tried to speak but I was waved off. Jane said I was very much put out because Miss Keyse did not give me what I expected and talked about leaving. They pushed and prodded at her to say more but she pressed her kerchief to her face and just shook her head. I suppose I should have been grateful she did not say more, it could have been worse.

They laid out a pile of stuff in the inquest hall that they kept waving about over the next few days. A hatchet and two knives, Miss Keyse's broken hair comb, some black rags, a shirt and my stained plaid trousers—strange to see them trousers there. Whenever Nott or Meech took the stuff out there'd be a great hissing and murmuration from the big crowd. I took to turning around and making madman faces at the girls in the front row. That would set them off screaming, 'n Hacker had to keep calling for order. Bloody young fool that I was then but I thought I might as well live up to that Punch and Judy show. You won't know what that is—a rollicking theatre, a mummer's play, you get it?

Doctor Kaiser: I think so.

—Eliza Neck got to her feet next. She gave me a sharp look as she went past. There would be no havering and hesitating from Eliza. She took the oath, speaking in a clear loud voice, and then launched into it. Said she was ladies maid and had as usual put a hot water bottle in the Missis' bed and laid out her night dress. She had bolted the first floor door leading out to where the water cask was. Said she woke once in the night but only got up on hearing Lizzie cry out. She went downstairs to the dining room and at the bottom of the stairs she ran into me. She said that I had asked her, 'What is the matter?'

I can still see her now, that skull face under a white cap coming out at me through the thick fume. I could barely tell the two old bods apart so at the time I didn't know if it was Jane or Eliza. She went on to say that she went with me through the choking smoke into the dining room where all one wall was afire. It was only when pouring water on that that she realized Miss Keyse was lying there on the floor. She said I was dashing about in shirt and trousers with my braces hanging down trying to fight the fire.

Juror Bendle, who fancied himself as a detective, asked if I was a heavy sleeper but Eliza said she didn't know. You couldn't get her to express opinions like them others. She identified the matches as ones usually kept in my room and said that she had found the candlestick on the dining room floor. That candlestick, it was strange how they harped on it. Indeed it was more significant than they could guess. If Eliza knew more she was not saying it then but kept her mouth shut as cramp as a cockle. She denied touching any lamp oil, she denied that I was with her when she found the body and said that there was nothing between Miss Keyse and the servants that gave her concern. All the questions washed off her like rain off a stone and in the end they dismissed her. I suppose I should have been relieved but her hard face on the stand there filled me with a fear I could not name. Something bad was coming. Everything was going to go scat. Come to nothing, doc. I knew it. Mainly though, I was hurting because it was so clear that Lizzie had turned on me.

Turnings

Life has a way of suddenly turning belly over. Things aren't what you thought they were and nothing is forever. When I was a kid I kept wanting to fix or freeze stuff to stop the world from changing. The trouble was that whatever I did everything glided on regardless. After the funeral we went out on Grandpa's boat, an old Lund he'd had for years. It was painted pale blue inside with mahogany seats. It was the same one we used for fishing big mouth bass and muskies in the cloudy Lake Pewaukee waters. My parents often came to the lake on weekends, walking and feeding the geese. Pa wasn't much of a fisherman. He was happy to wave me off on my boating trips with Grandpa. Still, we chose the lake because it was a special place for both my parents. We glided through the weed in the shallow parts until we were quite far out. Grandpa cut the engine: small waves were slapping against the hull and gulls were rising and falling. He opened the stopper on the big plastic urn thing and sprinkled the contents. Some bits sunk straight away and flecks of gray ash floated for a while. It was all that was left of them. He helped me throw in some flowers and we watched them drift off.

"That's it, son," he said.

SPOOL THREE
The jury makes their finding
St Marychurch, November 1884

—Back in the Market Street clink in Torquay I'd go through the long day's doings in court. How it would all puggle up in my young wits. No one would ever know what happened on that night, no one could know. The memory could not admit it. What could one say of the evil of it?

Doctor Kaiser: I assure you it would be best to let it out, to say what it is that has been troubling you.

—I'm trying to, believe me. But, Lord, it's hard because I've buried it deep. That night in Babbicam burnt a brand onto my mind: the horrible roaring of the flame, so much blood, black as ink in the orange light. It took two flints to make that fire, aye, true enough. Oh, my dead mistress. My head drummed as with a fever, 'n I kept thinking of when I was hurt as a boy and I in turn would thrust beetles into Ma's bee skeps to be killed by the swarm. My bones ached as they used to after Bartlet or Pa had done kicking me. The drop, drop, drop of the cab horse hooves coming back from the inquest knocked in my brain. While I slept my dreams wove with the racket in the cells. I dreamt of walking with Katie on the cliffs above a heaving bad sea; I saw again Granfer tapping with his heavy hammer. I used to scream out for them to be quiet there. Always racketing in the cells. Whenever I closed my eyes I saw the bees swarming in fury. They would kill all that were strange. The bucket delved down the Ladywell, I was afeared of what it would bring forth. I kept asking myself why would none ask me what I has to say in my defense. You remember Teacher Cornish once told me, "Man is wolf on man"? I saw that truth played out in the Marychurch Town Hall. Where was Lizzie? Why she was not locked up like me? And that Harrington? Not a sign of him in the crowds though I looked for him each day. Most painful was poor Katie who wept every time I saw her.

Doctor Kaiser: Was there no-one who spoke up for you in the inquest?

—Big old Dr Chilcote with his brushy hair and red face took the stand three or four days in. I thought when I saw him that now at last came one who would speak the truth. He spoke about the wounds on the Missis' body. Much I could not understand but he was clear there were two great wounds on the head and the throat cut so hard that it left a notch on the backbone. He said the burning happened after death. He used to nod his head in a funny way whenever he spoke, like a blackbird dabbing at a worm. He told them the head blows were what really killed her, the throat cut was done when life had all but gone. I could have hugged him for that. He said the head wounds were done with something heavy and rounded like a knob stick. He kept on bobbing his head when he said it. "Great force," he kept saying, "the murderer used great force". Nott showed him a small table knife. I recognized it at once as my lamp trimming knife. Nott asked if this could have been used on Miss Keyse's neck. Chilcote looked doubtful and said it was unlikely. Nott kept on at him about it saying it had been found wrapped in bloody paper in the butler's room. That knife was blunt as a bean. It could hardly cut string but still the coppers wanted it tied to my neck. The good gennelman doctor stuck by his judgment though and said that was not the knife and I was thankful. Nott then picked up the black rag and asked what Chilcote made of it. The doctor said that it was a chair covering and he thought it had been used to stem the flow of blood from the old lady's neck. It was a wonderment how clear-sighted he was in that.

It was only then that I began to dimly see what a role Sergeant Nott had in fixing everything against me. It was not that bold, loud Hacker who made the case against me but the slow-spoken Nott who had so quietly asked me to walk down to Market Street with him on that Saturday morning. Nott had come to me in the cells earlier, saying that Mary Ann Fey has gone missing and did I know anything about it. I told him that I knew nothing about the girl beyond she was not right in the head, a bit mazy. He said that lots of bad things were pointing at me. I said he should not speak to me like that and I would have my say in court. He said something like, "We will see about that." That showed his bad intent to me.

Doctor Kaiser: You think that Sergeant Nott was determined to prove you guilty?

—That damned peeler led Dr Chilcote on, to build a hanging case agin me. Chilcote, he stood bravely on the stand but I think now he was a man who was in truth afeared of making mistakes and unsure of his own judgment. His answers, though all wrapped up in fair speech, seemed cloudy and doubtful to the sharp ears of the jury. He couldn't make his mind up if the man who hurt Miss Keyse was right or left handed. He said it could even be a woman. He was not sure how long dead the old lady had been when he first saw her and was unsteady about what weapon might have been used. He did alright by me in talking of the deep cuts to my arm and saying that they would have been caused by breaking the window as I had said but he got me into deeper trouble when Nott took out a shirt, my best blue shirt for special occasions. Nott asked if the blood stains on the chest area and right shoulder of that shirt could have come from my arm wound. Chilcote looked at me sadly for a moment then back to the shirt. He shook his head, and said they must have come from some other source of blood.

Doctor Kaiser: Were you able to state your case? [immediate croaky laughter from Lee]

—No, sir. It was all sewn up already. A crowd of witnesses pressed on: Gasking, Richard Harris, the custom bluebottles, indeed it seemed every busybody in Babbicam had something to say against me. The inquest stretched out over three weeks and as the evidence began to pile, I took to playing with the crowd during the breaks. I pulled faces at them and once I wound a window sash cord around my neck and yelled, "This is what you want, ain't it?" Foolish young napper that I was. I think I'd nearly lost my wits by then.

They buried Miss Keyse half way through the first week of the inquest. The court had closed for the day. Bastin told me about it when delivering my dinner in the cells. Apparently a great crowd had gathered on the Downs. Gasking made a special coffin of three types of wood for the ole dumman. It was funny what care he took of her then after all their quarrels. The coffin was taken up Beach Road on the fishermen's shoulders, then Gaskin led a great procession with many gentry following in carriages and the whole jury marching along as well. They said that the Necks went to the funeral but Lizzie was not allowed—Mr Whitehead's orders. All the house blinds were drawn down Fore Street and the businesses closed. That was wunnerful, I thought. And that Gasking directing everything. Just wunnerful. With all the jurors at the funeral? Oh, what a perfection.

Doctor Kaiser: How did it end?

—There was a surprise for me before it was wound up. I had a visitor in my cell. It was most strange. Of all men it was solicitor Templer that had come to see me. His handshake was like a damp rag. He told me he was to defend me in court. I asked how this had come about 'n he said he was doing it as we owed it to Miss Keyse to see the truth come out. I found it hard to believe. I thought of Templer as an enemy, could he really be a friend? I remembered that Lizzie was afraid of him. He said it was his duty, the county did not like to see me undefended. He wanted no money for it and said I was not to trouble myself but I said I did trouble myself mightily. I was young. I did not know what I was doing. There were many there fit to hang me for what I have not done. I feared that the evil has been said in the court room that could not be unsaid. I had seen the faces of that there jury, I knew most all of them and they did not like me and never had done. What chance did have I now? They just wanted it finished. They had started clapping to hurry the Coroner back from the adjournments so they could get on with the verdict. Templer said I had every chance, it was an inquest not a trial.

Well, to me it felt like a damn trial. Who would speak for me? Miss Keyse would have but she was no more. That Harrington needed to be found but I knew not how to do it. Later, after Templer left, I puzzled over it. With Templer as a friend I thought that I must have enemies indeed.

Doctor Kaiser: This lawyer must have made some arguments in your defense?

—I wonder now if he took my case to do me harm. I sat back in the inquest after that as my sister, Gasking, Richards the postman and the police wove a four-ply hanging noose for me. Templer seemed to conduct matters very poorly, calling out in a shrill voice at the wrong times, always dabbing at his brow with a handkerchief, stammering like a village fool, seemingly angry and suspicious about small things and missing the big picture. He complained about the coroner to me in the holding cell then proposed all manner of grand plans to call this or that witness but he never actually did anything.

The witnesses kept pouring through. There were over thirty of them called. Gasking was the first, humpy-backed, all in mourning with a crepe band on his arm, his sly face fixed on Hacker. He could say nothing really bad agin me but told of me trying to fight the fire and moving Miss Keyse's body as if I was unwilling and fearful. He left an impression that I was a wrong 'un by the way he spoke of me. He said that he had to order me about to fetch water and such because I was so unwilling.

The customs also took the stand, four of five of them in their best uniforms. They said nothing too bad though they kept mentioning the damned hatchet, that one I used to chop the firewood. The customs men said how I had fetched it out so quickly to fight the fire as if I had it to hand all the time.

Richard Harris came to court still dressed in his sea clothes. He looked across at me and I seemed to see puzzlement and shame in his eyes. He tried to help but got me into further into trouble by making it seem that I had cut my arm deliberate-like. He told the inquest that I kept on mentioning that I had cut my arm that night. I suppose the idea of the jury was that I had hurt my arm to hide any other bloodstains on me.

Worst was that crow Bill Richards, the postman. Damn him in navy blue, all straight and stiff, the idle rogue. He swore that I had said to him that I was tired of the Glen and if the mistress did not give me a place she would bloody soon wish she had. Richards dragged up all sorts of other bad things I was supposed to have said. I forget them now but a tremendous commotion broke out in court when he said those things. I laughed it to scorn and tried to get Templer to do something. But Richards went on piling up evil stories about me and my knob stick. Hacker asked where this knob stick was. Nott said it was not in the house. I called out that I had thrown it away in Mr Horn's garden. Horn, sitting on the jury benches, shook his head as if to signify that this was untrue. Hacker began writing down more notes.

Then was George Russell, the chimney rat, making more of my words when I met him near Compton on that Saturday morning, telling I had said that Miss Keyse was burnt to death, that I was very sorry for it but as she was dead we shall never know how 'twas done. The jurors whispered together when they heard that.

That Nott is the one I remember most, moving to and fro in front of the jury, heaping up the evidence against me. Although nothing could be nailed onto me directly, each object that Nott presented seemed to point to my guilt. It was Nott after all that started that damned "only man in the house" label they stuck on me. He also showed how my pantry room was so narrow that it was hard to think of any person fetching out the oil cans in the night without me being woken. The sergeant was like the conductor in a House of Horrors. Everyone watched as he lifted up the exhibits, the hellish black stiffened rag of chair covering, the hatchet with blood spots on it, pieces of window shutter with blood and skin on it. Nott was the blood man. He spoke of spots on the hall door and the passage way outside. Blood on the door handles. A big pool of it in the hall at the foot of the stairs. Blood was everywhere, on the water barrel, on the nursery door, smears on the rock work in the garden and two bloody hand prints on the gateway to the Cary Arms. He kept pointing out the smears down the corridor near to my room, and blood on the drawers in the pantry by my bed as if they were red signs of my guilt.

Dr Steele pitched up also. Word at Babbicam was that he'd been taking Dr Chilcote's patients. He joined the crowd giving evidence against me and hammered in some of the last nails, although Lizzie was saved up for a final show. He took the stand with his gert turnip head and fussy little beard hanging below. Some said he used more modern methods than dear old Chilcote. He certainly made it plain he didn't agree with Chilcote about the nature of the old lady's wounds. He found an extra wound to the head not seen by Chilcote and he had stronger ideas about how guilty I was. He was happy to match the hatchet and the trimming knife to the fatal wounds. He speedily announced that the knife they were supposed to have found in my pantry was the one that cut the throat even though it was clearly so blunt it couldn't cut a fart in the wind. He also said that the hatchet head fitted the wound in the ole dumman's head. Both things were tied to me and it did not look well.

They brought Lizzie back but kept me in the cells that morning so I had no idea what she said against me. Templer told me about it later. I asked him why Lizzie was allowed to give evidence without me being present. Templer answered that the coroner felt that I had been threatening in the court when she spoke before. I was supposed to have tried to boss her by staring and by shouting out when she spoke. Templer said that Lizzie said bad things about me that second time. When I asked what things, he said something about Lizzie saying that I made threats against the life of Miss Keyse. "But no proof, no proof" he kept on saying.

Doctor Kaiser: It certainly seems an unsatisfactory business, this inquest.

—That's one way of putting it. All things end and that inquest finally wound up too. The jury were in such a stewer about the delays that they stamped on the floor to hurry Hacker to take his place in the hall. He still made a very long speech about all the evidence agin me. The only bit of it that I remember was when he talked of "the prisoner's menaces and threats". I turned off after that and stared out the windows. A sort of weak feeling came over me. Templer said nothing to defend me. At last the jury were told to do their duty and tramped out. I was taken to a back room in the town hall and asked Bastin how long it would take. He just laughed and said, "Not long, boy." He was quite right. Before half an hour was up Foreman Hanbury was standing before the coroner to say they had found that I had murdered Miss Keyse by beating her on the head and cutting her throat. The crowd gave out a beast of a roar and I was dragged away.

As I came past Katie I said, "Goodbye, my dear. We'll not meet again."

Doctor Kaiser: And did you? Meet again, I mean.

—Nay, not never.

I Invoke the Muses

Jenna's back.

I still like to call in at Picks of an evening but I don't really talk to her because I think the owner watches on security cam and I don't want to get her into trouble. She gives me a nice smile when she hands out my change and once she asked me if I was feeling better. I've taken her for my muse though. Have a passion for a woman? Then she can be your muse. My Erato, that's what Jenna is. She can join Kimmie, who will always be my main muse.

Jeez, I need some help, faced with this mountain of riddling stuff about John Lee. You need the precision of an artist to get through it. I'm also trying to deal with my own shit. Lee's description of his problems seems like a sort of lesson to me as well. Everything happens for a reason, right? He's teaching me something but I don't know exactly what it is yet. I'm getting anxiety dreams trying to handle it all. Last night I dreamt I kept a goldfish, one of those fat golf ball shape ones with flappy fins. I left its tank over a gas ring and I was boiling the goddamn thing up. I tried to rescue it and pulled it out of the hot liquid and ran with it flapping and gasping in my hands. I was fumbling with a faucet, trying to fill a container while the fish writhed in mortal agony but I'm not sure if I ever rescued it before I woke covered in sweat. My interpretation is that I'm screwing up this investigation of John Lee, it's turning out to be a botch, a total flub-out. Lee has led me into a maze. If I had a lick of sense I wouldn't have started this: that's why I need my muses to help me. Noli timere.

These tapes might seem a window on the past but they leave out a hell of a lot. For one thing Lee makes no mention at all of the other stuff he went through at Torquay after the killing of Miss Keyse. Fortunately I've got this heap of papers that tell the story from another perspective. Some of the newspapers gave a word-for word run down of what went on in court.

Let's try and get it straight. It seems that Torquay magistrates were really riled by Coroner Hacker. It is obvious that they thought he had been grandstanding to the press. The dragged-out inquest had grabbed the national news and had held up proceedings against Lee, so the magistrates rushed through Lee's appearance before them at a fast pace. The cops also came in for criticism. Their presentation of evidence at the inquest had been contradictory and confused at times. There had been talk that they had fixed on Lee early on as being guilty as hell and had cut out the possibility of others being involved. They didn't follow up any stories about that shady sister of his and her links to smuggling gangs. Instead they relied on her as their main witness. What also told against the police was that some of the evidence items at the inquest were produced late. There was confusion between the weeding knife and the lamp trimming knife as to which was the murder weapon. Lee's clothes mysteriously smelt far more strongly of kerosene days after the crime than they did on first examination. Something sure was fishy about that. Maybe someone had been faking up the evidence?

The same inquest witnesses were dragged in but there were a few new faces. There was a doctor sent down by the London Home Office (that's like our Justice Department, I think). Templer continued to represent Lee and continued making a lousy job of it. Reporters also recorded in a special edition of the Torquay papers that Colonel Brownlow turned up and sat on the top bench to see his former servant get a further dose of justice. Isadore Carter, a well known Torquay lawyer and a close friend of Miss Keyse, took on the prosecution case. He had been seen in the early morning of the day of the murder, poking around the smoking ruins of the Glen.

That doctor from the Home Office gave a lot of muzzy evidence about bloodstains but he was a disappointment to the prosecution. What I think hurt Lee the most was Lizzie's reappearance on the final day of the hearings. This time Lee got to be present during her evidence. She was still not dressed in mourning clothes for her mistress. Lee stared at her steadily the whole time but apparently she never looked towards him. The papers set down what happened word for word. Lizzie said in evidence, "I had conversation with John Lee. We were talking and reading in the kitchen. I said, 'I suppose Miss Keyse won't give you a character?' He said if she wouldn't give him a character he would level the place to ashes to the ground. I said, 'Don't burn me with it'."

Lee apparently waved to speak at that point but was ignored. Lizzie went on, "When Gasking called Lee to help shift the body he had to call him several times because he did not want to go near. He said once that he would set fire to the house and go to the top of Walls Hill and watch it burn."

The papers say Lee scribbled notes and passed them to Templer, who in turn tried weakly to speak up for him but they let Lizzie churn on.

"He called her 'the old woman', he did," she said. Carter asked when Lee talked about burning the Glen down.

"Two months ago," Lizzie continued. "He said once about murder. He said two should never be concerned in a murder because one—" Templer objected again and this time she halted, only shrugging when she was asked if she had more to say.

"Why have you not told all this before?"

"I tried to screen him," she muttered.

"Were you woken or called by anyone that Saturday morning?"

"No. I am certain there was no sound of anything but the wind of the storm. I lay awake for a minute before I noticed the smell of burning."

"And when you found the place on fire did you think of anything that Lee had said occur to your mind?"

"Not then but afterwards it did." Then she bent forward in

the witness box and began to cry silently. That was that, it must have hit Lee real hard. The papers say he just sat and stared at her.

That prosecutor, Mr Carter, seemed in control of the court room compared to the unsteady Templer. It seems he had been a buddy of Miss Keyse and was real keen on getting Lee hung. He told the court he thought Miss Keyse went to bed on the fatal night then was roused by something and came downstairs and was attacked by an evil person who smashed her head with two terrible blows then cut her throat. Then he pointed to Lee and said that the man who did this to the poor lady sits before you there.

Lee wasn't just giving his sister the stink-eye for saying bad things about him. I think she really destroyed him at that moment. Seems like he totally gave up after he realized she had fixed on making him take the blame for it all.

Spool Three
Found Drowned
Torquay, November 1884

—Oh, it's hard now to untangle all those trials I went through. I was like a rock washed by a bitter sea. At times it didn't seem to be me there surrounded by all those faces. The real John Lee had escaped to another place.

There was such relief to get back to the cells. I'd lie on my bed, listening to the carriages going down Market Street and farther off the fog horn sounding at the harbor. Life would be a-calling me. I'd listen to the hawkers cry out from the arches of the market next door. "Shoe black, shoe black, papers, papers, chestnuts, penny a score, russets fine, russets, be in time, be in time." I can still seem to hear those voices. It's just like where I am now in this bedroom. The real world moves on outside, all uncaring, going about its business, while a soul struggles for breath.

Doctor Kaiser: There was no appeal or way of telling your side?

—Templer came to my cell with his usual false friendliness, spilling out weak promises, saying that I would have my day in court and all would be set right. I'd stopped believing in it by then. No-one had asked me how it all happened from start to finish. Templer told me I was to go to Exeter Prison to appear at the January Assizes at Exeter Castle. It was to be a capital case, he said, I didn't realize what that meant at the time. He seemed stranger then than ever, always twisting his head about as if he imagined someone was listening to him. It was he who told me about Mary Ann Fey, how after her being missing for weeks after the death of her sister until she herself was found dead, washed up on Portland across the bay. That piece of news seemed like another doom-heavy stone being piled up on me. The poor mazy finch, in a way she was just one more person cursed by that Harrington.

ALL DEAD NOW

I've seen on the Discovery Channel about what it's like deep on the ocean floor. It snows white stuff there perpetually. That white crud is made up of bits of dead fish, silica, fragments of tsunami victims, filaments of every sort of thing dropped into the sea. It all rains down forever in the deepest sea to form a vast layer of ooze on the ocean bottom. Seven Mile Fair in Caledonia was a bit like that oozy ocean bed. Admission was $2. You could get most anything cheap: chickens, cowboy hats, mall ninja gear, T shirts with 'Bitch, I'm from Milwaukee!' printed on them. It was kind of a flea mart and swap meet combined. I went there a while back. A smell of Mexican food hung over the place from the burrito stands. I went there looking for inspiration, stuff the dead have abandoned: grimy VHS video boxes, old melted Avon lipstick, 1950s Air Force surplus jackets. It seems as if I had forgotten for a moment how dangerous it is to pick around in those junk fields. There was a dude with a rusty pick up who had spread his goods out on a tarp. He was offering compilations of black- and- white risqué photos from the Twenties and Thirties of the last century. I stopped to look closer.

"All them gals are dead now, man, all dead I guess," he said. It wasn't much of a sales pitch. Maybe he said it out of some weird gallantry, a protectiveness to the heavy-thighed beauties posing and arching on his pics. What he said did perversely attract me. I wanted to look into their faces and possess them. I wanted them gals to tell me what it's all about. They'd faced up to the mystery and they did not look unhappy. Did they still live somehow? I'm a transcendence hound sniffing after survival beyond the grave. I even bought a few photos off the guy without haggling, I wanted to hold on to their dead faces. I had a thought then—maybe I would take a pitch next to those minorities guys selling counterfeit schlock, MBA jerseys and Nike shoes. I thought I could dump that old cardboard container and the Webster and its boxes of wires and throw the whole lot back into the flow of discarded objects. Flip them back into the Sargasso and free myself. Let someone else deal with Lee's crud. It's good to let a thought out even if you don't actually act on it. By some weird connection I had the idea of contacting a medium while driving back from Seven Mile Fair. Yeah, a psychic medium. I didn't know why I had never thought of it before. I thought that it would be a new angle on the things that were bugging me. It didn't take long to find one, just saw the listings on Yelp and picked the nearest from the directory. She was called Mulvina Schott. She called herself by the tag line of 'The Happy Medium'. I got her on the phone after a few tries. She had a nice voice.

"What do you want from a medium?" she asked.

"I want to find a way to live with those that have passed," I replied.

She said she used psychometry and asked me to bring an object she could read. I thought at first I'd bring one of those red and yellow wire recorder boxes then I had a better idea.

SPOOL THREE
The sentence
Exeter Assizes, February 1885

—Judge Manisty put on his black cap. He had seemed a kindly old cove until he did that. All through the trial he asked me questions in a mild tone. Then he ended by saying something altogether more dreadful. He called out my name, John—Henry—Lee, and said that the sentence of the court was that I would be taken hence to the prison where I was last confined. And then he went on about how I'd be taken to a place of execution and hanged by the neck 'til dead. What a crinkle-crankle road had taken me to that pass. The old sprout then wished that the Lord have mercy on my soul. Ah, my soul, what was that? Ma would say, "the eyes be the window of the zaul".

I fixed on not showing I was frit, I was going to outstare the whole lot of 'em. That's why after the old todger had squawked out the death sentence. I leaned on the rails of the box and said to him that the reason I was so calm was because I trusted in the Lord who knew I was innocent. There was something about what I said that upset the judge. He gave a bit of a speech after the sentence and kept saying "I am surprised to see you so calm" but he went on to say that he had no doubt about my guilt. No one else had much doubt either it seems. That's why I could hardly pay attention to the whole nonsense.

Doctor Kaiser: You thought your innocence would be proven in some way before it was too late?

—I didn't really have thoughts like that. I don't think you

have them as a young 'un. Only feelings. You live with jumbled-up feelings. The whole trial went past like a dream. They'd let me stew in Exeter all Kirzmas and New Year then they dragged me out for the rattling speedy affair. It took two days—a Monday and a Tuesday—with summing up and sentence by Wednesday lunchtime. There was a tremendous congregation to see all come to pass. There was Hacker the coroner on the front benches, stroking his pointy beard, coming to see his work all capped off. Indeed there were many familiar faces in that court room. Poor Ma was there in black, toiling though the crowds, arguing at the gate to be let in. That beadle Whitehead, the brother, came to see justice done and I saw Colonel Brownlow and his 'andsum Cuban wife. Katie didn't attend, thank heaven. It would have been so hard for her to have to listen to our letters being read out again in public. They say tickets for entry were hard to get and much money was made by the court staff. They struggled to move me at all such was the crush and the great crowds waiting to see me. They sent a big old Black Maria drawn by four horses as a trick and the crowds followed that while I came in to court with Governor Cowtan by the back door in a hansom. We were so close to the streets on that journey I could sniff the free air for a moment. How it had rained, but it didn't put off the crowds, all promenading in their Sunday-gone-to-meeting clothes to see me condemned.

Those things that were once part of my life were shown again: shirt, trousers, socks, weeding knife, oil can and that damned axe. Much was again made of those things. They were passed hand to hand and held up for all to see. The witnesses they kept in a back part and I did not see them until they stepped out to play their parts. I was kept cooped in a holding cell below the dock then rising up suddenly like a jack-in-the-box into that sea of faces and the legal men in their white wigs. What a great crowd of witnesses was gathered about to see justice done, while the press men scratched away on their pads.

What a tayjisness it seemed. I was sick of the whole thing and wanted it done with. The story was the same, told thrice now. The same things brought up: blood blacker than ink, oil fumes, smoke-stained secrets, the old knife and the notched hatchet dragged out again and passed around. The same witnesses: the custom men, postman Richards, Dr Stevenson mumbling into his great beard, the Necks and that peddle-backed Gaskin. Chilcote who would not accept hatchet or knife was replaced by his little rival, the terrier, Dr Steele. The same opinions were trotted out but not attacked by my defense. I now had that young strapper Charles Templer, brother to soapy Reggie. A busy fool, he had come to see me on the Saturday before the trial saying that his brother had been taken ill and had to be replaced. I asked how ill he was and he told me he had gone to a place in Surrey in order to improve his health. I wondered what had ailed him? You had to be mortal sick to be sent to Surrey. I wondered what soapy Reggie had caught by his black doings.

Doctor Kaiser: Let me understand. Your defense lawyer got sick?

—Ess, I told you he was taken to a whatsit, a santarium.

Doctor Kaiser: What was wrong with him?

—I never knew. He alles seemed strange. Skin damp as a fish and he had the shakes something proper. Templer's brother was little better at the legal work than him. He had a breezy air born of nothing. He was vulishly keen and his only advice to me was not to say anything. He said we would get me off alright. By "we" he meant he and St Aubyn the same bearded, waxy-faced legal who had supposedly proved me guilty in my first sentence in the Brownlow case and who now had changed places and was acting this time for my defense.

Doctor Kaiser: Your representation certainly seems very strange. You say that the man defending you had prosecuted you in the past?

—You're beginning to understand, doctor what a world of trouble I was in. St Aubyn was high gentry in Cornwall, they said, and a parliament man. I well remembered him as the cause of me getting a long sentence at my first appearance in court. Maybe it was then that I first began to find a strange peace settling on me, I thought I'd just let it all happen as God willed. They say that the witnesses had travelled up on a special train together all prodded along by Sergeant Nott. Lizzie was among them. She was now seven months on, walking with a straddle gait. She had that air of knowing a secret that all women with child seem to have. She held a life within her that would go on beyond her. The lawyers kept saying that she was "unsaint". I had no idea what they were talking about until Charles Templer explained that it was French legal talk for being with child. It was then that I gave my only instruction to my defense lawyers. I asked that Lizzie should not be questioned in court about the babby she was carrying.

Lizzie stepped up as the chief witness, repeating her stories about my supposed threats. Richards followed her and also gave damning evidence about those careless words I told him in October. Sergeant Nott spent two hours on the stand detailing the evidence against me in every particular. In all of this there were no questions from St Aubyn. When I asked about this he answered that I should wait for his defense speech.

Defense? I had none for my case was in the hands of my enemies. There were some who could have saved me but they were not present. I kept looking around the court to see if Harrington was there or maybe out somewhere in that pressing crowd waiting for tickets under the arches in the Rougemont courtyard. Harrington's shadow had dogged me for so long it was strange that he was no longer there. After all, he was the only person who really knew what I was about. Now I felt dazed and dozy. I would sometimes look up to see my mother's black outline in the court gallery, aware of her eyes on me. I had taken from her example my cool scorn for all this vulishness. The press thought I was mad. Templer showed me a piece from the paper which said something about me having strange eyes like the ones you get in madhouses. Templer and St Aubyn certainly spoke to me as if I was an idiot, a gawking vul. Ma was what they called a scryer, she could read what moved on the surface of water and she understood dreams. That was not madness. That court was all a dream to me, a dream foretold. Those arrangements that bundled me along could be seen in that prophecy from the Ladywell so long ago. My name was always going to be on the lips of all in the country. No longer John Lee but 'Babbacombe Lee', forever. That was why I seemed so strange to them.

At the end of it all St Aubyn, once my enemy, now my so-called defender rose, adjusted his gown, and turned his great blind face to the jury and tried to block some of the bad things they had heaped against me. I barely listened I must confess, although I was angry when he dragged Lizzie's name into it and said more about her than I wanted to hear. I had told him to leave Lizzie out of it. He went on that there was doubt and when there was doubt the jury should not convict. Well, I could see on the faces of those Exeter rascals that they had no doubts at all. The old crabbit Judge Manisty came back from an adjournment to make his summing up. He cast his mild eye over me then stamped all over my defense saying that it was very far-fetched, very far-fetched indeed. He told the jury to weigh the facts—I could see how weighed up they were on their fat faces. I was led downstairs to the cupboard cell under the court. I heard the hum of a hundred conversations, the drumming of feet and scraping of chairs as the court cleared. Then silence and my breathing, guts rumbling, my brain a-scurrying. I lived in a new sort of time, an enemy time where hope was crushed out and nothing moved to a betterment. The account says that the jury was out for half an hour but for me it could have been half a day. Then came the thudding of returning feet, a key turned in the lock and I went up the steep steps into the noise of the crowd, knowing already what was going be said and done.

PASSED

I took Interstate 43 to New Berlin. When we were kids at Waukesha we called the place 'The Bubble' because nothing ever happened there. Mulvina Schott did home readings but I didn't want her to see my skank apartment. 'De mortuis nil nisi bonum', don't say nothing bad about the dead, that's what should have hung outside of her office; instead there was a poster there with a picture of an angel and these words—'peace will fall, time will pass, loving memories will always last.' Not great poetry but at least it was signaling that she likely wouldn't hurt me. Her workplace was a two story colonial in a conservation area. There was a flock of grackles in her lot. I find them spooky birds, always hanging round for a main chance with their drag-ass tail feathers and sinister greenish sheen to the black feathers.

Mulvina was an attractive woman with a round Slavic face and tilted eyes, in her 40s and real classy looking. I felt she was apprising me without being too obvious about it and I tried to control my tremor. She took my $75 dollars saying that we should get the ugly part over, then led me into her consulting room. It had soft pastel colors, was full of crystal objects and smelt of aromatherapy oils. I had the thought I wasn't going to get too many surprises. Mulvina explained how she worked, by 'channeling' spirits. I needed to be respectful and aware that spirits responded well to compassion. All the while she gave her spiel her intense dark eyes were boring in on me. Again she told me to relax. I told her I always shook like an aspen. She remained sitting for a moment and recited a sort of prayer. I asked if she was religious she said she was raised Catholic and gradually learned she could communicate with spirit after her mom died when she was 11. She said that's what she called people who had passed, they were 'spirit'. I really warmed to her then. I knew I was in good hands. She said the universe pushes us to find our true calling I said I could go with that. She asked me my object and I handed the bundle over. As soon as she had it I could see her smooth brow furrow. She looked puzzled and maybe a little worried.

"I think you're a sensitive too," she said.

Spool Three
On the brink of eternity
Exeter Prison, 23rd February 1885

—I thought of being dead and of the world moving without me. All I had known crumbled away. There were no choices left, no threats to make, no promises to give. I had gone to bed healthy and woken with a fever and all seemed strange. I felt Berry's eyes on me from somewhere close. Watching, measuring, calculating the drop. The warders treated me like an invalid friend whose condition should not be mentioned. Mr Rainford the Chief Warder had handed me a bundle of ribboned scented mail. He said such women often wrote to condemned men, "Somebody loves you, John Lee," he said in jest.

Sister Millie and Ma came to see me for the last time. I kept a light mood with them and Ma said that I looked as though I were going to a dance. I tried to show them a quiet goodbye in my eyes. Those last days gave me a sort of peace that I've never found again. I could see the years ahead without me, Ma sitting by the fire listening to St Mary's chimes, Katie finding other lovers, Lizzie's child going out in the world, the sea off Babbicam combing its shoals in all the nets of time to come.

Pitkin and Hine, the village priest, came to my cell also but they discomforted me much more. They had been called supposedly to melt my hard heart to confess. They both hammered on at me for hours until in a weak moment I wrote something on a piece of paper. They pulled the scrap away from me and held it to the lamp. I remember exactly what I wrote. It said, 'I was asleep that night, and woke to see Lizzie and a masked man creeping down the stairs. That man was Cornelius Harrington.'

Pitkin shook his head. He said it wouldn't do, but I'd had enough of them and sent them away. It was too late for bleating. The jig was up. A navy saying that, did you know? They said that the ship would sail when the sailor stopped dancing at the end of the rope.

Doctor Kaiser: You told them what really happened on the night of the murder?

—It was too hard to put it all into words but they should have paid attention to that note. After that it was too late. Big, bearded Berry came forward. His cod-fish eyes showed nothing. There was brandy on his breath.

"Poor fellow I must do my duty, step ahead, lad," he said to me. Then the three minute walk going slowly along the block corridor. The Chief Warder and the Chaplain were ahead and men to each side of me. I set myself to walk straight and keep my head up. The Chaplain's white gown shone in the corridor. He read aloud from his prayer book. What did he read? Something about how in the midst of life we were in death.

A bell kept ringing. Out the narrow door, into the cold air, and down the steep stairs to the Governor's garden; the bell louder now and the sound of rooks circling the prison roof. We moved along a path through the thin grass and up to the open shed before us. No scaffold, no steps, just a trapdoor and a bare room ringed by men. All of a sudden, I made out the beam and noose above me in the dark. It was just as in my dream.

A Reading

Mulvina told me she was an empathic. She picked stuff up, emotional and mental, from me and the object I had brought for her to hold. She told me she never knew what would happen in a reading. She couldn't guarantee bringing 'spirit' through. Apparently those that passed took their feelings and personalities with them, they could be having a bad day and not feel like talking. Did I understand? I nodded. She explained that spirit spoke to her and she jotted it down because often it came so fast. She in turn would relay the content to me. Sometimes she did a spirit portrait if the images came. She warned me she was not a counselor and if I needed psychiatric help it wasn't what she did. I again agreed. I could tell she thought I was a screwball. Maybe she saw that fear in my eyes because she then explained that she was only there to "communicate, appreciate and validate." She told me to chill out, feel free and be open to communicate. Hell, that was a tough one for someone like me. She said she did not know what spirit would bring. It might not be what I wanted to hear but it would certainly be what I needed to hear. She said not to interrupt her because the voices were often fast and whispery, they could be like psychic nudges, fleeting communications. I was getting tense with this build up and it was a relief when she finally got going with it.

I handed her my object: a pair of old twisted eye glasses wrapped in Mom's silk headscarf. Mulvina held it all tight in both hands and seemed to be rocking up and down, like a child trying to comfort itself. All of a sudden she opened her eyes wide and looked at me. Her eyes were spookily greenish in the light. She shook her head and began to mutter to herself real quick. I could hardly hear her. She put the scarf bundle down and began to write quickly on a pad. All I could hear was that scratchy sound of the felt tip on paper and her muttering. I can reconstruct some of it because she gave me the pad later. It went like this (I've put in the punctuation, there wasn't any in the original):

"He's here, my skirtful of hell. Banjo, banjo where are you? His collar. Got something? He'll show you the way. Want to protect, tree falling in a wood, like that. Saw a journey, letters curled, strange. There, a sudden parting. There are three of them wanting to speak, definitely three, one small, no voice. Are you lost? A tower, you're making your way there. Quit hurting me! My name is Georgia. You are trying, oh you are trying. Rigid for a moment, a voice saying… Can I get it? Bootiful oh my lovely boy, gone. Craters I call 'em craters, black sand is in his veins, weird shaking, find love, need to forgive. They are three of them here. They forgive because there's nothing to forgive, shadow. I feel I don't know what it means? Again threefold. Feel someone is dogging you. You see him also? Protect, this man Eebus, prison of your making, beaten down like pigeons, listen!"

"Phew!" said Mulvina, "I've never had that before. It was like headphones being switched on too loud and not being able to turn it off. It's quite short but that's all I could stand." She dabbed at her brow with a rolled Kleenex and lit a scented candle. I could see her hands were shaking.

"That was intense. Like a wind blowing through me," she said. She read out what she had written and told me, "I'm sorry, honey if it doesn't make sense. I felt a lot of spirit. Many voices but one presence. There was something else." She started scribbling and scratching on her pad again and showed me a weird cartoonish figure she had drawn. I found it hard to make out, there was a seated figure which Mulvina said represented me then there was another shape hovering over me. I couldn't get it, a big dark smudge maybe wearing a hat or was that a shock of hair? She also had a clump of figures to one side. They looked like those pictures of grey aliens with big eyes. Mulvina tried to explain that the figure over me was not entirely benign and the smaller entities, the alien figures, were trying to help me.

"Maybe you need to figure it out yourself," she said, "I can't explain it."

Truly, I was shaken up by it all but didn't want to show I was scared. I needed time on it. I asked her for her written stuff and she gave it and the picture.

"Maybe you need to look after yourself, eat better," she told me. "There is a road though and you're on it. It's leading you to the right place."

I said, "Thanks, I sure hope so, Mulvina."

She smiled. She really was beautiful with her dark wavy hair. She handed me back the broken eye glasses wrapped in Mom's scarf.

"Those are your parent's things aren't they? They've passed? I can feel that," I nodded. That's the only thing Mulvina really got right I guess. She asked if I had any questions. I asked her if there was a heaven. She said," Yeah, it always beautiful there." She went on to tell me about how sometimes she saw family groups there celebrating something for someone here on earth such as a birthday. She said that dead people call the place whatever they know it to be, some call it 'spirit world', it doesn't matter just like what we call 'God' doesn't matter. It's whatever you want or believe it to be. In the same way heaven is whatever they want it to be. Mulvina said sometimes she saw a beautiful garden with benches and big beautiful Greek- type buildings that look like they are made of marble. She said that they can create things only with a thought if they don't like it they think it away, and think something new. Sometimes, according to Mulvina, when a spirit has a very sick and tired body when they go to heaven there is a place they go where their spirit guides will perk them up with more energy. I said it sounded real nice. She told me the big old universe is pushing us along towards discovering who we really are, we may kick or scream and not like it and feel very afraid of being pushed out of our nests but we need to go on that journey.

"And Hell?" I asked. What did she make of that? She replied, "That's for those souls who are lost, honey. That's all I know." I thanked her and I really meant it.

SPOOL FOUR

The Eyes of the Lord Are in Every Place
Portland Prison Dorset, 1907

—I was on C Block South. They'd march us in column of twos to the exercise yard. That whump whump sound always filled the place. We'd go in a blue-grey line along the beaten track around the edge of the yard. High stone walls penned us in. We called the stone work 'ashlar'. You see, we ourselves built most of the walls that kept us in.

Doctor Kaiser: Where is this you're speaking of now?

—That was in Hell my good sir. Otherwise known as Portland Prison. On a headland it was, a crumbly limestone lump out in the sea, and that endless foot slogging kicked up the limestone dust. In Portland in summer you ate that dust all day and it made a sticky clay in winter. During exercise we had half an hour 'association'. This was the only official time that we could talk. It was a privilege you got if you were a long sentence man. Some prisoners had forgotten how to speak properly after being for years on the silent blocks, and many of the poor craiturs spoke in a strange way out the side of their mouths without moving their lips.

One long term man was Adolph Beck. He was in his middle years when I met him at Portland. He always whispered for the news when I came to give him his oakum each morning. He was all over the papers just like me. He had been mistaken for another fellow in a crime with eleven witnesses ranked up against him and with no chance of giving his own evidence at his trial. He got seven years and served every day of it, vulishly pleading his innocence to all who came across him. He served his time at Portland and was let out in about ought one but, most strangely, reconvicted again when he was once more mistaken for the same swindler that he had been confused with afore. They eventually changed their minds after a year or so of his second sentence when the actual man who did the deed had been identified. I heard that Beck drank himself to death after being released. According to the papers of the time there has been 'an unthinkable error of justice.' Ess, well, I knows all about unthinkable errors of justice.

I had nearly gone mad myself in the early days. Those nine months solitary in Pentonville and the Scrubs were a soul killer. It was a relief to go to the public works at Portsmouth despite the awful hard work, and later in Portland you could whisper to other men during chapel and on the work parties and there was that permitted half hour's association for long-sentence men with good conduct. After I had done twenty years inside, I needed conversation less anyway. I liked my cell time away from the other men, alone, studying the papers brought by the chaplain from the library. These showed little bits of how the world was changing outside. A new century had come. I had grown stronger over the years; stronger in character that is. I had hardened as a man and grown a horny shell. I wanted to live for my freedom. Thoughts I once had of escape and of revenge had burned away under a thousand workyard suns. I held to a strong will to win over the authorities and to steer my own fate. I was John Lee who could not be hung and could not be put away. I would prevail although so many were ranked against me.

Doctor Kaiser: How did you survive the experience?

—I became a good judge of character though I was surrounded by hard men. We long sentence men stuck together. The others sometimes spoke of what they had done to be in clink but most of them knew not to ask me about my offence for I was famous on the outside for the authorities' failure to hang me, and that had brought me respect. They knew that I had carried my innocence for twenty years and even the doubters respected me for that without believing in it for a moment. They looked up to me because of my strong spirit and my fight with the prison system. We spoke of the things we had in common, how the summer sun burned our heads and necks out in that bare exercise yard, how to lessen thirst by sucking stones. We always moaned together about the food. It was barely stomickable. Slimy bits of grey pork each day and split peas and potatoes with half an ounce of salt measured out separately. In the last years they started serving a sloppy vegetable stew which the men called the 'yellow peril' due to its roiling effect on our innards. I had lost most of my teeth and it was hard chewing on the tough globs of meat. Hog bristle tooth brushes were given out at some stage but I continued to clean my remaining pegs by rubbing at them with a flannel and a pinch of salt. How my teeth ached. Year after year the prison dentist called with his long, dirty apron and smell of ether, yanking out one tooth after another. Strong-rooted and black as coal, those teeth came out slow as if holding onto their memories.

I did not speak much to the other prisoners about my petitions and the work that family and well-wishers were doing on the outside. It was as if I spoke too freely about it then the hurt when those petitions for release were denied would be the more crushing. I did not want to fall so low as I did before when I really believed I would be set free after the twenty year period had passed. The Home Office had said 'no' to my application and that was the only moment that my will had really gone weak. For a while then I became a mazy-jack and wanted to let go my grip, the hold on hope that I had carried all that time. Then, I'd thought of throwing myself off the one of the sheer prison quarry faces but I soon pulled myself together.

Sometimes I spoke to the friendly assistant warder Crook from Crediton, one of two Deb'm men on the staff. Crook fed me news about my petitions and about what the papers said there was danger in revealing this knowledge. When I went before the Governor asking about the progress of my requests the Governor had set the chief warder Luscombe onto tracking down my informants on the prison staff.

Then all of a sudden one summer day in ought seven I was pulled out of a column at exercise and led through the yards to see Governor Briscoe.

They made me wait a long time next a sign that read The Eyes of the LORD are in every place. I knew the sign well as I'd stood outside that Governor's office so often over waiting on this or that, answers to petitions, requests for doctor or dentist. Ess, the Lord had worked in strange ways, saving me from execution but leaving me to that living death.

They pushed me into the Governor's office. Briscoe was scratching something into a ledger as we came in. He looked prapper angry about something and paid me no attention for an age. They said he had been an officer in charge of military stores at Gibraltar for twenty years. A man for figures. He dealt with the prisoners all the same way. He never shouted or bullied but he made it plain that you did not matter. Eventually he looked up and asked how I was behaving. The staff muttered their usual complaints agin me, how I thought I was cleverer than them. How I was suspected of contacting outside agents contrary to regulations but it could not be proven yet. Said I was on stone dressing gang duties. How I complained of my health and my teeth. The doctor thought I was shamming it. They had nothing good to say about me. The Governor looked at me as if he had found something on his shoe. It was hard to say what he was thinking. Some of the prisoners thought that he was afraid of them. He said he had a letter for me; it was from Ma. They never let me read my own letters because of my drumming up support and petitions for my release. I had requested release every one of the last fifteen years of my sentence and the answer always came back 'no grounds'.

The letter he read out was the usual one from Ma, written for her by Mary Bond from next door. I think she said in her letter that she had tried to get Solicitor Rowse in Newton Abbot to petition for me but nothing could be done. It seemed then that it was the usual hopelessness. For a while, after I had done about twenty years, I had really believed I would be freed especially after the warder from Crediton brought me the cutting about the crowds waiting for me at the station. I had the black dog on me when that disappointment had finally bit home. I grew thin and faint-hearted and they eventually sent for Dr Brayne from Broadmoor but by the time the doctor arrived my spirit had revived and they could not find reason to carry me away to the mad house.

Briscoe made me wait a while longer, he read out a few other pointless things, letters from Mr Bryan about lobbying members of parliament and the like. I had a good deal of friends like Bryan, do-gooders and kindly folk working to free me, I was not quite sure who Bryan was and why he had taken me up but I was grateful for his efforts. There had been many like him over the years. They usually had meetings in their home towns then got up petitions yet one after the other ran out of steam and all hopes were dashed. Why did they want to help me? I knew not but supposed that all the world loved an innocent man to prove his case.

Mainly, I did not want to show weakness but Briscoe was only playing with me on that day. They did that sort of thing all the time. He said there was one more thing then took out a letter with the Home Office mark across the top. Briscoe read out that the letter instructed him to remit prisoner L150's sentence and release him before the ending of the year. I was sure it was a trick at first and kept a face like a shut door. Briscoe said again that I would be released. The warders seemed to shrink away from me. Briscoe told me to deal with this news with good sense. He went on to say that I did not have permission to discuss this with anyone else and if I did so it would prejeediss the date of my release. He said also he was not going to let this news make for unrest among the other convicts. I asked if I could tell my mother but he refused. He said in due time I would be released, when that happened I would be able to work but not break my conditions, nor make an exhibit of myself, nor associate with low persons, nor would I bring the attention of the public to myself or he would be seeing me again. He went on about how I'd be staying on a while longer. Then he told me to get back to work. That's how I heard it, Doctor Kaiser, just like that, after twenty-two years in Hell.

Banjo

What could you do with the stuff Mulvina laid on me? Sure, I was dumb as a stick for bringing those family objects for her to get her vibrations off. That just stirred up the spirits to no purpose. Her reading was pretty obscure but I recognized some of it. Banjo, for instance. It's not that I had forgotten Banjo, it's more that I have pushed the memory of him to the back of my mind. Banjo was my dog when I was a kid, a mongrelly hound, whitish with a black ear. My folks bought him to draw me out and help me make friends, but me and Banjo never clicked. One time, I invited a neighborhood kid called Melvin Reinhard to our place. I wanted to impress Melvin and got out a crossbow I had secretly ordered by mail order. I fired the thing in Banjo's direction without really meaning to hit him but it went and stuck him in the backside. There was a lot of yelping and blood. Ever after the dog was real wary of me and hopped around with a limp. Dad was so mad with me, more angry than I had ever seen him before. Banjo got run over by a car a little while later. I was about 12 then. I always believed the dog had been hit on the road because he was running away from me, frightened of getting crossbowed again probably. So I wasn't too pleased by his return as a spirit animal. I thought that maybe he was still pissed with me. If my folks had sent him as a psychic emissary then that probably meant they were also pissed. Not that I believed that they were haunting me. What I really thought was that mediums were telepaths. Surely all they do is pick up all our mental sludge and broadcast it? That's why that classical stuff was in there. Was that a reference to Horace and the falling tree? Faunus, protect and all?

My own brain was full of fear and all that stuff had been echoed by Mulvina. I bet that picture she drew was of John Lee in his derby hat, glowering over me. That must come from me also. You might ask why I went to see her in the first place if that's what I think. Well, shit knows. I might have hope without belief; I want to use everything to understand what is spooling out. Lee secretly believed in spells and wise women, that Ladywell stuff is never far from him. Well, Mulvina is my wise woman. I want her on my side just in case. Now do you see how messed up I am? I'm in such a state of screweduppiness that botch, flub, foul-up and bollix all rolled into one won't cover it.

Okay, now I've made that clear and shown I have nothing left to lose I'm going to try again I'm going to surpass my own low expectations and deal with Lee rigorously. That's right, I'm going to employ some Edgar Allen Poe-type ratiocination. Somehow my own troubles and those of Lee have got tangled up. Those old ghost gods can care for themselves for a while— that's what Mulvina's zany word spaghetti referred to isn't it? She mentions "This Man Eebus", surely that's her phonetic 'Scansin version of what was in my head: Dis Manibus. It's laughable really. It's Latin, dudes. D.M. is on all the Roman tombs. Look it up, homies. Okay, I'll tell you. It means: 'in memory of the ghost gods, the Manes'. Hell, it doesn't take long for me to track back into the supernatural again, does it? Alright, Manes help me, what I want to do is to bottom out this John Lee hanging fuck-up. What the hell happened at his execution party?

Time for another coffee—no, better not, the shaking will be off the Richter scale—Mountain Dew it is then.

It's weird that Lee never said a whole lot about what had actually happened in the execution chamber at Exeter. Maybe it was on one of the spools that were broken or lost. I've have to piece it together from all the various published accounts. I've relied on what's written down, no flaky medium messages or Lee's unreliable memories. This is how it went according to the reporters who had a front view, sitting in a special pen on one side of the governor's garden. In addition, Cowtan described it in detail in a letter to the Chief Constable and even Chaplain Pitkin wrote about it in his memoirs called 'The Prison Cell In its Light and Shadows'. You can try and triangulate the truth by lining up all those accounts but whatever you do its still seems a freaky business. I come from the post-grassy knoll generation, I've studied the shape of the smoke clouds above the Twin Towers. The truth is hard to find although there are pictures of it from every angle. Some said it was the rain-warped drop boards swelling after the night's heavy rain that had bound together and so would not fall when Berry pulled the lever. Some said it was all on account of a spell put out by Grandma Lee of Ogwell who was paid to hex the execution. Others yet claimed they saw a white dove perched on the gallows cross-beam sent by the Lord who did not want to see an innocent man hanged. Those who liked a conspiracy said that it was convict laborers who set up the workings of the device and had cunningly fashioned it so that Pitkin would stand on a loose board which would then jam the drop lever. Here's how it actually went down.

The newspaper men, a dozen of them, were placed so that they could see the procession and look in through the open doors of the van-house-turned-hanging-chamber. It was a cold, wet February morning. The bell was tolling and the prison locked down. The procession trailed near to them before crossing the governor's grass lawn. All seemed caught in a sickly yellowish light. At the head was Chief Warder Rainford, then the robed chaplain calling out the burial service. Lee followed walking straight and erect, tied at the wrists. Two warders were on each side of him. The young guy looked ahead, his pale face was set in a determined expression. You had to hand it to him, whatever he had done, he had guts. It was so strange for them to view a conscious being that would soon no longer exist. It was such a privilege to see a man die like that. They said that it shook you up and made you really taste your own life fresh again after witnessing such a thing. The prison surgeon Dr Caird and Governor Cowtan came past and lastly the solid figure of Berry bringing up the rear. Berry stared intently at the back of Lee's head as if to forestall any sudden moves from the prisoner.

They could see the procession enter the shed. It was the same setup that had killed Annie Tooke six years before, she had been hanged by Marwood, Berry's tutor. There used to be a music hall joke that the journalists all knew: If Pa killed Ma who'd kill Pa? Marwood!

Poor Annie Tooke, she had screamed her head off as she was dragged to be hung. There was none of that from Lee. He kept a grim silence, not replying to Reverend Pitkin calling out the prayer responses. He wore his best gray jacket, the same he had on for the trial. They came to a halt and Lee turned to face the observers across the yard. They could see his pale eyes following a bird flighting across the garden then glancing up at the beam and noose above him as if taking a technical interest in the arrangements. Berry placed him on the drop boards. He had planned a six and half foot drop. He didn't want Lee's head yanked off nor yet to strangle him and have to hang on his legs. He strapped broad ankle bindings to the still figure and motioned two warders to step forward and hold him on each side. Berry took a white hood from his pocket and pulled it down over Lee's face. Usually he did this before the condemned man got to the gallows but Lee had seemed so steady that Berry must have decided to let him gaze upon everything without fear of him panicking. He spoke to Lee as he stood there with the hood pulled down and the rope adjusted and tightened below the left ear on its metal ringlet. Lee shook his head slowly, refusing whatever Berry had asked him.

The executioner moved fast to the left to grab an iron lever set in the floor. He signaled to the warders to let go of Lee and step back off the hatch. Pitkin, Cowtan and Dr Caird stood together to the right. Pitkin raised a shaky voice, "We therefore commit his body to the ground."

Cowtan nodded to Berry and he pulled at the lever with both hands. There was a grating sound and the boards moved a little but Lee did not disappear from sight into the pit as all expected. He remained standing, erect and unwavering. Berry wrenched at the lever again. There was the same grumbling of metal but no movement of the trap. The executioner next threw all his weight on the lever and yet again there was a loud graunching, the boards shivered but nothing else happened. The reporters were freaked and they looked at each other in amazement. That tableau of figures in the shed remained fixed for a moment before all hell broke out. Berry ran forward and gestured to the warders to lead Lee off the hatches. His hood and noose were taken off. The reporters could see him staring ahead while the dark figures milled about behind him. Cowtan and Caird frantically discussed the situation, Pitkin mopped his face with a kerchief and Berry, first of all on his knees peering at the locked boards, then prying at them with a metal pipe that had been one of the fittings of the coach house. The boards stayed wedged together and Berry began to stamp on the wood while great drops of sweat rolled down his face. After several minutes of prodding and banging he hurried back and pulled the release lever. The heavy doors fell with an echoing bang. Everyone jumped except Lee, who remained erect and still. Berry and the warders then leaned over the pit and drew back the doors with hooked poles. The trap was locked in position, Lee took four steps back onto the boards and all seemed set to launch him into the big zero. Pitkin started another wavering reading, "Man that is born of woman hath but a short time to live and is full of misery. He cometh up and is cut down like a flower…"

Before he had finished Berry yanked at the lever again. There was a grinding sound and the boards sagged down two inches. Lee, almost imperceptibly, raised himself on his toes to ease his neck from the rope's strain.

"This is terrible!" called out Governor Cowtan who made gestures urging Berry to do something. The executioner pulled and pulled again to no effect. He put his whole body into it so that the iron lever bent but there was no further movement of the trap. There were muttered voices and hurried movements as the frightened-looking officials scurried around the shed. Lee was again taken off, backwards this time. His hood and the noose were removed and his ankle ties loosed. He seemed to watch the wig-out frenzy going on in front of him calmly. Berry stamped on the boards, then made fat sweaty Warder Halse hang on the rope while putting weight on the trap. Berry moved the lever and the doors fell with a thundering crash leaving Halse dangling clutching the rope until other warders dragged him back. All was hurriedly reset and Lee was hustled forward, newly-hooded, bound and noosed. Pitkin read from the Psalms, his voice shrill and cracking, "God is our hope and strength, a very present help in trouble. Therefore will we not fear, though the earth be moved."

Berry put all his weight on the lever again. A grinding and a grating could be heard but nothing else happened. Lee remained a still dark figure with the white bag on his head. That is what the newspaper men would always remember—that unmoving white rectangle with the dark uniforms swarming in the background. More and more warders came running, some carrying tools, and the prison bell clanged on. Lee was unbound and taken to a small holding cell in the nearby blocks. From this place you could hear the crazy hammering and sawing as Berry made the warders cut back the edges of the drop flaps. At one stage Berry himself flailed at the wood with a hatchet. When they had whittled the wood back as far as it would go Berry ran to the lever and pulled it. There was a dull clank and the drop doors thundered down, to bang against the brick-lined pit. All now thought that the last block had been cleared and the whole nightmare farce was finally done. Berry fetched Lee from the cell where he had been standing in silence as if in a trance. Berry called out,

"My poor fellow. I don't know what I am doing. You must return."

Once more he stood on the drop. Pitkin voice was now scratchy and almost inaudible.

"Now is the Christ risen from the dead and become the first fruits of them that sleep."

The hooded man waited and in that moment a legend was born as Berry again pressed on the lever but the boards remained more stubbornly closed than ever. That was it. The fight went out of them. All of a sudden Berry slumped against the shed wall and called out, "I cannot carry on." Pitkin, who had run away in the last moments, squeaked from the yard, "Is it over?" and Cowtan began to argue with Berry. He wanted him to carry on and finish the job but the furious Dr Caird snapped at him, "In God's name put a stop to this! You may experiment as much as you like on a sack of flour but you shall experiment on this man no longer!"

It was a defeat for the system. Executions depended on a set process being carried out and no one seems to have considered during that half hour of turmoil simply pushing the noosed prisoner into the open pit and so finishing up the whole dang business.

The rain kept falling. Lee was led away and someone was told to stop that bell ringing. The newspaper men rushed out over the railway bridge and ran down the wet pavements of the High Street to the post office to telegraph their stunning copy. Lee was taken back to his cell as if in reverse time along those winding corridors that he had dreamed of the previous night. He still seemed to be in a sort of trance when Berry began to untie his wrists.

"Why am I not dead?" he had whispered, "I want to be hung."

Pitkin called out, "You should know by the laws of England they cannot put you on the scaffold again." Lee rubbing his numbed arms, blinking, staring about him. He croaked, "Every time that trap grated I thought I was gone." He was handed a glass of brandy but refused it. Pitkin took the glass and downed it behind their backs as they all stared at Lee, his cuff, belt and ankle bindings lying around him like the discarded casings of some amazing creature that had just hatched out.

I've listed some of the more fanciful explanations for what had actually stopped Lee from getting hung. It seems there had actually been a small but stubborn mechanical fault that had stopped the machinery from working on the day. A bolt was slightly out of line. Lee himself describes the technicalities in his next recording. Like any explanation it depends how far back you go to find the first cause. It's like the house that Jack built.

SPOOL FOUR
"In Debtor's Yard the stones are hard and the dripping wall is high"
Prisons, London, Plymouth and Portland, 1884-1907

—I've heard that in England now that they don't have a bell ringing during a hanging. Now they only pin a notice on the jug door. Crowds still likely gang up outside as if smelling the approach of death and that's the same all over the world. They ain't too particular here neither. A few years back you could see the pictures in the Chicago Tribune of that Ruth Snyder all bundled on the electric chair. You remember that?

Doctor Kaiser: Yes, of course. A disturbing picture.

—I'd heard later how Berry retired a few years later—or he had been sacked for selling his souvenir ropes, depending upon which paper you read. He later toured the country preaching against hanging and showing lantern slides about his doings. I was the only failed hanging out of a hundred and thirty-one. Berry even got to the States, selling his story. I'll tell you some more about that Berry fellow later if you like.

Doctor Kaiser: I want you to concentrate on what is helpful to you.

—Not sure who is helping who here, doc, [laughter]. I get the feeling you're getting something out of this also?

Doctor Kaiser: You're a good patient, Mister Lee. Just tell me your story.

—If you say so. Maybe I'm trying to avoid talking about prison. After the hanging business, it was hard to straighten it all out in my head. It was all too mazing. I had been half-way across the dark but I'd been called back, but to what purpose? I had been given something that all men wanted—the putting off of death—yet I was soon to find myself thrown into a deeper Hell. Believe me, I soon wished I had been hanged prapperly.

It was alright at first. They treated me to a port and steak on the night after the attempted execution. The guards made a fuss of me and I kept on wearing my street clothes for a while. I stayed on in the condemned cell that the prisoners used to call the salt box. Pitkin visited me every day. He took down all the details of the dream I had the night before the execution, the one about not being hanged and he told me about how Lazarus had been raised from the dead to bring change to the world. I received a letter from Ma saying that she too had a dream that I would not be hung on the night before. She said that all that night before the planned execution there was a rapping and a creaking going on all over Town Farm cottage and the bedroom ornyments danced around.

Everything still seemed like a dream to me. I passed the time lying on my bunk and going through it all in my mind. Warders Barrett and Milord read to me from Bible stuff left by the Reverend Pitkin. Once, I was taken out for exercise in the yards and noticed a pile of fresh dug earth. I wandered closer and discovered a pit there next to the mound. A warder said, "Yes, Lee. It is your grave all open and waiting for you."

Doctor Kaiser: How long was it before you heard that the death sentence was set aside?

—I waited a month to hear I was respited. I did not really know what it would mean for me. The warders told me I would probably do twenty years but none were very clear. One day I was called to see Cowtan. He told me I was being transferred.

He wouldn't say where. I was given duck canvas clothes marked with the government arrow which the prisoners called 'the devil's claw mark', or 'crow's feet'. That prison cloth were stiff and sharp and rubbed you sore. I was chained at the ankles and wrists, and Cowtan and two warders took me to the London train at St David's. They rushed me from the cab at the station. I could hardly walk because of the chains. A few folk saw me and called out,

"It's Lee!"

We took a closed carriage on the gert, green, steamer. I'd seen its name as we waited on the platform. It was the Amazon, an Alma class express; I'd watched it pile past on the Plymouth line many a time in the past. Now it took me east. I was still treated a bit special. At Salisbury they brought me a glass of milk and cakes. Those were the last bits of the outside world for a long, long while. At Waterloo I was pushed through the crowds who moved quick out the way of my brown heavy clothes and chains. A fast cab took us over the river through the city. I could see nothing as the blinds were pulled down. They stopped speaking to me. Once, Cowtan shouted out to the cabbie to ask where we were. He said it was the Caledonian Road. Shortly after the sound of the hooves changed to an echoey beat as we came through a gate into a walled yard.

"The Model," called out the cabbie.

Doctor Kaiser: What did he mean by "The Model"?

—That what they called Pentonville, the Model Prison, built thirty years afore. Us prisoners called it 'The Pent'. We came in under a spiked gate like into a castle. Cowtan told me to not let myself and him down. Then, with the forms signed, all connection was gone. I found myself being pushed along by new fierce warders under yellow gas jets. Everything was smooth, clean and shiny. The gaol corridors stretched out on each side like the spokes of a great wheel. They told me to give them any money, gold or silver, or they would take it. They also wanted letters or locks of hair otherwise they would find them and destroy them. I handed over the last of my things, letters from Katie and those from Millie and Ma, also the hair bracelet that Katie gave me on the night of the Babbicam Regatta. Then I was stripped and they peered up my arse for contraband. Disinfection bath came next then I was pushed into a narrow cell. It had a hammock slung from rings, a copper wash basin and a work bench all lit by a gas burner high on the wall. That night and all the other nights were spent there in hard silence. It was a place built to muffle up sound. The night warders shuffled past in soft overshoes. Couldn't hear nothing, only the hiss of the gas jet. Days were little better, the pile of old ropes to be picked to oakum fluff were throwed through the door hatch by a silent trusty and the half hour exercise time was spent alone, pacing in a walled yard.

About a week in, I started banging and screaming until the guards came. I wanted to see someone and speak so they gave me a kicking in reply and told me I would miss the meat ration that day for wasting their time. I heard one warder saying to another that he hated us boys the most. He said we were sad troublesome fellows until our spirits were broke.

Doctor Kaiser: How long were you kept on your own in a cell?

—I did nine months solitary. All long sentence men had to go through it. It pounded me to an inch of my life. The weight of those long silent hours and days pressed out all my spirit, forced me to live inside myself. After the first weeks when I would flail about and jabber and moan I slowly began to learn to be more still, to sink down into the oakum picking and let the time pass. I also learned to make out the faintest sounds and mark them. A special point came when I learned that towards evening if I stood on the work bench closer to the high window I could hear a faint whistle that rose to a point then faded. I reckoned it was the scream of an express pounding out of the city on the Northern Line and that sound gave me some hope of another life going on out there. The long nights were the worst.

The deadly quiet ate you up. Sometimes I burned a home-made candle made of meat fat and twists of oakum. Gar, I loved the smell of that secret flame and sometimes I burned my fingers with it deliberate-like to remind me that I was still alive. I still kept on thinking about that hanging business and what it all meant. I tried to draw pictures of what went on. I used the paper I was given for monthly letter writing. Those pictures were all taken away by the staff and in time I just kept everything in my head.

Doctor Kaiser: What kept you going?

—In solitary you needed to shift from living to being. You became like a craitur, a granfergrig, just scuttling along the stone floor and barely feeling the world. There were some who could not manage it, they were overmatched by it all. Sometimes on morning cell clear-out I'd see grey-faced felons along from me. Sometimes one of them would be missing, taken to the punishment cells for chucking their food or going for the crows—that's what we called the staff. Sometimes the poor lads went mad and stripped off and pounded at the walls. I held on. I saw it through. Nothing lasts. I knew that and know it now. It all comes to an ending some time. It could be very hard though. Bitter sad times, like those early summer evenings when you'd hear the whistling and chat of the crows going off work. They'd be going to lives waiting for them on the outside and all I could think of was all the maids I'd never have, those roads I would not cross again. I also used to think somewhere out there Lizzie would be having her babby and I wondered how they were faring.

Doctor Kaiser: You never left your cell?

—Nay, apart from half hour a day exercise in the yard, going round in a circle and chapel once a week. I looked forward to chapel. Can't say I have since. They used to sit us in wooden boxes screened from each other. I liked the hymns, specially "Stars In My crown" and "Nearer My God To Thee". It was the only time I really heard the sound of my own voice. Sometimes

I'd hear a strange tapping on the wood next to me. I wasn't sure what to make of it until a new trusty taught me about it, bit by bit, when he gave me my daily rope for picking. He whispered that you knocked out one tap for an 'a' and two taps for a 'b' and so on. Three fast taps signified the end of a word. It was a painful slow way to communicate not like the naval morse and heliograph that I had learned in the navy but still it made all the difference. I tried it first in chapel and the unseen fellow in the next box tapped back "Lee, we know you. Keep well." I became faster at it, and could rattle off the code. Knock knockety knock knock for, "Are you there?" And the rattling seven taps and two taps for "GB" meaning, 'God Bless' as a sign off. All would stop when you heard a thump rather than a knock, that meant, 'beware a crow'. I realized that some of the old prisoners went on like this all day between themselves by means of little coughs or clicking sounds or through noises made by brushes or tools.

Doctor Kaiser: And in time you joined the regular prison population?

—I was in the Pent for four months then in high summer I was moved to the half-built Wormwood Scrubs. It was noisy in the new gaol and there was less of the killing quiet that you had in the Pent. I got to talk to other prisoners more easily there though at night you had to tap along the pipes. I was given work sewing duck cloth uniforms to start with. I complained to one of the old tailor prisoners who brought me the cloth that I needed to find a way to kill time. He used to laugh at that and tell me to have a care because time would kill me in the end.

It was still a hard, horrible time. The days were spent picking at oakum from rope ends. It was as tough as catgut. Or sewing the ugly stiff prison jackets. When you didn't do that you had to turn a crank handle in your cell for hours while the guards screwed it tighter and tighter to make it hard to move. On account of that some of the prisoners called them 'screws'. Bad thoughts walked the night. For a while I made a four-ply rope from oakum thinking to fashion it into a noose and do it "good 'n prapper" this time. I carried that rope for six weeks until I eventually burnt it in my gas jet and crumbled it to bits. I remembered how Ma picked up bits of broken saucer and smashed them up as grit to feed the chickens. She said they had no teeth and needed help. I prayed to the Lord to give me teeth to eat the years. Then, ess, the full term nine months crawled round and I was spat out in October with fifty other men. We grinned secret-like to each other, we were survivors of the silent hours and we were going to the Portsmouth works prison.

I learned the real business of being a prisoner at Portsmouth; at least the hard work there pushed away my thoughts about the trial and the execution nightmare. First I joined the army of mud-brown convicts agnawing at the sea bed in the new dock basin for the navy. We toiled in the stink of harbor sludge and rotting sea weed all mixed up with filth from the town sewer pipes. I was more of a public figure there and the warders often pointing me out to visitors as 'Babbicam Lee'. That dreadful name had settled on me like a clammy shroud.

Doctor Kaiser: You managed more contact with family later in your sentence?

—News got through to me from letters, yearly visits from Ma, from other prisoners or the odd friendly warder. Poor Millie died. Dear, dear Millie, eaten up by the coughing sickness. Then I heard that Pa was killed by a conniption fit after a drinking do. He was gone and no regret. Ma buried him with all the family photographs as if wanting to sink a whole life with him.

Doctor Kaiser: You mentioned earlier about your campaign to prove your innocence. How did that work?

—I wrote letters to the Home Office about my case and to strangers who wanted to help. There were no end of petitions about my case and that made the prison authorities angry. My hopes were kept alive in many ways. Ma came about two years into my sentence and showed me a letter written in a poor hand. The envelope carried an American stamp. It was signed from 'a well wisher' and said that it was known that I was innocent and proof would come to light one day. There were the initials, very faint, 'CH' on the bottom of it. Some five years into my sentence a trusty showed me a piece from the Gloucester Journal. It said that I had been set free and pensioned for life at 30 shillings a week because Lizzie Harris had confessed all to the authorities on her deathbed. Well, I knew some of it weren't true for when I read it I was still working at the wringer in the Portsmouth prison washhouse for nine hours a day and sleeping in a dog kennel cell alongside forty men. And still and still, it made me wonder if something had really happened to Lizzie. I began to think that Lizzie really was dead, her merry mocking laugh, and her wild blue eyes no more. That woman who had held my heart in her hand. I thought perhaps Lizzie had gone and maybe her secrets gone with her too unless she'd told someone.

Doctor Kaiser: You must have felt you were a special person to have survived all this?

—I thought then that I lived on because the Lord had saved me, I knew not how or why. I still struggled with the meaning of that reprieve from death during the early time in prison. It was all mixed up with the dream I had on the night before the hanging and of Ma's account of her dream and the dancing and rattling of things in Town Cottage on that night. I thought maybe I could not be hung because I was special. I was a scryer like Ma. I could not be hung because the Ladywell had mapped out a different future for me despite all that was ranked up against me. That's what I thought then anyhow. Now, I'm not so sure, the track of life has got so knotted up. It's hard to make sense of it all. Maybe that's what I'm trying to do by talking to you like this. It seems now I'm getting closer to crossing the bar and finding out the secret that I nearly learned forty years ago in that shed at Exeter only the difference now is the sort of man I've become over those years in between.

Doctor Kaiser: Was it ever explained what happened on the day set for your execution?

—A long way into my sentence I was told that there had been

a check on the scaffold by an engineer set on it by Governor Cowtan. When they took the scaffold apart they found signs of rubbing on a draw bolt on the crank. The scaffold had been taken apart then put together again after the hanging of Annie Tooke. One of the draw bolts had been wrongly set back. It was out by an eighth of an inch and this tended to catch on the ironwork of the drop doors when weight was pressed on it. The report said maybe I had not been hung because my weight pressed on that eighth of an inch of steel bolt. Whether it was a bent bolt or the dove of the Lord it meant the same to me though. The fact was I had been saved and I still drew breath despite all that had been thrown at me but to what purpose?

Explanation

I keep going back to Mulvina's message like a dog to where it's just barfed. Leave it, dude! I am still trying to read her words as sludge from my brain that she has managed somehow to harvest. But there is stuff there I cannot account for.

I have a confession—I used to send out emails in my parents' name long after they had died, to pastors, neighbors, doctors, friends, anyone who knew them really. Even though they didn't live long enough to see the Net really get going. I created an account for them and used to say things like, "We have been here a while, we are so happy, love to all." I used to get some sort of comfort from it. Someone must have spoken to Grandpa after I'd sent out dozens of those e mails. He told me straight I was to quit doing it.

I tend to see Mulvina's communications as being like those phony emails of mine, they are made to make people feel better. Still, the one I got from her wasn't that comforting, it sounded more like a warning. They'd sent Banjo to help me. I needed leading though a wood, a crowded wood—I don't know what that's about. In Mulvina's scribbled message "there are three of them. Is that my parents and Grandpa also? Crap knows, this phony medium stuff makes me sick. The truth is brutal, ain't it? No crystals, no reiki will really help you. There are no Greek porticoes in the sky just dead meat down here. Plenty of memories though. Curse and bless me dear Mom and Pop, you are ash now, food for muskies and big mouth bass. What would you make of me striving and wordsmithing like this? Will I ever get to be your proud heir? It is ten years since I slammed the door on you both.

I'm in the mood for answers. I'm going to unleash enigmatic Doctor Kaiser to burrow out of Lee exactly what happened that year before the murder. I want to hear about that Brownlow business he keeps hinting at. Let's squeeze the truth out of the sick old bastard. Old Kaiser is beginning to show his sneaky methods. He can bore into Lee. You guys are all owed explanations even though I don't know you.

BROKEN SPOOL 5 FRAGMENTS

**What Really Happened at
Colonel Brownlow's
Torquay, 1882**

—When did my feet take the wrong path? When was it exactly, that bad turning I made? I had plenty of time to think of it through those twenty-two years of gaol time. It all led back to the Brownlow thing, all that crazy crinkum path. I had been trying to get back on my feet after the sorry mess in the navy but I was stuck in the dead end of the railway job at Torre Station.

Doctor Kaiser: Will you explain to me exactly what went wrong then, Mister Lee?

—Brownlow. What could I have been if not for that Brownlow business? The deadly hands of those twisters Harrington and Kisler had set me to it. What a stupid young tacker I had been to get onto a shameful path, a scoundrel's way.

Doctor Kaiser: How did it start?

—I had been barely a week into working at Torre—that's the rail station at Torquay. I was bored sick already, every day spent wheeling the tourists' bags and humping hampers and boxes of hotel goods. I was squeezed in with Aunt Millie and her noisy little nappers at Clifton Place at Tormohan. There was barely hammock space there and I was pleased when Miss Keyse's letter came, forwarded by Ma. Miss Keyse said in the letter that I was to go to Colonel Brownlow to take up a footman's post at the house called Ridgehill on Middle Warberries. It was only ten minutes from Aunt Millie's. It seemed a godsend at the time but one should beware such a gift lest it turns to a curse.

I found the great villa where the road winds up the hill from Wellswood among all the rich folks' grounds. Kisler met me at the servants' entrance. He was a big Frenchman in full butler's rig. I straightway thought I didn't like him at all. Kisler made it plain I'd been lumped on him and he was down on me from the start. He showed me my little room next to the plate room. He told me that Colonel Brownlow was an important man and I was never to speak to him or his wife unless spoken to first. I could hardly understand Kisler because he spoke with such an accent; I'd met Frenchies before, sailors and smugglers mainly; didn't like them neither. There was Susannah the cook and Clara the housemaid, she was from Plympton and had buck teeth, Eugenie, the Swiss maid, sniffy and thought herself too good for me. Kisler ran a strict house and kept going on about the cleaning or "netto yage" as he called it. I couldn't get away with sloping off all day like I did at Miss Keyse's.

Doctor Kaiser: What was your actual job there?

—Kisler kept me running about, boot cleaning, lamp trimming and message carrying and that was the before breakfast jobs. I did all sort of things a footman really shouldn't do. I thought I was a slave, a Johnny-for-all-jobs. I messed about with Clara a bit, she was willing but it was a pity about the teeth. I'd moan that the house was full of a load of vurriners and she told me that the mistress was Spanish or something like. She warned me about Kisler. Said he was fearful strict and had a son called 'little Michael'. He was a nosy varment and told tales to his pa. She warned me that Kisler would get in a right fizz when…

[Gap in the recording]

…not that bad though. My room at the top of the house was better than the cupboard at my Aunt's and better than Miss Keyse's pantry by far. I could see the moors from the top windows away to the north. I would hunker down there at night reading my Bear Hunters book or picking over my naval discharge papers. The days passed quickly enough. All the mornings were spent cleaning and in the afternoons I ran errands to town. Sometimes I took messages down to Miss Keyse at Babbicam. She would stop me and ask how I was faring and sometimes she gave me a penny to buy a bag of cherry gob sweets as if I was still a little boy.

Worst was serving those nobs at drawing room tea or dinners at Ridgehill. I'd hand out cream, sugar or cakes while the master fixed me with a look. He probably regretted taking me on because of my rough ways. I used to get in the pantry and stick my fingers in their cakes and puddings and lick them before serving. In the six months service there the colonel spoke no words to me at all but he got Kisler to chase me all the time on this thing or that. The young mistress seemed a lonely 'umman, always sitting in the conservatory, wrapped in a shawl, playing patience with those big Spanish cards.

The rich bellies came and went in their carriages all that winter season and …

[Gap in the recording]

…aid it was nothing but a passel of auld crams and had a good laugh about it.

I was off on one of my errands, hanging about near the villa gardens hoping to chaff with the house maids when I saw Kisler walking to the Ilsham junction. A sailor-looking fellow came up on the same side of the street. The only thing I marked about him was he walked with a bit of a limp. When he reached Kisler he turned on his heel and made to light his pipe all casual and at the same time he gave a good look around the street. I popped down into the laurels and thought I'd keep an eye on them. Kisler and that sailor stood together a good while. It seemed strange to see that stiff Frenchie with a poor rough sailor but I thought no more of it. A few nights later something woke me in the early hours. I crept down to see the glow from a shaded lantern and Kisler rolling something into the cellars. I had to be careful as young Michael was on the lower stair, watching over his father. I asked Clara about the cellar later but she seemed frit when I mentioned it.

Doctor Kaiser: What did you think he was doing?

—I thought he was watering down and selling off his master's cellar most like. I kept an eye on Kisler and his son but marked little else that late winter. Sometimes I laid a thread across the pantry servant's exit to the garden. Oftentimes it was broken in the morning yet Kisler kept up his cold prideful air as ever and gave no clue to whatever he was doing of a night. I saw the same sailor several times, once quite close to Ridgehill, sitting on a low wall close to a water trough just puffing on his pipe and watching.

Then, one afternoon, walking to Ellacombe to deliver dinner invitations, I heard a voice calling to me to hold up. He called me "my beauty" and asked if I worked with Frenchie Kisler. It was that same lean sailor man I had seen over those weeks before. He told me he was Cornelius Harrington and I would thank my lucky stars for meeting him. Aye well, I was a young vul then, a prapper mump aid. It's hard to fathom it, how he sucked you in and won you to his will. It's still a mystery to me though I've puzzled over it many a time. He took you in, and molded you like a piece of clay in …

[Gap in the recording]

…whatever the truth of it, I was easily netted. Harrington took me to The Man o' War down the road in Plainmoor. Said I was a careful lad, just what he was looking for. He said that Frenchie had a position to keep. Said that they needed me for something important. Well, no-one had needed me the whole of my short vulish life so far so that hooked me in. Harrington told me that he and Kisler had a business. The Brownlows would be going on their summer trips and that's the time their little arrangement got going. I was a slow wit about it and could not understand what business he was talking about. He kept on about the Frenchie schooners that came in on the new moon. I still didn't get his riddling talk of tipple for the parson an' baccy for the clerk until he spelt it out that he and Kisler paid for stuff that arrived on the beaches at night. Smugglers, you know? Stuff the revenue men have an eye out for. They needed the cash to buy so it could be sold on at a profit. That's where I came in according to Harrington. They wanted me to take the silver plate, pop it and then they would buy from the French boats coming in to Watcombe and Anstey's and I'd get a snip also. I really didn't like it. I was frit about the Brownlows missing the plate. Cornelius said that they had a ton of it and besides we would straightway redeem it from Uncle Peter, the pawnbroker. We'd sell the stuff at profit and get back the silver and replace it in the strong room and all would set right again. We would be the richer, they none the wiser. He asked if I got it and did I want a guinea or two or not. I wasn't sure that I did get it but somehow I felt obliged to go on with the scheme that those sharp fellows had cooked up.

Doctor Kaiser: Let me grasp this. The plan was to take and pawn the family's silver plates and use the cash to buy smuggled goods?

—That's it, and to sell it all on and redeem the silver before the family noticed it was gone. We were to pocket the profit. I thought there must be benefit in it. I thought it might be the leg-up I needed to make something of myself in the world.

Harrington told me that to reach him I should leave a note slipped down the back of the water trough set into the wall at the bottom of Middle Warberry Road. Ess, that same one I've spoken about afore. Before leaving, Harrington said to give my hand on it. I was to read in his eye and hand that we were together in this. "Mates and for profit," he kept saying.

Harrington turned out right about the Brownlows. Within a week in April there was a great commotion at Ridgehill, steamer trunks were piled and topped with hat cases and valises, carriages were drawn up and there was a rush about for the servants. The family were on the move: the Colonel and his wife, Hélène, and the maid Eugenie and a young nephew called Master Fiennes who ran about everywhere waving a net. Someone told me the net was for catching butterflies in the south of France. Imagine that.

The Colonel kept giving orders to Kisler right up to the last minute. We stood in a line on the gravelled drive and watched them go and said "Good riddernce" under our breath. Kisler said they'd be back in September and we still had work to do. He drew me to one side and told me to do his bidding in the house and to follow Harrington in all else. He said that if I obeyed him in this then all would be well. He still made it plain he thought little of me even though we were in business together.

That's how I ended on the down train from Newton Abbot to Plymouth. Kisler had given me the first bit of silver wrapped in brown paper. The train was full of sailor boys all laughing and ragging about, going back to their training ships on the Hamoaze after shore leave. Only a year before I would have been one of those careless lads; now I was about serious matters. Harrington had said I was to go straight in and get it done, to say no word to any man about the business and then I'd be seen right.

Doctor Kaiser: Why were you going to Plymouth? That was some distance from Torquay, was it?

—Harrington had chosen Devonport, his home town, not far along from Plymouth. I knew it also from my two years on the training brigs. He chose it as it was far enough away from any busybody's gaze and only twenty miles by rail.

I got off there and footed it along the Western Approach up towards the dockyards. It was strange to be back. I'd heard that Captain Jackson, who had signed my Bear Hunters book, was now Admiral of the Yards. I hadn't looked forward to coming back to this place where hopes and dreams had come to grief. The tub-sided Torpoint hulks still rolled in the tide.

I was supposed to go straight to Emdon's, the pawnbrokers, near to Gun Wharf. Everyone knew the place, said Harrington. I was not so sure. I kept away from such places as a cadet, never wanted to hock my kit for drinking money like some of the lads did. They were places for the poor, putting all their stuff up the spout. Like those yardies, the dock workers that us boy sailors used to look down on, they swarmed in and out of the pawnbrokers like flies.

I went past Stoneham Creek and thought on being landed there by launch, all swaddled in a blanket. I'd somehow caught the neumonee on the damp old Implacable and was taken past those green iron gates into the cool sheets of the Royal Naval Hospital. It did flood back on that journey up to Devonport. On I went, past the first dock yards, the mewies calling and with all that banging and hammering echoing out over the Sound. Like the carpenters on the wooden training ships always clappering away at something. There was gunnery booming away in the distance, like the training we did on the Foudrayant. Those quick firers were my favorite, letting fly at a dragged target. I had been best boy on Commodore Jackson's pinnace and had been going along fair and making progress afore I got sick.

Well, that was what I kept on telling myself though now I know it was lies. In truth, navy service didn't suit me. But in those days I kept a story in my head that I'd been cheated out of a grand career, screening out the truth like I screened out the fact that this Harrington business was knavery and bound for ill. So there I was, with hands full of silver and a head full of mumpsy ideas.

The parcel I was carrying held a pair of candlesticks, two snuffers and two silver trays—value twenty pounds. It was a tidy sum, twice what I'd earn in a year. Harrington has said 'Ordnance Street' but I wandered onto Fore Street as the dockyard signal gun went off at noon. I could see the great dock yard gates ahead of me and there was a shop front with the gold balls hanging and the sign in the window, "Emdon, Jeweler and Pawnbroker". I had a closer look and there were more signs about money being advanced on plate, jewels and all types of property. It was not Ordnance Street but quite near it. I thought maybe they had gone up in the world since Harrington had last been there. It seemed grander and more gentrified than I expected. I took the plunge and rang the bell. The jeweler came to the window and looked suspiciously at me then signed for me to come to the side door. I stood there at the side entrance while he looked out at me through a crack in the door. I said I had things to pawn and that he was recommended. The sharp little man wanted to know who had recommended. I muttered something about a gennelmen of Torquay. The narrow-faced pawnbroker kept up a sharp watch on me all the time I was talking.

In the end he let me in and held the candlesticks up to the light. He said they were odd sticks, an unmatched pair. I told him I could get a pair from someone I was in business with. He didn't say anything, only gave me another crabby look. He picked at the other things and spent time looking at a crest marked on the trays. He said he was going to fetch his scales. I heard a door open and close somewhere in the back. It was all taking too long. I looked around at the ranks of snuff boxes, foreign carvings, telescopes and such. It seemed too good a place, not like the heaps of old clothes and shoes from other pop shops I'd seen, nor was there any of the racket of the desperate poor. Still, Harrington must have chosen the place for some reason although the shopman clearly didn't favor me much. He had been gone a hell of a time when eventually I heard a door bang and the man came back. He spent another age weighing the items and looking at the marks with a glass. He then said he'd advance three pounds on it. I said it was worth twenty and that was never enough. He said that was his price. I was all of a diz and just wanted to get out and in the end accepted it. I said I wanted a better price on my other stuff. He began to write out a cheque. A cheque! Hell, the whole thing kept getting worse. I said I wanted no paper, I wanted the readies. He said he had no cash, it was Saturday and close of business. I folded up and let it happen. Everything was going to scat. I told him to pay the cheque to "Mr Lee for M. Kisler". I couldn't think of anything else. I tumbled out from the pawnbroker with that Devonport bank cheque. Everything had gone screwy and I did not like the look in the man's eye at all. I went into Tozer's outfitters next door to cash the thing but the clerk had pointed out that the date was two days in advance. I reeled out again. Gar, it was all a botch!

The yardies came clattering out of dock gates for their Saturday half day. I had walked back to Emdon's thinking to have it out again with that damned clerky shopman when I saw the pawnbroker pushing his way towards me through the crowds of dock workers. Beside him walked a big bearded man in a long coat. The big fellow held me by the wrist and told me to come along. He said he was Detective Slee, Devonport police.

Doctor Kaiser: So, you ended up getting arrested?

—Ess, the whole thing was a skiddy bum mess. I had made a terrible mistake. I found it out later. It turned out that I, the baffle-aided vul, had gone to Mark Emdon, jeweler on Fore Street not his cousin Eleazer Emdon who ran a much more rackety place in Ordnance Street, up snug to Gun Wharf. He was the man who Harrington knew would take in all manner of things with no questions and certainly no running to the police.

I was clapped in the cells and the police were at Ridgehill soon enough. I had put together the pieces during the trial that came after. Slee had gone to Ridgehill three days later. Kisler took the detective to the Brownlow's plate room and mocked surprise at the empty places on the shelves where the silver had once stood. He said how the footman had been acting suspicious of late. Kisler must have gone in my little box bedroom and palmed the spare plate room key under the mattress for the detective to find a few minutes later. So was my fate sealed up. I was charged with theft and rattled up to the magistrates then to the Assizes for sentencing. I never said a word about Kisler or Harrington but watched Kisler give evidence against me and I swore revenge in my heart. I got six months. No-one could understand why I did the crime. It had seemed such a senseless stupid thing to do, to steal from my employer and to think not to be caught.

"Mr Creed, my defense solicitor had said at the trial that he could not say why I did it. "Explain? How will I ever explain?" I said to Ma when …

[End of recording]

WHO IS HAUNTING WHOM?

Sometimes you can't help but feel sorry for him. He blundered from one disaster to another. At other times you know he's a meanball and you wouldn't like to be close to him. I have the feeling I should pay more attention to Lee's capabilities before I play Orpheus much longer leading his sorry ass back up to the light. I'm distracted though, that medium has definitely unsettled me. She's opened a door in some way and I don't at all like what's come in. I'm not great at sleeping anyway. Noises trouble me, something seem to scuffle in my yard and the apartment has these fruit flies that breed somewhere, gnat-like bugs that move about when the light goes out, I can sense them soundlessly maneuvering. They are waiting to land on my face. It got worse the other night, I was half- awake when I heard a whirling buzzy sound at first faint then getting louder. The sound stopped and I heard a voice, real distinct, say "That didn't work", it was a tinny little girl's voice but clear. It seemed to be coming from inside my head as if from a dream. I ignored it—or tried to. But it came again this time I heard the words "Don't hurt me, it's Georgia". I sat right up. Bummer! I've got schizophrenia on top of all my other problems. That's what I thought. Hearing voices was not good news. I stayed up the rest of the night and played Katie Scullin tracks on headphones to drown out any more of that shit. Same deal the next night. That whiny voice saying "I'm trying", over and over. The next day my ears seemed to keep buzzing with a high frequency modulating sound. A tinnitus-type problem according to my online symptom checker. I have no friends or confidantes. I sure wasn't going to see no doctors. All I could think was to ring Mulvina Schott.

"I'm not surprised," she said after I explained what was bugging me, "I told you that you were a sensitive. You evidently have some psychic ability."

That was not good news. All my life I've been told I'm out of kilter. Worse, she told me that little voice was probably my spirit guide trying to get through. Great, I thought, had Georgia on my case as well as John Lee. Mulvina told me to relax and go with it. The spirit world wasn't out to harm me. Little Georgia was my friend.

WTF did she know?

Spool Six

Will there be any stars in my crown?
Portland Prison, 1907

Doctor Kaiser: I think we dealt with your prison time last time we spoke.

—Not quite done with, doctor. Why don't you puff on that pipe of yourn while I tell a bit more about prison. Something important. I don't mind about the smoke. Quite like it in fact.

Doctor Kaiser: Very kind of you, Mr Lee but I'll leave off for now.

—As you wish, sir. Now, in clink, time crouched. That's what I used to think. Time was crouching in my cell. Everything was so frozen up when you were in jug. The rest of the world had forgotten you. Especially those long nights all alone there in Portland with the far-off sound of the sea coming to you. Time still went fearful slow even in the last months when I was waiting to be released. In a way, it goes slow now these last days also. I'm lying here all alone in my bed waiting for time to make his jump on me.

Doctor Kaiser: We are trying to help you…

—Don't think I don't appreciate all your time, doctor. Lord, you're a far cry from old Doctor Hood.

Doctor Kaiser: One of my profession?

—You could call him a doctor but most knew him as a butcher. That hospital bay there was usually full of the worn-out prisoners, too weak to be moved. Some even died after their release date. Dr Hood ran the place when he wasn't drunk, evil bugger that he was. I hope you don't mind me saying that, doc, but it's the truth. I saw men die from fevers, blood poisoning, runny guts and bad chests after being turned away by Hood for 'malingering'. He was no different and maybe worse than the usual run of prison doctors. I had particular reason to remember Hood. I tried to avoid him but he latched on to me when I was punishment block orderly. He used to call after me asking if was the 'Lee with the surprisingly intact neck?' He didn't actually say 'neck', it was some medical words that I didn't understand.

He knew exactly who I was. He said he'd been studying my case. Went on about how surely the famous Babbacombe Lee would not be afraid to dispute a little with him. I can see him still with his big red Irish face, calling out, "Come on Lee, just for the hellery now. Let's have no secrets." That type of thing. I kept away from him as much as I could but you can't hide for long in jug. Sooner or later he'd get me cornered in the blocks. He kept on asking me whether I did it and not. I'd argue with him as much as I dared but he'd tell me not to bandy with him. Said he'd worked with Chilcote as a relief doctor in Torquay ten years before, told me that Chilcote was dead, caught dysentery off what Hood said were those 'filthy charity patients' of his. Hood said that he often spoke of my case with Chilcote and followed the court reports in the papers. It seems Chilcote thought the evidence was wrong at the trial. He never would believe she was killed with a hatchet. Hood kept on nagging me, saying in a jeering way, "Innocent are you? Innocent as a sparrow?" If I tried to argue back he'd tell me not to kick unless I was truly spurred. He'd go on about the blood on my trousers, the only man in the house, the empty oil can in my room, the knife in my cupboard drawer—all the stuff I tried to push away. I knew not to fight back and I pretended to be an old broken-down thing but that only encouraged him. He said I might be all meek and mild now but I was a big lad in my time. He said her head was smashed and neck cut to the bone with a blunt knife. A strong man did that. Was it a strong man like me?

I'd have to stand there, cap in hand, and take it. He poured it all over me, going on about how Chilcote told him what a demanding old zaul Miss Keyse was. Complaining and full of opinions, she was. A creaking gate that had hung on too long. Annoying to a wild young man wanting to get on. Hood's main thing was to talk about what he called his "little theories". He'd prod at me to say yea or nay to them. He liked to guess at what he thought happened that night in Babbicam. His "speculations" was another name he called them. I wouldn't look at his toad face while he went on. I stared at the floor and let it flow over me. Hood rattled on about how those Devon beaches were a whirl of smugglers despite the revenue men. What happened? Hood asked. Did she stumble on a smuggler's meeting? Hood said he thought someone was startled when she came busy-bodying. Someone knocked her on the head with a truncheon or knob stick and then she was finished with a knife that was close to hand because she was threshing so much. He went on about how he wasn't saying I did it but he thought I was there. It all had to be tidied up once the deed was done. In all the panic maybe it was I who thought to fire the place? I'd say nothing and he'd laugh, saying that many a man's mouth broke his nose.

Hood seemed sure I'd tell him one day. After all, he kept reminding me I was stuck here in Portland for many a long year. Or he'd laugh and say that I had well and truly burnt my arse and now I must sit on the blister, whether I did the crime or not. Of course I'd not give him the chance of satisfaction. My silence gave him further ideas. He said he saw someone harder than me doing the deed with Miss Keyse. There was a little too much consideration in me to be a slasher or a basher.

Doctor Kaiser: Had he got close to the truth? Was that why you disliked his prying?

—Truth? Naw, not near it. He wasn't bothered about the truth anyway he wanted to grip on me and bear down. That's all. Even when I got returned to the main quarries he'd call after me in the block corridors, "Too proud to tell the truth, Lee?" Or if I was in a column of men he'd wave and tap his nose and shout, "I have you, sir. I have you!" Dealing with that Hood made me wonder if I actually got out what would be waiting for me out there if that was a taste of it? Do you think me a guilty sort of man?

Doctor Kaiser: I think you have been hard done by too but I

have not enough facts to form a true opinion.

—Facts eh? I thought I'd been boring you with too many. The only facts worth considering is who's to live and who's to die. Just like that fly in my room, a little cripple fly. A flick of spring sun has stirred it up from its hidey hole. I used to stalk those bluebottles in my cell. They grew to be great big buzzing things there. It was not the sound that annoyed but the waiting in between the bursts of buzzing that were a torture for a locked man. I'd whack 'em, those blue-arse flies, with a slam from my folded-over prison cap. Finish. Scat for Mr Fly. Now, we've got that Flit stuff. Addie goes around the place spraying away with it. It smells of paraffin like them lamps in the Glen and my stinking pantry room. I think perhaps I'll let this fly live a while longer. That's a little bit of control that I have left. Who is to live and who dies? Now that's a question. I can see now that all life is waiting for something to tread on you and squash you down. It's what you do in the meantime that matters.

It didn't look as if I had much of a future in those last prison days though maybe better than the poor look-out I have now. Now I just want to appreciate Addie and try and reach out. That's why I'm talking like this. To straighten it all out. It all comes round don't it, doc. All get caught in the end?

[No apparent reply from Doctor Kaiser]

BROTHER WHERE ART THOU?

Here's a question for you: how could Lee be so dumb and still survive? Let's see how he managed once he was let out.

Meanwhile, I've found a way of dealing with Georgia. She speaks to me during special sessions and the rest of the time I block her out. If I relax and let her in she comes to tell me things. Sometimes I play a relaxation download that Mulvina sent me: It's called 'Dolphin Chakra'. That was sweet of her.

Georgia comes into my mind when I play the floaty music. She has a tinkling kid's voice and keeps saying how there are three of them trying to get through to me, claiming it's your Mom, your Pa and your brother trying to get through (Grandpa clearly doesn't want any of it). I keep telling Georgia I've got no brother but she says in her tinkling voice, "You'll see, you'll see." I still don't believe it's a dead person talking. No doubt it's a bit of my unconscious that's trying to heal me and guide me to better things.

SPOOL SEVEN
Release and new birth
Newton Abbot Devon, 1908

—What do you remember of someone? Not their promises and not even their face or voice or way of standing. No, it's a general feeling about them, something about their character With Jessie, it was the way she tried to stick by me no matter what. All she wanted from me was a bit of something back, something to say she was loved—but I never really gave her that. It was all such a shame, a sickening shame that still hangs round me. There are some things I shut out my mind, 'n Jessie's face is one and our son's another. His fat tongue stuck out like a fig. Jessie now, she still pops out in my dreams whether I want her there or not. I've started to hate sleeping. I'm frit of those little slices of death. Those dreams of Jessie bring me back thirty years and more. I did not really know her when I was with her, not really noticing her smell, the feel of her skin, not knowing the 'zack color of her eyes. Maybe she is dead now, like her ma dying young perhaps and with this terrible war who knows what has happened to them all.

[The recording spool shuts on and off numerous times in this sequence as if Lee struggles to find words.]

Doctor Kaiser: Ready to go on?

—Ess, as ready as I'll ever be. At Kingswear when I started on the rail works they told me to go and fetch a bucket of steam from the engine shed. Mumpsy lad that I was, I went puzzling, scratching my head and dragging an empty bucket around and asking the artificers for steam to fill it. How they laughed while I wandered around with that bucket. They did it to all the apprentices. A joke played on the new lads. A bucket of steam. That's how the years seem. That's what my life seems to amount to now. A bunch of auld crams.

Doctor Kaiser: You must have been pleased to leave the penitentiary?

—I crept out of prison on my day of release in December 1907. My hands flopped at my sides because I had become used to having no pockets. I barely looked at the flinty sea off Chesil on the way down to Weymouth. There was a small crowd at Newton Station 'n I skittered though them like a mouse and was grateful when the Lloyds Weekly man ordered up a fast cab. We rattled up through Wolborough and onto Sand Pit Lane. It was only when we were going down that deep lane back to the village that I really believed I was free.

Then there was the village. So strange to think of it carrying on its quiet life all that while. The first thing I did when I came back to Town Cottage was to run up the stairs to my and Millie's old bedroom. I looked at myself in the mirror on the wall there. That skull face looking back at me was a shock. Outside, a pack of news hounds had gathered. Phillips from Lloyds Weekly arranged two photographs with me and Ma standing together outside and one with me with my arms round her. Ma wore her white apron and I still had my hat and coat on. The next day I was whisked to London.

Faster now, faster than I had ever been in life before, I shot back into the world. Newton Abbot, it seemed so much busier than I remembered. Everyone seemed to be hurrying at a hell of a rate. New buildings had gone up, the roads had widened and some of the old warrens had gone. The express to London thundered along at the devil's speed. It only stopped once at Exeter where I glimpsed the Castle high up on its hill. During the journey I roamed the new-fangled corridors between the coaches and could not stop switching the electric compartment lights on and off. Phillips led me through the mass of folk at Paddington and I took my first ride in a motor car. I gripped the leather straps tightly in the red cab as we went through all the horse traffic and omnibuses. I've been sold on autos ever since. At The Strand we came up to a very grand-looking hotel. I said the likes of me could not go in there, but Phillips took my arm and pressed me on. There we met Robert Donald. "Big Chief," Phillips called him. He ran the Daily Chronicle and Lloyds Weekly and much else besides. I sat in my old black coat, refusing a drink. The press king, with his big face whiskers and his face as red as a beet, raised a glass to me anyway. He kept talking of "mutual profit" and about making me the talk of the nation.

Doctor Kaiser: It must have been strange to see a big city like that after all you had been through?

—I was in a daze. They took me around the sights of the capital. I saw Parliament Square and Marble Arch, the new electric lights shone at the underground entrances above the pushing crowds. We went to the Bioscope to see newsreels of airyplanes, Peary in the Antarctic, Jack Johnson, a gert black boxer. He looked cocky and confident. A new world had grown while I had been inside. I wondered how a film of my own life would look. On we rattled to Fleet Street to see the Chronicle printed. I stood mazed watching the great thundering presses, a tangle of wheels and pulleys where men crawled like pigmies among the workings.

Doctor Kaiser: How did you set about telling your story?

—Phillips sat with me in my hotel room while he wrote out

my life. It took all of four days. I'd speak for a bit and he would write away madly. Some of the words he used were not mine, but who was I to say different? He wanted to call the piece 'The Man They Could Not Hang'. It was to be come out in two parts then to be in a book. It didn't say much about the Babbicam tale but dwelt on my hanging and on an account of prison. They also got an artist to make drawings. I was glad to be rid of them in the evenings. I spent the spare time reading old Lloyds Weeklies. The city made this constant humming noise, I could hear it day and night. Once or twice of an evening I went out into the streets but soon regretted it. There was something that frit me about that great mass of strangers. All the pubs seemed loud with voices and music, and my ears had got used to the dropping of silent hours in my cell for too long. Women kept calling to me, "Buy me a drink, dearie. Buy a drink." But I knew them not. The lights shone all night in the hotel and at times I wondered what sort of world I had been let out into.

I was glad to get back to Deb'm holding my fat check as the presses rolled and the whole country gobbled up my story. I found my feet a bit and started to lose the prison terrors—but it would be a long while before I laid them to rest. Those gaol lessons were long in the learning and long in the losing. Still, a sort of pride grew especially after the Lloyds articles came out and my book followed. Philips sent me a box of them and I laid them out on the floor of Town Cottages for Ma to look at. She said I was her bigabout lad, although that front cover, showing me all noosed up and hooded on the scaffold, troubled her. I've still got one somewhere if you want to look at it.

Cards, letters and gifts began to arrive, forwarded on by the Lloyds people. My story seemed to touch other people's hearts. Women especially wrote to me. My book carried a picture of me that was taken a week after leaving gaol. To me, it showed a hairless old man with a monkey face but the ladies seemed to like it. One letter spoke of my "untamed blue eyes". I liked that, "untamed", that's what I was. My fame grew and even the village noticed. Old Uncle George came hobbling down from Sunnybank with little cousin Fred in tow, holding a newspaper with my picture on the front page. They couldn't believe it. Ma grew sick of press men always rapping at the door. One paper brought Reverend Hine to meet me and to have our photo taken shaking hands. I hadn't seen the hooky-nosed priest since the night before my execution when he and Pitkin had tried to bully a confession out of me. Hine was still a gennleman in his top hat and gloves but time had rounded his shoulders and brought mild sorrow to his once high and mighty gaze. I asked him how he was going on and he said his wife had died five years before. That news cheered mezelf up a bit—how I had survived so many of them. Hine said to me that he hoped peace would stay with me and I was to fear not. I could tell he still thought I was guilty as sin. I told him I was not frit, not one little bit.

It got so I had to watch for who was about because of all those newspaper stories. Men hanging about outside the Seven Stars at Newton started to call out to me, "Go on, John Lee, you show 'em. Good on you, boy!", all sorts of things like that. Women began to stop me in the street to ask me to sign my book. I liked to put, 'Sincerely yours, John Lee', in there.

Doctor Kaiser: So, you became a novelty? Someone famous. That is remarkable.

—Even stranger for me, I can tell you. I cashed my Lloyds cheque. There would be a year's good living out of it. I got new vulcanite teeth to replace the prison rotted ones, a good suit and a day coat. I wore a flower in my button hole and bought a gold signet to wear on the left pinkie. I wore my hat at the old tilt and swung a cane with a barley twist and mother of pearl handle. The coppers at Newton police station began to joke with me when I came for my monthly sign-on as a ticket-of-leave man. I showed them a great bundle of letters I'd received with marriage proposals from women of all ages. They called me 'Lady Killer' for a joke. I suppose a kind of vulishness began to grow. I liked to be touched by women. It had been hard not being with a maid those twenty two years. The only ones that had touched me in all that time was the soft fingers of the queer prisoners, 'the mandrakes', they called them who shaved us prisoners every week. Prison neutered a man and even the whipping frame had a leather pad that cupped the privates so that they would not bump when the lash was laid on. It had been a long time since I had even looked at a woman close to. All through prison I kept thinking of Katie's words to me in that letter they read out in court, about how she would never get tired of waiting for me even if my lot was to crack stones in the street. Ah, poor Katie, I had cracked many a stone since then and she was long past taking me back. Instead of chasing old love I now became a new feature. My fame grew, fed by newspaper accounts that tracked my every move. Crowds followed me in the streets. Women came flocking, milliners assistants, dairy maids, the girls from bakeries and drapery shops.

"Wishee well, Jack!" They called out as I came strolling past in my new get-up. They often wanted just to touch me. Something drew them to me and sent them all of a diz, like the new Helter Skelter at Hancocks Fair.

"OO! Thikky eyes! They looked right through me!" They would squeak to each other after I had passed. I enjoyed that swelling fame and took advantage when I could but I did not lose my head altogether and seldom forgot that fame was a horse that would not run forever.

Sometimes I would hole up at Town Cottage for days while Ma went talking to her hives, telling them to rejoice because I was home again. I'd walk around the village. Sometimes I'd stop at St Mary's where Pa and Millie were sleeping together in the church yard. I met an old man once on one of these walks. His shoulders covered in a sack, under the dripping fingers of a rick. He said I had a bad name and no chillern. I was riding high now but life would go scat for me soon enough and I'd be all forgot. Miserable old crabbit, he was—still he made me think.

Doctor Kaiser: You were looking ahead?

—For the first time in my life I had something to lose. I sat up long into the nights puzzling over how much money I had left. Them great black moths they called "Old Ladies" came in from the night and used to bump around the lamp. Ma used to cry out to me to burn them because they were bad luck to enter the house. I wrote a gert many letters to well-wishers and replied to adverts that had businesses to sell. I thought about being a tobacconist. I also wrote a lot to the Home Office asking for permission to exhibit myself but they always said 'no'. I had a letter war with Mr Norris, the Queen Street photographer, for copying photos of myself that he had no right to and generally I tried to push myself forward, but my money was draining away and I had no idea what I would do in life. My best plan was to find some fat widow with money but even the plainest of my lady letter writers seem to think that I was the one with a fortune.

Jessie Bulled came along about then. My fame was white-hot and I'd been courting a girl in Brighton until her parents finally forced her away. Jessie was kin; we were second cousins, we found out later. There were Lees in her family from Witheridge way.

"Let us sing of the days when we were young, Maggie." That was the Henry Burr song then, you'd always be hearing it in the penny phonograph shops. Well, she was young or seemed so to me in her white nurse's uniform with those puffed-out sleeves. We met at a tea at the Congregational on Wolborough Street. I had been asked by the pastor to talk to them on God and prayer in prison. I had been happy to witness for them as I was still full of prayer then and liked to talk of how God had intervened mightily to save me. Jessie was introduced to me and told me about her work for the Guardians looking after the weak-minded women in the workhouse. Jessie called them "imbeciles".

She was no draggle-tail village girl. She had prospects and

was 'andsum too. I liked her mild grey eyes and her smooth fingers when they touched mine when she handed me a hymn book. Smooth as grapes her fingers were.

Many from the village had gone to the workhouse—the sick, the old and the idiots. Once in you were never out until they buried you, apart from the casuals—the baggabones tramps and men on the mooch. Jessie showed me round the wards once but I soon wanted to get out of those long dark rooms with their iron cots. Gaol has a smell to it, of dampness, sour bread and piss, and Newton Workhouse smelt like that too. What with the key jangling and all and those imbeciles I couldn't wait to get out. They kept creeping up to me with their moon faces and reeky breath, calling, "Maister, maister." I told Jessie that them craiturs were better off dead but she said they just needed kindness.

Later, much later, Jessie told me about her own ma. Dead twenty years before in an asylum in Kent. She had died when Jessie was a little girl. Her pa was now onto his third wife. Later still I began to think about Jessie's mother dead in the asylum for incurables, about how bad blood might have hid in her family.

I saw a bit more of Jessie in the hot summer of ought eight, although I was chasing other maids as well. I kept her on a string, she was my little piece close to home. Once, we went to the wishing well at Bradley Woods where they say the spring there never runs dry. I looked into the dark pool and asked her for a pin. She took one from her hat and I bent it and threw it in. I told her to make a wish. She said that she wished that all would turn out happy for us both.

In spite of all my chasing around I liked coming back to see Jessie. I also liked that we were blood family in a way. Jessie seemed a strong woman. I could also see she would be true to me. I needed someone on my side. It was good that she had employment although I did not like the smell of the workhouse on her. Sometimes the fingers of the past crept close, like when she came late to see me one day. I asked her what had stopped her and she talked about how two sisters at the workhouse called Fey had both fallen ill, and Doc Wiggins knew not what to do with them. I asked if she said "Fey" and she wanted to know why I knew the name. Her two were called Mary and Ann, two old Bishopsteignton housemaids gone weak in the 'aid. They must have been aunts or something to my two girls. It's strange how names run in families. I told Jessie that I knew some Feys once, but long dead now. Mary Ann Fey might have been long gone but she came back to me when I closed my eyes sometimes, still does, washed out far to sea and a-waving to me. Well, not long after that I asked Jessie to marry me and she said in answer that she would walk together with me always.

Doctor Kaiser: Wasn't she worried about your reputation?

—She believed in me but there were many that did not. We had a quick wedding that January. There were not many at the Congregational that early morning who actually knew us. Her father, a prudential agent in Plymouth, did not approve and refused to come. I didn't tell Ma, I only said I was going away for a while. Doctor Wiggins, the workhouse physician, had tried hard to argue Jessie away from the marriage but her mind was made up, although she looked whopper-eyed when making her vows. One sharp reporter from the Western Daily News had got wind of it and as we made off to the station asked me whereabouts we were heading. I said that we were going to Durham by way of Bristol. I had bought a business, a little tobacconist store, I said. But that was a lie. We did steam north but not to Durham, although we passed it. Instead we went all day by rail right up to Newcastle.

Ten at night by the Town Hall clock found us rattling in a cab in the deep gully streets and high buildings of that faraway Northern town. We came up Newgate Street in a sharp wind. The windows of the pub had handbills saying that Mr Wears presents John 'Babbacombe' Lee, The Man They Could Not Hang. When I saw my name there it gave me a shake and I knew I had really pushed the boat out good 'n prapper. They gave us a party that night at the Chancellor's Head. We were still in our wedding clothes. Mr Wears had already got a good crowd to meet his new attraction. He gave me £7 a week in advance and told me to be myself and all would be dandy. He was a merry soul, a big noise in the town and full of money-making schemes. Jessie and I were to live in the upstairs rooms. That first night we could still hear Wear's loud voice calling out "Howway, lads." They carried on late into the night with a bobs-a-daisy party downstairs. Jessie was already in bed waiting for me, her hair spread out on the pillow. To have another zaul lawfully part of my life and depending on me; this body to be close to another's; to belong to another. How odd, after all my lonely adventures.

It was a new world for us in those sunshiny first days. We were happy to stroll around and gawk at all the new things. Jessie liked Bigg Market. I bought her new hats and things at Fenwicks. The street sellers had funny sayings that made us laugh, they'd sing out, "Dandy candy, three sticks a penny," and the fishsellers went "Harrin! Harrin!" Jessie was happy for a while after she got over the strangeness and it seemed we could do anything we set our minds on then.

I began to exhibit myself to earn my £7 wage. I pulled pints and spoke to any that came up to me. At the start, they just stood and stared. I certainly seemed to be a draw with the howkies from the pit, the keelmen and the market porters all crowding in to take a keek at me. Wears was pleased, kept crowing that "The hoos was crowded oot." He gave me an extra pound on my wage because things were going so well. I was on show lunchtimes and evenings. The men were content to shake my hands and to stare in a good-hearted way; their women sometimes ran off, faces covered by their shawls, when I appeared. They kept going on about my "aaful hard eyes." I told them my eyes looked hard on account of what I had seen.

Some would call me "Jonty" and asked to see my neck as if

the rope had left a scar, but mainly they were very civil to me, always pushing me to take a thumping drink and to whet my kneb with them. Wears also ran the Bull and Mouth further down Newgate Street. This was a rougher place where they played billiards and men bet on the hoyling matches that were held on Saturdays on Town Moor. I was their hero and mascot. Three times lucky, Lee. Some of the men there liked to rub their hands on me for luck before making a bet. I bore it with patience for it was paying very well.

The only way to get some quiet was to go out and walk those winter streets. There was a gert big monument in the centre there, like Nelson's in London. The townsfolk called it Grey's. Anyway you couldn't often see the figure on top because of all that mist from the Tyne. I spent a lot of time on the elevated bridge watching the naval shipping go gliding out to sea. The girls that filled Castle Garth and Dog Leap stairs on my way back used to call to me to be a canny lad and go with them for a shilling, but they'd fall to silence when they looked into my eyes as I went past.

Doctor Kaiser: Why were they scared of you?

—Something about me frit them. Maybe I carried it with me always. I was death's man come back to life.

Doctor Kaiser: How did Jessie manage while you were exhibiting yourself?

—It didn't take long to find out Jessie's true nature. I guess the same went for her finding out about me. She started to show a sad and skittery disposition. She was lost without her nurse's job and spent her days sitting up in our cramped rooms while I plied the roaring crowds below. I fancied that she had become a little more plump and after a few months she stopped wanting to lift her nightie for me and began asking whether I loved her or not. She seemed to be frit of everything. She complained that the customers all wanted a piece of me but what about her? I'd find her crying or moaning that she was getting fat and there was nort she could do about it. Other times she seemed angry and addle-aided, railing at me for walking across a new-scrubbed floor. Once or twice I thought I smelt drink on her, but she denied it.

Ess, poor Jessie, she in turn had to put up with me staying as quiet as a crab all day. Sometimes I couldn't speak to her. I'd just wake up like that. My shut-mouth moods could last all day. She grew frightened of asking me questions about anything. I liked keeping the light on at night, for in gaol you were punished for hiding your face. Some nights I would wander around the rooms in my sleep like some dummy come alive. Jessie was too frit to do anything. I woke screaming from nightmares, thinking Berry was coming for me. Once I screamed at a vision of something horrible eating at me to find my own teeth grinning at me in a glass by my bedside. I tried to explain to Jessie that I was getting into a stewer worrying that everything would go scat but mainly I didn't tell her much. I was too used to living with secrets. If she found me sitting at the window looking out at Newgate Street I'd just tell her not to fash, not to worry about thinking because I'd do it all for the both of us.

Doctor Kaiser: Did the newspaper men not track you down given you were so famous before?

—The local press got to hear that I was in town but I did not encourage their attentions. A Newcastle Evening Chronicle man called Commons used to push his pug face over the Chancellor's Head bar counter to ask me foolish questions, like what I made of the new-fangled electric chair that the Americans were using for executions, or what did I think of that Indian being hung in the Pent for shooting Colonel Wylie. I said that condemned men should be treated with respect for some might be innocent like me and as for the others, well, God had decided to take them. I used to pace about all in a diz on those nights after that Commons had been bothering me. His blow-fly questions reminded me of that bugger Dr Hood, there was something sneery about him as if he believed in nort I said. I told Wears that I didn't want him coming into the Chancellor's Head no more.

Wears came bustling up to see me one day looking pleased with something. He told me that now was our chance to make a killin'. He had heard that James Berry was in town—Berry, the old hangman. He was putting on a show at the old music hall on Nelson Street that'd been taken over by the temperance people. He showed me a handbill that went on about sensational lectures and how you could make the hangman's acquaintance. I said 'no' to Wear's idea of a double bill, me and Berry. I said I still afraid of the Home Office finding out about me exhibiting myself but really it was Berry that frit me. Appearing in the pub was one thing but going on the stage was a step too far. I could not risk a return to prison. I kept the handbill though for it had a dreadful pull. To think that things had swung round in this arsey-versey world for both me and Berry to be entertaining the public.

Doctor Kaiser: You were not tempted to see him?

—I did go at the last moment, taking Jessie with me. Don't know why I did it, I just did. There was quite a bustle in the old music hall. The audience was mainly women. We squeezed in three rows from the front and looked up at a big banner that said, 'The Lord Healeth', or some such. Berry came onto the stage while the piano played the tune, 'Daddy wouldn't buy me a bow-wow'. Then, there he was. A gert block of a man eaten out by age and illness. He had on evening clothes with a cape. There was no mistaking the cold codfish eyes in the big melon 'aid. He spoke as if it was all a joke. Said he wanted to be called 'executioner 'because 'hangman' was for Jack Ketch, butchers and low folk, said he liked to deal with his 'customers' in a civil way.

That voice clawed me back to when I had last heard it. I was a mump 'aid to have put myself through it. Berry's voice seemed to reach inside me and scratch at my innards. He launched into his talk going on about how he couldn't stop executions but he tried to do them in a merciful way. He said that prisoners didn't mind hanging and being out the road compared to penal sentences for life. He was right about that. His main thing was drink. How it supported the gallows and created the crime. He mopped at his red sweaty face while the temperance crowd clapped like mad. After speechifying on his doubts about capital punishment Berry then turned to his lantern slides. I mainly remember the crowd moaning and groaning over the pictures. They fair turned my stomach, drawings of salt box cells, condemned men, hoods and nooses. Berry kept saying that this is what you get for breaking the laws of this country. He started to show pictures of the people he'd hanged. He said that Mary Pearcey was the prettiest woman he ever hanged and Moses Shrimpton was the most brave. About then I began to whisper to Jessie I couldn't stand it no more but then he showed a picture of the shed in Exeter with them all arranged—Berry, Pitkin, Cowtan and the warders and me in the middle, the white bag over my head. Berry said it was a strange case early in his career. How the rain at night had swelled the leaves of the drop and bound them despite the most careful preparation. There was a muttering in the audience, for many knew I was in town. Jessie told me not to make a fuss because people would see. It came to an end at last and the lights were raised to show Berry looking uneasy as if he had showed us something shaming about himself.

There were a few questions from the audience about temperance and the evils of drink and about hanging. One woman asked Berry how he escaped the convicts' friends and family who might be seeking revenge and he got a laugh by saying that he shaved off his whiskers and put on a dress when leaving prison.

Then he was gone, the strange old devil. Or I thought that was it but a voice called him back. I saw with a jump that it was Commons, that runty journalist from the Chronicle. He took Berry by the arm and led him to me by the side of the stage there.

"Mr Berry I present, Mr Lee. I believe you have previous

acquaintance," said Commons.

You could see he was all cock-a-hoop. Berry looked uneasy and told me he'd seen me and thought I was a ghost out there in the audience. He said he saw them all the time, their sad sorrowful faces, all them he'd hanged. He told me he regretted his terrible work. Said he was glad to see me. Who'd have thought it? I exchanged a few words with him 'n could see that journalist writing it all down on a pad. I told Berry I was tolerable well. He said it was the reverse of when we last met and that now he was mortal sick with heart trouble. He needed the money for his family and that's why he did these talks. He told me he had done well out of me although there was a fearful amount of trouble after he failed to hang me. And that was it. He gave us a copy of his book 'Thoughts About the Gallows' and held Jessie's hand and told her to look after me because I had been through a lot. Jessie said later what an awful wet clammy hand he had. It was like shaking hands with a beefsteak. I felt dirtied by the meeting, it was as if I had been rubbing up against the dead.

It was about at this time that Jessie told me that she was with child.

She was already two months on. She had not wanted to tell me before she was sure. It meant changes, new arrangements. We moved out of the pub and rented a house on South View near to the western road out to Hexham. It was on a hill, out of town, almost in the country. I missed the close-packed streets of Newcastle. Perhaps I felt more hidden and safer there. On walks near to our new house I came upon the grey gert blocks of Hadrian's Wall. The old Wall started there and marched away west over the hills. I took it as a good omen, like them Romans I wanted to outlast all. I was sure that Jessie was carrying a son. There would also be Lees to carry on, I thought.

Commons wrote a small piece about my meeting with Berry but the nationals did not pick it up and I wondered if my fame was dying away as sudden as it had risen up. After meeting Berry, I thought I should try and be more business-like about exhibiting myself. I saw an expensive law man about it who advised me that it I should be careful not to go against the terms of my release. Wears paid me well but the new house was expensive, there were doctor's bills for Jessie and I was frit that sooner or later I would outstay my welcome at the Chancellor's Head. Jessie's nerves seemed to improve although she was often ill and her legs all swelled up and became painful. I passed the time thinking of what my new son would be like. I would call him John like me. I thought perhaps he would do even greater things than me.

Doctor Kaiser: The confinement was successful I take it?

—It was a terrible long labor. It was a Sunday, and all day there had been crowds going past into town, brought out to hear speeches—for the whole country was full of election fever. It was cold, with snow across the hills. I could see at once there was something wrong with the babby. It had cross eyes and a tongue too big for its mouth and its ears were folded over in a strange way. The nurse said he was bonny and there was nothing wrong. Jessie said he was a flower that would unfold.

I paid out to see a doctor in his consulting rooms off Collingwood Street a few months later. He looked at our babby, turning his little head this way and that and looking into his cross eyes with a glass. At last he returned our son to Jessie and washed his hands in a basin and asked to speak to me alone. Once Jessie went out the room looking frightened, he told me that that he had to say was difficult. He was sorry to tell me my son was "defective". That's what he said, "defective". That word fell like a stone. He said he was incurable and I must rid from my mind any notion of improvement. He said he was a sickly infant now and if he survived he would grow to be a feeble-minded adult. When I got my breath I asked what caused it. The doctor did not know. He said a Dr Down had described the condition. Sometimes it's in the blood, he thought. I asked what should be done and he answered that I should put the child to a wet nurse and then into a home for the feeble-minded. It was best not to dwell on it, there would be other children. As I left he shook my hand and said that it was a sad fact that some are not fit to run the race of life.

Things were different from then on. Jessie would not accept what the doctor said. She doted on the boy and a wall was quickly built up between us. I could not get over the terrible disappointment, though now I feel bitter sorry about it. I could not help from thinking that it was something come from her that had made our son like that, maybe it was the curse of the long bony reach of her mother from that Kentish asylum.

Jessie drank and grew fatter. When she put out her hand to me I could not take it. I began to sleep back at the Chancellor's Head, pleading long hours. She spent long teary nights tending to the baby while it whimpered in the dark. She tried to keep things going. She made me meals but couldn't seem to do anything right. I ate them in silence, those awful dinners, then I would go back to town.

The customers noted my black mood. They kept saying that their Jonty's got the scunners. Mr Wears had to tell me to pull my socks up. The pub wanted jolly barmen to entertain the customers during Newcastle's glorious triumphs in the new Football Association cup. Besides I was no longer so famous. That Dr Crippen, the dentist who had killed his wife and buried her in the cellar then fled to America, he was front page news now and I ...

[Clicking on spool]

... is that Addie bringing me dinner? Don't want any of it. Leave it on the side. Full up with everything anyway...

Where was I? I made my mind up quick. By summer we headed south on a Great Northern express. We did not have much to take, just clothes and letters of introduction. Jessie had the babby in a carrying basket. Women sometimes made a fuss over him until they saw his yellow turnip face and cross eyes. Then they turned silently away. The steamer pounded south. I'd set on us going to London. We were falling into a new life.

HOMUNCULUS

Huh! I could tell Lee a thing or two about bad blood. At least he only hit his Pa over the head with a hammer. Georgia's voice has escalated to a warning squeak. She keeps warning me about a mean man who is after me. He wants to consume me or I him. I don't quite get what she's saying. I keep seeing a young guy in my neighborhood, an ordinary-looking dude about my age who is always pushing a baby stroller. He came past as I was loading up my SUV in the front yard the other day. I nodded and said, "Wassup?" and looked into the stroller. There wasn't a baby there, nor even a child. It was a child- shaped thing, shriveled and old with a thick head of black hair. The lips were drawn back to show yellowish teeth. It was a homunculus foundling of some sort. The guy pushing the stroller averted his face and passed by. I thought maybe that was what I looked like as a child. I was a sort of troll-kid when I was small. I did not belong in my folks' world and they had no idea how to handle me. Whoever's chasing me maybe it's me they need to watch out for.

SPOOL EIGHT
Right across the ocean blue
London, 1909

—Coming to the big city was a big jump. A theatrical agent at the Sunderland Empire told me about the Old King's Head on Borough High Street. I'd gone to him about exhibiting myself, and he said a lot of music hall acts stayed there and they also held events themselves. Bert Williams the landlord offered me a job as soon as I turned up. It was going to be just like the Chancellor's Head: I was to be barman and freak show all in one.

Doctor Kaiser: You came to London when?

—Nearly two year after my release. That's where I met her downstairs. I noticed her that first morning while being shown around by Bert Williams. I saw an 'andsum maid with red-gold hair chasing some little figures and flicking a bar cloth at them. Bert said they were Harvey's Midges, a dwarf variety act. He told me they were dirty, troublesome little tackers, always looking up ladies' skirts. [laughing on recording] The one doing the chasing was Adelina. That's what Bert called her. She was barmaid there. He introduced me to her as "Babbacombe Lee". She asked what "Babbacombe" was and he told her to start reading the papers more careful. I said that it did not matter, it meant she could make up her own mind about me. She said to call her Addie. We've been together ever since.

Doctor Kaiser: And what of your wife?

—Jessie stayed in the lodgings in Lambeth, mainly spent her days wheeling little John around the streets in his perambulator. She struck up a bit of a friendship with the Portuguese family two doors down. What were their name? The Nascimentos, that's it. They were a lively bunch of milliners who had a cripple daughter, all crabbed up and with a little head like an apple stuck on a stick. Mainly Jessie stayed on her own though. She didn't come to the pub, I told her the landlord wouldn't like it. They say that time turns love into corpses or wives. There is nort crueller than a dead love. I stopped touching or looking at Jessie, 'n our love vanished like the leaves from a frost-nipped tree. There was a sour quiet in the bedroom; I no longer watched her as she undressed; I turned my back and blew out the lamp. I was glad to hurry off in the mornings and come back late at night. Watching the pigeons fly off over the Lambeth rooftops from the cold bathroom when I shaved in the mornings and seeing my hopes fleeing with them. When she did speak to me it was often with bitterweed shrewish complaints about this and that. Sunday mornings were a torture, we used to wheel Baby John to Vauxhall Park then stand together by the pond, looking at the cloudy water, our feet all snared up by fallen leaves.

Doctor Kaiser: How were you earning your living?

—I got £9 a week from Williams as well as extra money from appearing at The Ring on Blackfriars Road. That was a boxing place. I worked long hours behind the bar. It was a busy drinking place and plenty of them came to gawk at me. I'd got the performing thing off pat by then. Nort they said fussed me and I stared coolly at them and smiled mysterious-like when they asked if I was innocent.

Doctor Kaiser: And Adeline?

—I started carrying out the crates of empties for her and wiping down the bar top until Minnie Williams told me off for taking a woman's work off her. Addie seemed to know how to laugh and I felt she really wanted to know what I had to say. After hours, we leaned together side by side at the bar rabbitting about the customers or listening to Minnie in her cups talking about her 'Cream City' where she was brought up. Ess, of all places, she came from Milwaukee. She filled our heads with talk of Broadway Bridge, whaleback steamers on Lake Michigan, trolley cars, St Jo's, holidays at Waukesha and all. Addie kidded her about exchanging all that for London soot and scabby old pigeons.

There were threads, at first small, but growing stronger and stronger and binding round to pull us together. We walked out together after work to watch the lights of the city wobbling in the river. Addie told me about her life in Croydon. One of nine children in a crowded house with not enough love to go round them all. Her dad had been a sergeant in the artillery in Burma. Three of her sisters had been born there. He came out the army after getting a jungle fever and took a brewery job that he hated. Addie was eighteen when all of a sudden he drank a bottle of carbolic. She saw his screaming fit and the foam hanging out of his mouth when he was carted away. Her Ma struggled after he died. They moved to a scrag end of town and she leaned on her elder brother who also worked at the brewery and they took in lodgers. A little while later her brother Henry took on a new cycle-making business in Scarborough and her family went with him. Addie tried jumping away into a new life and took to barmaiding.

We were together more and more often. We found any excuse to go out together on errands, fetching household stuff for the Williams or taking packages and post. Then, between work, we slipped away past Montague Chambers and down Borough High Street to the river. Here we liked to lean on the parapet of London Bridge with all the carts and omnibuses going past. We passed the time watching the river traffic go past. Addie knew all the big buildings, Fishmongers Hall, St Magnus spire—I can't remember them all now. I mainly noticed the big white front of Croll's American Merchants. I kept saying that was the place to go.

Over time we went further down Southwark's dark lanes and waterside places. Once, at Greenland Dock, we found a crowd gathered around a sale of dead sailors' clothing and effects. Lord, that was a sad sight, how everything could just go scat. Down Clink Street one time we came on a Lascar funeral. The Indian fellows seemed to be having a good time, singing and laughing around that open casket. I told Addie about how back in the village the sin eater would take onto themselves all the badness from the dead person. Maybe the Indians did the same. Addie thought that it was what you did in life that was important, grabbing your chance when it came. Although there was so many strange sights it was being with Addie that made the difference. It was so good being with her. Specially compared to those dreary sad Lambeth rooms that awaited me at night.

I began to put off going to Jessie more and more. She

complained about being lonely, said I felt far away. Lying in bed with her all I could think of was Addie.

I might have stayed for a long time being pulled between two women if I had not set on going to Deb'm one last time. I wanted to go back to the start of it all to work out what to do. I told Jessie in the back end of that year that I was going to see Ma and I could not afford to take her with me.

Doctor Kaiser: What were you planning to do in Devon?

—I wanted to look at it one last time because a plan was forming in my head.

The auld place looked much the same when I did get there, although new tractors were grinding up the fields and Ma seemed weaker and slower. The Bonds brought her food over now every day and it was pitiful to see her going all bent over and shuffling to look at her bees. She told me that no-one hung flowers on Ladywell at midsummer no more. The Newton Times somehow got to hear of me and sent a reporter to the village. I gave an interview at the cottage door about how people outside Deb'm were treating me fair, how I was making my way in business and had no plans to come this way again. On my last day I went to visit my kin, the Marles at Tormahan. Old Aunt Millie was dead now. They had moved to Grafton Terrace, a few doors down from where Katie Farmer used to live. Katie herself was long gone. I sent Addie a postcard from Babbicam. It was called Rustic Bridge: Torquay and showed a rope bridge over by the Palace Hotel at Anstey's Cove. I sent a cheery few words to Addie on it but I had chosen the card as a sort of sign. The Palace Hotel had once been the big house called Bishopstowe where the foreman of the St Marychurch inquest had lived. It was that inquest that had really done for me. In a queer way I had picked the card to signify I was making an ending. I weren't never coming back and "Babbacombe Lee" was going to be no more.

Doctor Kaiser: What were your intentions?

—I was going to skedaddle, as they say in these parts. When

I got back I went straight to the Old King's Head and Addie took me to the big church of St Saviour's nearby. She said I should light a candle to make peace with those that had gone. There was a memorial stone to William Shakespeare's brother there that Addie pointed out. Not read a word but I know folks think him the best. I used to think you needed your name in stone, to last, like those names I once saw in Kent's Cavern in Torquay long ago, scratched into the rock, outlasting the centuries. I think then I wanted my name to wash away. I wanted my name to be remembered kindly by family and that was all. Now I'm not so sure. Maybe that's why I'm speaking like this.

Where was I? I was telling about London...

The Williams kept on advertising me and we all made a bit of money from the last of my fame. I even did a turn at Southwark Fair that autumn. The Old King's Head made good business those days, people packing in to stare at 'the man that could not be 'anged', especially with the Crippen business all in the papers, about how he had buried his wife in the cellar and tried to escape across the Atlantic with his lady love and was facing the noose.

The Williams told us they'd be leaving in the early spring, going to South Africa to seek new fortune. Addie received letters from her ma begging her to give up the barmaiding and join the family in Scarborough. The Crippen trial at the Old Bailey came to its ending and the little dentist was hanged in late November at the Pent. The drinkers had a song about him taken from the music halls. I soon got sick of hearing it. How did it go? "...right across the ocean blue, followed by Inspector Drew. Ship ahoy! Naughty boy!" There you go.

In that early winter of 1910 if you had looked up at the pub front you'd see Addie's little flower boxes full of geraniums still blooming despite the sooty nip of London air. She could make love grow where it had no roots afore. The air smelt of cinders and the pigeons crept closer to the chimney stacks for warmth. Addie warmed my splintery heart though. She seemed to know how to live. I still think of her as I first met her.

Doctor Kaiser: How did you break it to your wife?

—It weren't pretty and I'm not proud of it. Jessie deserved better. The holiday season was a big rush at the Old Kings Head. It was Christmas Eve when Addie suddenly told me it was her birthday. We kissed for the first time that night and all the bells of the parish St George's, St Olave's and St Saviour's seemed to be ringing on my way home. That night I lay with Jessie for the first time in a long while. I filled her up although I was thinking of Addie's soft lips. Poor Jessie was happy that next day. I heard her singing carols to the baby thinking everything was going to be alright agin.

It all folded up quickly after that. The Williams were packing ready to leave. The new landlords, the Banburys, were shown round. Addie and I thought they were a sour-faced lot and not likely to give us a place. The boxing club boys from the Ring had a last do—Jimmy Clabby was just in from his Australian triumphs, middleweight champion of the world. Minnie gave him a party, especially since he was managed out of Milwaukee. She introduced me to Jimmy. She said I was the man who couldn't be hanged and I was wanting to fly to new pastures. He shook my hand for luck as he was due to pound Harry Duncan at the National Sporting Club. He also told me about how I could get on in the States. He said how I wouldn't get a fair do if I stayed in England.

Doctor Kaiser: And Jessie?

—In February I told Jessie I was going away on business for several months. She took it hard and screamed and clawed at me. As I struggled with her it reminded me of when Pa made me drown a young cat in the yard water butt, feeling its thin neck squirreling under my hand as it fought for life. I told Jessie not to take on so and it would be just for a while. For some reason, she did not tell me then that she must have been a month on with child. Straightaway after telling Jessie, I signed in at Peckham Clock House police station for my life license for the last time and found lodgings up in Islington. I took the rent book as proof of identity when we went to get our passports. Addie signed hers as 'Jessie Lee' and so our life of lies began. We kept on working at the pub for the last two weeks but moved in together in that little room on Copenhagen Street off the Caledonian Road, next to a home for orphan boys. It was not far from the Pent where I did my hard time. Our room was rented out by the Walters, a middle-aged couple who watched us as we dragged our bags up the stairs. Mr Walters gave me a wink and asked if I had been married long. I can never forget Addie kneeling to make a fire. Her hair was red-gold in those days and shining in the winter light from the sooty old windows. I'd already realized once before how a woman could take you so far down a road.

We came back for a last shift at the Old Kings Head and to draw our pay. Jessie turned up looking for me and I said I would be by presently. Addie's mother came from Scarborough to see us off. She was the only one who knew although Minnie suspected. Mrs Gibbs looked frightened and kept asking Addie if she really knew who I was and had she really thought of what she was doing. Addie asked her to be glad for her. She cried all the way down on the boat train to Southampton.

Doctor Kaiser: And no-one else knew you were going?

—Not a zaul. We took second class cabins. I should have taken steerage but I didn't want Addie to suffer the dirt below decks and the wandering hands of the crew. It was an old steamer with a German name, the Crown Prince something. Other passengers came on at Southampton to second class. We had to dine with them all each night and I taught Addie what she should say. I was a 'general dealer' seeking a business opportunity for a short while in New York and she was my wife. We were also in practice for lying to the American immigration. They did not like men who had served prison time. We did not want to be turned back at Ellis Island. We spent most of our time up on deck all muffled up, watching the poor steerage passengers rolling on the quarter decks below. It was blawing enough ver to take the teeth off a saw and cold too for late February. The English papers said that Niagara Falls was all frozen up.

One night, twelve days out, I pointed out to Addie the star Capella in the night sky and Arcturus showing the way west. I'd learned my stars from the sailor lads at Babbicam. Just then a white mewie came and flittered about the lights on the decks though we were far out in the deep ocean. One of the crew said it was a shearwater. I told Addie it was a blessing bird come to show us a new life.

Fetal Death Certificate

Kimmie and I weren't that great really. The main thing was I was so grateful that she was with me and that made each day a blessing. She stuck me for two years, she put up with my numb heart and cold fumbling fingers all that time. I still wonder what she saw in me. The only thing she seemed to appreciate was that I knew stuff, she liked me to read to her from the Latin. I read her Horace mainly, sometimes Propertius. Do you know Elegy 4, the one about the dead returning to chide him? Dumb question. Anyway, in it the poet says: 'phantoms have their reasons when they come'. Maybe I was remembering that line when I finally heeded little Georgia's nagging the other day. Acting on impulse, I dug out the family papers that Grandpa kept in an old army box, an ammo chest for .50 cal, I think. I scratched around in there all morning going through old snapshots, papers about the house that was sold and even some medical reports about me. I found it folded up with my parent's death certificates. It was a fetal death certificate—yep, there is such a thing. Apparently I had an unborn brother who died with them on that day. I never knew Mom was pregnant. Maybe they kept it from me. But Georgia knew. A bit of me still thinks that

Georgia remembers repressed memories but I'm beginning to swing towards Propertius—maybe ghosts do have their reasons when they come. A brother too—snuffed out. I keep thinking I've hit bottom but always there seems a way left to go.

Found something else in there. A cool, commemorative WW2 European Theater Colt .45 caliber auto with a silver nickel finish in an oak presentation box. It had some silver chrome bullets to go with it. Looked like Grandpa was fixing to shoot a werewolf. The gun itself seemed unfired. Maybe it was given to him by his veteran buddies. I've taken the pistol, I enjoy the sense of power when I heft it in my hand, I like to clack back the slide, sniff the purposeful gun oil smell in the chamber and look down into the zero of that recessed muzzle.

Spool Nine

The police come calling
Milwaukee Wisconsin, 1934

Doctor Kaiser: We have time for a session before my surgery.

—Whatever you say, sir… Been thinking of our old place on South 10th. We always seemed to be needing ice, even in winter. That iceman was forever coming to our door with his gert big blocks. Addie had a refrigerator that seemed to eat those ice bricks. I'd hold them in my bare hands once the iceman let go of his pincers. Addie nagged at me to use a towel but I didn't care. Ess, that old house on South 10th. An unlucky place. I guess I only wanted to numb myself after what had happened. I'd pay the man his 50 cents and take those blocks into the kitchen and stand there holding them 'til Addie slid them into the trays. Afterwards I'd look down at my cold hands. Grey as a plucked chickens. Old man hands. It was hard to believe they were part of me. You just want to be numb, don't you, doc? I think you know the same thing.

Doctor Kaiser: Yes, a bereavement can have that effect. What happened to you in that house?

—It was twelve years ago. I was half asleep on the front room rocker when there was a banging on the front door and the sound of boots on the walkway outside. It was the city police calling to deliver bad news. They asked if it was 922 South 10th and was I Mister Lee? They said there had been an accident. They stood on the step. There was rain dripping from their cap brims and the leather of their Sam Brownes gleamed under the capes. My eyes kept being drawn to the silver badges on their chests. All my life the coppers had been seeking me out. Like going down from St Marychurch to Market Street Station that November day, walking behind Sergeant Nott. They said it was my daughter and hadn't I better sit down. That was the moment our world had caved in. I will always remember the police there and Addie's face behind me in the doorway. She had already sensed what I could not grasp on that October afternoon.

Doctor Kaiser: They had brought you news about your daughter?

—Ess, they told me she was gone but I could not take it in.

[long pause]

That unlucky house was quite near the lake. It's strange how I've lived so close to water all my life. October used to bring early cold weather, mists and sharp east winds off the lake. I suddenly felt old in that house. I was older than Miss Keyse was when she died and she had seemed ancient to my young vulish self. When you get old it's harder to screen things out. Everything leaks through you. I'd stare out the front windows on South Tenth; the front yard palings were all twisted and bent. A hole had appeared in the yard one day. It started as a dip in the ground then it gradually became a gaping gert hole. Evie must have been about 14. It was that year a black boy, James Cameron, I think his name was, he survived a lynching in Marion, Indiana. The papers said his neck was scarred by the rope. Apparently, they took him down when someone said he was innocent. Anyhow, Evelyn asked me what that big old pit was that had just appeared in our yard. I explained to her what the county engineer had told me. You see, thousands of years ago all here was ice and a great glacier came sweeping down from the north and stored up a ball of ice under itself. Stored it like a babby in its belly. That ball of ice hunkered in the ground after all the glacier has melted. It waited and waited all secret like 'til long after the rest has warmed and ebbed away, but the ice remained there underground to melt in its own time and to leave an empty space there, hiding, no one knowing, creating a space that shows itself in its own time. Evie asked me why that sink hole had finally decided to show itself now but I couldn't tell her that. Things get to be hidden until the world is ready for them, I'd said.

The twelfth of October was going to live with us for the rest of our lives. I was never much good at anniversaries but we were stuck with that one. The first anniversary was the one that's clearest in my mind. It was the year of '34. I should have been working—Mister Lee, the shipping clerk in his long brown coat. I was seventy years old and still had a job though so many were laid off. I was good at what I did and I always liked working round machines. I loved watching the long lines of gleaming autos at Nash's, the flash Kenosha Dusenbergs for the quality market. I've been hiding all the time these last thirty years since I came to this country. Maybe hiding from myself. Early on, I thought I was making good and I felt strong. I was building a life that others thought I would never have. It all began to drift away after what happened to Evie. I kept on working for a while longer but there seemed no point to it. And then there were those October anniversaries.

The first anniversary in '34 set the way it was to go in all them other years. The geese always come over at about that time of year. They seem to signal that it was time to see her. I'd go out into the yard at night when I heard them yelping and I watched them go by in black threads against the moon. The geese were keeping to a way of doings things, just like me and Evie. Last year when I got sick was the first time that I had not kept the anniversary. I hoped she was not lonely. Never mind, I'll soon be there myself to keep her company. They follow you about, don't they doctor? Those that have died?

Doctor Kaiser: Yes, in a way they do, sure.

—For some reason I used to most sense her in the bathroom of the house on South 10th. It was a big yellow-tiled room. I'd be there shaving but somehow I kept imagining that there was Evie at my back. As a kid she's stay in the bath for hours. I kept on shaving day after day and sometimes I'd talk to her as if she was still there. I became an old man in that mirror. People said I grew much grayer and thinner in the first year after she had gone. What had happened in the world that particular year? I used to study the papers real careful. I was looking for some sign, something that showed that Evie had mattered at all to the world. Still the same stuff happened. The people still living in shacks in Lincoln Park; the strikes in the city; Mayor Hoan turning the tide; Dillinger shooting it out in Manitowish Waters where I had once took Evie and Addie on family outings; I think there was even a miracle story about the local boy who had fallen into a sewer and came out alive from a pipe a mile downstream. Well, there was to be no miracle for Evie and I could find nothing in the papers, nothing at all to show she was missed. Everything was a sink hole. A hole that bored into that horny shell I had growed around me.

Doctor Kaiser: How did Mrs Lee cope with the loss?

—Addie never wanted to come with me on my anniversary visits. Too painful. She preferred to remain at home as if nothing had happened and Evie was just going to come back through that front door from class or work. Addie would listen to the National Church of the Air on the radio or Betty Crocker Cooking Hour. She'd rather work in the house and stir soap flakes in the laundry barrel. That is how she coped. We didn't even talk about it. What happened to Evie put a space between us and that grieved me.

Doctor Kaiser: What had actually happened to your daughter?

—Gone and in the ground. Sudden as that. On account of a stupid accident, they'd said. I'm struggling to put it in words. I know I'm dragging on your patience.

Doctor Kaiser: Tell me in your own way, it's okay.

—All that was left was for me to pay my respects to her each year. I'd put on my winter coat and grey hat and call goodbye to Addie. She'd be in the hall maybe holding the flowers. She used to get then for me from Euler's, yellow chrysanths usually. Her face that had once made my heart run quick, it was so pale and handsome. Now a stranger would see she had the face of an older 'umman, as round and full as an old biscuit and with her green eyes hid behind glasses. She liked to fuss over me and tuck in my muffler. Then I'd be outside. I don't suppose I'll go outside again. Not 'til they carry me out that is.

I usually didn't take the Ford on my anniversary visits. I only really drove to work at the Cudahy yards once the family outings stopped. We had those wooden walk boards outside the house, 'n about then, for the first time in my life, I became frit of falling over and used to go real careful on those boards. We had a nameplate on the house. Addie wanted to call the house, 'The Hollies'. I think that's what her family house was called in Surrey back in her old life. For some reason I'd always remember that street in fall or winter, the catalpa leaves turning or dropping. There'd be snow slush and the sparrows squeaking and scrambling round the horse flop from the ash can man.

Mrs Donahue next door always seemed to leave her windows open whatever the weather. You'd see her curtains fluttering in the cold lake wind. The neighbors weren't bad considering that Addie and I kept away from folk. It was Evie that brought us out in the world. We saw the Hoelichs most of all. One

Independence Day street party Mike said a strange thing to me that I've never forgot. I think he was a bit tiddly. He said that "in da old country"—that's how he used to speak—"in da old country"' they said you get given a ghost when you are born, they walk beside you all your life and go with you back into the dark when your time has come. "What you tink of dat, eh?" He kept saying. I guess I've got more than one ghost going along beside me though I didn't tell Mike that. He worked at the Wauwatosa auto factory. He was lucky to have a job in those hard times. The City That Works, they said in the papers. I hit lucky I suppose in choosing this place as my home or I thought of it as lucky until what happened to Evie.

Those high towers of this city, the big shoulders of the MGL building, the city hall spire and St Joe's big onion, it all seemed a magic place once but there's a doomy sad look to it and a dirty sulphur smell in the air these last few years. Especially when I set out to Forest Home on my yearly anniversaries. I usually took the No 7, TMER & L Street car down Forest Home Avenue. No one would notice me, the other passengers used to keep their heads in their papers and there'd usually be a few high school kids chattering and laughing. Evie came home once in second grade and told me that Milwaukee meant 'gathering place' in Indian. Only she called it 'Muwahkee' like the other local kids. Milwaukee had been that for me, a gathering place. But for me it had been somewhere to grow the private man, a drawing of a family around me and a getting rid of that bad old public face that had stood in for me. America had been a new start. Lord, I've had a few of those 'new starts' in my time.

Doctor Kaiser: How did you get to come here in the first place?

—On account of Jimmy Clabby, the world champion middle-weight boxer. I'd mentioned him afore I think. He had set me up with my first job with autos at his garage in North Downer, in that same year that Schrank shot Roosevelt at the Hotel Gilpatrick. Clabby really looked out for me and was good to his word though I hardly knew him really. Jimmy was the best sort of guy. An 'andsum boy as they'd say in Deb'm. I don't suppose you've heard of him now? Just a name maybe.

Doctor Kaiser: I remember hearing that he had died.

—Poor old Jimmy died in the year after Evie. I read that they found him in a Calumet City flop house. I think he ran out of luck, lost hope and became a drunk. His fight place, the Elite Roller Rink on West National, also burned down about then. Jimmy carried the secret of 'Babbacombe Lee's' whereabouts. I know that the papers in England still run articles about me from time to time about how I am a publican in London, or how I'd been found in a doss house or discovered as a laborer or mariner somewhere. No one guessed I would be quietly working shipping out car parts in the Midwest.

In this town they don't give much of a damn where you are from. There's little care for the past. Everything here is always getting torn up and replaced, not like Deb'm where they hold onto things for years. I liked all that rattling change at first. Especially after twenty-two years of prison stillness. I had swum with it then, but in the later years here it began to frit me. It was stronger than me, swirling me along on with no bank to grasp onto. Just like the city whisking by that street car on the way to Forest Home. That south side of the city was always covered in smoke from the American Metal Products chimneys. It made all the people on the streets seem ghost-like. They said the unofficial city motto was "rip it up and start over", do you remember that? [no evident reply from Kaiser] Even when the city and the whole country were most in money trouble there were work gangs all over the streets on the mayor's employment projects, jackhammering and pulling up everything. Also in the depression days you could barely see anything except those billboards, realtor shop signs, and liquidation adverts. Everything was getting whisked off and sold cheap.

On the way to Forest Home cemetery that street car used to sail past The Riviera Movie House where Addie and I had seen

'The Valiant' in '29 with Paul Muni in it. There was something about that film that got to me. It was all about what happens before a man is executed. That night we saw it, for the first time ever, I had told Addie something of what really had happened at Babbicam. She had listened to it and said 'Oh, John,' at the end, that's all.

The trolley car generally stopped at Forest Home north gate. There was long drive there that went off away into the burying grounds. The whole place was like a gert wood in the middle of the city. I used to feel tired even by the time I passed the lodge house. Usually there would be no one about. There were stones all around even quite recent ones made of Wauwatosa limestone. They soon got eaten away to nort by the dirty Milwaukee smoke. I made sure ours would be of granite so they would last. I'd bought a family plot there in '27 for me and Addie both. I wanted to be sure that there was somewhere to rest for the restless. How could I have known that it would be Evie filling that place before us?

I learned how to mark it out among all the stones, a few steps from a stand of red chokeberries. Near to a big white stone with an angel. A mound of yellow sandy soil that slowly grassed over and flattened off as the years went on. There was a wooden marker with her name on it for a long time. We couldn't decide what to put on the stone. Addie wanted it to read, How Many Hopes We Buried Here?

I was all addle-aided but I sometimes used to call out loud in the thin air asking Evie if she was there. But it would stay quiet there by that heap of earth. I had been bothered by spirits all my life but I could never make out anything from her. Well, maybe ghosts have their reasons. It seems like death has made a hole for Evie leaving only emptiness behind. Poor girl, with us old, tight-lipped parents fussing over her. She had her grandmother's face but her voice was new and American. She could not understand how frit we were; nor why I used different names according to who was asking. She never really asked us about the past. She somehow knew in her gut that we couldn't talk about some stuff. I taught her some Deb'm words, 'ladybug' and 'flittermouse' and 'how be nackin' vor'. But I never told her that I was 'Babbacombe Lee'. I don't suppose it would have meant anything at all to her anyway. Bringing up Evie and putting everything we had into her helped rub out the past. I didn't need to prove anything while she was in our lives. It had all gone on in a far-away country and long ago, 'n scaffolds and hangmen belonged to another world. It's only since she's been gone that I've slid back to thinking about what happened in Babbicam and how to get things straight before the sun goes down on me.

Doctor Kaiser: Tell me more about your girl.

—She was called Evelyn after Addie's mother. She was a late swallow, I was fifty when she was born in 1914 with the old country we had left behind hammering on towards war. She was Addie's only child, something for Addie at last who had come into this country secretly under my first wife's name. Evie was loved like no other. And with love had come a frit feeling beyond anything I'd been through before. We were frit of losing her. We had a foolish false notion that if you worritted about the worst that could happen then it would surely never happen.

We kept her room as she had left it. Her Raggedy Anne still on the bed, a beret on a chair as if just thrown down there, her little ukulele against the wall, her South Div yearbook, her phonograph, her black button purse, some cardboard 20 cent discs she had bought and a photo of Ted Lewis. How she loved to dance around her room singing with him. In those last years she became a woman before our eyes. Her hair was bobbed and waved in a fancy style but she had her grandmothers hawk face and far-seeing eyes. She had a great liking for sweet things. She loved Snirkles Bars and Barque's root beer. She'd feast on them with her little Polish friends. They called her 'Lynn'. Their laughing and stamping feet filled the house as I sat downstairs on the front room rocker listening to them. She also loved the movie houses, I took her to see 'Gold Diggers of

1933' and Laurel and Hardy in 'Hog Wild' and sometimes we'd drive downtown to watch the famous light display outside the Butterfly Movie Theater.

Evie was easy to please. She liked everything: drives out in the Ford Tudor, walks by the lake. Especially trips to Jones Island. The city was breaking up the old shacks on our last visit there. We would walk along the beach along the lines of empty old wooden houses and I would tell her stories of the Great Lakes ghost ships. I could not help laughing at her antics. She had that gift to pull me out my mazy old 'aid. I knew then that she could be taken from me but I just thought it would be by some man. I was all primed up for boys in two-seater sedans, fast German boys from the West Side. Addie and I had talked of what we would do if she wanted to go out on dates but Evie had shown little interest in men. She liked those sloppy tunes though and maybe she kept her own secrets from us. That was the weakness of my selfish ways. My watching was for press hounds, for men with flash cameras and for letters with English stamps but the danger was to be quite different. Caw, my dear days, I'd got to be like a big old crab ahiding on the sea bed. I feared a pulling away of the shell I had built around myself.

Ess, there was no forevision although there was a turrible ache like the time Evie caught a fever after taking swimming lessons at Bechstein's Swimming School on the river. She had laid in sweaty sheets all night whispering "Sorry Pa… Sorry Pa…" over and over. I sat up over her until the fever broke. And once, in our first house on 5th Avenue right by the lake, she must have been six, I heard her screaming for me in the front yard. I galloped out in my shirt sleeves thinking that she had been hit by an auto. There was such relief to see her standing, with her black hair all tumbling in the sunlight. It turned out she had cut her bare foot on a piece of grass in the lawn and that was all so easy to fix.

Doctor Kaiser: And what happened? Can you tell me what happened to her?

—They used some sort of strong cleaner at work. Lysol, or something. I cannot bear to be near these strong killing chemicals now. They all seem to have a creosoty stink. They get you at the back of the throat like mothballs. Evie used that Neko germicidal soap for her spots and Addie had King Pine in its slope-shouldered bottle. They all had that smell. And the P & G naphtha laundry soap in its green packet, one dollar value for 25 cents, for soaking the woolens in the yard. The stink of the stuff—I should have seen it as a warning.

Addie had taught Evie the trade. She had worked as a cleaner to help with money right through our time here. Folks liked her English voice and her wage helped pay for Evie's music lessons and we could get little extras when Nash's cut everybody's pay. Evie was happy at her first proper job as a maid to Dr Kovacs, a doctor on West Wisconsin. Evie said that he was not a doctor, he was a 'physician'. Same difference. The job was a chance for her to buy herself things. Forty dollars a month didn't sound bad. We'd have wanted more for her, but we were happy to hide and not push ourselves forward. We'd had enough of that. Better to quietly get on. After her first day of work she came back all full of news about those rich Kovacs. She had been given the job on the Friday and started with them on the Monday. It was golden fall weather and she told us all about their swanky home. I grumbled to myself. It went bitter for me that my family were still servants in this country of freedom but I was happy to see her so merry.

By the Wednesday Evelyn had come back from work more quietly. She complained of being tired out and later she told us of having a headache and feeling sick after cleaning all day. We got her to take some cocoa that night but she ate nort and went to bed early. She was out the next morning as bright as usual. Addie had stood at the front door and watched her go up South 10th and turn one last time to wave back. Then the police came knocking later that day and later still Detective Bailey came asking more questions. Then there had been the identification of the body and more turrible things after that.

The inquest had been the first time that I had been back in court since the trial at Exeter but maybe it was worse for Addie with her memories of her father. Her Pa had drunk carbolic acid when she was young. Have I told you? Poor Addie, first her Pa, then Evie. In Evie's case the only insanity was a careless doctor. We found out that the Kovacs had set Evie on to cleaning the curtains using a bottle of naphtha cleaning fluid. They called them drapes in the inquest but they were curtains. I saw it on the table in the inquest room. It had a label on it that read 'Sunshine Cleaning Oil' with a little poison sign on the bottom of the bottle. You would think a physician would know better but it was that wife of his, pushing Evie to spot clean the drapes and to do them again and again. I thought of Evie's hands on the bottle, dabbing the stinking stuff onto gauze and wiping their rotten drapes with it in that warm little bathroom. I thought of her coughing, perhaps knocking the bottle over with the cap undone. Evie fainting, falling, great splashes of the stuff on her grey maid's dress. While she was blacked out the air in the room must have filled with the mortal stuff. Her body was burned red at the neck and her skin smelt of it when I bent down to kiss her in the morgue. And it remained on her clothes also. I would never forget the awful smell of her things when they were sent back to us in a brown paper package.

Reaching the Dead

I've been staring at a pic of Lee. His face seems like a big hole that grows and grows. I think the death of his daughter was his first real loss. That time death threaded his needle right through Lee's heart. Everything before that somehow seemed not to touch him very much. Evie's going wrecked him and he collapsed inward from his skin. I read in an archive copy of the Milwaukee Sentinel for 1934 that he attended the inquest but avoided the reporters. The story ended up on the front page. They headlined it, 'Terrible Poisoning Tragedy'. Poor frickin' bastard Lee, though there is nothing new in dying, grief is such a pot–hole. I think of him lying down on his daughter's grave talking to where he thought her face was. Pouring out all his bad dreams to the uncomplaining dead.

Maybe Lee is teaching me about living with loss. I told you Kimmie left me last summer. Just went back to her folks in Houston. I guess she got sick of the isolation here and my ambition and my cold water poverty. I used to keep that thirtieth Ode from Book Three of Horace pinned on my wall. The one that begins, "Exegi monumentum, aere perennis…" I explained to her that it meant, 'I'm going to build me a monument, higher than the pyramids, safe from the gnawing wind and rain and the scouring years, a part of me that will never die.' She wasn't impressed with that, nor with Shakespeare's Sonnet 55. She couldn't understand why I lived by that stuff and was damned sure she wasn't going to be no Muse neither.

Man, I miss her! Even spent three days driving down to that bayou outside of her folk's place. I sat and watched the lights in the house and tried to catch a glimpse of her. In the end a tropical storm passed over and beat down on my truck. The brown water kept on piling down the bayou and in the end I drove all the way back. All I have now is my invisible friend and persecutor—Georgia. She keeps on slithering out warnings, pleas and prayers. She assures me that there are three beings hovering around me that are wishing me well but she says I must be careful of a shadow entity. "One two – he's coming to get you," she keeps saying. The "Boogie Man" she calls him. I still carry that chromed .45. No use against invisible powers but it will sure work against mortal flesh. I really should be mad with Georgia. I spent my teens converting to the idea of scientific materialism. I not only got rid of God but all the accompanying fandang of ghosts, ghouls, demons and spirits. I did it to protect myself, to get away from the accusing dead and to piss off all those believers who made my life miserable at High School. I wanted to shuck off that body and spirit duality bunk and instead I have reinherited the whole mess.

It's weird how Georgia never mentions Grandpa. Maybe he and I understood each other and that's why he doesn't haunt me. He died very calmly. The illness took him quickly, all of a sudden he quit eating and seemed to shrivel away. Near the end, I asked him if he was scared. He shook his head without saying anything. I want to touch the death I saw in Grandpa. The calmness of it. I visit his grave sometimes. Yep, he wanted to be buried properly, didn't want to be scattered dust like Mom and Dad. He's buried out at Prairie Home. There's a bronze plaque on his headstone that reads 'World War Two, PFC 101st Airborne.' His veteran buddies leave a flag there every Memorial Day. I found a note in his desk drawer after he died—it's the same desk I write on now—"Blessed are the dead who die in the Lord. They will have rest from their labors for their good deeds will follow them." Revelations. I'm not sure why he copied it out. Maybe it was a message for me. Anyway, I had it cut into his headstone, it's there forever now.

Not sure what will follow me except bad stuff. I still have horrible sweaty nights, timor mortis conturbat me. I've wrapped pillows around my head to keep the noises away. Often the sweaty bedding gets wrapped in some way round my neck, I have red rings on my skin like a kind of stigmata.

I keep going by concentrating on getting a handle on Lee. I think now that he's not just teaching me about loss but about the line between life and death. A no man's land where we live all the time.

It's mind blowing to think that John Lee, born under the witchy spells and portents of a nineteenth century South Devon village, would live so long to inhabit a modern world that we can all recognize, a place of automobiles, peanut butter, cornflakes and movie theaters. In a way, it's easier to imagine him safely bound up in the past. It's strange how his voice actually gets stronger as you go through the spools in time order. He seemed to get something from the recordings, as if they made him grow emotionally. Lee made that amazing jump from Prisoner L.150 Portland Prison South Block to being a motor industry parts clerk and house owner in South Side Milwaukee. He wouldn't find it so easy to hide nowadays; Homeland Security would probably deport his ass.

As ever with Lee there are as many questions as answers. I'm sorry I keep jumping from one thing to another. It's the way my mind works. Also, maybe truth can only be found in piths and gists. These days we log into the Net for a few moments, fire our neurons for a few seconds then jump like a ninja to the next thing.

That long Lee narrative seems like a throwback. He's pretty sneaky and search engines cannot track him down. For instance, who are the Dingles? Lee listed them on his Ellis Island entry ticket as his address of destination, E. Dingle at 625 Vanderbilt Avenue Brooklyn. Maybe they were friends of Minnie Williams, the mysterious American wife of the landlord of the Old King's Head? Or a connection to Jimmy Clabby? It seems beyond knowing now—they certainly don't appear in any census or directory. I broke my usual habits, took a week out and hauled my ass all the way to NY to check that one out. Travelled Greyhound Express by way of Chicago, 14 numb- butt hours. I'm scared crapless by flying, you know. I'm frightened my spirit would get lost in the ether, maybe get jolted out of its zone should a jet break up all of a sudden.

I made my way to the address that Lee gave in Prospect Heights and stood under the honey locust trees in the street. It's a soda bar now. Everything is just surface upon which all exists. All I could see was my own shadow in the plate glass windows. Someone cloned my credit card when I joined one of the ancestry internet sites that lets you read New York phone directories from the past. I couldn't find the Dingles on there but whoever ran the site went shopping with my card in Union

Square and Nolita. They seemed to go for chi-chi clothes and jewelry mainly. It made me laugh. I wondered if it was somehow the psychic revenge of Lee, the name stealer.

I used to waste my time on dumb video games like King's Quest and shit. I'd spend days on them. You had to go up and down the levels solving puzzles, answering riddles and looking for magic rings and weapons. It was boring but I enjoyed the slow concentric accumulation. The riddle I'm trying to solve is: what is the genuine face of Lee? I'm looking for something within him that is undivided, a filiation where he finally gets to parent all the versions of himself. I find it hard to imagine how anyone can live without the consolations of art although millions probably do it. Maybe as a proxy to art Lee was looking for that mute undivided thing within himself. Was that what all those recordings were for? He was looking for the truth about himself? So often though he seems to flailing around, describing everything except the most essential and integral. I've often wondered how far could Lee swim out and keep himself intact.

From Devon to Portland, to Newcastle and Southwark and then to Wisconsin, Lee was always by water. Like my home town, the Rock River here floods pretty much every year. We are straight out West a short way from Milwaukee off Interstate 94. It's a land of hills and lakes and birch and sumac. The population of my town is 11,000 and one poet, moi. That sounds about the right ratio—it's an archaic profession really. I am one whose name is writ in water. I carry my clarity with me. Lee found me by a sort of process of convection, a property that is only possessed by liquids.

I think of my grandparents, a few miles out of Waukesha. As kids they might well have passed the Lees out motoring in their Ford Tudor on 1930s summer jaunts to the Dells and Black Hawk Island. That is before everything fell in for the Lees when Evie died. Memories get laid down in irregular clumps like crystals adhering; I think of the Lees perhaps mentioned in some diary or a scribbled-on calendar kept by those that encountered them, their neighbors maybe, or a calendar of 1933 like those calendar poems of Lorine Niedecker (she lived on Black Hawk Island, you know). I always seem to be looking for confirmation. Dr Kaiser's stuff is only a start. I'm thinking of those vacation snapshots taken by strangers where you unwittingly appear somewhere in the corner of a scene, now stacked in a shoebox or on some forgotten digital chip. The thought of other versions of Lee out there...

I've been digging around the things in that old box and had another look at an old chewed up album—from the 1920's at a guess from the pictures on the front. It's full of yellowed scraps of English newspapers. I've worked out that it must have belonged to Lee. Lee must have had the clippings sent to him by his kin, maybe Aunt Millie's son Fred Marles who lived in Tormahan. They include a piece from an English paper, The Daily Mail, dated 1912. The story told how Lee's wife Jessie had showed up at a South London workhouse in that year. The workhouses were awful places from what I've read and you had to be real desperate to go there. Jessie had a baby and an invalid kid to care for and Lee's cash had stopped. There must have been something so bitter to her in that desperate humiliation. Only two years before she had been in charge of the females' wards at Newton Workhouse; now it was her turn to join the wretched army of the old, the sick, the helpless and the hopeless. The paper described how the wife of 'The Man Who Could Not Be Hanged' was destitute. Her husband had been exhibiting himself until February last when he left the country. He had sent back money for a while then wrote to say that he was without a job. There had been silence since then. She had been struggling to manage and the children were going hungry. Her daughter, Eveline, had been born in the August after he left. Those were not generous times but the paper told how the deserted family were given some money and vouchers for the local charities (sort of like our food stamps, I guess).

There was also a cutting from the Plymouth Advertiser about

his old girlfriend Katie Farmer. She married a seaman two years after Lee's trial, endured five years of an unhappy marriage then ran off with a housepainter to live in nearby Plymouth. The press guys tracked her down years later after Lee's release. She spoke to them on her doorstep before shutting the door to her past. They recorded what she said about her old boyfriend, Lee: "He has suffered. I hope his future life will be happy. His way will not be my way for I am now settled in life. I hope he may be able to prove his innocence. I was then a silly, sentimental girl. I am wiser now. My friends told me that he would be kept in prison as long as he lived and a life's devotion would be thrown away. So I put him out of my heart."

Fred Lee, cousin to John, Uncle George's son, also wrote him. The letter was tucked in the album, still in its envelope with Lee's first Milwaukee address. The faded script informed Lee that his mother had died in 1918. Found dead in bed by the Bonds. It also said that people had been looking for him. One was a Mr Bryan who had helped Lee in prison. He had come wanting Lee's new address but Grandma Lee's guardians, the Bonds, had sent him away. Another, a seaman, who was also turned away by the Bonds, lingered in the Tradesmen's Arms. Tried to pay for his beer by doing card tricks. Asked again for Lee's whereabouts then stuck a piece of paper under Town Cottage front door. It read, "C. Harrington, care of Mrs Connors, 15 Granby Street Devonport." Cousin Fred also reported in the letter that he had called at the address a while later but the landlady had said that the gentleman had been on another binge and been taken to the pauper hospital fit to die. There wasn't much else in the album. Some advertisements for autos, a postcard of Jimmy Clabby in his younger days crouching fists out and an article about Sultana at Milwaukee Zoo—apparently, the first polar bear in captivity to have cubs. A search through the papers in the years after the First World War show that Lee's name kept on flickering up. People seemed to want the man they could not hang to keep on surviving. There were reports of Lee running a shop in King

Street, Plymouth, Lee a bar owner in London, Lee prospecting for gold in Canada, Lee in Flanders killing Germans. He was also reported dead many times, in a Devon workhouse, in Melbourne, Australia, in 1918 and in Illinois in 1931. They even made a movie about him and the movie-goers were greeted at the doors of the cinema by an actor calling himself 'John Lee' and wearing a prison get-up with crow's foot markings. I aim to seal him down though. No more reappearance antics or versions of himself. Like the way I caught those big fierce yellow jacket hornets in the back yard of our house on Summit Avenue when I was a kid. I'd lure them into a sticky jello jar then slam the lid on them then take them into the house and watch them press their fierce empty faces against the glass until they weakened and died.

Spool Eleven
Cab rides
Milwaukee, 1934

[Recording resumes after a break,
sound of a radio in the distance]

—Where was I? I'd go tumbling out the cemetery on those anniversary trips and more often than not I wouldn't go straight home. No, I'd stay on the trolley and go jerking North over the Bridges over the Menomonee. Past the breweries, the stock yards and rail yards. As we crossed West Wisconsin, I'd generally have a look towards those red-roofed houses of the rich where those evil Kovacs lived. It would be at the dead end of the day usually by then. How many times did I go on those awful trips? Eleven, I guess. Some Octobers stand out more. I'd get off eventually on Sarnow or Walnut and just walk and wander around downtown. I seemed to want to hang around in the rough areas of town.

Doing a sort of penalty to myself, I don't really understand it. The light would be about going. I'd just keep on walking.

I got well and truly lost that first time, I didn't realize the kind of neighborhood it was. Didn't really notice the men loafing about and the boarded-up shop fronts. On I went, block after block, all alone, like a terrier in a wet hayfield. Where am I? Forget now. I'm not so good today, doc. All that I'm leading to is that I heard a song calling to me on Walnut Street. 'Goin' down to the river to pray.' I could hear it playing from inside the building. That hymn sound seemed to promise healing, a sign for me to follow. Stupid it might seem to you I know but that's what I thought. It took me to the steps of an old clap-board new fellowship church. A black feller was out there calling out on the front steps about how he was happy, always happy and to come and confess your sins. Well, I had a lot to confess, that's true. So I went in like a sleepwalker and a lighted door swung open for me and I'm not ashamed to say I joined them in that singing.

Doctor Kaiser: Let me understand: you wandered into the poor neighborhoods and went into the colored folk's churches? And what did you confess to?

—There was no end to the bad things I'd done and sometimes it's the not doing of something that was so bad but the things you didn't do. It used to feel as if I'd been dragged through brimbles backward. Brimbles, you know, what you calls brambles. I was alive in my own prickly bush but I was burning and stinging. I'd pour out all kinds of nonsense then skedaddle for home. I was glad to catch those cabs appearing out of the night. Them cabbies liked to talk about how it was going to be a hard winter. They drove big old Packards mainly. They'd wonder what I was doing in Bronzeville, asked if I was lost. Ess, I was lost for sure. A sinner all wormed out with secrets trying to confess to anyone who'd have me, even them poor auld church niggers. I'd sit in those cabs and secretly thank those black fellers. The men in the work sheds at Nash's used to show me postcards of dead ones hanging from trees down

South. Heads swelled to pumpkins. In this country bad things can come quick if you don't fit. You can see it in the eyes of those black folks. You could dance real easy on the rope like that sheeny fellow lynched in the Mary Phagan business. It was in the news when we first came here. Lord, that rope and noose has chased me across the years. It's good to just try and forget. [sighing and coughing on the recording] The cabs would cruise along the downtown city, their glary lights moving over saloons, eateries, the white windows of the closed-down furniture stores. The meters clicked every four blocks and the big old Packards used to hum so smooth. So solid. I loved these machines and that smell at work of Rislone, grease, and rubber. I'd tell the cabbies they had good cars, real honeys. The best feeling I ever had in this country was getting my new cars each year. I'd be all lathered up after all that walking. It was good to sit and glide along. I'm glad those days are finished. Trying to connect with Evie each October was like putting my hand into a flame. It was a lot better to be all muffled up in everyday life.

Doctor Kaiser: Isn't it better to face up to the truth?

—The truth? Hah! I could tell you the truth if I could find it. [long pause] They had a shell game going at work. The mechanics used to lay bets. Find the pea. Find the lady. Find the lady. Once twice and again. Find her. Put one dollar down to find the lady. One of the greasers who worked as a cleaner he called it "dama ink—something ...inkeeta", that's it. It means 'restless lady'. Ess, that was a good name for it. Restless was what I was also. 'Unket' is what we called being lonesome in Deb'm speak. All on my unket. Damn! My mind was not right then and it's no better now! I really got bad in '29 though, jobs were going to hell and Addie got sick with pains in her belly. That and Evie being away at summer camp. I broke the habit of a lifetime and drank a half bottle of brandy. Then it all had burst out of me: a forty year secret.

[a long silence]

Things had become a mite strained. Evie had somehow taken

all our love and there seemed like there was less of it left to go between us. Even when things were good I was frit that it would all just vanish from under me. There had been such bootiful times at first in Islington and in the early years here. I loved being in America. That dirty smell soaking through the city that spoke of money to be made. The carelessness of everyone to where I'd come from. I'd also never seen so much food. Even the American robins were fat, big fat throstles, so unlike the narrow Deb'm kind of bird. The best of days were when I was working at the garage on North Downer. Then Evie was born just as Europe tipped into war. The relief that there was nort wrong with her; I was so much greyer and older than the other fathers waiting outside the maternity ward.

War was a blessing. It really boosted the auto sales and the jobs came along with it at Nash's and the Oshkosh trucks. I had kept ahead of my ghosts by moving so fast, like those cabs skimming along in the night streets. Driving in America in the dark you were never sure what was out there. I had the feeling that you could just drive off the edge somewhere beyond the headlamps. How I had tried to set my anchor but everything kept gliding on without stopping.

We weren't married but Addie was my woman and I grew to need her. The main feeling that came along was being frit, frit of losing her, yet at the same time I seemed to make a hole for our love which grew in the space around us. We couldn't marry—too many lies would be needed and birth papers, blood tests and explaining who we were. We lived under different names—to the authorities we were James and Adeline Lee. There, that's another secret out, doc. We shaped ourselves to this life and Addie did not question me about it. Evie took much of our life together and Addie spent the rest of her time keeping house and making an English garden despite the winters here and the sumac that came rooting into all her fancy plants. But the things I said in '29 nearly tore down our world.

Doctor Kaiser: What happened?

—Addie had been sick. She was taken to County General. I can't recall the doctor's name for it, gut trouble anyway. Evie was away at camp at Waukesha. It was the second night on my own and the nights were hell. I'd got used to having them around you see. Once they'd gone there was just me. We used to give Evie poppy seed syrup for night terrors and I needed something like that myself. In the end I drank the medicine brandy in the early hours and was still up and reeling around the kitchen when Mrs Hoelich came the next morning. Addie being away, the good soul had been worriting about me looking after myself.

She had bought me some pie. Everything had "and so" after it when she spoke. She spoke so local I could hardly make her out sometimes. I told her that she was a blessing and I tried to stand up, still crazy from the brandy, eyes all wonk and with a leaky head. She put the dish down and tried to get out the house, but I got hold of her like a mump 'aid and shouted at her to stay. Heaven knows what I jabbered out. It must have been bad for she has avoided me ever since. And she surely spoke to Addie about it later. I thought I told her something about how I had a horrible dream. I dreamed I saw Mary Ann Fey on that night at Babbicam, Mary Ann like the White Witch of the Moor, all dripping from the gale and holding my knob-ended cane. She was waving it and it was not rainwater but dark drops falling from it and spattering on the floor and walls. I screamed at Mrs Hoelich that I was all covered in blood and she tried to calm me. The brave soul told me it was crazy talk but I couldn't seem to stop spouting on. I went on about Lizzie and Harrington and Mary Ann coming back from the sea, and of the wash of blood that I could not stop and of teeth falling to rattle like dice on the floor. She managed to get free of me in the end, told me everything would be okay once Addie got home. I tried to explain to her that I had traded on my innocence all my life. I needed to believe in it. I could not help what one does in a dream. She must have decided that I was not dangerous then and she came round the table and held me around the shoulders until I was quiet.

Doctor Kaiser: The truth might set you free, Mr Lee. You need to let it out.

—You don't understand. It's not just me you have to contend with. I'm carrying stuff inside me.

Doctor Kaiser: You mean guilty feelings? You've mentioned feeling you're haunted in some way.

—Ghosts, doctor is it? There ain't no such things according to Harry Houdini. Just human lies and tricks. But I know better. Everything in my life has had a terrible twist to it. Every blessing has its shadow side. What was it for me? The price of living through that night in Babbicam for me was a lifetime possessed by a ghost. The price of saving my neck in Exeter was twenty-two years of hell. The price of a new life in America was the life of my dear child.

What is left for me to find? Find the lady, where is she, sir? Watch! Watch carefully! Once, twice and again. Something is moving. I feel the bed shifting under a new weight. Someone is sitting there. You might think me a mazy 'aided old man but I have felt a breath on my face, a tainted breath. I fancy I hear the clink of a watch chain catching on a brooch. A smell of a lost perfume keeps coming to me. Attar o' Roses. She whose life I have carried all this time. She who holds me still and grinds me bone on bone.

I want to tell both you and Addie about everything. To unburden and let it all come out. I had tried before but it had not come out so well and Addie did not want to hear me then. My Ma used to say that all life was cring-crankum—all zig-zag and twisted up but maybe time unravels everything you knitted in the end and returns all to its first state?

Can you hear, doc? Soon Addie's feet will come on the stair. You'd better pack up. She'll likely bring a tray of arrowroot biscuits and milk. I'm burning like a candle and need her to quench me. For once I really want to get through and find the love we have put aside somewhere. I don't know why I'm so weak all of a sudden. I'm a poor spider in a shoe box. Have I left it too late?

[music and clattering in the background then shutoff]

PINCH, PINCH

I move around this little town looking for the best wi-fi spot so I can watch those vids again and again. It might be the Beauty and the Bean coffee shack or it could be Lenigan's on Janesville Avenue or my favorite, Scottie's Eat-Mor on Main. Once I've settled into my viewing place, I order coffee and search out the execution vids. I often have to turn the sound down so as not to disturb the other customers, the old-timers lingering over coffee and pie and chit-chatting with the staff, the groups of young moms taking a break from shopping, looking at each other's vacation photos or poring over Kinderbreak adverts. I can't stop staring at those images on the little screen. It's not the human terror I'm interested in, it's the sense of otherness. Lee's execution drama took place in times before videos. In the States there were some newsreel of electric chair executions in the '30's and Lee mentioned the famous Ruth Snyder photos. There are those grainy French films of guillotining but for the real stuff you need to see the filmed executions from the 1940s if you have the stomach for it.

One of the most fugly and sick films is the shooting of the Romanian prime minister Antonescu and his ministers by a bungling firing squad. Apparently old Antonescu had danced too closely with the Nazis and so had to be offed in the old European style of government scene changing. You can get it on the Web. Just before being shot numerous times you can see Antonescu carefully setting his fedora down on a bank of grass behind the execution post (they did the same to the guy that followed him, Ceau whatever his name was, the vid of him and his wife getting shot is pretty grooly also). Then you can also see the real-life botched hanging of Amon Goeth, the German commandant from 'Schindler's List'. Unlike in the movie version, Goeth's actual Polish executioners were freakin' useless. They were fat dudes wearing Halloween masks moving clumsily around Goeth, who stands straight and still, just his raincoat flapping in a breeze. He drops down when the trapdoor goes but the rope snaps. Without a flicker he gets up out of the pit and lets them do it again. The rope snaps a second time and he continues living. As he gets out of the pit that second time you can see him give the executioners a quick look of total hate. I'm sure Lee gave out just the same look when Berry unhooked him. The third time the rope held for Goeth and he hung like a dummy, slightly quivering. Then, sated for the moment, I look up and register the everyday voices of the staff asking, "another coffee you might want, eh?" The red and white gingham curtains flicker slightly in the air from the extractor fan. Outside, a Cooper's hawk sits on a utility pole, Main Street conducts its business without concern. There is high cirrus in a crisp and tranquil sky and sunlight bounces off windshields.

I have a secret reason for keeping on playing those vids. One I sort of hide from myself. I'm looking to see if there is any sign or flicker to show the spirit flying out of those executed guys. I never seem to see it. Nor did I see Grandpa's spirit fly out when he passed two years ago. Eight decades had not thinned his rusty hair though Camel studs had warped and stained his teeth 'til they looked like old fence posts. All he said to me on his death bed was that he was surprised how quickly it had all come in the end and for me to look after myself. That was it. Then he turned on his side and died. The room was very quiet. I remained crouching by his bed for an hour or so watching the light move but there was nothing else. Only a profound stillness. I still grieve for him and with Kimmie going that has just made it worse. I've read somewhere that the sleep positions that you use are reflected in your personality traits. Some phony psychologist has analyzed the starfish position, the faller, the soldier, you get the general drift. What I am apparently is 'the yearner': I lie on my side, hands outstretched and clasped as if in prayer. That's also how Grandpa laid when he died. Now, I try and fit myself into his shape to give myself courage in the night.

Those fruit flies cluster at my apartment windows. Probably looking for an out. I keep the .45 under my pillow, it's comforting to run my fingers over its contours when I get scared in the dark. I sit sometimes with my face against Grandpa's desk. I swear I can still detect the smell of his Camels still caught in the wood. I used to get bad dreams as a kid and Ma would say that I should test out whether they were real or not by saying to myself "Pinch, pinch, it's only a dream." If the pinch seemed realer than the scary imaginings then it was only a dream. That doesn't seem to work anymore. Who are you, Georgia? Are you some bust-off piece of my unconsciousness or that little girl who was cruelly lost back in '47? I need answers, I'm sick of John Lee.

Drove out yesterday near to Rose Lake, and found a quiet spot near to the water. I started blasting at the trees with the .45. Blam! Blam! The black terns flew up in crowds. I got scared the wardens might show up and quit shooting after a while. I enjoyed seeing that birch bole split apart and start bleeding sap. It felt good and I stopped shaking for a moment. Think I'm going to make a final push to nail this sucker.

Lee seems to keep on remorselessly. It's as if after he escaped the finality of the death sentence he resisted further attempts to curtail or delimit him. Maybe I'm trying to believe that if I play his stuff just one more time I will finally get Lee. I need to catch him out, bum rush him in some way. He keeps giving me chances to understand the truth in his sound clips but never quite enough to fully grasp it. It's as if he has so many words but not the ones to name the unnamable.

Spool Twelve
Last steps
Milwaukee, 1945

Doctor Kaiser: Good morning, Mr Lee. Shall we begin?

—Begin? It's more like endings now. That's right, eh? Old Nurse Mulholland checks on me in the mornings to see if I'm still breathing. Often, I tell her not to worry and say I'm alright. If she says in answer, "I see," like she usually does, I try to get one over on her by asking her what is it that she sees? Does she see an old todger on his last legs? She never answers but her eyes tell me. All nurses try to hide the truth from sickly folk, don't you think? But I can tell in her eyes she doesn't expect me to last. That true, ain't it? Each morning she tucks me in real firm as if to stop me jumping out of bed. Fat chance of that. If I really get on at her she says that only God tells us when we are to go. She told me today my feet were looking better. She should not lie to a liar. My feet have grown as fat and purple as brimbleberries. You told me my kidleys are not filtering out right and so the filth drops to my feet like a sump. I've got that bit right?

Doctor Kaiser: Yes, I've explained your heart is not strong enough to perfuse your organs. It's pumping very weakly.

—Good word that, 'perfuse', I like it. I don't mind saying I'm worried about you, doctor. You work too hard and your eyes have big dark circles under them. You spend too much time here for one thing.

Doctor Kaiser: Thank you for your concern.

—My body might be shot but my mind's still good. I can tell you are in mourning. Seems like the whole world is wrapped in grief. I want you to know that I can take the truth.

Doctor Kaiser: I think we should concentrate on you. Please

tell me truly how are you feeling today?

—Tired, sickish all the time, dizzy when standing up, wheezy lungs, food tasting like ashes, feet all swole up, bumping in the chest when I move about. In fact it reminds me of long ago hearing Granfer moaning to Ma that he was feeling turrible and likely to croak dreckly. Doctor Kaiser, how long have I really got left?

Doctor Kaiser: You have serious heart sickness. The heart is failing on the left and right sides. I am treating you but there is no cure. The heart is not pumping and the veins are stiff. I cannot in all certainty say how long there is left. The treatment you are getting will prolong your life for a while.

— [sound of croaky laughter] I've certainly been prolonged. That's true! I've been prolonged a lot more than some folks would have guessed. Tell you what, I'll give you a prediction. I say I'll be gone before the leaves on that elm are fully out. That one out the window there.

Doctor Kaiser: We will all be arraigned before the Almighty one day, sir. I'd be failing you not to advise you to get your affairs in order while there is time.

—That's what I'm trying to do now. I've been clearer in my mind since I've got really sick. I've been in such a fever all my life now I'm as cold and clear as a newt lying at the bottom of a well. I'm all smoothed out and I don't seem to want or need anything. Once I was such a bigabout lad yet after these last few months there ain't too much of me left. I'm easily pulled around by Nurse Mulholland. My clothes are still ranked in the wardrobe but I will never fill them again. Lord, now all I ever really want to do is curl up under my sheets and let the busy world take care of itself.

Doctor Kaiser: Are you able to get up at all now?

—I have been marooned up here at the top of the house and had not come downstairs all winter. Sometimes I have got up to look out the window. My legs are all scambly like a broken-down hoss. Mainly I lie in bed and watch those elm branches there. It's a puzzlement that I can be so bored. I always used to be happy in my own company but now I miss seeing folks. We don't really know anyone now. We got a Christmas card from the dispatch clerks at my old workshops and some locals came to the door on paper and metal drives for the war effort. Addie sees a bit of Mrs Cepelka two doors down. Sometimes I watch her son, young Billie, from the top window. Billy actually called a few times offering to do errands for the school war fund. I asked Addie to send the little tacker up if he called again.

Billie did turn up asking for more jobs a month or so ago and Addie got him to come up to this here bedroom to see me. He looked a sharp lad in his red-check hunter's jacket. I could see he did not care too much for a sick old man. I asked him what was that uniform I saw him wearing outside sometimes. He said it was the Scouts of America. Billie also said his Pa was in Italy, fighting krauts. He'd sent back a swell enemy parachute helmet. It had dried blood on the inside. His Ma said it weren't blood but he knew. He reckoned his Pa had shot that kraut. He asked me if I'd been in a war. I said, no, not never. Not that sort any road. I wanted to know about his mates. He said that they were called Danny Bananas and Spitwad. Danny's real name was a spic name the boy said, but they called him Bananas, and Spitwad he lived further down on East Holt. His real name was Roscoe. I asked him, why Spitwad? The lad said that he guessed he spat a lot. I couldn't help but smile. Boys can't help showing you their real selves, don't you think, eh?

Doctor Kaiser: I guess that's true.

—Ess, I wanted to keep him there, I liked seeing such a bright fierce young craitur. Reminded me of what I used to be. I asked Billie what sort of things he liked doing. He went on about reading the funnies and comics. The American Eagle and evil Wu Fang or something. Well, I didn't know about them but I told him I'd got something for a lad who likes adventures. Told him to go over there by the bedside cabinet. He was a brave lad. No-one likes the smell of sickness. He rummaged about among all that invalid's mess there then pulled out 'Bear Hunters of the Rocky Mountains'. You know that book? I told you about it. The one that was gived me as a prize long ago in the navy. I told the lad that 'Admiralty' meant the navy. I showed him the ticket at the front signed by Commander Jackson. I told him he could have the book. He could make better use of it than I could now. I could tell he wanted to go but the good lad stuck it out a while longer. I liked looking at the boy. He was so fresh-minted and with eyes that looked through you just like mine used to do. I was passing something on at last. I told him my wife would give him something nice to eat no doubt and I wanted to say something else but could only come out with, "Don't be frit, boy." He gave me a look and said, "No, mister, I sure won't," then he was gone. I can't tell you the satisfaction of seeing that lad.

Doctor Kaiser: How else do you pass the time?

—Mainly, I read the papers. The Journal arrives with a bang; thrown onto the porch by the delivery boy. I likes to smell it. There is an outdoors scent to it. Nice fat newsprint, good American paper quality. Addie had bought me a magnifying glass so I can make it out better. I generally skip the war news and football and the bowling leagues. Life is a strange business, I likes to think of it flowing on without me. I like advertisements mainly. You can buy anything in this country: coolerators, cabinets, dinette sets, autos of every type—such wonderful things. Sometimes I dream that there is still time to buy more things for Addie. I feel I should reward her while I can. I wonder what happened to all the stuff, all those things in my life. Where did they go? The family bible gone with Jessie somewhere, Ma's pottery figure of Nelson gived her by Uncle Freddie, the mariner. Or that gilt clock of Miss Keyse which I had my eye on.

Doctor Kaiser: I think it's my duty to remind you that there is still personal business for you to clear up. Things that happened that night in England, the night of the murder. Is there anyone I should contact?

—Oh Lord no, doctor. You sound like a priest now, you do. The past is quite dead and everyone is past caring. I only like talking to Gabby.

Doctor Kaiser: Gabby?

—Gabby is Addie's cat. A braget cat in Deb'm speak. That's a grey tabby. She's a quiet friend to me. She sits at the bedroom window watching the birds and letting me rattle on. She tells me when someone is coming. I can see her ears flick when there is a foot on the stair or when Addie is whispering to Nurse Mulholland downstairs. Gabby will outlast me. She will go hunting the spring frogs calling in the ditches and her ears will twitch when they come to clear me away.

Doctor Kaiser: I feel you are not being entirely straight with me, Mr Lee.

—Let's not fall out, doctor. Like Lizzie told me all those years ago, the truth is dangerous if it is let out before its time. You don't understand. I'm protecting you. One day you will realize that it's me who has chosen you to talk to, not other way round. It will all be finished soon anyway. I have never really been so sick before, not since my lungs filled up when I was in the navy. My body has carried me so far though. Much farther than expected. Best not to think too much on it. Odd how the world is strange and mazy when you think about it then when you take a second look, it snaps back and lands on its feet again like a cat, all complete. You tell me to face the truth but I've realized that it's Addie I need to think of now. Bit late, I know. She keeps coming up to fuss over me. Sometimes I pretend to be asleep and just lie there and watch her through half-closed peepers. I still like to look at her lovely face, it's like a new moon lasting into day. I have led her to this country and now I'm leaving her. Poor Addie, even after I have gone, she will still have to hide because we have lived on false papers. I can hear her radio in the kitchen. Addie loves it but I cannot abide all the chatter and the beat music. The only music I like is hymns really. What is that program? Kate Smith, big fat Southern girl. She always signs off her shows with, "Thanks for listnin'."I often hear Addie singing Kate's radio hit song called 'White Cliffs of Dover'. I told her that there ain't no such things as blue birds at Dover. Bluebirds are American birds. Them Dover birds are swifts. We used to call them 'screechers'. She did not appreciate it and told me it was a beautiful song and I had no heart to make fun of it like that. I told Addie I did have a heart but it was made different from other folks. Anyway, I need to thank Addie for putting up with me for so long. She was so much softer than the others, especially that fierce Lizzie. Lizzie might have been the love that claimed my heart but Addie has been the best thing in my life. You too, doc. Thanks for listnin'.

Doctor Kaiser: I feel that we have not wrapped up everything that could be said.

—There you go agin. The only talking I've got left is what I keep saying to my feet.

Doctor Kaiser: Feet? I do not understand you.

—Ess, to my feet. I calls them "my boodies". Them yellow nails sit like horns on the purple plum toes. If they could for once be strong and firm and if my legs worked right I'd go to the lake shore to make an ending. I keep telling them that they'd better start working. Better to drop myself away than wait for sickness to point out the way. I've been watching those little flies in my room, they touch the light bulb then, Phut! They're gone and no fuss.

So many questions pop up now I can't move around. I think about what was pressed on me when I was young. You could say it was just how life rolled, some lived and some died. What is there to confess? The deed was done. That was it. I still find it so hard to put into words. Where was the feeling in it? After a life of regret and sorrowing over it the feeling is getting easier. I don't know why. But it does. What happened and did it matter? It mattered then and the pain mattered and the frit, the dreadful frit of a soul being forced out of itself before its time. But it all now seems not to matter so very much. Ma used to say that us better way be makin' hame. Bet you don't what that means... [wheezy laughter on the recording, no reply from Kaiser] How much longer will I lie here? Soon, Addie will be sleeping next to an empty bed. The money I built up will keep her safe for a while. She will go on tending the roses without me. The love between us has grown since I've been sick or maybe I appreciate her more. Sometimes at night I've crawled out of bad dreams and looked across at her sleeping beside me, her face all shiny from the cold cream. Still such a fair maid. So peaceful and all smoothed out. Wishee well, Addie. Did she hear me? Thanks for listnin'. Good bye and fare 'ee well then. Think I'll watch the snow a bit. There's the mewies flicking about...

GUILT

Dang! I've been so mad at him for seeming to bail on us so easy like that. In this last recording Lee just slides away. He is humorous in a way that he has not shown up to now. And all of a sudden he cares about Addie. Sickness has made him soft-headed and it hacks me off. I didn't expect a cryface Lee but I was hoping for some honesty at least. Instead he comes out with an unpitying, aloof voice that sees no need for the confessional. Perhaps it's all to do with that village folk magic stuff I don't really understand, something he got from his mother, stuff from the depths of the Ladywell. Maybe he thought he's already earned the stars in his crown, he was feeling secure because he's got someone to take on his sins like that sin eater business. I feel as if I've worked for a big fat zero. I've lost everything and blame him for filling me up with all this witchy crud, saddling me with Georgia and leaving me with zip.

Okay, focus. It looks like all I can do is fall back on my professional insight. Perhaps only a poet whose business is words can really trap Lee. My attic is full of words like coins all stacked up or, even better, like bees—yeah, that's it, words like bees with yellow eyes and dry rustling wings. I'm counting them off and putting one against another trying to find a way to make a picture of Lee. To help me I've been staring at his photo all the long months I've taken transcribing his recordings. His eyes burn out of that portrait. I'm sure he resents my poking and prying. The photo I've chosen as my inspiration is the one of him hatless in a morning suit. He looks like a middle-aged guy but with the sap still in him. His hair is wispy-looking, maybe still growing out from the prison barber's attentions. He refers to his hair as 'his feathers' in his ghosted autobiography. He has a gardenia in his button hole. That means it's got to be spring or summer because that's when they flower. I thought at first that it was a photo taken for his wedding to poor Jessie but that took place in winter. So the photograph has to have been taken in the warm months of 1908 because before that he was in jail and the following year he had flitted up north. It has to be spring to summer 1908. It's a publicity shot then, probably commissioned by him at one of the Newton Abbot studios. This is his public face. He looks a bit like a gypsy made to wear the clothes of a settled people. I scrutinize the picture, noticing the uncompromising set of the jut ears, the high voltage eyes that are ever so slightly skew. His whole face has a feral, varminty look, with something of the changeling about it. I'm like an old-time phrenologist trying to feel his bumps. I think I've detected his propensities—amative, destructive and secretive. That massy forehead of his butted against the world. I think it could be a violent face.

So far, so less clear. The photo glimmers on the edge of my desk lamp's glow. It's a stubborn pumpkin head like those put out to scare the trippers who pay their $18 to the Wisconsin Dells Fright Tours on offer in this town. How do you lay a spirit? I want to fix Lee and stake and settle him. Ghost laying is a village skill that's probably lost even in Lee's birth lands of South Devonshire. My fellow citizens seem to be creating a new cult of the dead and it's already getting to be a business opportunity. You can take Halloween ghost tours to see derelict cemeteries and old TB sanatoriums. You can pick over the vacant lot where the cannibal Ed Gein's cabin used to stand in Plainsville. At Maribel Caves you can probe for the revenant spirits of hoodlums, bootleggers and liquor runners. If you have more modern tastes you can go to the old Eagles ballroom in Milwaukee and try and tune in to Buddy Holly's last gig there before the plane crash. Maybe I should bring some Yankee greenback commercial sense to Babbacombe. Let's see, there's many a spirit we could scare up for the paying public. Babbacombe Ghost Tours! November 15th a high point, guaranteed appearances by Miss Keyse and the Fey sisters. Sweet! What a cash cow that would be for a poor holes-a-pocket writer. And I've not got to Forest Home Cemetery yet. Let's put that off awhiles. There is still some ground to cover.

Now here is another bit of verse, it's not very good but still there's a catch to it: "John Lee, the butler, is now sent for trial, Committed for murder there is no denial, Whether he done it, it is hard to say, It will be proved on some future day…" The author is not known, a hack Victorian song sheet producer most like. It was published in Bristol England in 1884. It asks the question that we are really after. Did he really ding the old lady over the head and slit her like a pig?

Don't we want the bones to live, speak, give forth secrets? Who was Lee really? Crime history is full of those about to be executed who plead their innocence with a straight face. They keep it up even when they are in the death house. Years later it gets proved by DNA that they were as guilty as hell.

When murder does happen here in the Dells it's a desolate business. Two teens went missing around these parts in 1980, a few years before I was born. They were a 19 year old farmer's son called Tim Hack and his High School girlfriend, Kelly Drew, just graduated from beauty school. Their bodies were found in a field near Ixonia. Tim had been stabbed and Kelly had been tied up, raped and strangled. There was a lot of police activity at the time but no suspects were identified. The case became known as "The Sweetheart Murders". Every August the family drove Tim's Olds Cutlass Supreme around Jefferson County hoping to jog memories. Thirty years went by until a cold case review matched DNA from the victim's clothes with an ex-con from Kentucky called Edward Edwards. At about the same time Edwards' own son contacted the police and fingered him for the Sweethearts Murder. Edwards was a lifelong criminal. He robbed gas stations in the 1950s and was sentenced to prison. He bust out of jail and became one of the FBI's Most Wanted for a time. On recapture, he said he'd go straight and even wrote a book about his reformation called 'Metamorphosis of a Killer' but it didn't take long for him to get back to crime. He drifted across the country between 1977 and 1996 and killed at least 5 people, probably more. There are some who think he might be the L.A. Zodiac Killer. He was a thief, forger and law enforcement impersonator and even posed as a psychiatrist in Minnesota, counseling trauma victims—get that. It turned out he was working as a handyman at Concord House Restaurant where Tim and Kelly were last seen. Edwards confessed to the crime once he was confronted by the evidence but he didn't elaborate or explain what had happened to those kids. He sat through his sentencing hearing without saying a word, ignoring the relatives sobbing their hearts out in court. I studied the photos of him and marked those frigid eyes. He acted bored—looking, yawning all the time, slumped in a wheelchair because he was crippled with heart disease. He had oxygen tubes going in his nostrils to help his breathing. I remember Grandpa saying they should have plugged those goddamn nose tubes into some natural gas and done everyone a favor. They sentenced him to life and he sparked out with a heart attack a few years later in 2011. They did a state poll at about then on the death penalty and it was the first time that over 50% in Wisconsin said they'd vote for death for murderers.

Maybe these boys have such a capacity for self-deception or they are so split off from their savage natures that they actually believe they are innocent. All our todays are made up of yesterdays. I'm not the forgiving sort. I've seen too much pain. I think killers should be offed toot sweet. Don't whine to me about innocence or squeal about their rights. I'll never forget the howl of grief from the mom of one of my high school friends who got run over and killed by a drunk. Nor am I easily fooled. Lee may have softened as he got older but I know that psychopaths can bend and morph if enough time and enough pain gets loaded onto them. That's where I would have set out my store on Lee. He was guilty as charged and good riddance. And maybe I'm there too. I need punishing. They say the best vigilante is someone stifling their own guilt.

I've been stalled up but I've made a further discovery. Something I hadn't noticed previously in that frayed old box I picked up in Cudahy.

I must have been so intrigued with the most immediate spoils that I hadn't looked in it properly. Weeks after I had transcribed the spools in their red and yellow boxes, I was picking about in the old cardboard container looking to see if the original microphone was there among the tangle of dusty old components at the bottom. I worked my way down through to the cruddy sediment there, dried moth husks, yellowed shreds of paper and a litter of burnt-out valves, tubes, wiring and decayed bits of the original casing of the Webster. I happened to flick back the folded edges at the bottom of the box and found wedged under the cardboard two more recorder spools. These had no boxes or labels and one was a flattened jumble of wire like a discarded fishing line. What they contained, once had I straightened them out and spliced them together, makes all the difference.

The first spool had Lee's voice. It wasn't the same as the other recordings. It's as if he'd done them secretly. Sometimes he's almost whispering. Maybe they were recorded late at night.

This is Lee's private naked voice, not that confident raconteur we've heard before. These words are like the axe to the frozen sea within him. There's stuff there he could never reveal in daylight.

Unnumbered Spool
Mutoscope
Torquay, 1908

—Feel like I'm stogged, bogged and can't move on. Addie's downstairs. She'll be there a bit, doing the ironing most like. Its dark now, one set of headlamps just moved across the wall, sounds like that big Buick Eight from two doors down. Chest is gert heavy tonight, feels like a stone on it pressin' me down. Keep pantin' and puffin' like an old ewe in lamb. Every time I close my eyes I feel I'm back on those Torquay lanes. Dark drang-ways, they were. I'm always going back down those ginnels, something's pullin' me there. I'm old and weak and grawpin' about. Can't make proper sense of it. There is no good in rakin' it all over again surely?

[Gap in recording]

… but I've been helped by talking into this here machine. Lord knows who will listen to it. Sometimes I shift it back and listen to my voice droning on. Maybe it has helped me get a grip on it all, but I've not really set on what matters. I've kept my mouth shut about the important stuff all these years for a reason. Once you let the truth out who knows what will come of it? The truth is full of knots Ma said and it can't be changed even though it's too bitter to be swallowed down.

I did go back once to Babbicam. It was after I was let out of Portland. That next spring I think. I had to go back at least once and look at it.

If I close my eyes then I see it. I'm back there, there's the clacketing of me stick down Babbicam Road to Wellswood. Can almost smell that coal smoke dragged down by a brisky sea wind. Can remember all of it like a film playing.

I could twirl my fancy barleycorn stick but at heart I was sick. Kept on asking myself, why the hell am I here? I was slinking really, even hiding from the butcher's boy in his cart and the women coming along past in their big hats and veils. Gentry probably, looking right through me I expeck. Somehow I reached Lower Warberry. That stone wall. Guess it's still there just ezzackerley the same. Stopped and had a good keek about. Last time I stood there was that November dawn when I was all blood-dabbled. Cabbage palms and the laurels had shot up over the years and tramlines had come up the hill but it still looked much the same. Further up was the Brownlow's place. I was wondering if that bastard Kisler was still there. It would have been almost worth another sentence to grind the end of me stick into his face.

I went on up little way to where there was a gap in the wall. The water trough was still there in that gap. Had a quick look then drew back and kept an eye on the neighborhood. Then leant in and rummaged right in the back of the trough. There was an opening there you understand, between wall and trough, a ledge no-one could see. Nort. Prodded down there again then hit on something wedged tight behind. Drew it out. It was not what I expected. It was a flat packet wrapped in oil cloth. Jammed it away under my coat then scratched around at the back of that thing again. Had to keep stopping as people came past, housemaids and such. Ducked down again when the coast was clear then prodded about again. Then I hit on it, stuck far down. Still there from where I put it all those years ago, the heavy end of it covered in rust and the handle all dark and slimy but still in one piece. Twenty three years since I last held it. I walked away with it tucked in my waist-band like a gun. Down past the big house at Bishopstowe to the Ilsham crossings. I thought someone was following me there but I think it was only a gapper-mouthed idiot boy. Saw him off with a chucked stone. Clear at last, I slowed and stopped by the hedge line, then sat on a milestone to unwrap the package. I peeled off the moldy oil cloth and greased paper to find a letter on brown crumbly paper, all riddled with blots and damp stains. It had no date to it and was quite hard to make out. He called me, 'Jack lad', and said if I was reading it then I must have made it out. It asked me to find him without fail by enquiries at the Dolphin in Devonport, 'n was signed 'your friend, Cornelius Harrington'. I considered the thing for a while then wrapped it up and put it away. Hard to say how long it had been there—it could have been ten years or more. That damned evil bugger Cornelius still hovering round me. I've always feared he'd fetch up here, even here in this country.

Back then, I forged on across the playing fields and old shooting ranges, past the big old place called Stoodley Knowle then the wind pulled at me and I could hear the sea. Looked out from the cliff top at Walls Hill, Babbicam to my left and Portland a dark shape far on the horizon. I drew out the hammer I'd hid all those years behind the trough—ess, Granfer's old hammer—then I hurled it as far as I could, end over end, spinning down to the waiting sea. Peered over the edge to see the waves boiling down there over Gaskin's Rock. There, that was done, the old business cleared. I also fetched out Harrington's letter, shredded it and lets the fragments spin away. I turned and tracked back to the main road using the All Saints spire like a compass mark.

The Bay seemed almost as I had left it. I thought I'd take a last look before catching the train back to Newton and to Jessie. Stupid really. So far, I'd felt alright. I thought, damn it, I have survived, no need to be frit of the place. There wasn't going to be no bony hand to shoot out and grab me. I stood by Lovers' Leap and regarded the sea all stretched out way below. There were new villas on the cliff slopes and a stone breakwater now stuck out next to the Cary Arms. A lot less sand on the beach. Maybe that breakwater had something to do with it, messing the currents. I ventured down the Beach Road—widened and gravelled—then cut through the beech woods down by the Vine. I didn't want the fisherman's children to spot me and start ragging. Stood there awhile in the woods with the sea rushing below. I could see the Cary Arms with green lawns and a bright new red tile roof. All spanked up. A few net drying frames and capstan drums still on the beach. Miss Keyse would still have something to complain about. Of the Glen, only a bit of the front wall remained. All rubbed away, 'twas hard to credit. Just the Music Room left: seemed to be a sort of boat house.

It was then, while standing under the Babbicam trees that I really began to feel all jiggered up. All of a sudden the gods-a-mighty sadness of it all came over me and I had to run. Went scammelling back to Torre Station as fast as I could. Sitting on that train my heart began to kick and jump with no warning. I felt I couldn't catch me breath, a sinking horrible feeling. Do 'ee know it? I choked, fanned meself with me hat. The carriage seems gert hot. The steamer chuffed at idle, then the train jerked. I was choking and fuddled. Kept thinking of that dreadful last run up to Compton in the November dawn. I wanted to tell Jessie all about it when I got in to Newton. 'Twas a terrible thing to live with a bloody secret for so long. I wanted to make it right but nort could. It felt like when those lads on the Implacable stole up on me and did a terrible prank. They sewed me up in me hammock one night while I was asleep. I came to, all hot and strapped up in the dark. I kicked and begged to be released. [sound of coughing] Keep fancying I hear a slamming noise, a trapdoor banging. Addie, are you there, dear? Help me, my chest, I—

[recording breaks off abruptly]

THE SECRET OF BABBACOMBE LEE

Lee sure is right: you need to be careful when you go searching for the truth. Is it the truth itself or the searching that is so beguiling? It's not as if I'm particularly addicted to the truth. When I was a kid I used to make up stories about what had happened to me on the way back from class. I'd invent attempted kidnappings, scary and weird events—anything to make me seem special.

This Lee discovery has been such a goldmine for me as an artist. He has led me on a blue-sky journey far beyond my usual haunts. I think I'm going to call myself 'Scoop'. Yet, when John Lee actually veers towards letting us know what happened on that fatal night in Babbacombe, I feel scared. I'm wondering how I will get on once I crawl away from under the S.O.B.'s shadow.

I thought today about how little I have in my life. A rented apartment, Grandpa's old deal table as a desk, some electronic gear, the old Webster machine, a beat- up Ford Escape and a few books. Not even a pet to connect me to life. I should really get a career, maybe take up teaching in writing school. Man, maybe I should join the other manqué talents doing creative writing classes? One thing's for sure, writing in itself is no way to make a living. It's a hard solitary road. I'm relatively young still, I don't know shit. Sometimes the writing does give you a high though, it lights you up for a while but it's the living between the highs which is so difficult. A hiatus between spasms, that's the scribbling life. It's also lonely, lonely to see your work in the bookstore all on its own in the poetry shelves, a bit of you split off and to what purpose? Am I the only one to really care about this stuff? Words, books, dreams of the past, fragments in a mirror, they give you nothing. Sometimes I feel all fake-ass, especially when a real bit of life hits you in the face.

Like last week when I drove way north to Stevens Point on the Wisconsin River where the river is dammed up and broadens out into a lake. I went to Bukolt Park, walking by the river and thinking of portage sites, Menominee Indians, river guides, my usual junk. There was a cold nor'-easter blowing down river, November coming and the leaves were pell-melling off the trees. I walked by the brown surging water and stopped at a grove of bankside trees—black ash and big tooth aspens mainly. The tree trunks had perspex cards nailed to them. On each card was the name of someone who had died, their dates and a memorial message.

I watched as a father and young son came past and launched a kayak. They wore camo gear and hunting hats. The father was giving a whole lot of orders to his scared-looking son. The kid was about eight or so. It was late to be on the river and they did not look too familiar with their craft. A bunch of turkeys came flying over from the tree line and the father gave out a whoop. The kid looked white-faced, he wasn't paddling, just gripping the sides of the kayak. I went on a while and paid them no mind. I was looking at the signs on the trees and reciting the names of the dead like a poem in my head when I heard this screaming. It was the father calling out "Earl! Earl!" His calling was a jabbing electric sound that went through you with a jolt. Some youngsters from the nearby skateboard park were helping him get back up the bank. He was soaking wet and he'd lost his hat. I could see the kayak upended and spinning far out. The father began to run wildly down river looking for his son. He jumped back in the water and grabbed at something but it was only a paddle and all the time he kept up this sobbing scream.

The skateboard dudes and I rushed further down and spotted something. It was the kid, face down in the water with the orange loop of his lifejacket sticking out at the back. We snagged him using a tree branch and dragged him out by the loop. Water was pouring out of him and he didn't seem to be breathing. His father gave a shriek and started shaking him. I didn't want to do

CPR in case I got it wrong and one of bystanders eventually took over, pushed me to one side and worked on the kid. Someone must have called 911 and responder vehicles began to arrive. I hoped the kid was okay. I last saw him all huddled in blankets with an oxygen mask. I felt like an interloper, a voyeur. The father's scream seemed to keep on echoing inside me. I drove home with my legs all wet and stinking from the kid's vomit and the sour river mud. In fact they seemed not to dry out at all the way back home seventy miles and more on I-39. I felt chilled for days afterwards. It was hard to sit to my desk for a while after that. It had been a shock, the first real thing that had happened in a year of book work. That father's scream seemed so much more powerful than anything I could imagine.

Sometimes I fall asleep at my desk, my hair stirring in the warm breath of the laptop exhaust fan. I usually wake all cricked. In one such fitful sleep I dreamt that I was walking with Grandpa down a road. It got darker and darker. I grew fearful but he said it was only an eclipse. We came to a crossroads and he told me to keep my coat on until the sun came out again. He said that the roads divided there and he had his own road to go on and I had mine. He said, "You go this way, son. Go down the road to the people who love you." I said that I couldn't see any people down that road. He just replied, "There will be, son if you travel far enough." Then I woke.

Yeah, I am lucky, I've found Lee and he has found me. It's a contest though as to who is the stronger. Seems like a spirit war is going on in my apartment. There's Georgia for one thing. She makes the place rustle like a pile of wind-blown leaves. There's that Latin poem—Animula blandula vagula—"pale, fleeting, wavering little soul"—that's Georgia. She shimmers up in the mirror behind me, a vagrant spirit. She shakes her little pigtails and keeps saying, "No, that's not it, it s not it." I wish she'd quit bugging me. I should ring Mulvina to get her to exorcize the place.

It was a strange moment loading that last spool onto the

Webster and wondering what was on it. The thin metal wires kept whipping back as I tried to wind it on, leaving score marks on my clumsy fingers.

Unnumbered Spool
I have hid myself in the flame
The Glen, Babbacombe, 15th November 1884

—I was fast off but hadn't meant to be. All of a sudden Lizzie was there shaking me awake and saying it was time. Her candle flame jumped like billy-o in the draught. I asked her what time it was and she told me it was one and thirty and I must be quick. There were no kisses, no touching, just our plan pulling us on. Outside the sea was all boiling up. It was as if the air was sucked out of the house to feed the storm. I was already dressed. Lizzie kept telling me to come on. A bit of me wanted to fid-fad around and pull back. I was frit of what we had to do. Those flags were cold through my socks—no boots, I wanted to go quietly over the floor. Gar, that it had come to this. I had let Lizzie take over and my common sense had said goodbye.

Took my hammer from under the pillow and put it into the waist band of my trousers. That was in case of trouble, I thought. It would have been better if I'd buried the thing with Granfer. Shook out a pillow case and took it with me, came out the pantry. To the right was the kitchen corridor, a dim red glow from the range at the end. Lizzie has slipped away ahead of me 'n I followed her ghosty shape as she moved towards the stairs. The dining room doorway was a black pool that I feared to enter. I'm not sure if I thought of dear Katie as I began creeping about but I should have. She'd be tucked up in her bed in Tormohan. The poor maid could never give me what I needed; Lizzie's fiercer flame had drawn me back in.

First, the dining room. The wind was streaming in through

the half-open terrace door. Papers danced about on Miss Keyse's desk. If the outside door was open then who had come in through it? Hell! I dreaded to think who might have entered. I prayed it wasn't that harpy, Mary Ann. I had seen her the previous night, flitting over the terrace.

I tried to listen and get under the sounds of the storm. Nort else seemed to be stirring. I thought maybe the door had only budged in the gale. I pulled it to but did not bar it. The room got quieter. I felt along the mantle, took down the carriage clock and put it in the pillow case. Candle sticks, and shiny things she called "mice-in", they also followed into the sack. Some silvered snuff boxes joined them. Take what's owing, that's what I kept thinking. This would teach her to dock my wages—the ole dumman.

Lizzie came to me, put her mouth to my ear. She whispered that someone was in the house and pointed back to the hall. My throat went dry, 'n I already wished I'd never started it. Lizzie rested a warning hand on my wrist and put her finger to her lips to quiet me, then slid away. I began to curse at myself for ever getting into it. That Lizzie had put a spell on me. Promising to make me as happy as a man could be in more ways than I could dream. Those promises and the child within her, that's what led me there.

Lizzie had slipped away back into the darkness. I slid the heavy pillow case under the ottoman. The cold made my feet ache, the dark walls seemed to bend in on me. I could hear something—something was going on in the hall, ess, something was definitely going on in the hallway. I crept to the door. Lord! I could make out shapes. A man's voice was muttering and there was a lit bulls-eye lantern on the floor. I could hear Lizzie saying, "No!" and again, "No!" then the low mumbling from the figure. He had his back to me and Lizzie was crammed up in the alcove. I had to do it but I don't mind saying how frit I was. I snatched at his shoulder. The figure turned and jabbed me in the guts, kicked my feet from under me and pushed me backwards. I went to wrench myself back up but he was on me. The fellow was strong and fast. I could hardly breathe and I thought my heart would jump out of my chest. Thrashed and kicked from the floor but I was straddled and held down. There was a masked face above me with fierce eyes, someone come ready for trouble.

I struggled and bucked and kicked but felt the strength going out of me. Lizzie started mauling at the man's head. He pushed her off and jumped to his feet. I then got a kick in the ribs that rolled me across the floor. He pulled down the scarf. It was Harrington and he was mad enough to gore me to bits! We clamped and roiled around again. I pushed him back for a moment but he was so much stronger than me. I hauled out my hammer and waved it above my head. I told him to go to Hell in a whisper from a mouth as dry as paper. 'Twas strange to be fighting and whispering at the same time. Nort seemed to stop the varment. Harrington feinted a jab then caught hold of the hammer and twisted it right it out of my grip. He got me against a wall with the shaft of my own hammer jammed across my throat. He set to squeezing me to blackness.

A voice came flying out. The voice called out, "What is it?" That sound stopped everything.

"Who is there?" There was a light moving on the stair and a creaking of the boards. The pressure eased off my neck. It was the Missis coming down the stairs holding a candlestick. She must have heard us despite the storm. Harrington pulled away from me and all three of us ranged back. None of us said a thing but Harrington crept out of sight into the alcove under the stairs. Miss Keyse stopped on the landing and raised her candle to see us better.

"Wickedness!" is all she said on seeing me and Lizzie standing guilty-like in the hall and all dressed in our day clothes.

Then Harrington, reaching up quick from the alcove, dragged her down the last few steps to slam forward onto the floor. It happened so fast and so unexpected-like that there was no time to move. Lizzie also kept me clamped in a strong grip.

Miss Keyse landed on her knees, her dropped candle stub spinning around on the floor boards. Everything was lit clear by the bulls-eye lamp. We could hear her crying out, "Oh! Oh!" and scrabbling on hands and knees. She began to mutter something like, "Oh God, thou wilt not… John! Are you there?" She made to clutch at the banister and tried to drag herself up. Harrington punched her hard on the side of the head. She cried out but clung on to the stair rods. At first I was rooted to the spot with it all then I tried to get to the villain and smash him but Lizzie held me hard. Then Harrington was above the Missis, his arm raised. There was a sound like a pumpkin being dropped. The Missis fell instantly. Harrington stood over her and gave her two more heavy whacks to the head while she was on the ground. Then I saw what in his hand. Dear Lord, it was my hammer. There were trails of wet and dark stains on the walls behind. Miss Keyse was very quiet and still for a moment but after a few seconds a horrible powerful noise started coming out of her.

Oh, how she groaned after Harrington hit her. She made a beastly grunting sound that started low but got louder. I asked Harrington what he had done. He stared back at me with goggle eyes and said that he had to do it. I told him he was a mad snake and he was going to get us all hanged. Lizzie asked if we could stop the noise the old lady was making. Harrington raised up the hammer as if he was going to hit her again but then he let the thing fall to the floor with a loud bang. He slowly put his hands to his face. Lizzie was the only one with nerve enough to look on it. She went to the shaking figure on the floor and rolled her over onto her back. The horrible rattling moan came even louder then. A black stain opened out around the head. Lizzie went to Harrington and told him he must end it. He seemed about ready to heave up. Lizzie next came up to me and told me to finish it. I said I could not, she was my mistress. Lizzie hissed at us that we were not men. She went to the hall, rummaged about, then took out the weeding knife that was always kept there. She looked at it and tried the blade then tossed it back down. She went to Harrington with her hand out and told him to give it to her. He slowly drew back his coat, took something out, and handed it to her. Lizzie came up to me. She had his long sailor's knife. She pressed it into my hand and said that I was to finish it for the Lord's sake. I shook my head and she said even more loudly that I must help the ole dumman.

"Finish it, Jack—do it for me," she kept saying. Somehow I began to move near to the shivering shape on the floor. Lizzie pushed me closer.

I crouched down by Miss Keyse. The beastly snoring sound rattled loudly. Close to, I could see her peepers were open and she seemed to be staring at me. Her hands were stretched out stiff in front of her and her whole body was shaking. It seemed like she was begging me. I put the blade out to touch her neck and asked her to forgive me. I pressed down a bit but could not do it. I told Lizzie I could not go on. Lizzie leant right over me, pressing me down. Her strong right hand clamped over my knife hand and the other grabbed onto Miss Keyse's hair and drew her head back. Lizzie told me to go on and at the same time pressed down hard over my hand, making the knife jerk mightily to and fro like a saw. Miss Keyse' heels drummed on the wood floor. Then something gave way and the blade sunk home. I felt her breath puff out of her for the last time. I pushed down further until the blade grated on bone, and a hot wet wash went right over my hands. It felt like something went out of her and into me in that moment.

Lizzie took the knife from me, the blood kept pouring out, a black flood in the lamplight. I asked her how we could stop it. She gave me the cloth covering from Miss Keyse' chair and I tried sopping it up but it was no good and I knelt there and began to cry out at the pity of it. Harrington seemed to have been puking in the corner, he wiped his face on his sleeve and said that we were jiggered and should run while there was time Lizzie pulled at me to get up. She gave me a shake to bring me back my senses. I turned to Harrington and told him he was a bastard and asked why he did such a thing to the ole lady. He just shrugged. Lizzie told us not to fall out. She said it was done and couldn't be helped and we were in it together. She seemed to take charge and we let her. She kept her head through it all. She told us to burn the house quick. Flame everything and 't would all be an accident and none would know. First she got us to shift the body out the road. Harrington took the Missis' heels and I had the other end. Her head kept bumping against my legs as we moved her. We dragged the body into the dining room and laid her in front of the ottoman. Harrington cursed at me to cover her face so I put a newspaper over it. Lizzie ordered us about as the clock ticked away during those last terrible night hours. We pulled out more newspapers and piled them into a heap onto the body. Lizzie started tipping the lamps over and emptying out paraffin onto the furnishings and carpets. A stink of lamp oil began to fill the rooms. I asked her about the Necks, still upstairs there. She said to let the old birds roast. When I looked doubtful she said that they cared nort for us. I crept up the stairs and went to the left and into Miss Keyse's bedroom. I was frit to go in there. I thought somehow her spirit would rise up out of her fourposter to ask me my business. I pulled down the servants' bell cord to make it seem like she was giving alarm for a fire. Emptied out a lamp onto her bedding. Tried to light it with a Lucifer. The damn thing wouldn't go until I'd added some papers from her bedside cabinet. A yellow flame grew then faded then caught again. Outside the wind boomed over the roof.

Downstairs Lizzie was setting fires here and there in the dining room. The terrace door was wide open and I found Harrington with his knife in his hands stabbing it into the earth of the flowerbeds. I asked him what he was doing and he answered that he was cleaning up. He sounded then as if he hadn't a care in the world. He wiped the blade on a piece of cloth. It looked like a shred from off Miss Keyse's nightdress.

He started to go on about me taking Lizzie from him but I told him he was a cuddy, bastard, murdering rat and to keep away from me.

There was a rank smell of scorch and lamp fuel. I got on my hands and knees and tried to swab the worst of the blood off the hallway. I found one of Miss Keyse's stockings and a slipper all sodden and could only think to thrust them out of sight under the hall mat. It began to get all too much for me. I tried to get up, slipped in my wet socks on a patch of blood and began to cry out to Lizzie that I couldn't stand it no more and asked if we could just run for it. But she would have none of it, saying to pull myself together, get on and hurry. My foot banged against something. It was my hammer, dropped by Harrington. I swabbed it with paper and put it head first into my trouser pocket.

We ran from room to room trying to fire everything. A bitter thick smoke began to fill the corridors but the wind continued to howl outside and our fires keep blowing out as if the gale was trying to stop them. We struck match after match and make heaps of newspapers and eventually Lizzie fetched out the can of Alexandra oil from under my bed in the pantry and slopped it over everything.

She poured half the can over the body of Miss Keyse and at last the flames begin to really take hold. The ottoman was well alight covered with sparking orange flames. At one stage I heard a wail and a pale flash passed me. It was poor old Tib the cat fleeing from some hidey hole and all on fire.

When was it I saw the Necks? Maybe they had watched everything from the beginning, maybe peering down through the banisters as it all went on? I first ran into Eliza on the smoke-ridden landing. She looked frit as if she would flee from me but I called out to her that I would not let her burn. I led her downstairs through the thick fume. She shouted out that the Missis was on the floor when we got to where Miss Keyse was lying. Pieces of burning wood began to come off the dining room ceiling and everything was lit more brightly for a moment.

Once the flames had really got a grip then we switched round and pretended to fight the fire. Lizzie went upstairs and called to Jane Neck. She threw a bit of water on the flames using her bed pot.

I led Jane Neck down the stairs with an arm around her shoulders. I felt her shaking. As soon as I got her out onto the terrace she began to scream, "Fire!" The wind drowned her calling. She went back into the dining room and began to try and stamp out the flames by the body. We were both coughing something terrible from the smoke.

I smashed my left fist through the glass of the dining room windows and rammed the right one in also. I wanted to get rid of those hands, to mix my own blood with that of my mistress. The pain was devilish and I moaned to Jane about my arms as she reeled about the blazing mess of the dining room. Lizzie came out the smoke, got hold of me and whispered to remember that there was the fire and nort else. I was asleep and there was the fire. Nort else. She again said we were together in this. I asked her where Harrington had got to. She said the coward had gone and he was never here. Did I understand? I understood alright and I have vulishly kept to that story ever since.

The last moments have become a mazy blur. Mainly I tried to cover up everything as best I could, crawling through the smoke and throwing bloody towels and paper onto the fires. The body of my poor mistress was well alight then. I also pushed my pillow case into the fire and with it all the things I had aimed to take away with me that night. As far as I had known I was only going to take some valuables and run away with Lizzie to a new life that night. Instead what I got was bloody ruin.

It seemed like everything speeded up in the end. I put the empty oil can back in the pantry. My cut arms were killing me and my blood kept trickling onto everything. Gert flaming lumps begin to drop on my head as the ceiling caught and the dining room fire ate through to the upstairs rooms. Lizzie told me to go out and to get Gaskin. I ran to the Cary Arms and called out to him that Miss Keyse had been burnt to death.

The whole thing then opened up. Gasking was dressing and shouting questions to me, lights were beginning to appear at windows. I went back to the Glen next to the angry sea and saw Lizzie running to get Harris and the coastguards further up Beach Road. That's how the whole …

[recording ends]

TWO
INVESTIGATIONS

To Each His Own

I've replayed that particular loop many times. I suppose I should get it digitized in order to preserve it. The sound of the Webster machine has a weird clarity to it, you can hear each deep gushing sigh and gasp Lee made. He also seemed to be tapping something—there is a tickety-tack sound that recurs throughout this last one. I've wondered if it's the way he's gripping the microphone particularly tightly and maybe he's rocking to and fro and knocking against something. My transcription has not really captured his spooky breathing and groaning. It sounded like he's in some sort of chamber. Perhaps he crawled into the bathroom to make it. He seems as if he was at the farthest reaches from us when recording this yet maybe he is the nearest to telling the truth. The whole sad business threatens to infect you when you listen to it. It seems to filter into one's empty spaces like blown sand. At least it does mine. It really was a grue-fest, that night at the Glen.

I don't mind saying that I'd always thought that Lee was guilty. It's been my unconscious assumption that the male has a tendency to dissemble, distance and deny. It turns out that I was partially right. Lee had indeed ended Miss Keyse's life but he seems to have done it out of the motive of easing her suffering. That and being unable to say 'no' to Lizzie. His sister had obviously got her claws back into him and dragged him into the whole mess. I'm still not sure if she planned for Harrington to be around on that night, perhaps as insurance in case Lee failed to go through with the plan to rob Miss Keyse and scram. More likely I suppose was that Harrington had sensed Lizzie was betraying him and had turned up to confront her on that night. Lee wasn't much given to charity, though his mistress' agony evidently did touch him on the murder night. It took Lizzie's hard and forceful hands to drive his knife hand down.

No wonder Lee felt able to believe he was innocent yet still labored under a blood-guilt all his life. The horrible events on that night and Lizzie's betrayals help explain his disconnected state during the inquest and the trial. Lee must have felt that he carried Miss Keyse within him forever; she became part of him. It seems likely that Lizzie remained his dark angel all through his younger life. It's clear even at the trial that he was still crazy about her even as she strung that hanging rope around his neck with her evidence. I reckon that he would have kept on looking for her after being let out of prison if not for that 1908 article in the English newspaper saying that she had made a death-bed confession.

I never went to my own parents' funeral. I guess people thought I was still in shock. I was thirteen. The last time I saw my dad was that terrible moment when I punched him and he fell backwards into the book case and there was a splintering of glass. I used to get those True Detective magazines as a teen. I'd stare at the pictures of the dead. Victims of killings. I wanted to understand what had happened to them. I'd try and get closer and closer to the images until they blurred out into black dots. The dead, they turn their faces away from you even though you can never get rid of them.

I'm not sure when Lee made those last recordings, maybe the early weeks of March, 1945 before he got too weak to move. There was one more fragment of wire recording left unplayed. I was greedy for more revelations and couldn't wait to spool it up and run it.

What I got seemed like a blank recording then halfway along came the rich breathy voice of an old-time radio announcer introducing a new tune, "Alright, listeners, let's sizzle with the Modernnaires," then there was a flourish of twirling strings and a syrupy song played. It sounded like music you get in shopping malls or elevators. I worked out the song was called 'To Each His Own'. It was apparently a hit in 1946 for a number of singers including Tony Martin and the Ink Spots. It seemed a total bummer to have such a wild card stuck into the rich pack of Lee's recordings. It must have been recorded by Doctor Kaiser at least a year after Lee had died. Maybe he made many recordings and this was only a chance survivor. I wasn't sure why he chose it. The song implies that there is a coupling in the universe, that for love to flourish it must be reciprocated. The song lyrics are full of paired images. It's a clunking, sickly ditty. I even took to playing it loudly in my apartment, crooning along to, "if a flame is to grow there must be a glow. To open each door is a key. I need you I know, I can't let you go, your touch means too much for me…" The more I listened to them however, the words began to grow a new significance. The lyrics stuck with me and became strangely catchy; sometimes I imagined it was John Lee singing them to me.

At some stage those faintly mocking lyrics of 'To Each His Own' pushed me into the sudden ugly thought that this whole thing might be hoax. The idea was like a fish flopping in my chest. Maybe someone with an infernal talent for mimesis had created the wire recordings and planted the stuff in the box. The whole thing could be an obscure con like the Maybrick diary they tried to sell a few years back. I was relieved to argue myself out of that notion—for one thing that old Lysol box in the yard sale was clearly due for the trash bin if I hadn't come along. Usually one wants to profit from the labor of an elaborate hoax. Surely there was enough weight of evidence there to anchor me to the truth?

Whatever, that's the end. There's going to be no more John Lee. His time had run out and there are no more recordings. I should be relieved. After all I'm still standing. I've out-stared the mutha and not blinked. Trouble is I still can't rest. Georgia's little feet keep on tap dancing at night and now I keep seeing a strange light, a sort of lemon-colored glow coming from the other room, like the light you get when an icebox door is left open. It's a freakin' spook-light. I'm sure Georgia has a hand in it. Same as that strange tapping and donking sound I hear when

I'm beginning to drift off. I'm keeping it all together by staying up as long as I can. At least 'til daylight. I get Modanifil to keep myself snappy. It's $4 a pop off the Net. Suck on that, Lee.

That reminds me, I haven't told you what else was in that box that helped me identify the recordings as those of Babbacombe Lee in the first place. Okay, there was a scrap book with pictures of 1930s racing cars on the front which was filled with newspaper cuttings sent by Lee's family in Devon. There was an old rubberized stamp device with a wooden handle which when inked up gave the imprint, "Howard B. Kaiser M.D.". There was a sheaf of medical notes about Lee in hard-to-read medical shorthand; a faded receipt to Dr Kaiser for $88 for the Webster from Schuster's Department Store; a battered copy of 'The Man They Could Not Hang, The Life Story of John Lee Told by Himself', an original with stiff decaying pages from 1908. Inside the front cover in faded ink was the signature, "Sincerely Yours, John Lee"—I'm not sure if this was an original signed copy kept by Lee to remind him of his glory years or whether he signed it in 1945 especially for Dr Kaiser to thank him for use of the Webster. Lee had actually died on Monday, 19th March 1945. I know this because it was listed in the Milwaukee Sentinel although Addie put him in as 'James Lee', still evidently following a lifetime of caution instilled in her by Lee. The death certificate lists 'heart failure' as the cause of death. Kaiser's name is on the form. Lee was buried at Forest Home Cemetery next to his daughter. Under his real name that time.

THE VERSIONS OF CORNELIUS HARRINGTON

I really need to deal with Harrington. Or at least take a fix on him. I have an uneasy feeling that he will get away from me whatever I do. Let's try and settle on what I do know.

He came from Plymouth on the English Devon South coast,

thirty miles from Torquay. He is called a 'Janner' in the second spool. Apparently the term is still in use to describe someone from Plymouth. One authority on the Babbacombe murder has him being born in 1864 which would make him exactly the same age as Lee, but Lee made clear in the recordings that Harrington was an older man. There were several Cornelius Harringtons in the area at the time. Maybe it was a family of Irish origin that named all their males Cornelius? I think our Cornelius was the one that appears in the 1901 census for Devon who is listed as being born in Plymouth in 1861. That would make him aged 22 or 23 when Lee first encountered him at Colonel Brownlow's. That seems right.

Lee does not really describe him physically. He defined him by what he was not. Lee implied he was somehow slant, gimp, walking with a limp perhaps or maybe just rolling like a seaman. These descriptions may be a mirror to his character as much as an actual picture. He was both ugly and handsome at the same time. He had a snaky charm and showed an uncanny knack of getting under Lee's crusty shell. He had the sly scamming insight of a con artist. He seemed to be always horny yet we know he burned a special candle for Lizzie.

All we actually know of him is that he was involved with Butler Kisler in smuggling in 1883 and he was a fisherman in Harris's boat crew in 1884. What else we know can be inferred from Lee's account. He must have lived in lodgings somewhere in that small huddle of dwellings on the slopes of Babbacombe Bay. Somewhere close to the Glen anyway.

He liked his liquor and the habit probably caught up with him in later life. I think he feared dissolution and was scared that he would never really amount to anything. He was always looking to build himself up. He would scam folks by seeming to reveal personal stuff about himself in order to fake up a closer relationship with them then he'd generally rip them off in some way once they thought he was buddies with them. Maybe he unconsciously accepted his own dark nature although on the surface he would deny it. Maybe he wanted both Lizzie and Lee to appreciate how special he was. Maybe he has a fantasy self and admired Lizzie's stone-like clarity which was in contrast to his own mixed–up feelings. Inside, he was likely a shifting kaleidoscope of stuff. He could never hold onto and be true to anything good. I assume that he tried to connect with Lee through the letter he left for him behind the water trough because he still wanted to con him into some other cruddy enterprise or maybe he wanted to be sure Lee would keep his mouth shut. Also, Harrington may have sought him out again because both men were united by something they had in common. The woman that had lured them both on had also abandoned the two of them.

I guess that despite his charm Harrington knew at heart that there was something very wrong with himself. When it came to the moment he was a wolverine. He struck without hesitation at Miss Keyse, he likely did something nasty to Bartlet and he certainly brutalized the Fey girls. No doubt he had a whole heap of excuses to distance himself from his bloody work. He would never enjoy the sort of life he thought he was owed.

I sometimes think of him striding up the beach to greet the dismayed Lee on Lee's return to the Glen in '84. A slight man but strong and wiry, with thick, dark rumpled hair. He held a direct gaze though he carried the head lowered as if always searching for something on the ground. He spoke easily and had a honey tongue but his mouth was like a slit. He had a big beaky slice for a nose, a strong jaw and green eyes that drove into you. His ears were low set, his hair thick at the back of the neck like an animal. He had an angular Irish face with features that sloped like chevrons. A face like a bag of chisels, his kin would have said. A small man but with presence, something steely about him and bristling with malign purpose.

Maybe that is not him at all, I need to beware my urge to fictionalize. The facts are rich enough. I know this story and how it will all turn out though the characters remain ignorant, making their way through it like unknowing sleep walkers. I seem to see Harrington in my dreams—maybe Georgia brings him to me.

I've wondered what Harrington did on the early hours of the 15th once the fire had blazed. I think he probably slunk up through the woods onto Babbacombe Down then watched the proceedings. At some stage he would have had to get rid of his bloody clothing. Perhaps he saw Lee go running up Beach Road in his long coat and holding a lantern at 5 am? He does not feature among the fire fighters and witnesses at the inquest. I think he might well have been a sort of double agent working for the customs men, and they would have wanted to protect him from scrutiny. Harris, his boat captain, was dragged up for evidence but not Harrington.

I found a telling newspaper article in that online archive of Brit newspapers. The East and Devon Advertiser for 1885 had a piece about a long knife being found on the slope above the Glen and close to the highway. The piece said that the blade was bloodied and had a significant notch in the blade. The piece openly speculated that this was the actual knife in the Keyse murder and mentions the corresponding marks on the old lady's neck bone. Maybe they were right. That was very likely Harrington's knife. He probably fled the smoldering Glen and slung the fatal weapon over a stone wall into one of the wooded enclosures at the edge of the Mount Temple estate.

As to what happened to him afterwards it is hard to say. Police Captain Barbor mentions that Harrington was at sea when the Home Secretary ordered an investigation following Chaplain Pitkin's 1885 suggestion that Lee might not be guilty. The 1891 census showed no trace of him in Devon and I've not found his name in ships' crews or immigration lists. He must have left his letter to Lee between 1885 and 1908. Lee mentions getting a letter with an American stamp in the late 1880's. It could be him in that census of 1901. He appears to be living then in a lodging house on King's Street in Plymouth. Many of the other lodgers have Irish names and are listed as being hawkers, road menders and laborers. You'll remember that letter where young Freddie Lee told Lee that he had been to check on the presumed Harrington but could not find him.

It would be good to trap Harrington in death's cage, to draw the curtain on him and say goodbye for sure. Here is where he gets all tricky on my ass. There is a Cornelius Harrington listed as dying at age 70 in Plymouth in September 1936 but the dates don't fit our man. I've found a death report about a Cornelius Harrington in the Idaho County Free Press, for November 26th 1903. The report says that 54 year old Harrington, a gold miner, died of heart disease in his cabin. Or take an Australian newspaper of 1891 from Walhalla, Victoria, which reported a Cornelius Harrington arrested for kicking his wife to death. The paper said that "The body was pounded out of shape, and the room in which it was found was saturated with blood." The paper later stated that Harrington was sentenced to 15 years imprisonment and died in jail.

Or here is yet another version of Harrington from the New York Times in the early years of the last century about a Cornelius Harrington, a thief, killed by an Eyrie Basin policeman when caught in the act of stealing rope. The policeman managed to break his skull by hitting him with an oar during a struggle.

That's it, take your pick, dudes. You decide which one is the right Cornelius Harrington. I guess it doesn't really matter which one he is. 'Abyssus Abyssum Invocat' should be on his tombstone wherever it stands. Deep calls to deep: it's a translation in the Latin vulgate from Psalm 42, and more explicitly it means, 'hell calls to hell'.

LONELY

There's no more Lee to distract me. No more crawling drag-ass transcription to keep me occupied. How am I going to live without him? It's the end of August. Georgia rules the night so I sleep only in the day. I don't even go to Scottie's any more. I feel that people are looking at me. I'm existing on take-out red boxes from The Golden Corral and bags of Funyuns. Crudalicious! I've had thoughts of driving out to Waukesha with Grandpa's commemoration Colt automatic and going looking for my high school bullies. They're probably working as order clerks or dishwashers now. Yo, guys! How ya doin'? Remember me? Kapow!

Lighting Out

What did she do to you, Lizzie? It's not as if Miss Keyse had come scratching at your bedroom door in the night like she did to your brother. I guess she was a querulous, demanding, miserable old bitch but she gave you a job. She hardly deserved the treatment you meted out. No doubt it was your choice of men that really burned your bridges, Lizzie. You had juggled with brother Jack, with dangerous Cornelius, and the diseased bonehead Templer, all at the same time. Everything was going to come crashing down at some stage. Maybe you thought to boost some of the old woman's valuables then light out somewhere abroad. If Jack could keep up with you then he could stay with you but if not, you would journey alone. Yeah, you were pregnant but you had coped on your own for a long time. You had conceived that child in the August, in Regatta time. Did you even know who the father was?

Sexy, resolute Lizzie Harris, I can't help admiring you. I've studied the drawing that the court artist made of you, a face like a carnal apple. I can see why those men wanted to look into your pale, still eyes. Born 20th August, a Leo, brave, sensual and good at keeping secrets according to the sun signs book I've had for years. Crummy to look at astrology I know, but you have to believe in something.

You carried such a stately name, Elizabeth Hamlyn Esterbrook Harris. Though really it was a sign of shame. The Hamlyn-Esterbrooks were gentleman farmers on Dartmoor and one of them must have knocked up your mother. Your rotten ma dumped you out of her life but she wanted you to never forget the circumstances of your shameful birth so she saddled you with that name. You were born in a one-horse flyspeck of a place called Torbryan. Then you were farmed off to kin and brought up alone in that gloomy farmstead by the marshy estuary of the Teign. But you survived and made your way despite the family neglect and your bad name.

Some would paint you as a Lady Macbeth or a Lizzie Borden, a crazy and ruthless woman sacrificing your dumb brother. Brave also, you kept on refusing to wear mourning clothes for Miss Keyse even though it told against you. Maybe you really did hate Miss Keyse for something? Your brother was a partial witness in his recorded memories of you. Besides, what abandoned lover is ever happy with the disappeared one? You "carried your character with you" he said of you in his last letter home before the planned hanging. But I think he still loved you all of his life.

A reporter for the Torquay Times of January 30th 1885 spotted you leaving Torre Station on the way to the murder trial at Exeter. He noted that it was a wet day and Sergeant Knott had difficulty rounding up the witnesses to board the train. You are described as being "in fairly good spirits and talking gaily" with your companions. You were in dark clothes but not in mourning. He said that you looked thinner than at the inquest but your resemblance to Lee was more striking than ever. The reporter followed you into the carriage and watched as you stared out the window the whole journey.

Lizzie, what did you think about when you were leaving Torre Station? You had the presence of mind to joke around with the Necks—perhaps you wanted to distract yourself from the grim business that was waiting for you in the witness box.

You had to nail your brother down, he was good for nothing else. Perhaps life at Aunt Millie's in Tormohan was tough. You were eating for two now also. It must have been a relief when the trial ended. Another reporter saw you standing in Exeter Assizes courtyard after the guilty sentence, you were dabbing at your eyes with a handkerchief then you tucked into a tea and bun. At some later stage you admitted yourself to Newton Abbot Workhouse. I guess after the weird reprieve of your brother everyone turned against you. Maybe your neighbors had begun to think if God had saved Jack then His finger was pointing at you as the true guilty one.

Beatrice, your daughter, was born in May 1885. Maybe you had picked the name because Queen Victoria's daughter, Princess Beatrice, had been married in that same year. You stayed only long enough to nurse her for seven months into winter then you slipped out of Plymouth Sound on an emigrant boat. Beatrice was left behind despite her hopeful aristocratic name.

There wasn't much of a life left in England was there? Who paid for your ticket, I wonder? What did you have to do to get it? You can't have had any wages left after eight months out of work. Maybe you sold Beatrice like in some Thomas Hardy novel and comforted yourself that she would have a better life? Or more likely you left the kid behind because she carried bad blood and you didn't want to be reminded of that for the rest of your life.

You arrived at Maryborough on the Queensland Fraser coast after a hundred days at sea. The name of town has the echo of the St Marychurch that you left. I found you listed aged 31 arriving on the iron-hulled, full rigger, The Eastminster, in 1886. It was an old ship that was mysteriously lost at sea four years later. You got away Lizzie, sailing to a new life with all your secrets packed away. It couldn't have been easy. I have no idea what you had to do to survive those first six years. You seem to have stayed in bustling Maryborough, a port on the Mary River which took in twenty thousand emigrants in those years. You fought your way among that crowd and in 1892 you married Robert Dukes, an English laborer from the East Riding of Yorkshire. He was ten years younger than you and had already married a young local girl. Maybe the previous woman had died or moved on or maybe you replaced her. You knew how to please a man after all your adventures. Whatever the reality, you managed to hold on to a settled life. You had two daughters and a son. At some stage the family moved to the small frontier settlement of Broweena a little way inland but in the end you came back to March Street, by the river, close to the center of Maryborough. No-one seems to have found you or linked you to the Babbacombe mystery.

I found a passenger listing of a Cornelius Harrington sailing from Southampton to Sidney in 1914 so maybe he was still sniffing on your track even then, but I can't believe that he actually found you. The outside world did intrude though, your twenty year old son Robert was called away to war and died on the Somme on the Western Front in France in 1916. You lived on. After the war, the Australia newspapers featured the human interest-type story of a devoted Devon couple who had lived together for 86 years as man and wife and who had died within a week of each other. Their names were William Easterbrook and Anne Hamlyn, late of Torbryan. They must have been close kin and William might even have been your father. I wonder if you noticed the story.

You could not fail to have heard of the good reviews of a new movie production, made in Australia in 1921 and touring all the country. It was a movie of 'The Man They Could Not Hang' with an accompanying live performance by the actor Arthur Sterry playing the celebrated Babbacombe murderer, John Lee. The sell-out production appeared at the Wintergarden Palace Theatre on Kent Street, not half a mile from your house. Maybe you never went to it because you couldn't tell your husband about your past. When you died in February 1926, aged 70, he filed you wrongly as being born in Kingsteington and gave a fictitious name for your father. Maybe you never told him the truth.

There probably still is a picture of you somewhere in a family album, an old lady with a gypsy face shielding your eyes from the fierce Queensland sun. Someday I'd like to go to the Fraser coast and look up your grave. I'll stand among the weeds and the sallow grasses among the emigrant dead, trying to sense you. You don't need to be scared. I'll be a friendly presence, maybe I'll leave some flowers and a handful of red Devon soil as a greeting. You should understand, I want to make my peace with the dead of this story

Caesura

Outside, the day calls to everyday folk. Old Glory snaps in a norther sent straight from Canada down Main Street. I stare out the windows of Scottie's Eat-Mor. Yep, I've rallied and gone back there again. An eastern redbud rattles in the wind. It's the sort that Grandpa called a 'Judas Tree'. It has a few last copper-yellow leaves hanging on at the tips of each branch. Old guys come into the diner. One says, "I don't mind them salads as long as they've got cheese and bacon in 'em, eh?" My mind stalls. For some reason I keep repeating Keats' words, "thou foster child of silence and slow time." The wind gnaws at the sign outside that reads, 'Wow! Friday fish is back'. This small town threatens to dissolve my floor of memory. I think I'm going to drop through everything and somehow fall into another dimension. At night I wake from drowsing with a jerk to find the TV playing 'I Love Lucy' shows back to back. I noticed today the quamash bulbs I planted in a pot in the yard a month ago. Then, they were dried-up lumps of matter but now they have violent, white roots roiling out the container despite winter's advance.

What I'd like to do is to light out like Ambrose Bierce. He wrote his family that he would not be a burden then went to

Mexico. Ostensibly, he went to take notes on the civil war there in 1913, Pancho Villa and all. But really he went to disappear. No-one knows what happened to him. One Bierce history freak even built a gravestone for him in a Mexican mountain village. But it could have been quite another spot where he met his end. It's a bit like the Babbacombe Lee story, you could make a mark and say it all ended here. But you'd be wrong.

I'm the young gringo set to follow my own journey to its mysterious ends. Only I've got no family to write. I so admire that short story by Bierce, an 11th grade English high school staple, called 'Occurrence At Owl Creek'. If you don't know it, it's about a man set to be executed by being hung off a bridge. We follow how he escapes when the rope apparently breaks and he dives away down the hungry river. The physical world seems intensely real for him for the first time in his life as he swims along and glories in his reprieve. He eludes the bullets of his pursuers and flounders out the shallows and heads for home. He resolves that he will now appreciate everything about his life. We jerk back to the fateful bridge and find out that it is all taking place in his mind in the last moments before his neck is snapped.

That Bierce disappearance idea has real appeal. Georgia won't let up. She keeps bugging me about something. When I pay attention to what she's actually saying it seems she keeps telling that I've missed something important. She keeps saying something that sounds like "seize her". I guess it's only a mind glitch, one of my many mental malfunctions. Just to be sure I'm fixing on asking Mulvina if she can rid me of my ghosts.

WHO WAS DR KAISER?

This whole Lee deal has become a drag. I've written no poetry since it started. I just want it over but I don't know how to end it. I thought when I had played Lee's recordings and transcribed them that would be it. I would cut this sucker to the bone, write a short pithy crime book about the mystery of Babbacombe finally revealed and then sit back and rake in the sales. Instead I'm faced by more questions than ever. And I seem to have inherited some spooks of my own. I had a thought that I needed to go back to first base. You can start with the problem about who exactly was Doctor Kaiser and why did he record Lee?

Let's again go over those other things in the old cardboard box along with the spools and the Webster wire recorder machine. First, there was the name stamp, I've mentioned already. Kaiser must have used it to sign off his official correspondence or to mark his prescriptions maybe. There's the scrap book with English newspaper articles. John Lee or Addie could have given it to Kaiser for it to end up jumbled up with Kaiser's things. And the same for the old copy of Lee's Autobiography Kaiser surely had got off Lee or Addie directly and it shows that Lee must have become more than a patient to him. Not forgetting the invoice from Schusters, the big old Milwaukee department store. Kaiser must have been on the ball to buy the Webster, one of the first wire recorder models to be available to the public. Maybe he just liked gadgets or he was thinking to use it for his medical work.

Then we have the medical notes. They were written on pieces of lined card and were really hard to read. The ink was faded, the writing crimped and willfully illegible and some of it was in medical shorthand. I've had to look up no end of stuff to understand them. This is my transcription attempt.

Home visit. Exn. 02/03/45
James Lee. 454 East Holt Avenue. 81 yrs.
Complains of nausea, weight loss, tiredness, (illegible word), breathless ++
Exn.
Weight 94 lbs
Height 5' 11"
Edentulous
BP 90/69
85/63
Pulse bounding, 100-120
Temp Norm.
Scattered rhonchi
Systolic murmur
Percussion revealed moderate enlargement left ventricle
Pitted oedema both feet
Hist
Married. 1 daughter † 1933 (Acc. Poisoning)
Immigrant,
resident 35 years
? Pneumonia/TB age circa 18
Old injury scars on l. & r. Arms, - healed rib fractures, cause?
Infarct probable 3/12 ago
Nil else of note
Diagnosis
1- chronic congestive heart failure 2- atheroma with secondary renal impairment
Treatment
Digoxin tab 125mg x1 daily
Mercuhydrin 0.5cc im x1 daily
Trinitrin prn
<u>Prognosis</u>
Poor

There you have it. Lee's poor health captured in Kaiser's brutal shorthand. However you read it, it didn't look so good for the patient. His heart rate was going like a machine gun and his blood pressure was in his boots. Especially when he stood up. His arteries were blocked and his heart's pumping action was weak. The doctor did not have it easy, I bet. Lee was a frickin' liar on many occasions. He didn't give his right name to start with and I'm sure he would have tried some BS on the doc about his symptoms. I wonder when Kaiser started to find out who his patient really was. Kaiser started seeing Lee at the beginning of February 1945 so the recordings must have been made in February and March of that year.

I was staring at those medical notes under a lamp at my old deal desk when I noticed there were indentations coming through the paper from the other side. Turning the notes over, I could see that there was something faintly written on the back. I managed to make the writing clearer by rubbing a soft pencil over the marks. The words out of the first group spelt what looked like "brag …flash …holdfast" and a little lower at an angle as if jotted on the knee, was the word, at least I think it was a word, "agepannies". It took me a while of mumbling these over and searching online before I could work them out.

There is one of those whacky British sayings which goes, "Brag is a good dog but Holdfast is better". You can find it in Dickens' novel 'Great Expectations'. I guess Kaiser's note refers to this strange expression and was something he heard Lee saying which he did not understand. Lee probably used it as part of his ordinary speech. The phrase apparently means that it's alright to be flash, brash and blingy but tenacious, quiet purpose is better. Doc Kaiser must have puzzled over this and jotted it down. I think Lee might have been kidding around with his doctor to come out with it in the first place. Maybe Lee was intimating that he wasn't expecting to make spectacular progress but "holdfast" would be as good as anything given his sick condition. The mysterious word "agepannies" was harder to work out. All I can think of that it was Lee's mispronunciation of 'agapanthus'—a blue-flowered garden plant. Why he mentioned an agapanthus I'm not sure. They were popular in Victorian times and maybe Lee grew them for Miss Keyse. I know they get burnt by the hard winters up here, maybe Lee was saying that his body was like the agapanthus after a cold winter—all burnt out and frosted, gone mushy to the roots.

That's as much as the old Lysol box yielded up about Doctor Kaiser. I looked him up on-line to see what else I could find about him. There were a few Howard Kaisers, including a sex offender in Colorado, but not my man. Doc Kaiser inhabited a pre-digital age. I got on better through an initial genealogy search. There was a group of Kaisers from Philadelphia in the 1890s and I found a Howard D. Kaiser born there in 1905. Tracking him along, I could see that he married a Lina Weidman in 1925 and had one son, Clyde Kaiser, born 1926. I cast around in other sources and found an old Milwaukee city directory which had a Doctor Kaiser listed on Fond Du Lac Avenue. I drove down there. All the old properties have been torn down, and it's the Marquette campus there now. There was a heavy vibe on the street and some bad looks so I did not linger. If you look lost or out of your territory you are a target.

Bronzeville has expanded greatly since John Lee's day. The divisions between folk have different manifestations but they are just as toxic. Now, you have the Hispanics also, South Side is their big territory and the gang stuff is rampant. Each outfit has its own territory, whatever you call them, Latin Kings or the Cobras, it's the same stupid deal. Let's not dwell on our own ugly times, the murder of Miss Keyse seems genteel compared to Jeffrey Dahmer's activities for example. He also lived not far from Kaiser's old surgery on 924 North 25th Street.

Still, one murderer at a time please. Let's stick to the sawbones. Genealogy can be an uncertain trail and there were so many Howard Kaisers. The web archives at The American Medical Association put me on the right track. It seems that a Howard D. Kaiser graduated from North Western medical school in 1936 and practiced as a community physician in South Milwaukee up to the end of the 1940s. He seems to have switched direction and worked in public health at the Milwaukee Veterans Hospital in the '50s through to 1978. There was no note of death nor any obituary that I could locate. I looked around the Veterans Hospital. There was no plaque or building named after Kaiser. I guessed he had just gone off and retired somewhere.

Darleen Engstrom pushed me on in my Kaiser-hunting just as I was losing traction. I hit on an old article from the Sentinel Journal about a woman who had retired from the Veterans Hospital after 55 years as a medical transcriptionist. The piece sketched out a lively character study of the gutsy old lady so dedicated that she had started work in Eisenhower's presidency and had served through the period of 11 other presidents. According to the article she had remained single, had rarely taken a vacation or sick leave, and had walked to her place of work every day. The newspaper piece was only two years old so I thought there was a good chance she was still around. I looked her up on White Pages and yes indeed there was a Darleen Engstrom, listed as aged 65 plus and on Becher Street, not far from the VA hospital. I rang a few times before I got an answer. When I did get her she confirmed that she was the same Miss Engstrom who had worked for Milwaukee VA Public Affairs. She had a giggly, girlish manner on the phone. She asked me if I was from a dating agency for seniors then laughed as I hesitated and said that I mustn't mind her, she was just kidding. In truth, I was afraid that she had dementia or something. I told her I was doing some research, a family history of Dr Howard Kaiser. Did she remember him?

"Kaiser, Kaiser? Oh yes," she said. "He was on the staff when I first came in '57. Yes, I see him now, quiet and serious with a grey streak in his hair in the front there."

I asked her what she recalled of him. All the while I tried to control my voice. "Very quiet and reserved," she replied, "He never got over his son, you know,"

"Clyde?"

"I never knew his name. He was killed in the Pacific. Doctor Kaiser kept the anniversary every year. They said the grief broke up his marriage. He lived for his work. He was polite and pleasant to us secretaries. He bought us donuts sometimes. A distant man but a good doctor. The boys liked him, the patients, he could never do too much for them."

She said he had retired in the '70s. He didn't stay local, she thought. He had maybe died in Florida in the mid'80s, he went somewhere south anyway. She said she might have read it in the VA newsletter.

I could not get much more out of her. She said I should come over and talk about the old times. She knew of no connection of the doctor with England and could suggest no one else from that time who knew Dr Kaiser. They had all passed, she explained. She told me she was on her way to her voluntary work, she was a "get up and go person", that's what had kept her young. She worked with the animals at Wisconsin Humane. That kept her going. Before I rang off she said, as a kind of afterthought, "What I do remember about Dr Kaiser is he made our lives easier in transcription. He got us those IBM Selectrics, as soon as they came out in the early '60s. Before that we had manual typewriters. Good on new equipment he was, Dr Kaiser. It made all the difference to our secretarial work. Of course the computers are marvellous now."

That call got me boosted. I was sure that was my Kaiser, the gadget man. I could almost touch him, and the information about Clyde being killed made sense when I recalled that Lee had spoken of the doctor wearing a black arm band. Both men knew grief then. Maybe that was what had linked them.

I was all fired up after that success and went back to online genealogy with renewed enthusiasm, although I got ground down again after a while. You need to be a methodical type to trawl through the lists. It was easy for me to start follow the line of some other Kaiser or get distracted by the suggestive names that called out to me. That ancestry searching began to kill me financially. It was $10 dollars a pop to look up original records and it was eating into my meager pot. There are some dudes who really like this stuff and after once more faltering in my searches for Kaiser and his family I found a website called 'Roots Web' where you can post genealogy enquiries and good-hearted enthusiasts answer your queries for nothing. It's called "free look-ups". I posted a query about looking for the family of Howard D. Kaiser, born 1905. Someone who used the tag-name of "Whizzbang" took up the case, bless his hide.

I waited for him to complete his work and passed the time looking at streaming video of the web camera at Babbacombe Beach all the way over in England. The low-definition camera seemed to flick on at an image every second. You could see the light winking and ever-changing, the waves beetling in slow-mo and the black jerky shapes of dog walkers on the shingly beach.

Within a couple of hours I got a ping back from Whizzbang. It read, "Hey buddy, looks like I found a younger sister and brother of your man Howard Kaiser in census records. Both born in Pennsylvania. Hermina Kaiser b. 1918. Orville Kaiser b. 1917. In 1920 the family was in Milwaukee but by 1940 they had moved to New Athens, Illinois, leaving Howard behind. Their 1940 address was 60 South Elizabeth Street, New Athens. It seems that Hermina married a Randolph Parks. I can find no issue from Orville. Good hunting. W."

New Athens was in South-Eastern Illinois beyond Springfield, six hours drive away. I wondered why on earth the Kaisers had gone there? A quick look up on White Pages revealed 23 Kaisers in New Athens even though it was a small place. I could find no Orville Kaiser among that throng though. It seemed too draggy to ring my way round all the Kaisers in New Athens and so I looked for Hermina Parks instead. That turned out to be a whole lot easier. There she was listed at the same 1940s address that Whizzbang had found for me. There was no associated name listed at the place so I guessed that she was now widowed.

I suppose I should have rung first but I was impatient to get started and it was late at night when I found her online. That next dawn I dropped some guarana tabs, filled up the Ford and headed South on 1-39. There were hours of driving in the soapy light, straining to see through the wipers going full tilt and dodging the big looming rigs. I kept telling myself that a journey has no merit unless it tests you. Past Litchfield, Edwardsville and Troy, I followed the blue and red shield sign of the Interstate 55. For some reason I kept on repeating the phrase from Virgil's Aeneid which begins, "I beg you, let me be mad with this madness before death comes." Its deep echo in Latin was pleasing to me and I said it out loud again and again. I think I must have some high-functioning syndrome the way I lock onto things. Sometimes I just open my mouth and chimp-out. Yipping and hooting noises or loud screams are my favorites. If you repeat anything long enough it finds its own meaning. I find it strangely soothing to shriek and gibber like that.

I came in to New Athens over the big white bridge that spans the Kaskasia. The whole place was watery and low-lying like my own home town. I'd read somewhere that those south eastern Illinois lands belonged to an Indian tribe called the Tamaracks. There was a green sign for "New Athens, population, 2000". The hamlet sat in the bend of the river among vast bare fields. A fitful sun came out to celebrate my arrival. There was no sign of the Tamaracks now only the looming white tadpole shape of a large water tower. I got passed by a pick-up with a gun rack, full of hunters in camo who eyeballed me as a stranger. Duck feathers flicked up out the back of their vehicle and came eddying around my dirt- crusted windshield. Following the route of the old state highway onto Spotsylvania Street, I passed a brick building which had a sign on it saying it was the first house in the settlement, founded 1847. Hell, that was only 17 years before John Lee was born. We are such a young country compared to Devonshire. This place only recently wrenched from the hold of the rivers and the Indians.

Elizabeth Street was a left hook off Spotsylvania. There were not too many other streets to get lost in. The Parks place was a woodboard one-story house. It looked newly painted. A snakebark maple lifted up its arms in the front yard. The street was empty of all inhabitants, not even a dog around. I got the impression they were all hiding or watching me. Out the travel-stained SUV, I was hit by the smell of wet earth and the raggedy cheeping of sparrows. The silence seemed exaggerated by the noise from the birds. I went up and knocked. There was no answer so I wandered to the side of the house. I could see no movement through the ground windows. At back there was just a washcloth jittering in the wind on a rotary clothes dryer and an old box left out on the grass. It was packed full of discarded women's shoes. I sort of slumped then and thought, "Now what? You tard. You've dragged your sorry ass all the way here to this void." I might have stayed there an hour or a week while those sparrows squeaked on. I'd somehow run out of ideas as to what to do next and decided to hang tight and wait for inspiration. It's just as well that at some stage an old timer came out from the next house, peered me for a while from his porch then came out to speak to me.

"You lookin' for Hermina?" he said, "She fell over 'bout two weeks ago. She's in Memorial Hospital up in Belleville."

Nurse specialist Tammy Pozner addressed me at the entrance to Orthopedic Trauma. I knew it was her name because her badge tag wobbled around at eye level. She was a big woman.

"Yes, Mrs Parks is an in-patient here. You're family?" she asked.

"No, sort of friend of the family," I muttered, "I'm really not sure if I—"

She interrupted me, "It does her good to see folks, I'll have to stop these though. We don't allow flowers on the ward; we find they harbor bacteria."

I gave her the bunch of bronze and gold chrysanthemums I'd brought and she immediately plunged them into a clinical waste bin. I moved obediently down the ward behind Nurse Pozner but I kept thinking that I shouldn't be there. I should have stuck to book and internet knowledge and not got involved in reality directly. I tried to veer off but Nurse Pozner ushered me firmly into a room and all of a sudden I was confronted by an elderly lady in a blue-flowered smock, sitting up in bed. Mrs Parks' round apple face looked doubtful on seeing me, and her gray eyes blinked uncertainly.

"I can't quite place, you, son, come closer." I reluctantly approached her and said quietly,

"I've come here to ask you about Howard."

"Howard?"

"Yes, Howard, your brother."

"Gee, son, Howard? No one has mentioned him for years." She smiled, "Now I see, you're one of his doctor buddies. You seem mighty young though. You should have said. Now then Howard, yes, he was always going to be something special. I knew that from when he was small. I'm his big sis."

"What happened to Howard?" I asked, "Can you tell me where he went after retiring from the VA?"

Her gaze sharpened to sudden suspicion "Why are you asking me that? You should ask Howard yourself. He never visits me. If you are his friend how come you don't know where he is? I think I'll ring for the nurse. Ward D7, they will know. You call that nurse back in here at once, young man. Do it at once. D7, they'll tell you."

"I'm sorry to have disturbed you, Mrs Parks," I said, "I just wanted to hear more about your brother."

"I'm not listening to you no more. You are definitely not a friend of Howard's." She grimaced as if in pain then yelled out,

"Find D7. Get hold of Ward D7 at once!"

"This is Ward D7," I said. That did it. She really became agitated then. She kept struggling as if about to rise up out of bed.

"Let me up, let me up," she called out. She pushed behind her with her thin arms but could not raise herself, then searched for the bed buzzer, which had fallen out of reach. Thankfully, the old lady began to tire. Her head dropped back onto the pillow and she closed her eyes. I could see her chest rising and falling with shuddering breaths. I sat for a while and looked at the TV. It was showing Sesame Street. Mrs Parks seemed to have gone to sleep and I watched the screen as the room darkened. It had been a long day's travelling to get to this. After a while, I became aware that Mrs Parks was speaking again. She seemed calmer.

"Poor Howard got wrecked by his no good wife Lina. She left him you know. That and Clyde getting killed. He spent all his time on his doctoring after that. Lina ended up in charge of the Majestic Theatre at Madison. She told us she had shaken the hand of Leonard Bernstein. That's all I know. Guess she's passed now. I've not seen Howard in a long while. I heard he went to California. I think maybe he's passed. My poor Randolph has gone also you know? Did you know?" She looked at me and I nodded back at her. Mrs Parks looked saddened to have her fears confirmed.

"My husband, he worked at Lehr's meat market. He came home for his lunch every day. He was a man of regular habits. I can't get used to him not being around. I've been on Lost Dog Road ever since he's gone. Guess I'm on Lost Dog Road now." Tears gathered and fell. I handed her a Kleenex from a box on her bed table. She rallied after a while.

"How is your mother?" She asked brightly with a little shake of the head.

"Uh, my mom she's dead," I said and I tiptoed out.

Hospital security caught me in the exit atrium as I was

trying to haul ass out of there. Two heavy guys all in black. One held me by the wrist as Tammie the nurse pointed at me and a middle-aged woman in a North Face vest kept saying, "Who is that man? We don't know him. Why has he been allowed to see my mother?"

Later when it all calmed down a bit I was able to explain that I had come seeking to explore family history and I hadn't meant to cause distress.

I spoke to Mrs Parks' daughter outside in the parking lot. Her name was Carla Sokal. A middle-aged divorcée with soft gray eyes like her mother. I thought maybe they were Kaiser eyes, though Carla told me the Kaiser side of the family had died out. She said her mom had fallen but a scan had showed up a crumbling hip bone. She was being eaten at by bone cancer. Her advanced age would slow the speed of progression but it wasn't looking good. The doctors thought that she showed signs of dementia as well. I told Carla how sorry I was about it all. It was a mistake coming. I was a harmless researcher looking into her family history. Come to think of it, maybe I wasn't so harmless—you should beware the single-minded. Even the crudest grip on history would tell you that.

Mrs Sokal was too preoccupied to ask me very much about what I was doing. She thought her mom might have told me something once but it seemed unlikely now with her memory problems. Carla herself had met with her Uncle Howard a few times. She believed he'd died of a heart attack while sea fishing in Southern California. The family had thought it odd because as far as they knew he had never shown an interest in fishing before that. He'd been cremated and his ashes were spread on Clyde's grave. I asked where Clyde was buried. And she told me, Milwaukee. He'd been brought home, you see. She took my phone number in case she thought of anything else and as she leaned forward I could see she wore a silver medallion round her neck. On impulse, I asked her what it was. She said it signified "Our Lady of the Snows". She told me that the national shrine to Our Lady of the Snows was there in Belleville. They even had their own replica Lourdes Grotto there, had a million visitors a year. No miracles yet but many had been healed. She and her husband were oblates. I only realized then that Doctor Kaiser was probably Catholic also. I had presumed he was a secular scientist type but maybe he hadn't been like that at all.

I rolled into the Super Eight Motel on East Main. It was low end but with wi-fi. It was hard to chill. I didn't really like staying away from my own small rented corner of the world. Some Herbalife Calm Compound helped take the edge off of it. I lay there uneasily on the blue check counterpane.

I didn't know what an oblate was so I looked it up on Wiki. It turns out oblate came from Latin 'oblatus'—to offer. An oblate is a secular person who offers up a private dedication to a religious calling. I liked the idea. Maybe I could be an oblate in my own style.

I missed the routines that usually lapped around me. My fixed habits held me from chaos. I didn't even like changing my breakfast cereal. I quite often had it at night. It was the melatonin in the milk that helped me sleep, I guess. I've always had Barbara's Bakery Corn Flakes at $4.59 a box, I liked their yellow natural color. Then they changed it and put 'new improved taste' on the box. It's weird how much that upset me. The new product was dry, brown and alien.

I must seem like a goober with all this obsessional crap. I believe I will center myself one day. Maybe love will cure me if I find the right person. Anyhow back to that motel room: I tried to short-cut sleep and dropped another natural herbal tranquiller, some valerian and chamomile that time. I lay back on the king size and did my usual sleep routine. I have these special memories that I deliberately play in my mind like a relaxation tape to soothe me. They are always the same: riding the John Deere in sunshine at Grandpa's place and me lying with Kimmie in a wooden vacation cabin by the lake at Minocqua. She got me used to being touched by a person.

I was woken by my cell phone ringing. It was Carla Sokal. She told me she had got to thinking after meeting me and had dug out some stuff she'd kept since her Uncle Orville had died. Orville was a brewer who had come to work in the Pilsner brewery in New Athens. It had gone now, burnt down, she said. She also said she had papers, letters and such originally belonging to Doctor Kaiser. I was welcome to look at them if it was helpful and if I was still in town, though she wanted them back.

We met in the motel entrance hall. She was carrying two heavy-looking canvas tote bags. She said she had quickly collected up a few things she thought would be useful to me. She always planned to do something with them herself, but she was always too busy to make a family history. She asked me again what I was interested in. I said it was for a book about a doctor, and I asked her if she had seen any wire spools. No, and she didn't know what a wire recorder was. She thought Uncle Orville must have thrown out the rest of Howard's stuff. The doctor had kept a house in Cudahy but spent most of his later time in California. He had heart disease and it was thought to be more healthy down there. I guessed that the original Lysol box that I had found must have been discarded by Orville and must have passed through several hands.

I wished Mrs Sokal good luck with her mother. I've always found it so hard to say the right thing to folks, that's why I stay alone. When I try and break out of my box then my intensities tend to scare everyone. Carla said that if God had not taken her Ma yet then it was not in his plan. I asked her if God's plan ever got messed up.

"Oh no, it might seem to be messed up but it's always working its purpose out," she replied. It was late. She had to get back as she was teaching school in the morning. I said I couldn't sleep too well. She told me if I went to the "Our Lady of the

Snows" for help I could get healed.

"Will the Lady cure anyone?" I asked.

"Sure," she replied, "That is the miracle of it all. Even if you don't believe in her, she will cure you anyway."

I laid out all the contents of the tote bags on the king size bedspread. There were many letters and quite a few articles clipped from what looked like medical journals, also heaps of photos, a whole album with a frayed fabric cover, some faded high school pennants, medical certificates, military stuff and a naval telegram. I stayed up all night studying it and marking up the stuff to be copied. I got it scanned at Office Max the next day, two blocks from the motel.

It turns out Kaiser retrained as a shrink shortly after John Lee had died. He attended Wisconsin Psychiatric Institute in Madison and went on to do a residency at the Menninger Clinic, which was linked to a VA hospital for neuro-psychiatric casualties. It seems an enthusiasm for Freudian psychoanalysis had swept through psychiatric practice at the time. You can see its traces in Kaiser's work but he seems to have kept his feet in the biological wing. There were notes on neuro-surgery treatment programs, on the treatment of chronic pain and the use of insulin shock for locked-in cases. He seems to have experimented with stuff called sodium amobarbital as a truth serum and relaxant to enable veterans to access repressed war trauma. There were many notes about mentally disabled returnees from World War 2, Korea and early Vietnam.

One whole bag was full of more personal items. Photos: Kaiser, pipe in mouth, with that gray streak in his hair, standing with faculty members; colorized photos of Lina smiling on a porch, Clyde squinting into the sun with shiny plastered-down hair, holding a pup and posing next to an old automobile. There were so many of Clyde, with one whole album dedicated to him. That included the last pictures of him in uniform along with the cards and letters he sent from military camps. There were older pictures of unknown people in woolen swim suits at a swimming hole. I thought one of them might be a young Hermina. I found Kaiser's staff name tags stored in a tin of St Bruno tobacco. There was also a large number of note books filled with his crimped, precise writing.

What I really focused on was Kaiser's articles. Some seemed to have appeared in the Journal of the Wisconsin Medical Society and others that looked like they were intended as discussion items for medical students and colleagues. I got to recognize the lucid measured style. Sometimes they were informal think-pieces under the pseudonyms 'Wise Owl' or 'Suum Cuique', sometimes they came out under his own name. There were no major academic or research papers. Kaiser seems not to have been ambitious. He seems to have remained a resident doctor on the house staff most of his career. It took me a time to recognize that 'Suum Cuicque' comes from Cicero—it means, 'To each as they deserve' or 'To each his own'. It's the idea that we should all achieve to the maximum of our abilities, although it also has the more somber sub-text that 'we get what we deserve'. It was a while before I connected it to 'To Each His Own', the song by the Modernnaires on the last spool of the wire recorder. Kaiser must have recognized the connection of the catchy hit tune to the bleaker Ciceronian quote and that is why he recorded it. Maybe he enjoyed the irony of it.

Kaiser's life seems to have been completely discarded, shelled off, lost and washed away. I'm a snapper-up of forgotten bits and pieces. I could have spent time on him to reconstruct his life but I really wanted to focus on Lee as my revenant. Kaiser's role was to be my guide and signposter on the way. I noticed a particular article he wrote in 1956, just a piece to be read at an academic meeting I guessed. It was typed on thin paper, maybe done by Darleen Engstrom for him. He called the article: 'Three May Keep a Secret: Confidentiality and Clinical Practice on Mentally Disabled War Returnees'. I guessed the title referred to the Benjamin Franklin quote, "Three may keep a secret, if two of them are dead". The article covered how the doctor had managing the freaky and upsetting material that psychologically damaged war veterans brought back. Those guys kept on having flashbacks to all that death, horror and repressed guilt at the things they had done, stuff like leaving buddies behind or shooting prisoners. A lot of the material was from the Pacific war against the Japanese. Later in the piece there was reference to more specific stories of lighting up Japs with flamethrowers, loosing Marine Dobermans on the prisoners, cutting off Jap heads and sticking them on jeeps as hood ornaments. Gnarly stuff. The article suggested that the patients should be helped by allowing them to ventilate bad thoughts, sometimes with use of sodium amobarbital to empty out their more clingy secrets.

Kaiser seems to have treated trauma like a grieving progress. The piece described in long words how the libido bound up and hypercathected with the past. Hypercathexis is a shrink's term for the intense emotional longing for something. Sort of like being intensely in love. Kaiser described how his serviceman patients held desperately onto a crippling mass of feelings about their war experiences. They were in love with their distress, he thought. He saw his job as starting a sort of mourning process where the ego has to learn how to get away and become free again from its grabby, intense attachment. The treatment encouraged a process of hyper-rembering and obsessive recollection. The therapist's job seemed to be to rev up the hyper-remembering process. It appeared that he was encouraging an almost fictive process, a deliberate recreation of the past.

I could see at once that Kaiser's wire recordings of Lee looked like an early version of this unloading. I got a tad lost in the technicalities of the piece. The gist of it was the survivor was helped to bring the past alive again, replacing an actual absence with an imaginary presence. This magical restoration of the lost objects and experiences helped the mourner to get a hold of the value of what happened in the past and understand what he had lost by moving away from those experiences in time. By dragging out the existence of the lost past at the center of Kaiser's grief work with his screwed-up soldiers then his patients came to understand that the past experiences no longer existed and had no power over them. In the phony- sounding language of Kaiser's article—mourning and guilty agitation then could come to a decisive and spontaneous end and the libido was free to attach to new objects and experiences.

Okay, so far, so complicated. I can't say I got all of it but what jumped at me from the pages of that old typescript was Kaiser's introduction, He commented at the beginning:

> *"Every patient is unique. Even the general practitioner will encounter the extraordinary within his everyday practice. I well recall a patient who confessed to me that he had committed serious crimes many years before in another country. In fact it turned out the fellow was notorious in his home country. This patient was in end stage cardiac myopathy, my treatment was confined to the palliative yet his chief concern was this confession about killing two women. The man was confused due to renal failure, I did not have a clear idea of the truth of his beliefs, but that was not my function, I was there to allow that hypercathexis, the intense desire to dwell on the things that bothered and perplexed him. My role was to help him complete his object and make a confession. I realized that if I was to help my patient then it was my duty to allow that secret to come out, and so to free him. What actually happened in historical time died with the patient, but the dilemmas posed by that case stayed with me."*

Two women? What the hell did Kaiser mean? It surely had to be Lee he was talking about in that article. Miss Keyse we knew about. Had Kaiser remembered it wrong? It seemed unlikely.

There was nothing else about Lee's case in his papers although I searched through them all night. That was it. Two women killed? Yes, Lee had annihilated some people in a metaphorical sense. He had grievously damaged Jessie Bulled and Kate Farmer emotionally for example and he was dead to his kids by Jessie but specifically a killing? And a woman?

I fell asleep in the early hours among all the litter of documents and awoke as if Kaiser had been my spirit Orphic guide during the night. In a dream it had come to me, the answer about two murders. I realized at once when I woke that it was not just Miss Keyse who had died in those early hours of the 15th November. Something else had happened. I think Lee told us an alternative version of the truth in those wire recordings. That bastard frickin' Lee, the mendacious shit! Why couldn't he just level with us?

Maybe Mrs Sokal was right. It was God's plan to put all this into my head. I pieced it together on my drive back home. I realized that Lee only wanted to believe in his good avatar. Who doesn't? That was why he did not tell the whole truth on the wire recordings. Kaiser, my guide, he had been walking beside me all along, giving me clues and trying to lead me to the truth. The good doctor was in mourning for his own lost objects and so was I. I guess we're all mourning the people we were before the bad stuff happened.

A Casting Out

Mulvina sat me down in her consulting rooms. A poster on the wall read, 'Live life to express not to impress. Don't strive to get your presence noted just make your absence felt.' Yeah, John Lee sure took a leaf out of that book. Mulvina looked hot with her dark hair tumbling over a crisp white blouse. I'd asked her to get rid of my bad spirits. She'd sounded a little doubtful over the phone at first but said she could do a "cleansing and a blessing" for $200. When I got there she lit some candles that puffed out an acrid smoke. She said that was sage; apparently, the Native Americans used that for driving off bad spirits. She told me to be open to the experience, said that the ego was arrogant and shut down the voice of spirit. We sat facing each other. I liked looking at the frieze of tiny, cute moles on her neck and the way her dangly earrings glided over her skin. She explained that the spirits that haunt you are immature souls, they get a kick out of scaring you. A negative spirit is a stubborn and controlling one. They want to stay in the earth plane, they are lost but it would be cruel just to kick them out. You need to gently move them on towards the light. Well, I thought, that's not going to work with a baddass like John Lee. Mulvina asked me about who I thought was haunting me. I had quite a choice but I ended up saying that it was Georgia, a little girl who had died young. Poor Georgia, she sure was lost. Mulvina said that it was not only about getting rid of ghosts. I needed to get my life straight at the same time, be practical, render unto Caesar as it said in the Bible. I asked what 'render unto Caesar' meant and she said that it was paying attention to worldly matters as well as tangling with spiritual affairs.

"Okay, shall we proceed?" asked Mulvina, but she looked puzzled as if she sensed I wasn't entirely leveling with her about everything. I nodded. She explained that it was important to name the spirits I wanted to leave. That was the best way to get rid of them. She went on to say that you need to help them on their way. All people need to know they are forgiven and loved. Mulvina said life never ends, the dead have folks that are waiting for them. I repeated it was just Georgia who was bugging me. I guess I was afraid of naming anyone else, especially Lee. Maybe I didn't want to send my family away, that would have been wrong. Besides I've not settled my business with them. I asked her to focus on Georgia. What the hell, I thought, one ghost at a time. I watched Mulvina's cute face in a haze of sage, chanting, inscribed Georgia's name on a candle and burning it. At the end, she walked me to the door saying that I was free now.

THE NIGHT VISITOR

The condo is empty and lonely without Georgia's lisping little voice and the sound of her feet in the corridors. I should have known that she wasn't the problem at all. Maybe I had to get rid of her as a sort of practice run. I'm not saying still that I do believe in all this psychic crud. Let's proceed as if it could be true. I realize now that that drawing that Mulvina made way back with that figure looming over me did not show Lee as a threatening spirit over me. No, I've been clear about him. He has always come face on to me. Mulvina was trying to draw someone else, a big man with a grey forelock to his hair. "Render unto Caesar" is what the medium was trying to say. I know now that meant Caesar or Kaiser, the chieftain. Maybe that's what Georgia had been warning me about.

The realization came to me in the early hours; something woke me, a sound. I could see in the bedroom a shape by my bed just to be made out in the ambient light. It was a figure, a male figure standing with one hand cupped under the chin as if contemplating me. I could also make out the edge of his eyeglasses gleaming. Then it was gone. I felt cold but the bedclothes were wringing wet and there was a lousy taste in my mouth. Weirdly, I wasn't scared and in the morning I was filled with an odd certainty. I guess it was a kind of "walk-in". My dreaming brain seems to have produced a sort of hyper-remembering. I wrote this next piece straight out as if by dictation like one of those psychic guys who write undiscovered Beethoven sonatas straight from the composer's invisible hand or like the poet James Merrill and his tea cup receiving messages from the dead. I'm letting Kaiser have a chance. I feel that's what he wants. It came to me after I had studied Doc Kaiser's papers. It could have happened like this. I'm not saying it did happen, but I felt Kaiser at my elbow correcting me, messing with his pipe, tapping its mouthpiece against his teeth with a warning click whenever I strayed too far.

KAISER'S STORY

"A telegram, chief," is all the cabbie said. It was signed by Vice Admiral Randall Jacobs, Chief of Naval Personnel. The message number that could be seen through the window of the envelope was circled, indicating a death message. Telegram deliverers were normally coached to look for this signal and to be cautious in handing the telegram over. Judgment was called for—as a minimum, one might at least tell the recipient that it was a death message. In this case, a cab driver hadn't noticed or didn't care. He just handed it to me and hurried away.

The telegram read:

The Secretary of State for War desires me to express his deep regret that your son Ph. M. 2/c Clyde Kaiser attach. USMC was killed in action on February 19th in the Pacific Theatre of Operations. Letter follows.

We had been apprehensive because Clyde's letters had stopped coming, but the blow was sudden and savage. Clyde, Clydie, our only son. We had poured everything into him. He'd turned out smart, lively, humorous and unafraid—everything that I was not. A child of his times, frank and optimistic and given to snappy phrases like, "killer diller" when he was happy and, "'T weren't me McGee," when denying some minor infraction. His favorite song was "Little Rock Get Away".

I had wanted Clyde to be a better doctor than I was; I had wanted him to find the happiness and success in love and work that had eluded me. But the war had hurried him down a different path, and he came home one night smelling of beer and told us he had enlisted in the navy. He resisted our arguments. He was nineteen that autumn of '43.

Clyde went through months of training. We had hoped that

the war would be finished and it seemed likely, The Nazis were about done and the Japs were being hammered. Surely it would not last much longer and he would be spared. After completing basic training in August 1944, he went to the Naval Hospital at Great Lakes to become a corpsman. He reported his new schedule to us:

> *A.M.*
> *05:00 - Get up and take the three S's (shave, shower, etc.)*
> *05:30 - Exercise*
> *06:30 - Chow*
> *08:00 - 1st class (Minor Surgery)*
> *09:00 - Nursing*
> *10:00 - Hygiene & Sanitation*
> *11:00 - Inspection*
> *11:30 - Chow*
>
> *P.M.*
> *12:30 - Classes - Materia Medica*
> *13:30 - Bandages*
> *14:30 - Anatomy & Physiology*
> *15:30 - Chemical Warfare (study of gases)*
> *16:30 - Chow*
> *17:00 - Work in barracks & wash*
> *19:00 - Hit the sack.*

I reasoned that this training would stand him in good stead after the war when he could pick up a medical career again. The sense of discipline and purpose would help him. But in reality Clyde was becoming a soldier and moving further away from any life we could imagine. That list of his daily activities showed he was being trained to be a combat medic. His training schedule frightened us in its uncompromising purpose. Clyde remained still boyish in his letters home. He went on to the

Marines at Camp Lejeune, in North Carolina, learning field treatment. He sent me a postcard from there which announced: 'I got 273 out of 340 for rifle practice—that's good Pa!' He said also that he was reading Zane Grey westerns. Then they moved him to Camp Pendleton where he was assigned his unit, the 4th Medical Battalion, 4th Marines. Well, surely it's some sort of hospital behind the lines, I thought. Then Clyde came back on leave. On the surface he was cheerful but he remained solitary and he didn't want to see his high school buddies. I found him lying in bed on his last day just staring at the wall. He had no sweetheart and never had a girl as far as we knew. That was also a sadness. In the last batch of letters there was no hint, nor premonition. In his final note to us he spoke of changing his war bond allocation. Clyde included some uncharacteristic folksy expressions in the letter and I then worked out that the first letters of the words spelled out 'Maui Hawaii'. Clyde was letting us know where he was. Then there was silence.

February 19th 1945 was the first day of the battle for some Godforsaken island of black volcanic sand they called Iwo Jima. So many other young men had died there. Later, there was that photo of those boys with the flag on the scarred peak of the mountain—Suribachi. It was on every billboard. We got our own flag also. It was handed to us by a marine lieutenant at the memorial service that they held two weeks later at First Baptist Church. It was a month after receiving the death notice telegram.

I still went back into Clyde's room every day, touching his gaudy high school pennants, the heaps of his civilian clothes, trying to sense him, aware of nothing, a withdrawal. I still called his name although I knew the answer was silence, a silence that grew out and through the house and down the street.

A little while later, I got a letter that explained more.

Dear Dr Kaiser,

This is the hardest letter I have ever written, because I don't know how to say what I want to. I would have written sooner but have been in the hospital and unable to correspond with anyone.

First of all - I was a friend of Clyde. We have had many long talks together - I liked him from the first night he came into our outfit and I got acquainted with him. We used to go topside - at night- when aboard our ship and talk. He told me such nice things about his family that I felt at the time, I should like very much to meet you. He told me one time "Bob - I have the best Dad in the world - because he treats me like I was a Pal" He told me many other things that I don't recall at the moment.

Clyde and I hit the beach at Iwo together - side by side - I have never seen a fellow with greater courage and more faith than that guy had. About five minutes after we landed, he was hit in the arm and we tried to get him to go back. He just grinned and said it was a scratch and that he had work to do. When I left him he was taking care of some fellows in a big bomb crater and I waved at him. He waved back. When I returned, he was no longer where I had left him and later I learned what had happened. A Japanese mortar shell landed near him and took the life of one of the finest fellows I have ever met. May I share your grief and sorrow. Please accept my most tender sympathy for your loss. I realize and you must also know that it's guys with guts like Clyde's had that is winning this war.

I hope I can meet you and talk with you sometime when I come to the States.

I am married - two boys - and live in San Angelo, Texas, but plan to visit you some day when possible. If you receive this letter, let me know. Write

> *me and I will answer any questions or be of any assistance I can.*
> *Sincerely yours,*
> *Bob Warrell Mills H A 1/C*

I never got to meet Bob Mills after the war. I'm not even sure that Mills survived. I kept on working through that terrible spring. Work has that purpose sometimes, to help with the heartbreak. Lina dealt with it in her own way but we had not been close for years now and what happened to Clyde drove us farther apart. I went back to my practice, and saw the usual dreary trail of cases: scarlet fever, gumboils, whooping cough, influenza, sprains and bleary eyes. I was lucky to have a practice in Bay View that was well paying and with fewer chronic diseases than the poor wards of the city. Patients built me up. I'd always enjoyed that bit of the job. Their obligation and their gratitude filled a void. Maybe all doctors seek that payback. Later an ambition to treat the psychic wounds of war veterans would grow but it had not occurred to me yet.

Mr Lee did not initially strike me as being that desirable a patient. Firstly, the dying were rarely grateful and could be resentful. There could be no alliance through which healing occurred. Lee was an elderly man, slowly fading out from heart failure. There was little for a doctor to do apart from the palliative. Lee had lived a full life span. At least he had had a chance to have a life. Not like Clyde and all those young boys being consumed.

I thought of diagnosis as being like a good navigator. You plotted the course and balanced all the factors. You then applied your knowledge to determine where you were and in what direction you wanted to go. You did not need to be a medical genius to determine that the future for the old man looked bleak. Not that he seemed much disconcerted about his fate. Lee was keen to talk, but had little interest in treatment. He seemed to know that he did not have long. He barely listened while I explained to him how to put the TNT pills under the tongue whenever he had chest pain. It was as if he had been waiting to see me on quite another matter.

I first came to Lee's house one early February evening after surgery. My patient had a grey complexion in the lamplight with spots of hectic red on the cheeks. He was bald, with prominent ears and eyes that were red-rimmed and puffy but still a startling vivid blue. His oversize oedematous feet stuck out the bottom of the bed sheets. Lee seemed to be watching me, sizing me up. He had a strange accent that was hard to understand, rural English, his attentive wife said, mixed with a touch of Wisconsin. They had a smart home in a good area. At first sight, there didn't seem much to stand out about him.

After he had submitted to my initial physical examination, Mr Lee had said, "So, not playing hokum then am I, eh, doctor?"

"Hokum, sir?" I queried.

"Ha, that's prison slang, means fakin' it, sick on the sly, doctor."

Prison, well that explained the old rib injuries—he was an old jail bird and had taken some knocks.

"No sir, you are indeed quite sick," I told him.

I found myself wondering just exactly what the genial old guy could have possibly done to go to jail. Mainly I concentrated on his symptoms. It did no good to be too involved in patients who would not be around for long. I told Lee he could not be cured but he could be alleviated. Lee laughed at that. "Never mind, doctor," he said, "Brag is a good dog but Holdfast is better."

Bit by bit, Mr Lee gradually got worse. I needed to reduce the fluid in order to lighten the load on the heart but I had to bear in mind that the patient was losing weight. The toxic organomercury I used as a diuretic weakened Lee's kidneys further. Lee couldn't maintain calorific intake due to the nausea brought about by renal failure and a vicious circle formed. His heart pumped weakly, the body filled with toxins, he could not eat to maintain his strength and all went downhill. Lee kept a sharp mind though, until the last week.

My patient began to grow more compelling and I found myself thinking about him in my off-duty hours. As if waking from a long sleep, Mr Lee was wanting to convey something important to me. Early on he'd said, "At Babbicam we had in the gardens the blue lily of the Nile, what Miss Keyse called 'agepannies'. After a hard winter the pots would be full of roots, all boiling about, but the tops would be quite dead and soft. That's like me, doctor. The body's shot and has run out of future though my innards keep on working regardless." I had no idea what he was talking about. Mrs Lee said, "He's not soft in the head, doctor. He's speaking about the past, in the old country. Things that were important to him." I had little interest in the past, or in horticulture for that matter. I saw Europe as a place where pointless conflicts started. Before the war I had supported Lindberg's isolationist pitch.

I did not need to say much to my patient. Mr Lee always seemed real pleased to see me. I tried to speak to him about his disease and the progress of treatment but he just laughed. He came out with a lot of odd expressions and had a strange story to tell. He wanted to confess something. I began to conceive of the idea of recording him using the new Webster I had recently bought. Lee said once as I was applying the stethoscope, "You have an honorable job, helping people. As for me, I have done naught for others. I've feared being a naught. Selfish I've been. I alles feared it would just go scat, doctor."

I said, "You have married, Mr Lee. You have a fine house. You have provided for your family and made your mark in the world." I was trying to comfort him.

"Oh, doc. You have no idea, how many I have trampled on to last so long."

Once when I asked him if he had eaten, Lee looked me in the eye and said, yes, his appetite had picked up, but his wife contradicted him, "No he hasn't, doctor, he has turned away everything I have made for him." When I gently chided him about the untruth later, Lee spread his blue and trembling hands out on the sheet,

"Well doc. What can I say? We are all innocent until others know better," he said. I took to seeing Lee during lunch visiting hour, giving him his shot of diuretic then sitting with him for a while. I was aware of those new cardiac operations just available in Boston which could save this patient or at least delay the inevitable but I did not really keep up with new trends. Cardiac treatment has moved on even the last five years—wars are generally good for medical advances. When I was taught cardiology at Northwestern it was all about seeing the heart as a pump. If the pump was damaged then it needed to be rested. The old man's pump had taken him a long way. The digoxin would make it work a bit better but not for long.

I also found myself reflecting on the ambitions I once had to be a great doctor, a specialist. But I seemed not to be really been good at anything in particular. I thought perhaps I should retrain, find a new interest. Hard to do anything with such sadness dogging me.

Lee kept watching me. He seemed keen to check on the progress of a kid from next door and kept telling his wife to give him some money. He once asked, "Have you got chillern, doctor? It's important, that there is another to carry a piece of you on."

"A son?" I answered absently, "Yes, I have a son... well," I corrected myself, "no, I had a son." Lee nodded. It was if he knew, and his vivid gaze softened as he said, "Ess, doctor. I also had a son...once."

Lee's wife started to bring me sandwiches and coffee as I sat up there with him. Sometimes, I could hear the radio downstairs. It was strangely soothing to hear the ordinary world going on. Quite often I could hear Mrs Lee singing along to a tune on the radio:

> *'There'll be joy and laughter and peace ever after,*
> *Tomorrow, when the world is free.*
> *There'll be blue birds over the white cliffs of Dover,*
> *Tomorrow, just you wait and see.'*

That corny song. Seemed like I had been hearing it for the whole damned war. Still, it somehow hit the spot. When there was no meaning to the cruelty of the world maybe a childish hopefulness was all that could be left. At some stage then I'd brought my new Webster with me and told Lee he could say something into it if he liked. I sat up with Lee for hours as he murmured into the machine. I might seem to be listening to my patient but mainly I was just replaying Clyde dying again in my mind, the bursting of that perfect skin, a Pacific noon chipping out the light, the breakers coming in perfect and straight.

I watched Lee as he poured out his strange stories. Even though the man was dying his body's cells still worked to renew themselves. Skin is with us for a fortnight before being replaced entirely, gut cells for a mere five days. Intercostal muscles linger for fifteen years and bone for ten. But the brain cells, they are with you from birth. They remain within the vaults, slowly hardening like a reef.

Lee seemed unsurprised to find me by his bedside. He'd wake and say, "You again, doc. Thought you were the old man."

"The old man?"

"I have seen him before, doctor," he said, "I have seen his face and he spoke to me."

"Who is he, Mr Lee. Who did you see?"

"He comes to collect you and hear what you have to say. I saw him before, you know, when Granfer died. I also saw him years ago when I thought it was finish for me. In that cellar room in Exeter."

I mentioned the conversations later to Lee's wife.

"I think he is becoming confused, Mrs Lee. It can happen, you know, with renal impairment."

She smiled.

"Oh no, doctor. He means it literally. You see, he still has beliefs. Not the same as yours and mine, village beliefs that he holds to, though he laughs about them to your face."

Another time Lee waking and saying, "I didn't do anything, doctor, did I?"

"Do anything?"

"Ess, in my sleep. All my life I've been afraid of doing something at night. I used to walk in my sleep as a lad and feared flailing about and causing hurt, all unknowing-like."

"There is no need to fear now," I said. "You have not harmed me."

"Ah well, that depends on what happens when we go finally."

"In what way, Mr Lee?"

"You wouldn't want me to be a-haunting you and a-dragging my chains around your bedroom of a night?"

"Now, we know that's not going to happen."

"It depends what happens when we go through that door. It might be like going to sleep or just winking out sudden, like a trapdoor going bang. Or you could be all restless, like a lost dog without a home. Addie now, she believes we get the chance to join the company of saints, if we are good enough or if we are forgiven. Heh! Heh! That rules me out then, doc, don't it?"

I smiled along with my patient although I was always thinking of those telegrams being sent out about Clyde with his brothers-in-arms, their faces like petals floating on the Pacific tides, all those young men.

I had been looking after Lee for two weeks in March and he seemed to be bumping along on a plateau. I'd begun to pay more attention to my patient's stories of the past, playing them over at night to myself on the Webster. There seemed to be real history in his tales. Then came a sudden change and there was no more recording. Lee became sweaty and fevered and he refused even the thinnest of soups that his wife could bring. His blood pressure dropped and he struggled for breath.

"I'm on fire today, doc but it's ice tomorrow, oh, ess," he muttered. "I wants to tell you something, doc. Something no one else knows. It wasn't just the Missis there that night in the Glen. The bloody 15th. Oh no, I've not told everything, not even on that there recorder thingummy of yourn. You see there was not only Miss Keyse that died there that night. There was that Fey girl also, Mary Ann, ess, mad as a loon she were."

I told him to go on. Lee spoke of how that night, after Miss Keyse was dead and after the fire had really got a hold, Mary Ann had come flittering up seemingly out of nowhere. He had encountered her on the narrow strip of garden between the sea and the Glen, that bit of lawn which kept being burned by the salt spray. Mary Ann was staring in through the shattered dining room windows at Miss Keyse's body all lit by the flames and she had begun to scream, "Murder! Murder!" Lee said he had to shut her up, Lizzie was upstairs pretending to fight the fire with the Necks but someone was bound to hear the mad witch. He ended up struggling with her and she clawed at his wounded arms. Lee said he pushed her away in desperation and she just sort of spun away and went right over the sea wall and into the waves. He hadn't meant to do it but maybe he was so desperate he didn't care what happened to her. He looked over the wall afterwards but could not see her. The wind was shrieking and the waves heaved and thundered. Nothing could live in there. She had been there and as real as a stone and then she was gone. Lee told me that he had imagined later that it was all a dream and sometimes he doubted it had even happened and his attention was overtaken anyway by all the other hellish carry-ons in the Glen. Lawyer Templer informed him later that Mary Ann had been found washed up way over in Portland. Everyone else thought she had drowned herself because her sister had died of gut fever and besides you had to remember she was out of her mind. But Lee always knew different.

Lee reached out and tried to hold my hand but I moved away. I didn't know what my patient would come out with next.

Lee moaned hoarsely that Mary Ann kept coming back to him at night, all sea-washed.

He suddenly became weaker after that and had to be helped to turn over in bed. I stopped the treatment. There didn't seem much point in going on. Lee suddenly tried to pull at my hand again. He said, "Can I ask you—don't let my wife bring a priest. Can't stand 'em. I know she wants to."

"Well, no, of course, your wishes should be met, but I'm not sure if I can promise," I replied.

"A man can promise and stand by it," said Lee with a glimmer of the steely man he once was. "Sometimes he stands by his word and by what he is chosen for, whether he likes it or not."

After that his thoughts became more muddled, and he began muttering something over and over again. I tried to catch it. I thought Lee was saying some nonsense words. They sounded like, "Gone a plowin' with your slippers on," repeated over and over. And once I thought I heard him say, "Lizzie! Where are you?" At one stage he sat up and said he'd seen his mother moving about his room.

Then came a stupor out of which he sometimes surfaced a little to toss around and pick at his blankets. I interpreted that as a sign of distress and gave him a shot of morphine. As I took the syringe out of its case and swabbed the needle I heard Lee mutter something. He said the word, "naphtha" quite clearly. It was the last thing that Lee said as far as I know. I knew that the morphine would soon see him off by depressing the breathing. I warned Lee's wife that he would not last long and arranged for Mrs Mulholland to sit up with him in the night. Lee fell into a sleep from which he didn't wake although he lasted into the next day, the 19th. Mrs Mulholland told me later that Mrs Lee had disobeyed her husband and called in a priest from the Anglican church on Juneau Avenue. He came and said the prayer for the dying. When he pronounced, "deliver your servant from all evil and set him free from every bond," Lee gave out a strange cry and raised his hands then he lapsed back into stillness. Apparently the priest said, "They always do that."

Next day I came to certificate the death. I entered the still room, lifted the sheet and introduced the stethoscope to listen to nothing. Lee was lying on one side, the purple hands melded together as if praying. One eye still open and going milky. Mrs Lee made me do a strange thing. She brought up a glass of beer and slice of cake as I was packing away my medical bag. I tried to refuse but she insisted and so I politely sipped a little of the beer and ate the cake there in the room next to the deathbed.

"My husband would have wanted it," was all she said about it. As I turned to go I noticed distinctly for the first time that the elm tree outside was covered in tiny green buds in the sparkling March sunshine.

"You must send me your bill at once, doctor," said Mrs Lee, "You have been very good to us." She also told me to fill in the death certificate properly. "Not James Lee, Doctor Kaiser. That's a name he went by. Let's use his real name—John Henry Lee. John 'Babbacombe' Lee actually."

I did not attend the funeral although I felt strangely drawn to go. Lee was buried at Forest Home Cemetery. He was a man who had two graves dug for him though he occupied only one.

His wife joined my list as a patient and in time I got to know her much better. She told me soon after, "Strange how still the house is with him gone. I was half-expecting objects to move and dance about like he described happening in his parent's house the night he was due for hanging." Old man Lee's strange story stayed on with me. I moved into a new career and became a professional healer of trauma. But I could not throw Lee off even if I wanted.

I arranged for Clyde's body to be brought back home. Family could elect for that from the war graves people. Clyde was buried in the Forest Home annex for servicemen not far from where John Lee and his daughter lay.

What's in a life? I say, 'to each his own', it's not a matter of holding all the best cards, you play your poor hand the best you can.

A Killing

It's weird how life gives you a jog to remind you what it's all about. I'm ghost-less for now. Kaiser seems to have faded away once I let him out the box. That news that Lee had offed Mary Ann Fey as well hardly surprised me.

It had been getting colder here. Snow dusting the bluffs above the Wisconsin River. It had been nearly a year since I first found that box of wire recorder spools in Cudahy. With the cold weather the birds were getting hungry and I liked to feed them. It's something Ma used to do and I feel I've got a connection with her when I do it in turn. The trouble was that a pesky squirrel had kept on turning up and stealing from the feeders. I think he came from Memorial Park across the way. Wherever he was from that glossy carefree robber was a darn nuisance. He hung there emptying the feeders while I raged and yelled. He gauged the limits to my interventions and bounced away at the last moment whenever I rushed outside. His flicking tail seemed to be giving me the bird. He really riled me when he pulled some of the feeders down completely. I thought if that went on then pretty soon I wouldn't be able feed the birds at all. I spent a good while hanging everything on thin wires to deter him but he leaped onto them and ransacked the feeders within the hour and that is when I began fixing on murder. I couldn't use the .45 of course so I went to Dicks Sporting Goods instead and selected a Black Widow catapult with quarter inch steel balls.

"Got a critter problem?" said the clerk.

"Sure have," I replied grimly. I held the clerk's gaze a good while. I don't usually manage that with folks.

My first shot went high. It put him on the alert though and he stood up on his hind legs to look around him like a prairie dog. My second shot just skimmed him and he got alarmed, shinned down to the ground and was beginning to hop away. My third shot caught him in the head with an audible smack and spun him around. I could see he was in trouble and jerking about on the ground. I approached. The beast had lost all coordination. I could see it staring up at me and the whole of its eye seemed to be flickering and winking in agonized spasms. I relented then and felt ashamed of my cruelty. I leaned forward and tried to pick up the animal. The squirrel convulsed and tried to crawl away as my shadow fell over it and I could see that the thing was mortally hurt so I hit it hard with a piece of old lumber I found lying in the yard. It still was quivering so I gave it two more whacks. All was quiet then. I looked around to see if my neighbors were watching then went inside. The mailman came with a parcel of more nootropics. He did not seem to notice my blood guilt,

"Cold day, snow we might have, huh?" he said. I had a shower, ate lunch, even walked with a little swagger. Killer, diller, that's me. I could see how murderers quickly become detached from what they have done. I put off getting rid of the corpse for a while though I could see the mute silky tail sticking out of the fall-bleached grasses. In the end I wrapped it in plastic and dumped it in the trash. It all became business- like then. There's nothing like a dose of death to wipe away solipsism. That night I typed in my Evernote journal, "only as creators can we destroy". Next day another squirrel was on the feeder. I eyed it coldly and muttered, "You next, buddy."

Adelina Gibb

That leaves Addie. Women seem always to be living with the crud their men leave behind. She stayed in that house at East Holt Avenue, Milwaukee for more than twenty years after Lee died. It is so incredible that she lived on through the Kennedy era to the cusp of the moon landings and Woodstock. Lee had hidden his traces well and no one seems to have come back from the past to confront her. She seems not to have wanted to return to England. She sent food parcels to her sister, Grace, during the war but most of her family thought of her as good as dead since disappearing with that criminal in 1910. It seems that Kaiser kept contact with her for a while and she certainly gave him some of Lee's documents. Addie never said anything publicly about her notorious "husband", but perhaps she never really did know much about him. I like to think that he just told her that he was asleep on that night in the Glen and woke to find himself covered in blood and with Lizzie calling him, that's all, he couldn't account for any more of it. Adelina spent her last few years at Elm Lodge Nursing Home in Wauwatosa. She was buried on January 20th 1969. She had actually died on January 9th but they had to wait for a thaw. The hymn, 'Stars in My Crown' was sung at the service at All Saints on Juneau at her request. The heirs of the Rosaleks had been keeping her gravestone all that time since Lee first bought it after Evelyn's death. Then all three were laid together at Forest Home.

SIN EATER

How can I put it? Semper idem, it's always the same thing. We know we are going to get popped one day. We humans are the walking dead. We scope it early but we don't fully realize it. We usually figure it out as kids unless we are special dumb. We understand in some way that we are historical beings and we begin to construct our lives as stories. If we are lucky we get to have beginnings, middles and ends. It doesn't worry us too much when we're young because we think the end is a long way off. Or we choose to forget about it. 'How quickly we forget', yeah, too right my Roman friend. We are transgressors against the laws of life. We have all gone to the afterlife and had a good look. Now, the sin eater is like the poet. He is more ready than most to go to the zone and live with the dead. I keep looking on YouTube at those Mount Everest climbers. They call it the death zone up there. Some come back and some don't. The top is littered with those dead climber dudes, preserved forever. They have a sort of immortality. I understand now the sin eater deals with guilt, that's the thing that fouls everything up. The dead walk because they have too much crap to deal with. I want to be a poet to inhabit the death zone and the life zone both. I want to free myself up and tell you what really happened to my parents but still I can't put it into words somehow. I have to find a way to eat my own sin. As a first step I went back to our old house on Summit Avenue in Waukesha. I left some flowers on the roadside there. I can't tell you about it yet. I don't know how to. I'm keeping the Colt though. That's insurance in case I flub this.

Three
A Travel Journal

November 10th

I've been looking at the 'amenity kit'. You get given it in a blue bag. There are some socks, an eye shade and strange plastic gizmo. It took me a while to work out that it was the handle for a dinky toothbrush. When did I last brush my teeth? My body clock has all gone to hell. Was it 12 hours ago that I left my little place? I could sense the accusing silence already building up there as I moved with my bag to the door. Kept saying to myself, "Crap knows why I'm doing this anyway." I thought maybe the journey would explain itself to me. All I had in my mind was that I wanted to confront John Lee in his own backyard and that meant going through a certain amount of turmoil. Feel the fear and do it anyway—they used to say that in my anxiety management classes. Well, I'm sure crapping myself now at thirty-two thousand feet. It's night over the Atlantic. I have a pounding headache. It could be excess adrenalin or maybe something to do with the three straight Bourbons I had before I got on this thing. Can't remember the last time I drank booze before that. There is the low thunder of the engines, the sound of curtains being switched back and forth by the cabin staff. The lights are low and no one else looks the slightest bit worried and certainly not as scared as I am. Couldn't eat my seared beef dinner. Keep thinking of those jets like the Pan Am 103, that TWA out of New York or those Malaysian planes just exploding and dropping us all to vortex down. Four minutes to flail in the air like that. Those poor fallers. The engines are changing tone again. Time for more Bacopa pills and some Gaba for good measure.

I've popped one of those suckers from its orange bottle. Maybe the anxiety neuron transmitters will damp down at last. I'm scanning the crews' faces. They don't look the least bit concerned.

Time? Been turning over my talisman in my fingers, it's strangely calming to feel a bit of Kaiser with me. Could see a few lights down there in the dark, a ship? A burning ship?

Everything I really knew slid away, the familiar streets, Memorial Park, Old Glory flying outside Scotties. I left the good old Ford Explorer in Lot D for extended stay at O'Hare. I was already worrying what I was going to eat over in Brit land and sweating over how much of the inheritance from Grandpa would be left. Before leaving the apartment I had got it into my head that I needed some sort of talisman to take with me and help protect me. Looked around. I couldn't see anything. There was that photo of Kimmie in a frame? No, better not. That might not be too lucky; nor Pa's eyeglasses—I want to keep away from spirits. I ended up putting the small wooden nameplate stamp in my pocket. Hope he'll stay with me. I'm fingering the worn wooden handle, the small, backward letters that spell—Howard Kaiser MD. Ut spiritu tuo protegas me. Those Romans believed in the Veteres, the ancients, the guiding ancestor spirits. I've got my parents, but maybe they are still angry at me. There's my dead fetus sib and Grandpa of course. Further off there is Miss Keyse and Mary Ann Fey—not Lee though. I'm pretty sure he's a bad spirit.

Passengers talking on their phones; wish I had someone to ring. Kimmie, what you doin' now? What if I rang you out of the blue? It would sure surprise you to see me here, it took everything you had to get me to go to Kmart with you.

Drowsing under the airline fleece blanket: dreamt that everything went pop in a cloud of orange dust. I'm falling into the blades of a spinning jet engine.

Plane altering course, engine pulse changed slightly. All alert again. Don't even ask how this idea all started. The idea of a pilgrimage, a confronting, a squaring.

Flat-toned English accents of the cabin crew, so different from the slow, rich voice of Lee I've listened to all these months.

Dude, I hope to crappin' crap we get safely down. I prayed like a bastard to the Lady of the Snows as we launched at forty five degrees against the moon. No terror like that moment the plane banked over Chicago, the lights glittering like death below. It all begins in the belly, the icy, chilling horror. I keep going to the restroom, dodging the 'occupied' signs. In the yellow light my sickly terrified face appears in the vague mirror, the belly goes through peristalsis whatever.

November 11th

Came in low over London, the city packed in squares and whorls around the slow scribble of the Thames. Gray light, our wings clipping the shreds of puffy cumulus. A dim wet cloistered light so unlike our bright Midwest skies. I was numb with tiredness. Let's just get this over.

Customs raked through the tablets in my carry bag. Guarana, Bacopa, Lion's Mane, Herbalife memory EPA. They particularly didn't like the Gaba. They took that away, customs man said it was not on his permitted list. Hell! How am I to manage to find my own equilibrium? Wonder how easy it is to get nootropics in the UK?

Green fields and old world trees. The birches I could recognize with their butter-yellow leaves. Fall not much advanced here. Everything packed in here real tight, houses each with neat squares of backyard made into gardens. Toy towns with roads jammed full of cars. Boxy new commercial buildings with corrugated walls. Forests of TV aerials.

Searched for my candy in vain at Waterloo Station. Asked the clerk if she had any Tootsie Roll or Peanut Butter M & Ms. She didn't know what they were. Strange accent, kind of Middle Eastern face. Thought of Lee being dragged through the crowds there, manacled in his snuff-brown uniform with Governor Cowtan, on his way to prison. Saw 'Exeter St. David's' on a big sign board. Now we were cookin'. Soon as I saw that sign I felt better, felt that something might open up for me.

I'm not sure how to speak to folks at the best of times and I don't know what to say at all to the Brits around me. No one seems to look at each other in the rail carriage. All they do is look at their phones or gaze out the window. There's a black bro' a few seats down who keeps pulling his braids round and sniffing at them. Maybe he is as alienated as I am. I feel proud of myself though to be here. Something changing.

Destination: Plymouth by way of Exeter. How Lee dug his trains. Their rattle was never far from him wherever he lived.

On the train to Torquay, and here it is at last—Lee's land. Small, sloping green fields edged about with trees and neat clumps of woodland. All is scarp and slope and deep green pasture, the rivers run red and full, and there's a misty light on the undulating fields. These are Lee's birth lands. The white stone houses tight to the ground make our stateside houses look temporary.

Torre Station in the drizzle is shabby and neglected-looking. I took a slow stopping train that let me off there. I waited for that one special train at Exeter.

"Not a lot come by Torre nowadays," said the cab driver. He told me the town council wanted to change the name of the station to "Torquay Central" to make it more popular. "But we won't hold with that," he said, "It will always be Torre to us."

Damn right, I thought, it will remain Torre for me also. So many of the characters in Lee's story made their entrances and exits there. Lee himself in a GWR uniform toiling in the baggage rooms, him with the Brownlow's silver under his arm, slinking off to Plymouth, the trial witnesses going to Exeter herded onto the train by Sergeant Knott in the rain and Lizzie lighting out, bound for her emigrant ship.

"Don't get many tourists in November," the cab man continued in his burry Devon accent. In St. Marychurch, he lowered his window and called out to an elderly buddy, "Alroit, boy!"

Jet lag, lolling, sick with wrenching change, half-amazed to find myself here. I read once that 'amazed' comes from the English country belief that you are 'mazed' or had a spell cast on you by a place or person. I guess that Babbacombe and Marychurch has cast such a maze on me. I seem oriented, I know my way like someone returning to a childhood place.

The cab dropped me on Babbacombe Downs and I booked in at the hotel. I am writing this in my cramped room mainly occupied by a double bed. The hotel is one of a Victorian row of houses, once great villas I reckon. I have bought many old postcards of Babbacombe off the Net and scanned them. I think my current hotel is one of the buildings in an old card I have from about 1890. I recognize the chimneys. You can see the bluffs dropping to the sea with the Cary Arms barely visible tucked down under the cliff and the mole that sticks out into the Bay. It was built while Lee was in jail. Lee must have walked by this building every day, on his way to drop the post into the box on Babbacombe Road. It has morphed into a weird hotel, done out with white rough plastered walls and wrought iron fittings in a faux-Spanish style. A sign on the door says it specializes in honeymoons. I guess that's why the huge bed and the giant wall mirror. It also advertises, "Pink weddings a specialty." It took me a while to realize that meant gay weddings. Gee, wonder what John Lee would have made of that? No sign of any other guest though, gay or not. A wind straight from the sea presses against the window.

I went out onto the cliff path as soon as I could. This was the moment I had been waiting for. All those hours listening to the recordings, the months of research trying to figure it all out. A deep recognition of place. Afternoon misty light, dog walkers limned against the skyline, that iron fence on the cliff edge looking the same as the one in the postcard. The view out to sea that had drawn so many, the sad insistent sound of waves on Oddicombe Beach far below, the dark bluffs dropping to the heaving back of the sea. A couple of freighters at anchor a mile or so out. Too hazy to see Portland. That view was one to die for. I thought of Miss Keyse looking out there for the last time on the 14th November, John Lee standing behind her, 130 years and more ago. The pleasure grounds at the cliff top, Victorian patterns overlaying more ancient tracks, all the houses packed in along the front, lop and slant and jammed together under a stone-colored sky, the streets folded and stratified like rock in this little town. Christmas lights swayed and clanked, strung up on the old gas lamp holders, and their constant creaking and clinking made it all more spooky.

I walked down Beach Road by the Babbacombe theatre built in 1920 on the site where the Prussian band once played for the Regatta, going down into Babba's gulch. Space is a central fact for man born in America, and here everything is folded, sunk, cramp and secret. I felt dropped into an ancient place. It was a troglodyte world below Babbacombe Cliff: ancient, goetic, groined and damp. You are wrapped in the smell of wood smoke, wet earth and leaf mold and the lichened breath of the sea licks over you. The wind bustled on the cliff edge above but down there it was still as death. I've spent time wandering over the old grounds of the Tamaracks and the Indian Mounds back home but I had a sense of something immeasurably older here. At Kent's Cavern round the headland they have found fossil human bones from half a million years ago.

The yipping gulls flickered around me. How close it all was to the sea. I'd imagined a long empty strand where all that murder drama was played out but no, it's a pocket-sized patch.

A few paces and I was going past the Cary Arms, now a thriving bar and hotel. I couldn't afford to stay there. It's so cool the joint was doing the same business as in the time of Gaskin, the ruthless entrepreneur. I was sure that flinty bounding wall was the same one as in Lee's day. My hand trailed over its rough barnacled texture and I leaned with my back to the three red rocks that Miss Keyse said looked like sounding whales. A dog barked across the way and the noise rolled out over the water. The bay was a natural echo chamber. I realized that everyone in Babbacombe must have heard the sound of Lizzie retching in the mornings and yeah, surely they'd heard Mary Ann's screaming.

Only someone young and dumb like me would think that truth from the past could be pried out of this place. Still, I told myself I'm going to give it a shot. I was going to sniff out that genius loci. A milky sea hissed on the shingle; I imagined Mary Ann carried away out still screaming under the water. Cormorants stitched in and out of the dimpling wavelets as I stood on the stained patch of concrete, now a civic car park, where the Glen once existed. I wondered stupidly if some fragments of Miss Keyse's DNA still lay lodged in the mossed roots and crevices of the beach cliff. Sea–rod fishermen paid me no mind, hunched there on the rocks, scanning the water as if also looking for ghosts. The waves glubbed and sighed under them. All of a sudden a man came past me with a dog. He said something like, "Arthurnoon, commin on rein." I nodded, not really sure what he'd said. I felt suddenly dead beat from all my travelling and far, far from home.

I came up the steep slopes through the thick woods where the house called the Vine once stood, past Victorian garden seats coiled about with weeds and ledged with fallen leaves. I thought these were the remains of the old pleasure grounds of the Glen and imagined Lee sullenly sweeping down those paths in his long coat. Near the top of the bluffs I disturbed two figures who had been embracing or maybe having sex on one of those old seats. I could just see that it was a man and a boy. Black shapes sprang apart and scooted away. They left something on the bench. It looked like a kid's blue T shirt. The smaller of the two must have been really quite young, a child maybe. They fled away through the trees. I had the sense of having stumbled on something ugly. I'd been looking for ghosts but maybe these dudes were the real guardians of the dripping trees. Maybe that fleeing man was one of Lee's true inheritors. After all, Lee used to maul at Liza Maile up there, taunting her to show him her bubs. Perhaps I was in cold hell, in thicket there, ya, selva oscura, lost in a wood.

I look for the truth but I keep missing it or it misses me. I keep thinking I'll know it when I see it surely? Rinsed by weariness, fear has ebbed a bit. What am I afraid of anyway? Is it failure? A failure to recognize. I lay for a while in the lousy, cold, English hotel room, and got under the covers. Mushroomy smell in the room, streaks of mold down the windows. I watched TV but it's like in a code I can't quite get, we're separated by a common language sure enough. A lengthy weather report. They spend a lot of time on the weather here. Lay down again, tried to draw my routines around me but there were none to grip onto. Real stupid to come here. To be an oblate means to accept new rules and commit to them whether you like them or not.

I slept and dreamt of my Ford Escape SUV, dreamt of flying like a bat down a narrowing tunnel or journeying somewhere by night on a strange route. Fine dry Wisconsin snow ticking on the windshield, then the road blurring out, tires churning in a rut, headlights darkening and no light behind.

Woke late, maybe nine at night. A storm had come up, strings of lights clashed and jerked in the forecourt outside and the palms vibrated their leaves in the sea wind. I went out. Lights were visible out along the coast, must have been Teignmouth and Exmouth. The moon laid a milky path on the black sea for a moment then clouds dragged across it. I walked in the rain through St Marychurch, past the Babbacombe Corinthians sailing club, along by the marble obelisk to Doctor Chilcote and then past the Town Hall where the Lee inquest was held. The place was now remodeled to shop units and a real estate office. I seemed to find my way easily, the town fell open to me like a book. Dinky windows, thick walls, close alley ways and St Mary's flat-toned bell sounding out the hours. I thought, I must go and see Miss Keyse's grave tomorrow. Felt really hungry and the hotel didn't do food at night, so I looked for a convenience store. I might have known the dark narrow streets but I couldn't find anything to eat there. I was looking for da Pig, ya know, a

Piggly Wiggly or something. Kept going round the same blocks and seeing the same guy in a hooded jacket drinking from a beer can in a dark alcove of a shop doorway. Each time I came past he gave me the same dead-eye hostile look.

In the end I went into the Crown and Sceptre pub. Kind of a Dickens scene in there with low benches and a log fire trickling smoke. The walls were festooned with strange objects: bed pans, old record sleeves, dolls with cracked faces, antique urinal bottles. There was definitely a toilet theme going on. Even had items of clothing pinned up there. Maybe stuff the customers had left over the years? A few locals came and went. They greeted each other with a muttered, "'Ow you been?" Their blunt-faced dogs were strapped up in leather harnesses, and fixed me with their mean little eyes as they crouched under the tables. I asked one owner what sort of dog he had. He said it was "a staffie". Her name was Daisy, he said. Huh, Lady the brach, might sit by the fire and stink, I thought. Don't suppose they know their Shakespeare here nor Latin neither. Still, I guess that truth's a dog who must to kennel, he must be whipped out in any man's language.

I sat and listened to the murmurous Devon voices. Each table had a big dome of melted candle wax, supersize lumpy candles formed out of generations of smaller candles melting and molding one on top of the other. Bit like this country. Generation after generation stacking down and staying put. A shrouded people. Their dogs might stare but none of their masters seemed to look at me directly—they all were watching, I guess. I wondered if Lee had ever come into the Crown and Sceptre. If he had it was only to do deals, he was no drinking man. Maybe to meet Cornelius. I'm sure that jerk Cornelius would have known the place.

I drank cider. It was thin and acid and looked like piss. I felt woozy after one glass and tried to order some food. There was a low rumble of laughter from the drinkers. The barmaid said, "No, we don't do none. Try the chippie, my lover. Hanbury's is what you want. On Princes Street."

First night at Babbacombe. Feel sick and floaty. Cider and jet lag. Smell of fat on my fingers from the food. Holding Kaiser's name stamp, protegas me.

November 12th

Woke after a fitful sleep, and felt better. I sat at my window with crappy powdered coffee made from the kettle in my room. Outside the wind jigged the strings of festive lights, crows patrolled the Babbacombe Down. The cliffs here are a startling red and the sea a deep dark blue.

I began to feel like making a poem, each line beginning with 'because'. How would it start?

Because pain, because of a peeled mind,
Because feeding, because sick sheets,
Because life folds down to a circle.

The piece had a way to go, I thought maybe I'd call it 'Looking for the Muzot Tower'. It was good to be forming poetry again; the words had been shaken loose by travelling. Perhaps I'll send it to Del Sol Review when it's done. Poetry has helped me, the doctors pressed me down with diagnoses when I was a kid, autistic spectrum, conduct disorder, developmental disorder, social phobia. Poetry saved on all that Advil and Zoloft they wanted to give me. Poetry and the study of Latin have given me a way to survive. I have lived through books.

Not that the critics have liked me much. They've spoken of an uneasy blend of the toxic and the beautiful in my work. One said of me "The poet is squatting in the shallow water, searching for something to give us, a breadcrumb trail out of that hostile desert back to the life that's still waiting for us on the other side." That's been my only good review.

I walked down into Torquay, the same track Lee used to take

going to see Kate Farmer at Ellacombe. My breathing is easy in this town, I'm getting the feel of it. I've started nodding to the passers-by and saying, "Marnin', marnin.'"

Man, I'm going to do a lot of walking before I'm done here, I'm not confident on using the buses yet. There are so many cats, big fat ones that seem to sit at each front gate, guarding their territory. I went past the green and cream bulk of the Palace Hotel. I thought it must have originally been the mansion they called 'Bishopstowe'. There was a bronze plaque by the hotel entrance and I stopped to read it. Yep, I was right:

Bishopstowe, a great house in the Italianate manner built in 1841.

Sampson Hanbury lived there in'84, a rich dude, Miss Keyse's buddy and foreman of the inquest jury a.k.a. lynch mob. He made real sure the hanging rope fitted round Lee's neck.

I was looking for Torre Abbey, the oldest building in Torquay, a medieval monastery originally but now a museum. Lee had little reason to go there in his day but I had seen on the online catalogues that they held a piece of art work by Emma Ann Whitehead Keyse called "A View from my Window". It couldn't be anyone else, could it? I wonder if someone had snapped up the piece in that beachside auction of the Glen's fittings held in the year after the crime. I was hoping that it would give me a further clue to her personality. I got a bit lost and asked the way of a big guy dressed entirely in motorcycle leathers. His bald head was circled by a striped necktie, worn like a headband, pirate-fashion. I must have been dumb to think of speaking to a nutcase like that but he courteously pointed out the way. An oblate does not choose his helpers, they find him.

Torre Abbey was an impressive place, guarded by towering columns of yew. There was that name 'torre' again. It seemed to haunt me. I'd looked it up online. It meant 'tower; as in the Spanish 'Torre de Babylon' or Tour de Muzot for that matter. It was also a Celtic loan word meaning a rocky outcrop. The place looked closed, there was only a gardener raking leaves, and a sign said that major repairs were taking place. I came to a big wooden door like the castle door in my old computer game—King's Quest. I kept thinking of those lines: "Childe Roland to the dark tower came". A cleaner appeared and told me the museum was being restored and everything was shut. I said I'd come all the way from the States to see something, was there anyone in charge to whom I could speak? Strange how being abroad made me more confident.

I waited a long time. The cleaner said there was someone working in the art gallery but everyone else was gone. I first heard her feet clopping down the flagged stairs of a tower, coming closer and closer. Then she was standing in front of me, a pale face in the shadowed hall. She held her head slightly cocked to one side. I stuttered out some bullshit about coming from the University of Wisconsin, doing some research. I even waved my old student card. She listened, her green eyes seemed amused. She said the staff were not there, she was a visiting archivist assessing and cataloguing the art collection, and asked what piece of art I was interested in. She was quite tall, nearly my height; her voice was husky yet smooth. God knows why she gave time to a stuttering bum like me. I felt I could look into her eyes. She told me she did not immediately recall the Keyse piece but there were a lot of pictures in the collection. Nor had she heard of the Babbacombe murder. She moved to the reception desk with a graceful swaying motion and asked me to write down my name and number. She said she'd let me know although she had no authority over the collection.

My hair is thinning, a definite widow's peak is emerging. I've been looking at myself in the mirror of my moldy bathroom. A fluorescent tube runs across the top of the mirror, it blinks like an unsteady heartbeat. My older face in future years comes swimming out to me like some terrible fish. You've only got ten more years left, buddy; then you'll be real ugly. I miss the sacraments of a lover.

Cool girl today. Woman, I should say. There was something

mature about her although she was younger than me, I think. I felt instantly at home talking to her. She made a face when I spoke of the Babbacombe murder, she obviously cares nothing for killing—maybe she's a Buddhist or something. She told me her name was Hannah. I was flustered so I missed when she told me her other name. Too busy staring at her. Dumbass! What is my malfucktion?

Big coaches arrive outside of the hotels along the front, unloading old timers. Some wear festive gear, paper hats, sprigs of foliage. I wandered round Babbacombe and Marychurch, poked about at All Saints Church which Miss Keyse so despised. Its brash spire still looks like an interloper over the rooftops. Nearby was Compton House where the half-sister lived. Plane trees formed a palisade around it, all pruned down to knob-ended stumps. High stone walls surrounded the gardens there. I thought of John Lee running along those streets looking for somewhere to throw his club stick. I looked at Chilcote's memorial in daylight: in affectionate remembrance of a noble and unselfish life. You couldn't say that about Lee, could ya? Up Fore Street to St Mary's Church. Miss Keyse used to wander the beach at night listening for its midnight chimes. I searched all over the place. It took a long time to find. I eventually discovered some fragments of the memorial laid in concrete by a path.

I had been looking for a big tomb as described by the newspapers of the day but then I remembered reading about how on 30th May 1943 a German FW190 fighter bomber came in just above sea level over Lyme Bay and strafed Babbacombe Down. It flew so low that empty bullet casings fell on the ornamental gardens outside where my hotel now stands. The plane then gained height a little and released two bombs. They landed right on St Mary's the Virgin church, blowing the place apart and killing twenty one children and three teachers who were attending afternoon Sunday school inside. They repaired the church so you couldn't see the damage but maybe Miss Keyse's tomb got shattered on that day also and that's why it's in pieces and laid in the grass.

Spent the early afternoon in Torquay library archive in the John Pike rooms. They even produce a leaflet on the local hero. There he is on the front cover, a circular portrait from about 1910 in his derby hat, his pale eyes glimmering under the brim. There's that gardenia again. I don't want to see that feral face no more once I'm done here. I flipped through more old newspapers. I felt bushed and took some guarana in the library restroom. Some old guys in flat caps were eyeing me. Look out! Long-haired pill popper in the john! Then I got a text from Hannah. "Hey, I've found your picture. Give me a call. Hannah."

We met at the Cat's Whiskers, a coffee joint in Torre. She'd directed me there, so I asked her if she liked cats in particular. She said, no, she had no pets or anything. People are hard enough to deal with, she said and gave me a nice smile. Irony, that's a Brit thing right? I get it but I have to work hard at it. Just like I have to work hard at being normal. It's a fictive process and takes effort like everything else I do. I had a coffee but she went for roui bush, something exotic. It smelt like old socks. She told me she was an independent expert, she catalogued collections and assessed the condition of items. I asked if she usually met people in coffee shops. She said no. She thought I looked desperate but harmless and anyway the museum was closed. She had such a calm presence and a husky deep voice. Her coppery-red hair was cut short and spiky. Un coup de foudre. That's the expression? Blam! I felt I could live forever in her green eyes. She was holding a cardboard tube and drew something out of it. She unrolled the paper with those cute fingers, pale fingers like grapes.

"Here's a copy," she said.

It looked as if it was taken from a sketch book. I pointed out how Miss Keyse spelled Babbacombe in the old Devon manner with an 'i' instead of an 'a'. How crowded with boats the bay was in her day. It was dated '76, so she must have been sixty years old when she made it, yet the whole thing seemed somehow immature as if done by a much younger person. The view was looking north from the Glen towards the Oddicombe cliffs and Watcombe and Shaldon beyond though actually no window looked that way from the Glen. The place was tucked so far in you could not possibly see that view from Miss Keyse's window. The thing was a fantasy. Those three-masted luggers also would never be so close inshore, it's too shallow in the Bay and the Babbacombe seiners would have probably driven them off. At the top of the drawing it showed the thatch of the Glen peeking into the frame. That stuff would burn like hell on the night of the murder. I wondered if the glass panes in those iron-framed windows looked the same as the ones downstairs that Lee thrust his hands through. Sergeant Knott detached some of them to exhibit in the trial. I wondered aloud what other drawings by Miss Keyse survived. Maybe she sketched Lee at some time? The picture in front of us was drawn about two years before Lee came to the Glen, before the half-savage boy met the fantasist.

"Wow, you really know your subject," said Hannah. I told her I'd lived with the Babbacombe case for a year but wanted to be free of it now.

We got on so well. There was a spontaneous understanding between us. It felt right. She came from London and was staying for a week like me. We compared shitty rooms but I wasn't paying full attention. Ovid's slender arrows had entered me. I kept asking her stuff.—I've learned to ask questions of people, it makes me seem less strange. Most of my interactions are some kind of performance.

I asked her about those old folks I had seen getting in and out of coaches on the sea front hotels. She told me they must be 'turkey and tinsel' trips." She explained how they were a pre-Christmas experience for those who wanted to replay the festive season several times over. Jeez, I thought that was sad, to want to have a Christmas under your own terms because no one would give it to you the way you want. I said I didn't much like

Thanksgiving or Christmas. I said I hated anything formulaic but Hannah guessed the real reason. She said holiday times were lonely times for some folks. She looked as if she understood loneliness. I was going to tell her that loneliness in Latin was 'infrequentia'. An unfrequented place, that's my inner world. But I decided not to. It might scare her for me to go on about Latin. It seems like we spoke a long time, though it was only for the span of a coffee. She said she had to go, and I said kinda casual that as we were both on the loose she might like dinner tomorrow night? She looked surprised and said okay. Don't know why I said tomorrow rather than tonight. Guess I need to prepare.

November 13th

Today I'm on the brink. Meeting Hannah makes me think that I'm really going to get a break. I felt so pent up I couldn't write last night. I can't wait all day 'til I see Hannah. Miraculosa die, the sharks have truly padlocked their jaws.

I wandered around this morning, and went to the Torquay Museum. Walked round the exhibits, dull Neolithic pots, whole loads of fossils, and rooms where you dress up as a Tudor peasant. Nothing about Lee. There was a tourist shop. Back home we'd say it was for 'tourons'—a combination of tourist and moron. A little 'Scansin joke. The shop sold chinaware, plastic swords and potpourri sachets of "Elizabethan" fragrances. 'Grockle-bait', John Lee would have called it. Just because I'm a Yank doesn't mean I don't know shit about the past. I thought of all those lost objects I'd really like to see in a John Lee museum: Miss Keyse's diary, the Lee family photographs buried with his father, the note Lee gave to Pitkin before his execution, that presentation copy of 'The Bear Hunters of the Rocky Mountains'.

I asked the guy on the cash till about John Lee. He said that everyone knows about him but you'll find no mention in the museum. He said that when Lee was let out of prison he was strolling on Torquay sea front and he tipped his hat to a man who seemed a bit familiar. That man was James Berry, the hangman who had tried to kill him. They both looked surprised to see each other but they shook hands. I said that I hadn't heard that one. The clerk shrugged and said that he couldn't guarantee that it was true. Later, I walked to Lower Warberry by where the Brownlows had lived, and found a niche in the sandstone wall where the water trough once stood—the one where Lee's hammer had lain hidden all that time. It's as if I'm always looking at a space where things used to be. Fallaces sunt rerum species: it's the nature of things to be deceptive.

I've been staring in the mirror again and know I look a mess. I asked a guy at the hotel what the swankiest restaurant in Torquay was. He said 'The Passage to India' on Torwood Street.

I decided to get serious on my sartorial ass. After all, as Propertius noted, every lover wages war. I bought a suit at a place on Cary Promenade after looking at my balance at the ATM. The salesman told me it was a wool mix and was made in the most fashionable narrow cut. It sure was expensive. I could still wear it with my Redwing boots, it would be a funky combination. Next, I went to the "Wild Hair" salon next door. The girl asked, how did I want it cut?

"Fashionable," I replied.

She suggested a short crop with a bit of a 'jagged peak', as she called it. I agreed. Maybe a new cut wouldn't show up my receding hair line so much. She was a heavy girl with a peachy complexion, a bit like Kate Farmer must have looked. I watched her in the mirror as great clumps of my hair fell to her scissors. While I had been waiting my turn I had read in the local Herald Express paper about a Torquay man, Kieran Mogridge, 21, who had been charged with the stabbing and attempted murder of a man. The accused had been remanded to appear at Exeter Crown Court. There you go. Still the same deal going down in this little town. Everything changes, nothing perishes, according to Ovid.

"Bootiful," said my lady barber when I tipped her a ridiculous amount.

Hannah looked shocked when we met.

"Is that you?" She said, "I can hardly recognize you."

"Even a poet needs to get cleaned up once in a while," I said.

"Poet?" she said. She looked worried. I could see she was regretting agreeing to meet me. I tried to pull back from being too much of a jerk and things got better after that shaky start. I got her to explain all those dishes to me. The Brits are crazy about curry. I can't remember any of the courses that she told me about except 'bhindi', that's 'lady's fingers'. It has a silent 'h' apparently. I said we called it 'okra'. It's what trailer trash ate. I told her the only food things we knew about in Wisconsin were types of cheese and beer. We knew a lot about those. I didn't much like the curry. The spices made my head feel itchy—or maybe that was the razor cut. Everything chilled between us; I said I hoped I hadn't scared her.

"Thought you might be a bit batty," she said as the evening progressed.

"What's that?"

"A bit crazy," she said.

"Uh, crazy—I might be, but batty, definitely not," I replied and she laughed. She laughed a lot at my dumb jokes. I took that as a good sign. She asked me if I was writing poems in Torquay. No, it's a prose trip, I said. I told her I was looking for the truth about a killer, and described John Lee and my discovery of the wire recorder. She thought it must be great to be writing and researching. On the contrary, I said. It was hard work, a lot of grind. In fact it was often torture, like putting sand in your eyes and grinding it in slow. She said I must be a patient sort of guy.

"Yeah," I said, "Flash is a good dog but Holdfast is better."

Hannah didn't much like dwelling on crime, she preferred gentler things. I was happy to agree with anything she said. I tossed back more and more wine. I had told the waiter to order the best. I think I got louder and more animated, I guess it didn't mix too good with all that full strength guarana. I told Hannah about how I had tried to save a boy from drowning. How I gave him CPR but it was too late.

"How awful," she said. I enjoyed stimulating her compassion. I wanted her to feel something about me and indeed we did seem to have a connection. I asked her birth date and found she was a Gemini. Mutable is what they say about them, quicksilver and charming. She said she thought of herself as being a bit dull. I told her I was a Sagittarian, a teacher and explorer. I said how we got on well with Geminis. Fire and Air combined. She said she found it hard believe in astrology.

"It's not necessary for you to believe," I said, "It works out true whether you believe or not."

I paid the check. It seemed really cheap but I got in a tangle about how much it was in dollars. For me, words and languages and it's all gravy, but math—no. I waved my American Express card although I was not sure if there was anything left in the account.

I felt giddy during the cab ride. Was this being in love? I didn't really need to bluff and lie so much with Hannah. She had been put there to save me, that's what I was thinking. I told Hannah I was so grateful for her dragging my ass out of solipsism. I began to murmur, "Hannah, would you…?" and tried to kiss her, but she put her hand to my cheek in a tender stalling gesture. She told me she was sorry but she should have said before: she lived with someone in Kennington. Where the crap was Kennington? She said she lived with a woman. Did I understand? I flinched and felt like I couldn't breathe for a while. We rode in silence. Hannah's hotel was near Ellacombe. She held my hand in the cab and asked me to walk her to her hotel door, and slipped her arm through mine in a consoling gesture. Her hotel glowed with shimmering blue festive lights. She drew me to her and embraced me.

"Friends?" she said.

What a frickin' asshole I have been but she was sweet to me. I somehow couldn't feel angry with her. I paid off the cab with the last of my money and walked home through the spooky streets, my feet echoing like I was in a cave. "Let us live, Lesbia, let us love". It was laughable really to be passing along those English indifferent streets clenched up in my tight new suit. My head is so cold and literal. I'm always trying to dig up stones with a pry bar but the world is much too fluid for that. I so much fear not being real, not being lovable. It all seems like a sort of test. I thought I could hear Lee laughing.

November 14th

Dawn over Portland, sea mist spilling up over the bluffs at Babbacombe. What are those lines from Peter Abelard, the castrated lover?

I got up and looked into a mocking bathroom mirror: stubble-headed as a penitent. Oh yeah, I remember them now, est mihi pallo in ore, my face is pale from love's disappointment. How was I expected to feel? I did feel something. Maybe that was the point of it. I should thank her for that. I still felt stupidly tender about her. My love had been like a cactus flower that had bloomed for one night only.

The tide was out. I walked across the shingle towards the pier that Leveson Harcourt built in 1889. Prisoner L150 Lee might have quarried those Portland blocks. Harcourt was kin to Home Secretary Harcourt who had commuted Lee's death sentence. The mist cleared to reveal a greasy swell far out. Cormorants stood sentry on Harcourt's pier. I saluted the webcam on the café roof that I had spied through all that year; now I in turn have become a stuttering image for unknown eyes. My feet trod down on squeaking pebbles, crackling wrack and shells. I have certainly fished by obstinate isles. So strange for my Redwing boots to stamp hollows down on real Babbacombe Beach. Wave-smoothed brick, chips of green glass, whisps of bast: I picked up handfuls of it. Fragments of the Glen in there, I reckoned. I'm set on building up a torre with those fragments, exegi monumentum. Yep, I will build me a monument. I have a male brain. I can accept it now, its asperities drum at my temples. It's not much good at love but dandy for facticity.

You realize how eccentric Miss Keyse must have been when you feel the closeness of the sea there. She must have been crazy to live in the cottage on the beach and not in the more spacious Vine up the hill. All that is left of the life of the Glen are remnant buttresses and pediments. You can only see indentations behind the devouring ivy, shadows of buildings that once were there.

I've been studying another one I've saved. It's my favorite old postcard of the bay from John Lee's day. The picture must have been taken from the path leading up to Walls Hill. It's more treed up there nowadays. There is no Harcourt pier to disfigure the curve of the bay. You can see the red cliffs of Oddicombe to the right. The outcropping Blackball Rocks lurk in the middle. There is no sign of Babbacombe Down or St Marychurch behind the trees on the rim of the bluffs. You can see the pale lozenge shapes of fishermen's shacks to the left of the Blackball Rocks. The Cary Arms roof is the main focus of the picture. It is still thatched. That thatch burned in 1906 to be replaced by the red tiles it now carries. At the apex of the crescent of shingly beach you can see two buildings belonging to the most northerly parts of the Glen, the Music Room and the Boat House, where Miss Keyse's body was laid out immediately after the fire. The Glen itself is invisible under the trees. It is a space, an elision in this photograph then and as it is now. You could put a sign there, hic iacet aenigma, here lies an enigma.

There was a weird incident near to the Blackball Rocks this afternoon. I came across a pack of guys chasing two girls. There were five of them, young but strong-looking, their faces barely visible from the hooded jackets they all wore. They were throwing stones and shouting stuff at the girls. I'm sure I heard one yell that they were gonna rape them. They kept on throwing wood and stones and one of them pushed the girl's dog into the sea with his boot. The dog yelped and swam in circles. The girls looked scared. They didn't see me at first. I came out the shadowy woods and screamed at the boys to get lost. They looked surprised and seemed even more freaked when I came up close to them.

"Fuck off, mate," said one of the larger guys.

"Yeah, why don't you fuck off?" said one girl. She didn't look too pleased at being rescued. Maybe I'd misunderstood. Pretty soon all of them had turned on me. Those kids thought they were hanging tough but compared to the gangstas of South Milwaukee they were small fry. I picked up a piece of driftwood.

"Ya want some?" I slapped my leg with the wood. I pointed at them. "Which one first? You? You?"

Pretty soon they beat a retreat, pausing only to shout at me from a safe distance. I had no idea what they were saying and didn't care. They hadn't had a chance. I had a feral Lee on my side. He'd taught me a bit. Wish I had him with me when I had those bullies at High School, that Cody Breadgood with tattoos up his neck and the fattass Lanette Blair. They were so shitty to me. It felt good to run the kids off my beach. Yeah, run, you jerkass shitbirds. Jesus, the Brits sure do a line on skeazy deadbeats. Maybe my problem has been fear all along. Hitting Pa like that must have choked off my confidence.

Had to walk a while to ease the adrenaline rush—I had no high strength Gaba to calm me thanks to Her Majesty's Customs & Excise. I stamped around on the groaning shingle reciting exegi monumentum, the one great part of me that will never die. There have been consequences to my pilgrimage here but I've not quite figured out all their ramifications. For one thing it came to me that Lee had internalized his guilt because he felt responsible. Maybe he had so many bad thoughts he imagined they had leaked out into the actual world. "I will make an end of one," he had raged. What had mattered about his story was his transfiguration.

Tonight Hannah rang me, checking I was okay. We talked like old friends. She sent me some texts which she signed with an 'x'. There are many kinds of love. We have agreed to meet tomorrow and drive around some John Lee sites.

I've come to understand something real important. I've been going in circles looking for the truth but maybe there is more power and beauty in a secret that is well kept. Everyone makes a big deal of ventilating their thoughts these days but I think Melville wrote about a different way in his Notebooks. Something about Captain Pollard of Nantucket and his terrible secret. I would check but I've not got my old books with me and this is something the online world has not noticed.

That's it, I've now remembered. Melville wrote: "To live with a secret may have more power than to bask in the full light of the truth." That's what Lee did, he learned to swallow down his secret and live with it. An unknown heroic act by which he earned his crown of stars.

November 15th

I stood outside Torquay Library waiting for Hannah to pick me up as the Torbay citizens went about their Saturday morning business. They were a strange sight in the muddy light. The old people had guarded faces, they slunk along without looking right nor left, especially avoiding a gaggle of young shitbillies hanging outside Riley's snooker hall. Quite a few old timers rode on scooters, they were everywhere here. In fact, every third person looked disabled in some way. The Brits have given up on the gentleman thing. Their newspapers and TV seem now to celebrate swaggering scuzzball soccer players, and the well-dressed Englishman has been replaced by a crumple-faced, ill-dressed inheritor. My old postcards show the streets of Torquay full of snappy dudes in boaters and the women in crinolines and bonnets but now they are filled with a sullen, bundled, shabby people with guarded unhopeful faces. Only the black folks here seemed to walk about with an animated stride and bustling confidence. Maybe they are on the up. The English have retreated to their last redoubts. I saw a sort of fear in their eyes. It seems like they didn't know who their neighbors were any more.

I had most connection with the street bums selling magazines and such. We had loneliness in common. I felt they were my homies and I gave them money, solid English coins like bullets. I tried out my John Lee slang on one of them. I said, "How be you nackin' vor?" He stared at me as if I was crazy then replied "Alright, mate. What's on?"

Hannah told me to stop talking to guys on the street. I might get into trouble, she said. I didn't tell her about the beach incident.

Her car was real small, we had to move the seats about to fit me in. She found it funny. Her sharp white teeth showed as she laughed. She's so beautiful, my heart still does a back flip to see her.

First off, we drove on the coast to Teignmouth to look for Templer. He had died in that asylum in Surrey but they shipped him back home for burial. We wandered up and down the big burying ground on a hill above the town but he eluded us. In the end we admitted defeat. He was always sneaky that Templer— syphilis-wracked buddy to Miss Keyse. Whatever was he up to when he volunteered to defend Lee? I guess maybe he decided to do such a spectacularly poor job of it so that Lee was bound to get hung.

"Well, that was a good start," said Hannah as we left Teignmouth. Irony again right? We went on towards Exeter by way of the coast, through folded West Country hills with their small packets of fields. Red trails of mud leaked across the twisty wet roads.

We stopped in Dawlish for lunch. The rail line there ran on

buttresses right along the sea front. I thought of Lizzie Harris looking out the train window there on the way up to the Exeter hearings to condemn her brother. A high tide slopped and swirled at the sea defenses as we walked past the shuttered amusement parlors by the front. The eatery had prints of foxhunting scenes and they played sounds of bird calls and cow bells in the rest rooms. I guess the English seem always to be looking for a vanished rural past.

I saw a stagshorn sumach growing in a front yard. I sure was far from home and my old comforting routines. I seem to have lost my fixity these last few days and I've only now noticed that my essential tremor has calmed down a lot.

As we travelled, I entertained a fantasy of me living in Torquay. Maybe teaching in writing school and living in a threesome with Hannah and her friend. They could be my own Gertrude Stein and Alice B. Toklas. Only a lot better looking. Creative writing, huh? I read a handbook once, 'A Guide to Narrative Craft', I think it was, it said the business of writing was 'the study of humanity'. For me that is not enough. In our post-human times we should write about humanity confronted by the relentless facticity of the world. Lachrymae sunt rerum, the tearfulness of things is the bitter truth of men. Maybe I should quit literature altogether, live on a torre, be a gardener in Torre Abbey, yeah! Or fish for lobster in the murky waters off Babbacombe Bay.

We poked around Exeter Rougement Castle. Hannah seemed interested in everything although I got the impression she humored me some of the time. Sometimes she gently corrected my misperceptions of her country. Once or twice, she laughed outright. Especially when I asked if a cool white dog we saw was some kind of special English hunting dog.

"No, it's just a poodle," she said. She seemed to find that real funny though she tried to hide it.

Rougement was where Lee faced his death sentence. The cells that he once occupied in court have become chi-chi apartments and the court rooms were being ripped out for a shopping mall. We could see Exeter Prison a half mile below, just visible through a screen of leafless sycamores. That at least was still being used for its original purpose. I told Hannah about how the last witch of England was hung off those Rougemont battlements in 1680 something. Thereabouts anyway. The luckless Alice Molland. There was to be no fuck-up with her hanging.

We came looping back to Torquay by the back roads, stopping at Bishopsteington. The village sits on a rise overlooking the wide curving estuary of the Teign. I had a memory that the Fey sisters hailed from there, and I had a hunch we'd find them in the burying ground around the old church. Crows were fidgeting and calling in the churchyard trees as we searched. Hannah said they weren't crows they were "rooks". We found the girls close under an old tree. They were buried together.

It was hard to read the lichened sandstone. There was a butterfly motif at the top. Hannah said that represented the freed soul. I had to feel the letters to read them.

> *In loving memory of Sarah Elizabeth Fey aged 17*
> *Also Mary Ann Fey Sister of the Above died 17th*
> *November 1884.*
> *To die in Jesus o how sweet*
> *You need not shed a tear*
> *You need not wish us back again*
> *You have no cause to fear.*

Those words seemed like an invocation to stop a haunting, as if someone was scared of the girls becoming revenants. The date 17th November was from when Mary Ann was found washed up off Portland. Sarah had died on about the 13th according to Lee. Only I knew that today, the 15th November, was the real anniversary of Mary Ann's death. Hannah left two posies by the grave, made up of wild blue asters we'd found still blooming.

Our last stop was Abbotskerswell, the home village.

Modernity has overwhelmed the place. Rows of new houses have crept up the valley, even the old cob-walled houses had spanking new thatch and vinyl double-hung windows. I stared up at Town Cottages but could feel no presence. Ma's bean rows and woven skeps had been replaced by neat front yards, faux rustic benches and rose arches. The churchyard had weeds that were knee-high. The Brits seem to have stopped using their churches. We stumbled round in the dusk and found a sullen group of Lee kin clumped together. The last Lee grave was from 1951. There was one marked with the white Portland stone they use for military graves here. It was for Freddie Lee, the sailor, killed in a fire on H.M.S. Eaglet in 1920. On Freddie's grave was written, 'Resting where no shadows fall.'

Streetlights began to light up. We found only one other authentic survivor from the past: the Ladywell at the far southern end of the village. The pool was still there, enclosed within an ivied recess and guarded by a mysterious door. Inside was a circular translucent brimming circle of clear water seemingly cut into the bedrock. Hannah threw a bent safety pin into the unsteady waters. I asked her what she saw there for us but she would not tell me.

"Nothing bad," was all she'd say.

Night of 15th

I am in my hotel room, it's late, my leg is throbbing like a bitch and I am inputting this left-handed.

It being the anniversary of the Babbacombe killings, I thought somehow that I'd tap into the night vibe down in the Bay. I really didn't know what I was looking for—searching for the authentic I guess. England takes on its old guise at night, once you move out from the dull orangey glare of those sodium street lights. I went down Beach Road off Babbacombe Down. All of a sudden it got old world creepy. There was a misty uncertain light, and I kept bumping into wet breathing walls and jumping when the shadowy trees creaked and shifted. I could hear bursts of laughter from customers at the Cary Arms away off by the shore, and the sound came now nearer, now more faintly as the wind shifted. I blundered along through the woods. All of a sudden a gunshot moon flared in a space in the clouds, lighting the scene. I could make out the shadowy structures of the Glen gardens. I didn't want to go ass-over-teakettle into those old cellar pits so I hunkered down on one of the benches by the side of a path with my feet tucked into the fallen beech leaves.

It seemed peaceable at first, and I told myself to chill. Nothing was going to harm me now. I thought I'd tune into the night sounds for a while then go back to my hotel. The sea kept up its low rhythmic wash, wash. Sometimes there was a fleeting call of a sea bird which was then abruptly stilled. What did Lee call them? Oh yeah—mewies. The wind dropped and it became quiet. I felt kinda comfortable, even a little drowsy. I settled back, arms folded with the back of my neck resting on the smooth old bench. Once, something zipped across between the trees in the moonlight. I thought a raccoon maybe. Then I remembered they hadn't any of those here. Maybe it was a rat then or a small bird even, like the one the Devoners call 'a crackety wren'. Whatever, they were only critters settling for the night. Nothing to get fussed over. I sunk back in peaceful contemplation.

Then I was on the alert. Something was moving on the wooded slope above me. A distinct, non-natural noise. I sat up. There it was again, then a new sound, a creaking and clanking of an iron gate. I thought that surely was the gate at the top of the gardens, a secret back way to get to the Glen but I was pretty damn sure it was kept secure with a big padlock. Silence fell again. I strained to listen then it came clear and unmistakable— the grating rhythmic crunch of a solid footstep. Yep, holy shit, I realized someone was on the move towards me, a person with something heavy on their feet like hiking boots or maybe hobnails. It was getting louder. I had sudden sickish thought it was that pedophile guy I had seen earlier, a badass who was gonna be resentful of me squatting in his woods. It seemed too late to back off out of it, I'd make too much noise groping about. Nearer and nearer came the brisk purposeful tread; whoever it was obviously knew their way in the woods. Then I picked out movement against the pale dirt of the path. He was coming straight for me. I reached for Kaiser's nameplate stamp, still in my pocket, and bunched it in my fist. The noise stopped. The intruder was somewhere to my left. Maybe whatever or whoever was trying to sniff out where I was crouching. Two more loud crunching steps then I saw him. The moon came out the cloud a moment and lit him up: a long dark coat, circular hat tipped right back and a mole-like, feral face glaring at me.

"'Ow do, me boody?"

That low growly buzz-saw voice was shockingly loud. I knew it at once.

"'Ow be nockin' on there? All conferable on thikky bench?"

My heart was stammering full belt. I just wanted to get outta there and away from that freaky thing. I tried to speak but my throat went dry and crawly. The air seemed cold all of a sudden and my breath came out in pufflets like dry ice. All I could manage was a feeble, "Who the hell are you?"

"Nay, 'oo do you think? Whose me? Now, what a question after I've come special to see thee."

"I don't know you," my voice had become a squeak by then,

"Caw my dear days! What is it? Are you frit o' me? Do you think I'm a spirit, condemned to walk the night? Ha! Well, I'm not."

The figure moved. It seemed to be pointing at me,

"I'm out and about because I've been called. You wanted to see me though you look wisht to see me. Do you know what wisht means, boy? No? I can't hear 'ee, what the matter, has kitty cat got the auld tongue? Well, it means bewitched, whisht does."

This was turning out to be the mother of all bad trips I can't say I had thoughts as such at the time, they were panicked flittering notions, fragments of thoughts. A dream? A phantasm? A heavy-duty neuro freak-out? Whatever it was I wanted it to stop. Man, I knew I should have kept on with the Gaba. I should never have left Fort Atkinson for that matter neither.

The figure seemed real though. I shut my eyes and opened them again and it was still there. I tried opening only one eye, same result. The figure's gaze shone back at me like coins under the ellipse of the hat brim. It seemed impatient, I think it was tapping something, a stick maybe, against its leg. The head kept moving and twisting as if freeing itself from a tight collar, making angry jerking gestures. It had a thick, strong-looking neck.

You'll say I imagined it all, I might have thought so too if it was not for the smell. I was about ready to crap myself when I caught a whiff of the distinctive acrid stink that came downwind off the figure. It was the sticky, sweetish, yellow smell of kerosene. I knew that cloying candle-burning stench well enough; Grandpa used it to light a lamp in his woodshed. That was it. After a whiff of that lamp oil I stood up, whatever it was I was pretty soon going to run from that horror show.

All of a sudden I yelled out, "I don't know what you want but I want you get the crap away from me!"

"You've got it all back-ze-vore, boy, you wanted to see me didn't you? And here I am."

"Back-ze-fore?" I repeated like a dumbass.

"Ess, back-ze-vore, back ter front, you gert mump 'aid. You been lookin' for somethin' cauchy, something with no value to it. You've been lookin' under stones everywhere. I've seen 'ee out on the beach there and trying to raise them dead Fey girls. There's no point to it the secret is in yer hand already."

"I hold the secret?" I couldn't believe I was conversing with the thing.

"Ess, you paper-skulled mommet, Thee! Lord, Do I have to

make everything plain? I've come to help. Tho I've got plenty o better things to do. You need to listen. You're like a tawd in a bucket, boy. Stuck, in other words, unless you do what I say."

"Get da freakin' shit away from me, you're not real."

The figure took a step forward.

"Not real! Yu'm an owdacious young 'un. This world still be full of knaw norts. I've come back and found one more. It's thee who are cursed, don't you see? Kaiser, that quack has laid it on. Ess, it's thee who are mazed though you don't know it. Just like it happened to me. Miss Keyse mazed me. Her breath came into me and brought me unrest all my life. She was a strange bird. I ate her sin and Kaiser ate mine. You've got to find someone who will take on your troubles in turn. It is the only way to help yerself. All I wants in return is for 'ee to go where I'm buried in that city across the seas. Go and see me every whips in a while. Take a dash of beer and slice o cake in my memory. If you do that, young tacker, I'll think well of 'ee."

"It's all crap! Get lost ya spooky murdering deadbeat!"

The shape convulsed and rippled. It seemed to be glowing with fury, and one yellowish hand clawed out at me.

"I'll show 'ee. Come here, mump aid. This is what it is about…"

I didn't wait to find out anymore.

I bounded off like a scalded dog. I was scared out of my pants, and had to get away from that Halloween crud. I hauled ass uphill. My legs were not working too good. I took a smash in the face from something spiky, fell, got up, went down again. Keep on moving, that's all I thought, keep moving! I crashed on through the brush for an age it seemed, chased by all the demons I could imagine, straight up to that Victorian cast iron fence. Didn't wait for anything there, just grabbed those big old spikes and twisted myself up an' over. There was a ripping pain right through my leg, I hung there on the top for a moment then something gave way and I was falling slap down, bang into darkness.

I came to somewhere on the circular path that skirts Babbacombe Down. (I only know this now). An elderly woman was bending down and trying to talk to me. There was something wet on my face. It was her Chihuahua licking me. Everything hurt and I couldn't see right. The old woman was saying something about had I too much to drink, young man?

"Call 911," I murmured before fainting again. Wee-woo sounds bouncing off the bluffs, quite a fuss for Babbacombe. I still lay there. More dog walkers arrived. Lights. Someone asked me my name. Shit if I could remember it just then. Got lifted into the ambulance. More questions from a green-uniformed woman, and she attached a wire to my forefinger. A machine was bleeping somewhere; back in the land of the living. The ambulance woman's fingers were on my arm, cool fingers of rationality,

"Have you been drinking alcohol tonight?"

"No, I've not been drinking, ma'am … no, I don't have epilepsy neither."

"Tablets? Any medication?"

"Uh, that's a tad more tricky…"

What could I tell the medical staff after they transported me to Torbay Hospital and put me on a gurney in a booth surrounded by vinyl curtains? What could I say? I've been living in a dead man's shoes? I'd been building up a cairn from the broken things of the past? No, we stuck firmly to the somatic. I got some stitches for a scalp wound, left parietal area. Two broken fingers on the right hand were splinted together. A severely bruised and grazed left thigh was cleaned and lightly bandaged. I refused a skull X ray; I was scared of what radiation would do to what was left of my wits. Apart from that I seemed to have got away with it. I was the man they couldn't hang, reprieved! Guess we're reprieved every day. Only we don't appreciate it.

I limped out to an outdoor bay where they unloaded the ambulances. Some patients were smoking out there and using their cell phones. My pants legs were flapping from where the ambulance people had scissored them. I rang Hannah and asked her to fetch me. Said I was real sorry. It was just before midnight.

Hannah picked me up. So great to see her lovely face coming towards me in the rackety emergency rooms. The harassed Asian doctor told her I must rest up after a blow to the head like that. He said I should take no alcohol and seek help if a severe headache developed. Concussion could be a serious thing, he said.

I apologized again to Hannah and said she probably regretted meeting me. I told her that Miss Keyse was murdered this day. And Mary Ann Fey. I'd celebrated the anniversary by nearly getting killed myself.

We drove away in her dinky car. I really owe her, she calmed me right down. I was still a bit scared of Babbacombe so we drove to the Torquay sea front, by the harbor. We sat and watched the lights gliding over a black sea. She held my hand. I told her I thought I'd met the ghost of John Lee in the Babbacombe woods and described how he'd told me to go to Forest Home cemetery and take food and beer at his grave. I said it seemed real. What did she think of that, huh? Was I having a psychotic break? Hannah kept a straight face, seemed to take it seriously. She told me she didn't know what had happened to me but it was clear to her that ghosts could only tell you one thing—that they were dead. She said I had overdone it, my nerves were shot, I'd been working too hard. I was far from home and disorientated. She said daylight would bring sense.

It's then that I told her all the other stuff that's been dogging me. All the bad crap I'd been carrying and never told anyone. How as a kid I had been a holy terror, breaking stuff, running away, lying, making up stories, setting fires in the yard, punching other kids, hurting the pets and playing hooky from school. How I was abusive to my parents—gentle folk who had struggled every day to help me. How I'd worn out legions of psychiatrists and psychologists. They had put me on all sorts of regimes: Adderall, special diets, hugging therapy, behavior mod. I kept on playing hell whatever. I harrowed them and it all got worse as I got older, stronger, more resourceful and destructive. Then, about this time of year, a week short of my 14th birthday they were trying to give me boundaries. I wanted to go out and Pa said I couldn't. He told me I was grounded. I turned on him and punched him hard, far harder than I ever had before. He fell backwards onto a glass-fronted bookcase. I'll never forget the hurt look on his face. He cut his wrist in his fall and while Ma was bandaging it I ran away outdoors, just hiding. Don't know what was in my head. It got dark as night came on but I thought I'd punish them by staying out. I'd teach then for trying to ground me. Apparently they went out driving around, shouting my name, going round the neighbors and calling the cops. In the end they drove out to a junction on the highway. Guess they were too busy looking for me; they got hit by a big rig which flattened their vehicle and they were both killed. I've lived with the guilt of having been responsible for their deaths ever since.

I found my face wet after telling Hannah all that. I've never cried about anything before, so perhaps I'd got concussion. Lachrimae sunt rerum, Latin bullshit, tears for things. I told her how I went to the wreck site and found my father's eyeglasses, you know, by that roadside still there a year later along with all those chunks of plexi in amongst the roadside grasses. Felt I could never be trusted again, could never really have a life.

Hannah said I shouldn't say 'never'. Life might be kinder than I thought.

I said there sure was going to be one 'never' for me.

"What's that?" she said,

"I'm sure as hell never eating no cake or beer over John Lee's grave."

We both laughed. I told her then it was late and she'd better get me back.

It's real late now. I've had the realization I've been sick, literally sick for a long time. I've been the lord of my own desiccation. Decided now to take things as true only if they guide me in this inhospitable world. Everything else was just a bunch of old crams.

I've not figured out what happened in those woods, but it's a resurrection of sorts. Now I'd better find something to quell this throbbing head or maybe get some sleep. You know I just realized something, I never told Kimmie I loved her…

16th November
Dartmouth to Newton Abbot, stopping train.

Not looking for endings any more; only looking for beginnings. I left the library picture of John Lee in the hotel guestbook when I was checking out and wrote "Thanks for the stay. Wishee well, sincerely yours, John Lee." Just kidding them but I do believe that Lee will keep on dogging me. I still don't fully understand the meaning of our connection. Love is a kind of possession also, ain't it?

Now what?

In Torre Station I waited for the Exeter train. A windy morning rattling the plastic bags caught up in the track-side sycamores. Pale sunlight, the Victorian metalwork of the station once painted a garish salmon pink and now going flaky and gray. Weeds flourish in the planters. The platforms are deserted apart from one woman waiting for the Exmouth up train. There are a few cycles left locked to the railings. Looking south, you can see the sea glinting in Torquay Bay as it must have shone for hopeful John Lee coming here to start this story. We are invited to an execution every day of our lives. What we so admire about life is its calm disdaining to destroy us just yet. There'll be no hanging today then. We Yanks like a positive ending but mainly I'm relieved that things haven't turned out worse than they could have been. Maybe John Lee's world has won out in that sense.

Cumulus drift, rusting iron in the embrace of brambles. The rail lines curve away to the north then disappear round a bend in the track towards Edginswell. The smell of soot and spent oil. I imagined a big, oldtime, puffing, steam train cranking along that track. 'Leaving Torre Station', would be a good title for a book. It's always been a passing place not a terminus. It will be the same even if they rename it "Torquay Central: Gateway to the Sunshine Coast" or something". It will always be Torre. "Everything that has been shall be again". Who was that? Yeah, W.B.Y., you have it right.

Birch trees keep shedding off a yellow torrent of leaves. Weird how they fly upwards and not down. A diesel hooting, a flat English sound not the lonesome wail they make at home. I feel I'm ready to go home. That old sign for Torre has vegetation crawling over it: nothing persists, go with it, kid. The woman waiting for her train paused in her texting to watch me. I've been grounded long enough on this rocky outcrop. Now I'm moving off.

Hannah gave me a ride to the station. Sweet of her to have done all that for me. She plans to drive home to London later. I've delayed her work with all my crud and she has a report to write. We hugged. I said I'm still searching for Torre Station, still looking right to the end. She said maybe the secret is that life is the train not the station. Damn, she is so darn sensible and with a beautiful soul. Said she'd got me a gift and handed me something wrapped in pink tissue I've just looked at it in the carriage. It's something she must have bought from the Exeter Cathedral shop when we visited. I saw them there, polished stones with an inspiring word incised on them like "Courage", "Faith" or whatever. Hannah had bought me one which says 'Forgiveness' on it. I was strangely moved by it. The stone is gray Devon granite. I'm holding it, warm and solid in my hand.

The smell of this train and its molded seats; the scent of

sealed space, vinyl, acrylic and fabric cleaner with a base tone of old shoes and body odor. An amplified voice tells us the next stop is Newton Abbot; refreshments are available. I can see my huddled reflection in the window. There is a blond girl across from me. She has earphones on and her lips keep parting as she soundlessly sings along to something. We cross a river, must be the Teign, tawny reed beds, gull drift. Fare thee well, Sarah and Mary Ann. Green fields flicker past, a sign for 'Nissan', young birches sprouting on the railside gravel, red earth and white houses. November rain flecks the dirty windows. The blond girl is texting furiously. Her fingers are a blur. Maybe my generation can't feel direct experience any more. Stupefactibus. A deliberate dulling of the senses. Maybe I'll give Latin a rest now. Don't need to be outré any more. Go with the flow, son.

What am I carrying back to my life? I have Hannah's stone, my research notes and a crack on the head. I hope I've spat out all the mazy spells that have been put on me but I expect there are a few more. What was the secret of Lee? It wasn't solving the murder but how he lived with it afterwards. Life only belongs to the survivors. All my moments are summations ready to be overturned at the next bend in the track. It Could Be You! Some sort of advertisement for a Brit lottery. I'm switching on my old Sanyo Talk Book micro cassette recorder. I'm going back to analog. That worn silver machine fits real comfortable in the hand.

The train gathers speed. Whoosh, speeding thru those Devon fields trying to get ahead of John Lee. Perhaps I can start over. If Lee was not there it would be necessary to invent him. Think I'll make a new version on tape. Let's see, let's get it right. It groans and rattles over a crossing. Gonna start it again and do it right this time, click: "Starts with Ma I s'pose. Ma was a scryer, see …"

Author's Note

This book is fiction but it would not have been be possible to write without the work of those trail-blazing John Lee historians, Ian Waugh and Mike Holgate. Torquay Library John Pike archives have also proved to be an invaluable resource as has the Milwaukee Public Library Historic Photo Collection. I am indebted to Carole Broomfield and Nina Pickup for generously sharing family history relating to Adeline Gibb. Thanks to Nick Heard for researching the Fey sisters. I also thank Marsha Knightsmith for her photos of Wolborough, Celine Antier for her advice on French usage and Chris and Emma for help with contemporary Devon slang. This book has been greatly influenced by Jon McGregor. I owe much to him for his invaluable mentoring and advice. Thanks also to author and publisher, John Lucas. Amazingly, John's father actually saw 'Babbacombe' Lee in person. John's acute eye and sharp pencil have greatly shaped this work. Thanks to Henderson Mullin from Writing East Midlands for his early encouragement and help and to Robert Peett for taking a chance on this unusual book and for his decisive editing of the final draft. Most of all, to Sharon for her support through the long years of the writing and for all those searches through Devon churchyards.

Rod Madocks,
Nottingham & Babbacombe 2015

About the Author

Rod Madocks was born in Broken Hill, Northern Rhodesia in 1952. Neither the place nor the country exist under that name any longer. Spent a restless youth wandering Europe and lived in Texas, U.S .A. Held down a wide variety of jobs including hypnotherapist and professional gardener. Completed a Phd in the work of the writer Vladimir Nabokov. Retrained as a mental health professional and became a forensic specialist within criminal psychiatry.

Rod is based in Nottingham, England and is now a full-time writer. His novel No Way To Say Goodbye (2007) and short story collection Ship of Fools (2012), both published by Five Leaves Press, are centred on the world of mental health and high security institutions. He was nominated for the Crime Writing Association John Creasey Dagger in 2007.

Babbicam is his second novel.

Lightning Source UK Ltd.
Milton Keynes UK
UKOW02f2328080515

251179UK00002B/7/P